DAUGHTERS OF TIME

KAALII CARGILL

For all the mothers and daughters since the beginning,
and for the Earth, mother of us all.

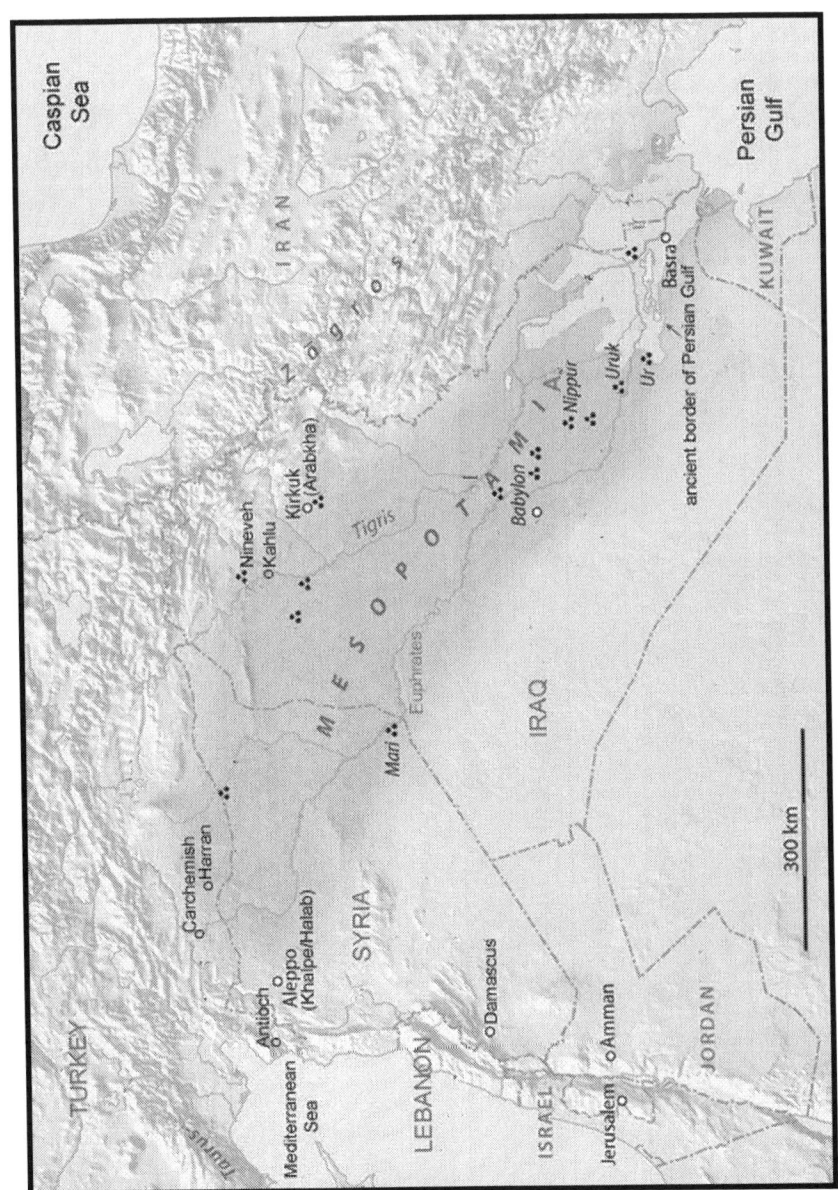

For man without woman there is no heaven in the sky or on earth. Without woman there would be no sun, no moon, no agriculture, and no fire. **Arab Proverb**

PROLOGUE

The city of Urim (Ur), Ancient Sumer. c 2000BCE.

The last days were upon them, and still the child had not come. The great city of Urim would fall, and the way of Inanna, Queen of Heaven and Earth, would be lost.

"All things must pass," whispered the river.

Nin-lil-la, High Priestess of Urim, stood naked at the river's edge, alone but for tourmaline-feathered ducks and tawny lions. The stars faded. Like a boat of dreams, the crescent Moon sailed gently from the horizon.

It was here at the river that Nin-lil-la came to wash away her fears and savour the stillness. When the lions began their raucous welcome to the Sun, Urim would come to life, and Nin-lil-la would belong once again to the Temple.

Graceful, unhurried, Nin-lil-la immersed herself in the sweet water. Her long, black hair moved like eels with the current.

When the lions turned to face the East, she left the river,

wiped the moisture from her skin, and wrapped a square of white linen around herself in the pleats and folds appropriate for a High Priestess. She twisted and coiled her damp hair and secured it with a length of reed. Skin tingling, she began the walk back to the Temple just as the lions began their celebration of the Sun's release from the Underworld.

Nin-lil-la, High Priestess of the Temple of Nanna in Urim, climbed the steps of her Palace. She paused to look back over the Buranun, glistening now in the first light of day. The great river ran like a ribbon of gold from the North to the Pars Sea that lapped at Urim's Western Harbour. She frowned as she saw, yet again, the vision that had been haunting her: where now there was water, bringing life and riches to the city, one day there would be sand, dry and lifeless. How the great Sea could disappear was not something she could explain, but she knew beyond doubt that her vision was sent by the Great Ones and was, therefore, true. One day Urim would stand alone in the desert, all splendour faded.

With the vision came the face of a girl with eyes like a gazelle and courage enough to walk through Time. Had she even been born yet, this girl-child who haunted Nin-lil-la's dreams? Would she come in time?

CHAPTER I

Philadelphia. February 2014CE.

The USGS estimates that several million earthquakes occur in the world each year . . .The NEIC now locates about 50 earthquakes each day, or about 20,000 a year.[i]

Tsunamis are long-wavelength, long-period sea waves generated by an abrupt movement of large volumes of water.[ii]

"Awesome! You should see this, Mum."

Were all thirteen year olds so damn noisy? Lili blocked out Josh's voice and scrolled down the web page. Amazing how much there was on Inanna; five thousand years old and still getting hits: Queen of Heaven and Earth; First Daughter of the Moon; Sibyl; Soothsayer; Seer; Mighty warrior, fierce protector . . .

"Mum! Come here! Quickly!"

What was it this time? Another crop circle? Unexplained lights? Why had she ever thought the Discovery channel would keep him quiet while she worked?

"Mum! This is serious!"

Lili pushed away from the desk and walked to the lounge room. Josh sat on the edge of the couch, fists clenched, body rigid, staring at the television screen. He looked frightened.

"What is it now?" asked Lili impatiently; she had a report to write before tomorrow.

The television screen was awash with scenes of chaos: water streaming though city streets, traffic jams blocking highways, wind-tossed trees toppling on houses.

"Tsunami," whispered Josh, eyes wide.

"Where this time?" asked Lili, turning to go back to her desk. Why was he so upset? There had been tsunamis in the news for years now!

"Everywhere," said Josh.

Lili stopped. A shiver rippled up her spine, stirring the hairs on her neck. Everywhere?

Josh whistled through his teeth. "Tsunamis all over the World. Here, Australia, India, everywhere. There's never been anything like it."

"Not since the great Flood," said Lili, sitting with Josh to watch the reports. They were still there when Joel and Mish came home twenty minutes later.

"Have you seen the . . ." Mish sat on the arm of the couch, biting her lip like she had when she was young enough to be scared of the dark.

Joel walked through to the kitchen. "I guess coastal property just fell in value," he called over his shoulder.

"Guess so," said Lili. It was an old joke, arising from his work in real estate.

"We called Aunty Jen," said Mish. "It's not so bad on the West coast."

"Everything's going to be salty," said Josh. "There's sea

water everywhere."

A pulse of heat passed through Lili's body like a fever. That's it, the words from the translation: *And bitterness floods the land.* The ancient Sumerians called river water "sweet" and seawater "bitter". She had thought it might refer to warfare or some natural disaster: *And bitterness floods the land . . .*

The tsunamis and flooding of the last decade were a disaster, but there was nothing natural about them. Sea levels had been rising and earthquake activity increasing in all the hotspots; global warming and aggressive mining said the environmental pundits. Yet there had never been so many tsunamis at once.

Lili left the others watching the news reports and went back to her desk to finish her report on Sumerian mythology in the twenty-first century. Instead of working, she frowned at the translation Blu-Tacked to the wall above her computer screen:

> *Seven times the Guardian spoke*
> *Taking each time the sacred me.*
> *Hidden in stone soaked in sweetness*
> *Riding the wind burnished bright*
> *Seven times the Guardian spoke*
> *Taking each time the sacred me.*
> *When men forsake the task of life*
> *And bitterness floods the land,*
> *Daughters will come marked at birth*
> *To find the me, remember the Queen,*
> *Restore the Balance for eternity.*

From a shelf below the translation, Lili picked up a clay tablet the colour of old bones. Someone in ancient Sumer had marked the words into wet clay. Baked hard, it had survived two millennia. But how had it come to her? And what did it mean?

Lili shook her head and carefully placed the tablet back on the shelf. It should be in the museum, but it had arrived at her home address two weeks ago--in a brown-paper parcel from an anonymous sender--and she still hadn't taken it into work. If she had, it would just be sitting in the basement with hundreds of other tablets and fragments from ancient Sumer. Before consigning it to that fate, she wanted to know who had sent it, and why they had sent it to her.

The mainstay of Lili's life was logic, and the tablet was one of the most illogical things to happen for a long time. Why now?

Turning fifty should have been a celebration, but last year's birthday had left a pall of doubt and dissatisfaction that Lili had dealt with by working longer hours and taking on more research. It wasn't helping.

She lived in a beautiful home, had two intelligent, well-behaved children (even if neither were shaping up to do Medicine or Law), and a marriage that had stood the test of time. She was slim, fit, and highly respected in her profession. Shouldn't she be happy?

She scowled at the tablet. "I'm sick of you! I'm taking you into work tomorrow, and you can gather dust in the basement!"

And yet there was something about the inscription . . .

Lili read the last lines of the poem again: *Daughters will come marked at birth To find the me, remember the Queen, Restore the Balance for eternity.* She rubbed the birthmark on her wrist; with a bit of imagination it could be a star, and the eight-rayed star had been the symbol of the Mother Goddesses from Inanna through to Mary, mother of Jesus. The literature said the crown with eight rays was probably a reference to

Venus, the morning and evening star revered in ancient Sumer as the star of Inanna, Queen of Heaven and Earth. Lili had seen the symbol on game boards excavated from the graves of Ur, and she had lived with the birthmark all her life. Her mother had a similar one on her thigh, and Mish had one on her ankle. Daughters marked at birth?

Nonsense! She was just a miserable, old woman looking for something to distract her!

Joel came in and rubbed her back in the repetitive circles Lili hated. Was he trying to erase her? He pressed harder than usual, his hands tense.

"Looking for answers in the past again?" he asked, kissing the top of her head.

"No, not really. Just distracting myself." Lili turned away from the tablet.

"Have you thought about what to get for Dave's wedding?" asked Joel. "It's next week, and I won't have a chance between now and then."

Lili sighed. Dave was one of Joel's many nephews, but she always bought the presents, wrote loving messages on the cards, and kept track of the names of the children when they were born. Why did Joel always bring it up as if he might just do it . . if only he had time?

"You seem tired." Joel rubbed harder.

Lili squirmed away and found herself looking at the tablet again.

"Is that from work?" Joel reached for the tablet.

Lili blocked his hand. "It's fragile. Best not to touch it."

Joel shrugged. "What does the writing say?"

Lili repeated some of the poem.

"Sounds like one of those New Age prophecies. How old did you say that thing was?"

12

"Four thousand years or so. Maybe it's a message from back then." She didn't believe that, but it would piss Joel off, and then he might leave her alone and go and watch television.

"Yeah, and maybe on the back you'll find the Powerball numbers, too!"

"Maybe," mumbled Lili.

"Come on, Lil, I was joking. Remember when we used to joke?"

"Hmmph."

"You seem tired," he said again. "Why don't we take that holiday we've been putting off?"

"With the World going to shit, I need a holiday?"

Where had that come from?

"Okay. Okay. No holiday! Just let me know when you get over whatever's bitten you."

He left then, and Lili swung her computer chair round and round like a child, kicking her legs and scowling. What was the matter with her?

Tears burned behind her eyes, but she swallowed them and turned back to the report. The tablet beckoned again. *Daughters will come marked at birth To find the me, remember the Queen, Restore the Balance for eternity.* What could it mean? The *me* were the seven sacred vestments worn by Inanna when she journeyed to the Underworld to meet her sister, Eresh-ki-gal. The Queen of Heaven and Earth meeting the Queen of the Underworld. But what did it have to do with anything, and why had someone sent it to her?

Lili sighed miserably. She was one of the few people who had actually been to the ruins of Ur in the south of Iraq at Tall al Muqayyar, a student goggle-eyed to be walking in the footsteps of the great Leonard Woolley and the team who had unearthed the treasures of Ur in the 1930s. She had held necklaces and

13

armbands that may have been used in sacred rites. But that had been years ago, and most of her colleagues would say the *me* never even existed outside the stories. Yet she couldn't help wondering . . .had the *me* been found and stored away in basements in Baghdad or London or Philadelphia?

Lili bit her lip and stared at the tablet. There must be some way to make sense of it!

CHAPTER II

Melbourne, Australia. February 2014CE.

In 2007 the Intergovernmental Panel on Climate Change (IPCC) released their fourth assessment report, concluding that:
   * Warming of the climate system is unequivocal
   * Humans are very likely to be causing most of the warming that has been experienced since 1950
   * It is very likely that changes in the global climate system will continue well into the future, and that they will be larger than those seen in the recent past.
These changes have the potential to have a major impact on human and natural systems throughout the world including Australia. http://www.climatechangeinaustralia.gov.au/

"Lamb chops, salad, fetta, tzatziki, flat bread." Paula ran through the supermarket, saying her shopping list aloud as she grabbed what she needed. She had twenty minutes until school pick up.

She paid, packed the food into the crumpled, ecosilk bag she carried everywhere, and ran for the car, hair blowing wildly around her face.

Wind tore through the car park, hurling a discarded plastic bag up into a tree to hang there like the corpse of a bird with shattered wings. Paula threw the shopping into the back seat, threw herself behind the steering wheel, and sped out of the car park. She broke at least four traffic rules on the way to school and parked in the pick-up bay just as the bell went. With a deep sigh, she pulled out her hair clasp, retwisted her long, dark hair into a tidy enough knot, and secured it firmly. A normal, organised mother, right on time to collect her daughter . . .

Mary ran out with her friends, laughing and chattering, her long, dark hair as unruly as Paula's. She looked younger than her friends, petite and ethereal, as if she hadn't quite crossed over from somewhere else. Paula felt the pang of protective love that had squeezed her heart the first time she looked into Mary's eyes. It was different from the fierce love she felt for the other three, as if Mary was on loan and could be taken at any moment.

Mary pulled open the door and tossed her bag onto the back seat on top of the shopping. Nothing ethereal about that.

"Can we go home along Beach road? There'll be hundreds of white horses today," said Mary as she sat down and fastened her seatbelt. "Please."

"And hello to you, too," said Paula, leaning across to kiss Mary's cheek. She smelled of school lunch and childhood. "Everyone will be going slowly because of the wind. You can see the waves another day. I have to get home."

"But they won't be as big. Look at the trees moving!" Petite and ethereal--and stubborn as an ox.

The trees were swaying violently, and the car shook with each gust of wind. What next, a hurricane? After a decade of drought, bushfires, and floods, anything was possible.

"No waves today," said Paula firmly.

Mary sulked all the way home, making little grunting noises to show her displeasure. As they turned into their driveway, Paula's mobile rang.

"I'll get it." Mary emerged from her black mood to rummage in Paula's bag for the phone.

"Hi, Dad."

"No, we're not. We're home."

She handed the phone to Paula.

"Hi, Thom."

"Thank goodness you're safe. Beach road is flooded. Cars washed away. Crashes. Are the others home yet?"

"I'll check." Paula ran up the path to the front door, heart beating wildly at the urgency in Thom's voice; he was usually the calm one.

Rinna opened the door and threw herself into Paula's arms.

"What's happening? Are Jon and Hayley here?"

Rinna shook her head.

Paula held her by the shoulders to look at her face. "Are you all right?"

Rinna nodded, but she clung to Paula's arm as if she were drowning.

Paula remembered Thom on the phone still clutched in her hand. "Rinna's here, but the others aren't home yet. Jon had tennis practice."

Thom told her to stay inside and said he'd collect Jon on his way home. Paula put the phone in her pocket and looked at Rinna again. She was shaking, her eyes huge in a too-pale face.

"You look terrible. What's going on?"

"I thought you'd been washed away. There's tsunami's everywhere."

"It's just Beach Road," said Paula. "Damn! I left the shopping in the car." She turned back to the door.

"It's not just Beach Road," said Rinna. She sounded scared. "It's everywhere."

Hayley ran up the path, school bag bouncing on her back, hair flying in the wind. "Have you heard the news? There's tsunami's everywhere!"

Paula gave up on the shopping and walked through to the lounge room. The television blared out the news, volume too high as usual.

She stood with her hands on her hips, glaring at the screen. "Bloody fools! Don't they know it all works together: air, water, heat, the whole Earth? Just tip the balance with one, and it all turns to shit!"

"Mum!" Rinna was shaking her arm. "Who are you yelling at?"

Paula took a deep breath, pulled out her phone and called Thom.

"Got him," said Thom. "We're nearly home."

Paula sent Hayley out to bring in the shopping, told Rinna to turn down the volume, and sent Mary to change out of her school uniform. She stomped into the kitchen, turned on the grill, and burst into tears. Was there going to be anything left for the children?

Thom and Jon ran in, clothes and hair dripping wet. Jon went to join the girls in front of the television. Thom found Paula in the kitchen and held her close.

"It's okay. It's going to be okay," he mumbled into her hair.

"It's not going to be okay, and I don't know what to do about it."

"Let's start with dinner," said Thom. "I'll get dry and give you a hand."

After dinner, Paula left the others watching the news reports and retreated to her study. Of course there were tsunamis. Of course Australia was having the worst drought and the worst floods on record. Of course it was going to escalate. There was only so much the global ecosystem could be pushed out of balance before the catastrophe was irreversible. She thumped her desk, making her laptop jump. Governments were talking about sea walls and tidal gates, desalination plants and wind farms, but no one was addressing the fundamental problem at the root of it all: the determination of human beings to dominate Nature. Well, almost no one. She logged on to the Gaia forum.

The site was alive with activity. She went to the Environmental Science blog and scrolled down the latest entries. Colleagues from all over the World were discussing the tsunamis. She added her bit and then checked out the other pages. The word "prophecy" caught her eye. Weren't ancient prophecies, conspiracy theories, and Doomsday cults banned from the site?

The entry was by an archaeologist from the University of Pennsylvania. UPenn was Ivy League; no way their research program extended to prophecies!

Paula frowned at the screen. Ancient Sumer? How had the moderator let that one by?

She logged off and settled down to edit the final chapters of her PhD. She had set out to compare how cultures with female deities and those with male deities treated the environment. The literature reviews revealed a pattern of cooperation vs domination demonstrated in artwork and artifacts from archaeological digs all over the World. The most notable finding was the absence of weaponry and images of war in cultures that seemed to have walked lightly on the Earth. She had also documented how the concept of Nature was incorporated into the various cosmologies; the differences were striking: "We are an integral part of the world around us" vs "We are separate from the world around us"; "It is our (duty, task, destiny) to cooperate with the rest of Nature" vs "It is our (duty, task, destiny) to subdue and rule over Nature (and people less developed than we are)".

There were also clues about how the prevailing cosmology of a culture impacted on actual practices, but what she really needed were some hard data, like a survey questionnaire from a decent-sized sample of Late Bronze Age women. She could just see it: a group of unkempt women sitting around a fire, marking their responses on animal hide.

Paula smiled for the first time in hours; she could imagine what those Bronze Age women might say about the modern practices that contributed to climate change, loss of biodiversity, land and water degradation, and escalating stresses on food-producing systems!

CHAPTER III

The city of Urim (Ur), Ancient Sumer. c 2000BCE.

An astrological age is a time period in astrology which is believed by some to parallel major changes in the Earth's inhabitants' development, particularly relating to culture, society and politics . . . The Age of Aries ushered in efforts to replace polytheism with monotheism.[iii]

"Do you know the magic of becoming?" whispered the wind.

The first time Nin-lil-la heard that question she had been ten years old. Fresh to the Temple from a farm on the river, she had absorbed the lessons like the red soil soaked up water in the Emesh heat.

"Do you know the magic of becoming?" Her heart had thudded once and then seemed to stop. Between one heartbeat and the next she had glimpsed the cycle of life and death that makes up the magic of becoming. The High Priestess had come to stand by her, smelling of sandalwood and frankincense.

But that had been forty years ago, and now she heard the question in the reeds, on the wind, in the flames and the water. Her life had unfolded, and she had walked her walk from acolyte to Priestess and then High Priestess when her time came. Nothing to regret in that, although sometimes she wished she was an ass trader who could make the long journey to Kemet and Zara to see the fabled marketplace where all the colours of the world could be found: saffron and indigo, white lead and lapis lazuli, and the purple taken from sea creatures for the robes of Kings and Queens, Priests and Priestesses.

Nin-lil-la shook the thoughts from her head; it was a small regret, all things considered. Releasing the memories to flow away like the waters of the Buranun, she climbed the stairs from the river and entered the coolness of the inner rooms.

"All things must pass," she whispered to the walls. The words were true, but there were some things she would give her life to preserve.

The morning song of the lions carried across the city from the river, a distant thunder that echoed through the corridors of the King's Palace like a warning.

In the paved courtyard by the Palace wall, an old man paused. Manark had risen early to listen, not to lions but to crickets. Trained meticulously in the infallible number systems of six and ten, he had selected the loudest cricket song and calculated the temperature of the air from the number of chirps in a minute.[iv] The figure was impossibly high. Manark's skin felt no hotter than it had the day before and the day before that, but the crickets were singing up an inferno.

Like all mathematicians, Manark believed in the

orderliness of numbers; yet for all his years in the House of Tablets, he had never heard the crickets as strident or as desperate. That was the word for it: desperate. Even the caterwauling of the lions sounded more urgent than usual. Had the ancient city of Urim ever heard the like of it?

Urim was, after all, a place of memories. The foundations were said to have been formed in the very first days of the World. Memory, ancient and deep, roamed the dark lanes, brushing against pillars and gateposts. Perhaps, if the city could speak . . .

Shaking his head at the foolish thoughts, Manark climbed the worn mud-brick stairs to the flat roof of his rooms. The air was dense, the walls warm beneath his hands.

What was the matter? Too many nights listening to the river instead of sleeping. Should he curl up on his sleeping-mat and ignore the portents? But he was a Mathematician and Astronomer, trained to interpret the signs of change! If not him, then who?

Yet the signs were not clear. The crickets sang more insistently every night, but the frogs had subsided into uncharacteristic silence. The star of Holy Inanna, first daughter of the Moon, dimmed in the Heavens, and a new tale had arrived last month from the East. It told of the death of the Bull and the rise of the Ram. No surprise in that, but the tale told also of the dimming of the seven stars, favoured of Inanna, holy Priestess of Heaven. Signs! Portents!

"What do they mean?" Manark asked the silent walls. He knew he was not alone in his unease; the people of Urim were restless. Someone from cooler lands might have blamed the heat, but the sleepers on the rooftops were immune to the scorching power of the Sun. No, it was not the residue of the day's heat that caused the people of Urim to moan and whimper, turn and toss. It was change.

Manark felt it gathering in the shadows of the date palms and the carved stone columns of the city. Change so near that even memory stood still, waiting . . .

"But what is it that comes?" he asked of the dawn.

Behind him, a serving boy spoke. "The High Priestess approaches."

There was awe in the boy's voice. Manark smiled; he had been like that once, in wonderment at the powerful ones of the city. Now he just nodded once and stretched his arms to bring life back into his body.

"Bring dates and tea," he said.

He walked stiffly to his rooms, holding the wall for support. Bit by bit his body had stopped obeying his mind, and now the High Priestess must cross the city to meet with him. In his youth he had run to the far side of the city, through the Market square, along the street of Physicians, past the lane of Magicians, to the Palace of the High Priestess. But that had been seventy years ago and a different High Priestess.

His world was smaller now: the two rooms granted him by the King, the rooftop, the courtyard below, and the slow stairs between. He still read the tablets carried from the House of Tablets by the boys who came for a day or a week to serve him, but he no longer bothered to learn the boys' names.

Manark settled himself on a stool by the small table in the front room. Built of precious cedar wood from the North, the table was where he worked all day, recording the omens and rereading the records scribed by others. He drummed his fingers on his knees like a boy awaiting examination. With a tired sigh, he stilled his hands and held them up: relics of another time, spotted and scarred by life, veins showing blue through the dark skin. They had been strong once, almost too strong for the

24

delicate reed pens of the Scribes. He curled and uncurled his fingers against the tightness of the joints.

When the boy returned the High Priestess came with him, poised as ever. Black hair piled high, Nin-lil-la wore the pleated robe marking her rank, white linen bordered in purple, not a fold out of place. Crushed lapis lazuli brushed her eyelids and the tops of her feet.

"The High Priestess comes to consult the Mathematician," said Manark, bowing his head.

"She does." Her voice was low and resonant, trained by years of ritual intonations. Her face was beautiful but cold, eyes dark and inscrutable, like the statues of Inanna.

"And Nin-lil-la comes to see an old friend," she added, voice and face softening.

"Old, indeed," Manark said.

"Old enough to know what it is that comes?" she asked.

Manark gestured for her to sit on the stool by the window. Open to the East, the carved lattice glowed with the Sun's first light. He poured tea, mint and tangerine, into glazed bowls. Tiny ants crawled on the dates.

"I have heard the crickets' warning and the silence of the frogs," said Nin-lil-la. "What do the latest omens say abut the Age of the Ram?"

"I truly cannot read them," said Manark. "There has not been a turning of the Age in two thousand years. Even I am not that old."

"What of the tales from the East?" Nin-lil-la stood to look through the lattice. The Sun made the black of her hair shine like polished coal. "What will become of Urim if the seven sisters are gone? Long have they watched over us."

"The tales say the seven lights are dimmed," said Manark. "The young Astronomers say the stars are not the sisters of

Inanna but fixed points in the Heavens. They do not see Alo-ne, the Queen who wards off evil, Astera, the Stubborn One, and Elek-ra, the Shining One. They do not see Ma-ir, the Great One, and Tar-ge, the long-necked one."

"What say the tales of Inanna?" asked Nin-lil-la.

"The tales are of battle and conquest," said Manark. "The hero, Gilgamesh, slays the Bull."

"The horns of the Bull are the crescent Moon, eternally renewed," said Nin-lil-la. "Will the Ram serve us as truly as the Bull?"

"Not if the portents speak true," said Manark, the weight of the change pressing on his shoulders.

"So there have been signs." Nin-lil-la's tone was cold, her eyes piercing.

Manark shivered. It was said that the Priestesses of Inanna had walked the path of no return, had looked into the eyes of Eresh-ki-gal, Queen of the Underworld. That they could turn the eyes of death upon a man, and he would be taken.

He forced himself to hold her gaze. "Truly, the omens are unclear, but the Ram is marked for war. The Hunter takes the axe, the quiver and bow of Anshan, buckles the sword to his belt." He recited the tale as he had read it in the tablets. "First he slays the seven watchers. Then Gilgamesh thrusts his sword between the neck and the horns and slays the Bull." [v]

"We have failed, my friend." Nin-lil-la spoke the words as a lament. "The glory of Ki-en-gir will pass into memory, into legend, into myth, and be forgotten. Who will remember Inanna? Who will sing Her praises? Who will remember the Balance?"

She stayed that day, walking in the garden with him, sitting on the rooftop. They ate dates and sipped tea sweetened with honey from the bees dancing along the riverbanks. They spoke of Urim, of the past and the future. They sat in silence and watched the Moon rise in the indigo sky.

Nin-lil-la walked back alone to the Palace by the North Harbour. As she passed by the river, the ducks asleep in the reeds fluffed their feathers and snaked their heads deeper into the downy darkness under their wings. The lions were silent. Only the crickets in their shallow graves dared disturb the stillness.

CHAPTER IV

Philadelphia. Updated March 15th 2014 11.52am UTC

The death toll is slowly rising as information trickles out of Peru after a huge 8.9 magnitude earthquake struck late yesterday, flattening buildings and triggering a tsunami that is menacing the Pacific rim.

"Did you see *Hair?*" asked Mish, pouring herself a coffee from the plunger and adding liberal amounts of milk and sugar.

"What?" Lili shook her head to clear the dullness that came from lack of sleep.

"The musical," said Mish, bouncing around the kitchen like she was eight instead of eighteen. "Did you see it?"

"I'm not that old," said Lili. "*Hair* came out in the seventies. I was only Josh's age."

"I wish I'd been alive in the seventies. The dawning of the Age of Aquarius and all that." Mish whirled dramatically around the island bench, dark curls falling around her face. "Before

28

global warming and water shortages. Before tsunamis."

Lili sighed. "It was all starting then, but we didn't know it. Didn't want to know it, mostly. Anyway, it's still the dawning of the Age of Aquarius. It takes centuries for an Age to turn."

"Really?" Mish sat down abruptly at the table. "When will it happen?" She sipped her coffee, suddenly grown up and serious.

"You change like the wind," said Lili. "If you can sit still for two minutes, I'll tell you about the new Age."

Mish smiled sweetly. She looked so like her grandmother, Miriam, that Lili had to smile as well.

"A New Age is meant to start a couple of centuries before the end of the old millennium and to last for quite a while afterwards. We're in the middle of it right now."

"Great! I was afraid I'd missed it. What do you think will happen?"

"It's already happening with all the global crises; there's usually something momentous going on at the start of a new Age. In ancient Sumer, the change from Taurus to Aries was a catastrophe. The last flowering of the old kingdom ended, and their culture was lost."

"But you've been digging it up again," said Mish. "So it wasn't completely lost."

"If only that were true. We still don't really know who the Sumerians were."

"But what will the Age of Aquarius bring? Do you think we'll make it through the next two thousand years?"

"Maybe we need to find a prophet," said Lili. "Like Christ when the Age of Aries turned to Pisces two thousand years ago."

"We'd probably end up with Buffy or someone!" said Mish, nibbling a piece of dry toast.

"Are you eating enough?" asked Lili.

"You're so funny," said Mish, rolling her eyes. "One minute you sound like an archaeologist, and the next you sound like a Mummy."

Lili smiled. Mish and Josh had invented the Mummy jokes years ago when she was doing her PhD in archaeology: "Our Mummy's a Mummy doctor." It was odd to hear it again today; last night's dreams had been full of crashing waves, shadowy figures and ancient tombs. Joel had grumbled about her whimpering in her sleep.

"I'm off to the Library," said Mish. She kissed the top of Lili's head and ran to the door. "I'll pick Josh up from school this afternoon. Love you."

"Love you, too. Take care."

The door slammed, and blessed silence filled the house. Leaving the coffee cups, Lili went to her desk and lifted up the clay tablet. The small rectangle of baked mud looked dry and brittle, the cuneiform barely legible. She whispered the translation, as she did every morning:

> Seven times the Guardian spoke
> Taking each time the sacred me
> Hidden in stone soaked in sweetness
> Riding the wind burnished bright
> Seven times the Guardian spoke
> Taking each time the sacred me.
> When men forsake the task of life
> Daughters will come marked at birth,
> To find the me, remember the Queen
> Restore the Balance for eternity.

Maybe Joel was right when he said she needed a holiday. Last night's dreams had all been about opening endless doors looking for a treasure she couldn't find.

Her mobile phone rang. Her mother.

"Hi, Miriam."

"Hello, darling. How are you?"

"Good. Working at home."

"I won't keep you then. Can you and Mish come over this weekend for an hour or two?"

There was something odd in Miriam's voice, but Lili didn't ask; her mother revealed things in her own time.

Lili checked with Mish and called Miriam back to confirm a visit on Saturday afternoon.

Miriam was at the door to meet them, looking even more petite than usual in an oversized, emerald-green cardigan. She perched there like an exotic bird, hands fluttering like tiny wings, smiling tightly. She took Mish by the hand and led them into the front room. Miriam's smile always stopped before reaching her eyes, and today it was even more fixed than usual; Lili fervently hoped this wasn't going to be another lecture about her neglect of Judaism or the perils of Mish marrying out.

The afternoon light turned the front room golden. It was Lili's favourite room, with Miriam's desk by the bay window and a tall bookcase filled with old editions of Homer, Virgil and other classical works. Lili had spent many happy Sunday afternoons curled in one of the winged armchairs, beginning her love affair with the ancient world through The Ilead, The Odyssey, and other epic tales.

Miriam had tea and biscotti set out on the low table, with

three of the delicate, flower-patterned china cups she reserved for special occasions. Lili sighed; they must be in for a particularly serious lecture.

Mish chattered happily to her grandmother about some new colour she'd been experimenting with, as if she wasn't about to receive a diatribe about her responsibility to continue the line of Abraham. And why should she worry? Lili had always been there as a buffer, and Mish was a whole generation removed from the Holocaust. Lili sighed again and poured herself some tea.

When they had all eaten some biscotti and finished their tea, Miriam sat up straighter and clasped her hands protectively over her heart. "There's a story I've never told anyone. I didn't mean for it to be a secret, but it grew into one over the years."

Lili sat forward. A shiver ran up her back; like someone walking on her grave, her father would have said.

"When I was a girl," said Miriam, "we lived in Budapest, as you know. My Bubbe and Zayde, my mother's parents, lived in the same street. The house had been in the family for hundreds of years. Bubbe Mari, my great-grandmother, lived there as well. She was over eighty and stayed in her room all day. One day I was sitting in the front room at home when I heard the strangest tapping sound, like a woodpecker at the front door."

Lili held her breath; Miriam rarely spoke of her childhood, except in terms of loss and responsibility.

"It was Bubbe Mari, tapping her way up our front steps with her walking stick. I brought her inside. She pulled me into the sitting room and talked so fast I could only understand every third word. She was very excited, saying over and over that I was to keep the family treasure with me always, show no one, and take it to safety when I left. She'd always been a bit odd, and I had no idea what she was talking about. As far as I knew there was no such thing as a family treasure, and I certainly wasn't going anywhere. I was eight years old.

"She pulled an old leather pouch from down the front of her dress and handed it to me. 'The Queen's gift. It is yours now,' she said. 'For your daughter, and her daughter after that. Take it to safety. It is the Queen's gift. To remind us.' She wouldn't say any more. She just told me to hide it and keep it safe. Not to show anyone." Miriam sighed. "It was so long ago."

She reached into the deep pocket of her cardigan and produced a leather pouch. She unwound the thong and tilted the pouch. A bracelet slid out onto her lap.

Lili gasped. Pu-abi's headdress. The stars were like Pu-abi's headdress!

Mish leaned forward. "It looks like gold, Bubbe. Real gold."

"I think it is," said Lili. "Beaten gold and lapis lazuli set in pitch." It was hard to focus, as if she was floating up near the ceiling, looking down on three women and an impossibly old bracelet.

"It's very old," said Miriam, handing it to Mish, who held it as if it might bite. The gold glowed softly in the afternoon light.

"How old?" asked Mish.

"I don't know, but I think it might be quite ancient," said Miriam softly.

Lili reached across and touched the clasp: a hook coiled to slide through a solid ring. She knew what she was seeing, but she couldn't believe it.

"It could be about five thousand years old." Her voice sounded like a stranger's, high-pitched, racy. She took three slow, deep breaths and reached across to her mother. "You've had this all these years?"

"I don't know why I haven't shown you before," said Miriam. "I didn't even show my mother before I left Hungary." The old grief was there in her voice. It was always there when she spoke of what she hadn't shown her mother, what she hadn't said to her mother.

Mish turned the bracelet over and over in her hands. "It must be worth a fortune," she said.

"If it's genuine, it's priceless," said Lili, her voice trembling.

"Perhaps it is," said Miriam. "But it can't be sold."

"No, of course not. It belongs in a museum," said Lili.

"No!' said Miriam. "No museums. We have to keep it."

What now? Did Miriam have some crazy idea that the bracelet held memories of her past, memories of what had been lost?

"We should at least show someone." Lili had seen enough fragments of jewellery to know the furore this piece would cause at the Museum.

"No!" said Miriam again. "It must stay with us. With me or one of you. Daughters marked at birth."

"What?" Lili leapt up from the couch, knocking the table. One of the precious cups fell to the floor, bounced against the table leg, and shattered into small pieces.

"Mum!" Mish grabbed her hand.

Lili shook her off. "You said, 'Daughters marked at birth'. Where did you hear that?" She stood over Miriam, hands on hips, heart racing as if she had been running.

Miriam stared at the broken cup, face white as the broken porcelain. "That's what Bubbe Mari said: the Queen's gift for daughters marked at birth. I thought it meant my birthmark." She shrugged, a delicate, vulnerable gesture like a wounded bird.

"What does it mean?" asked Mish. She sounded scared.

Lili clasped her hands to stop them trembling. "It's on the tablet! Daughters will come marked at birth . . ."

"That's too weird," said Mish, rubbing her arms as if suddenly cold.

"Are you sure that's what Bubbe Mari said?" asked Lili, suddenly wanting to hug Miriam, apologise for breaking the cup and acting like a bully. Instead she sat down and took some deep breaths.

Miriam shrugged again. "It was a long time ago, but that's what I remember." She knelt to pick up the pieces of the cup.

Lili took the bracelet from Mish. It was heavy: eight thumbnail-sized rosettes of gold strung on a gold cord of interlocking loops. In each rosette, eight pieces of dark blue stone--lapis lazuli--set in pitch, like the petals of a flower or the tines of a star. Only three of them were cracked.

"It's very beautiful."

"I've never worn it," murmured Miriam, kneeling to collect the shattered porcelain.

That was surprising. Miriam's love of semi-precious stones was legend in the family; she owned some wonderful pieces. She placed the fragments of the cup on the table and stood.

"It didn't seem right," said Miriam. "Like I was only taking care of it."

Lili slipped the bracelet onto her wrist.

Mish and Miriam stared at her, mouths open in surprise.

"What? Do you think I'm going to disappear or something?"

"Maybe there's a spell," said Mish. "Like the cloak Medea made, or Hercules' shirt, or the Pendragon's scabbard."

Lili touched the bracelet. It was just a piece of jewellery, no spells, no magic. Mish had a very active imagination; she had read every book on myths and legends in the school library and had a whole wall of fantasy novels in her bedroom.

"There was magic in the scabbard so he couldn't be killed," said Mish. "The Queen made it."

"The Queen's gift," said Miriam, echoing her Bubbe's words from more than half a century before.

"But which Queen?" asked Mish.

Lili's skin crawled, as if insects were running over her. "That's on the tablet, too: remember the Queen. There were two Queens in ancient Sumer: Queen of Heaven and Earth and Queen of the Underworld, Inanna and Eresh-ki-gal ."

"Huh?" Mish touched the bracelet. "Is this as old as the tablet?"

"Could be," said Lili. "It looks Sumerian. I've been researching the *me*, the vestments worn by Inanna when she journeyed to the Underworld. One of them was an arm band."

"You think it's from Sumer?" said Mish. "Like it was used in Temples or something?"

"If the *me* really exist, then this is exactly the sort of thing I'd expect to find."

"What do you mean: if they exist?"

"We don't know if it was just a story recorded on the tablets, or if the rituals were enacted."

"Did Inanna really exist?" asked Miriam.

"Most scholars would say she didn't," said Lili. "No more than Aphrodite really lived on Mount Olympus."

"And you? What do you say?" asked Mish.

"I would have said she was just a story, but I'm not as sure of anything lately."

"I've been thinking of Bubbe Maria," said Miriam

quietly, absently arranging the pieces of the shattered cup. "I know it sounds strange, but it's as if she's been calling me."

That's the least of the strangeness, thought Lili, slipping the bracelet off and placing it back in the pouch. They spoke a little longer, but about other things like Josh's tennis and Joel's fishing trip.

When Lili and Mish stood to leave, Miriam made them promise to keep the bracelet safe. Lili hugged her good-bye; she seemed smaller and more breakable than ever before.

That night, as Mish searched Google for references to Queens and the gifts of Queens, Lili leafed through her textbooks. She expected to find the bracelet on every page, but there was nothing quite like it. Had Miriam's Bubbe really said *daughters marked at birth*?

Mish's Google search for Queen's gift produced pages on horse races and knighthoods but nothing about a necklace.

"Which one's Bubbe Mari?" asked Mish, looking at the framed photograph on the wall: a sepia-coloured shot of three formal-looking people sitting awkwardly on an overstuffed couch in a dark room.

"The one on the right." Lili pulled out the genogram she had drawn up when she was younger than Mish, trying to reclaim something of her mother's lost family. "Mari Zeiblin, born May 5, 1849, the oldest child of Franz and Maria. She had a sister and three brothers: Zinna, Joseph, Frederick, and Hans. That's all I know."

Once again she came face to face with the great, gaping hole where her mother's family should be.

After Mish went to bed, Lili sat for a long time, holding

the bracelet, wishing it could speak . . .

CHAPTER V

Melbourne, Australia. Updated Sunday March 16th 2014 2.19pm AEDT

In Sydney, hundreds of people have lined the promenade at Bondi Beach, waiting to see what impact the Peru earthquake will have on Australian shores. Beachgoers were directed off the sand shortly before 8.30am AEDT and the beach was closed. Much of Australia's east coast was put on tsunami alert late on Friday with boats urged to return to harbour. A massive 8.9 magnitude quake hit Peru yesterday, killing 834 people and triggering a tsunami that rushed across the Pacific. -ABC/AFP

Paula tiptoed past the children's rooms to the front door. The night called, whispering secrets on the breeze. She pulled a shawl from the hallstand, opened the door, and stepped outside. The air smelled deliciously fresh after hours of homework and bedtime stories.

Paula walked slowly to the far corner of the garden, breathing deeply, scuffing her feet over the uneven tufts of grass. Her toes itched to feel the softness of the moist, green lawns of her childhood, but lawns had become unsustainable since droughts and water restrictions, and these days the growth in the front yard looked more like a bad haircut than anything else.

Paula bent low to enter a small alcove under the drooping branches of the old plum tree, enclosed by the unclipped wilderness she called a garden. The eternal hum of the city segued into mysterious possibilities: the droning of bees on a riverbank, the fall of spring rain on green grass . . .

She stooped to pour water from a round-bellied ceramic jug into a wide clay bowl half buried in the ground, a libation to the Goddess who sometimes came close at night under the trees. She put the jug down, sat on a flat rock under the tree, and closed her eyes. Time changed, and she was six years old again, cocooned in velvet darkness, watching the moon rise round and golden over the trees as the frogs sang their secrets to the night . . .

"Mum? Are you there?" Rinna stood on the verandah, backlit by the hall light, peering into the garden. "Mary's awake."

Paula came abruptly back to the present, left the bower, and ran across the yard to the big, rambling house and her four children.

"Was she screaming again?" she asked Rinna, holding her close as they walked down the hallway.

Rinna nodded. "What's the matter with her?"

"I don't know. We'll sort it out."

The light was on, Mary sitting up in bed, her eyes round as an owl's, with scruffy, old Fair Bear clutched to her chest like a shield.

"Another dream?" asked Paula.

Mary shrugged.

"Come on, let's get you two back to sleep. School tomorrow."

She lay down with Mary, snuggling against her back. The girls' breathing settled into the steady rhythm of sleep, and Paula's thoughts wandered over the day.

Jon's first driving lesson; a milestone, like taking the first step, learning to swim, the first day at school, first night away from home. How she loved it when they took those steps and survived!

Hayley's first that month had been a boyfriend, Chris. "But, Mum, we have to talk for school." "For three hours every night?" "Well, it's a really big project!"

Rinna, serious little mother at twelve, so like her at the same age. And Mary, nine years old, going on ninety nine, with her huge, solemn eyes and strange nightmares.

Was Mary picking up on Paula's own dreams? Every night for the last month, Paula had been woken by a woman's voice saying, "Many are called, few are chosen."

It had been pleasing at first, a promise of being special. After five or six nights in a row, it had become something else, shameful somehow, as if her need to be special had called forth the dream.

"Many are called, few are chosen." Paula had Googled the words; they were biblical, and they made no sense to her at all. She had disavowed Christianity as a teenager, as much in rebellion against her mother's medieval morality as for any deep, philosophical purpose. Had it come back to haunt her? And Mary?

Paula shivered. She wouldn't put it past her mother to come back from the grave and torment her into returning to the fold of Catholicism and having her children baptized. But even a haunting wasn't going to make that happen; what had begun as rebellion had developed into a deep commitment to her own spiritual wisdom. Over the years, Paula had developed her own sacred practices--like pouring water from a jug into a bowl under the old plum tree every night while the children slept--and had learned to listen with her heart, to feel the sacred rhythm in her bones and blood, to recognise the divine in the rustling of the wind in the leaves, in the moonlight, and in sunlight glistening on water. She secretly thought of herself as a priestess of the Goddess, and her mother's ghost, or whatever it was that disturbed her sleep, was never going to convince her to worship a disembodied father God.

Paula shivered. Her mother was probably looking down from Heaven, calling her "strega", making the sign of the cross, and muttering curses in Italian!

"Peace, Mama," she whispered, pulling herself away from the familiar maundering. The girls were sleeping like angels, and Paula crept quietly out into the hallway. If Thom had been home it would have been tempting to go to bed, lie against his back, breathe in his warm-biscuit smell. They might make love in the slow, deep way they had settled into over the years, and fall asleep together . . .

But Thom was away with his mates, fishing and drinking and pretending to be eighteen again, and she had work to do. Her thesis needed at least a few hours from her, but first she clicked open the Gaia site. Another entry from the archaeologist, calling for ideas about a mysterious tablet. There was also something about matrilineal cultures, so Paula joined the discussion, contributing her ideas about how people had lived in cooperation for millennia when the life-giving power of women and Nature was respected.

She was surprised to see a response from the archaeologist in Philadelphia almost immediately. What time was it there?

"Interesting ideas. Do you have data?"

Paula sent through some links and references, and she also gave into her curiosity about the tablet. "Do you think the words on the tablet refer to the present time?"

"Definitely not," wrote Lili. "I just thought someone might have an idea where it came from and how it got to me."

Beyond logic, beyond reason, Paula wanted to argue that the tablet had come to Lili for a purpose, but she hardly knew the other woman, and most people found her intuitive hunches a bit crazy. Or infuriating.

"I think we need something from left field to deal with what's happening in the World," she typed, trying to be moderate.

"Modern science has more chance of fixing the problems than some so-called prophecy from ancient Sumer," wrote Lili.

Paula took a risk. "I think we need all the help we can get! The World's going to shit, and there won't be anything left for our kids unless we fix it!"

"And how exactly do you imagine a poem can help fix it?" asked Lili.

Oops! Paula rolled her eyes; she really shouldn't be so pushy. "Sorry! I just get excited about ideas that come from outside the normal channels. I think we need something to take us right out of the mindset and beliefs that have got us into the mess we're in. Something to restore the balance."

No answer.

Paula shrugged and turned back to her work.

A few minutes later, her Skype pinged. Who would be calling so late?

Inanna1234, said the Skype name. Inanna?

"Hello," said Paula. "Who's this?"

"Is that Paula Matthews? From Gaia?" A woman with an American accent.

The Skype picture resolved into a very pretty women with amazing blue eyes and dark curly hair. She looked miserable.

"Is that you? The archaeologist?"

"Oh, I'm glad it's you," said Lili. "I looked you up on Gaia and then found your Skype name. Or a name I hoped was yours. What time is it there?" She spoke so fast, Paula had to wait for the meaning of the words to catch up.

"I guess that's what I get for using my real name on these forums! Look, I'm sorry if I upset you. I just get these feelings sometimes, and I shouldn't say anything . . ."

"No, what you said, about restoring the balance; that's on the tablet, those exact words: restore the balance."

"Wow! That's amazing."

"I know. That's why I called."

"But you don't think it's a message or anything."

"I don't know what to believe, but it was strange to hear you say those words. A coincidence, I guess. I mean, how could it possibly be a message from the past?"

"Well, there's Nostradamus, and the Aztecs, and all sorts of other things."

"Not exactly scientific!"

"No, but science isn't everything."

"Aren't you an environmental scientist?"

"Yes, but with the emphasis on environmental."

"Fair enough."

"Did you just call to tell me I got the words right?" asked Paula.

"No. No. I called because you're the first person who's

shown any real interest in the tablet. I mean, I get a four thousand year old letter, and no one thinks it's amazing. Except you."

"And I'm a crazy environmental scientist obsessed with matrilineal cultures!"

"Yes. Or, I mean no. Oh, I don't know what I mean! I'm having weird dreams, I want my husband to stop rubbing my back, and nothing seems to mean anything anymore."

Paula didn't know what to say.

"Yeah, I know. So I call a stranger across the other side of the World. Now who's the crazy one?"

"I guess it's never crazy to reach out; I'm just not sure what I can do."

"Maybe you can help me sort it out. It's easier to talk to someone I don't know."

Paula shook her head in amazement. Americans! She'd barely spoken with the woman, and now she was asking Paula to be her best friend! Well, why not? Anyone who supported the Gaia forum was probably not too bad.

"So, do you think it's the tablet that's been disturbing you?" asked Paula.

"I don't know," said Lili. "Maybe it's just a mid-life crisis."

"I think we say that about far too many things that are actually important," said Paula.

"See, that's why I called you: you take things seriously, as if they matter. That's sort of unfashionable where I come from."

"No wonder you're miserable!" said Paula, and immediately wished she hadn't.

"I am miserable, aren't I? I live in a beautiful home, I'm in an okay marriage, have two great children, a good career etcetera, etcetera. And I'm miserable. And ungrateful!"

"I don't know. I think we women need to feel miserable to remind ourselves that we're not just wives and mothers etcetera. It's too easy to fall into the expected roles and lose ourselves."

"Do you lose yourself? Are you married? Children?"

"I lose myself all the time; that's how I know about it! I've been married for twenty nine years, and we have four children, but I think it's bigger than that. It's what happens to women in a culture that doesn't respect nature and the feminine."

Lili was quiet.

"Now I'm off on my hobbyhorse," said Paula. "Sorry! Tell me more about your prophecy."

"I've been calling it a poem, but if it's a prophecy, it's the sort of thing you'd expect to read about the World today."

"See!"

"Maybe."

Paula sighed. Passionate as she was about the true cause of the environmental disasters sweeping the World, her ideas were more intuition than science; no wonder Lili was doubtful. But someone had to do something before the rivers ran dry, the ice-caps melted, and the sea covered even more land!

Lili smiled tiredly. "Anyway, it's good to actually see you. Isn't this technology amazing? What time is it there, by the way?"

Paula laughed. "Everyone says I do that. Now I know what it's like."

"What? Oh, changing the subject. I do it all the time. It's just the way my mind works. Associations." Lili shrugged, rolling her eyes.

"Can I see the tablet?" asked Paula.

Lili held up a piece of flat clay about the size of a small, oval plate. The marks looked like bird tracks, and Paula had no idea which way was up.

"You can read that?" she asked Lili.

Lili nodded.

"I'm very impressed by anyone who can decipher languages no longer spoken by the living," said Paula. "I think it goes back to school days. I had a wonderful Latin teacher, one of those classical, older women who loved learning. I wanted to please her, probably to be like her, but most of the class just made fun of it. *Latin is a language as dead as dead can be; It killed off all the Romans, and now it's killing me.*"

"I remember that one. Isn't it strange how much easier it was to learn that silly song than *amo, amas, amat*?" said Lili, smiling.

She read Paula the translation. "I have no idea what it means, for then or now."

"It really does sound like a prediction, like Nostradamus, or something. Do you think someone knew that the Sea would rise and flood the land, that men would forsake the task of life?"

Lili snorted. "Not likely! Do you really think this was written four thousand years ago for us to read now?"

"For someone who doesn't believe in prophecies, you seem fascinated by the possibility," said Paula.

Lili shrugged. She did have serious doubts about anyone who believed in so called prophecies, and the sheer age of the clay tablet made her even more sceptical; four thousand years was a very long time! It was a miracle that anything at all had survived the two or three hundred generations of warfare, natural disasters, and the human tendency to destroy anyone and anything that was different. So much could be lost even in the space of one generation.

"Well, I'm voting that it's a message for now," said

Paula.

Lili wondered if it was time to end the call. Paula was probably one of those kooky women who channelled Isis, or something.

"Just think! It could be from a time when there was a Goddess, and the life-giving power of the feminine was respected. When Inanna was Queen of Heaven and Earth," said Paula.

That made more sense to Lili, but it probably just meant that Paula was channelling Inanna rather than Isis.

"Look, Paula," she said, taking a deep breath. "I know I called you, but I'm starting to think maybe I should go. I'm usually the one who sees all sorts of patterns in history, and I think there's more hope for the World with a Goddess than a father God, but . . ."

Paula interrupted, excited. "That's it. That's what the words mean. On the tablet. It's about hope for the World."

"For the World now? But why not something back then?" Lili's heart thumped with excitement despite her misgivings.

"I don't think so, although you may be right, of course," said Paula. "The mess probably started when Gilgamesh cut down the cedars and turned the Garden of Eden into a desert, but I think it's a message for today. Mind you, my colleagues roll their eyes and laugh behind my back."

"Garden of Eden? You lost me there. I know the story of Gilgamesh, of course, but cedars? Anyway, I hate the way people dismiss what they don't understand; it's happened so often with new theories." Lili remembered some uncomfortable moments of her own at the University.

"You'd know of Marija Gimbutas?" asked Paula.

"Of course," said Lili. "When they were finding all those statues of women with big breasts and buttocks, she knew they were symbols of the Mother Goddesses. Most of the other archaeologists thought they were some sort of sexual fetishes. Twenty thousand of them! Can you imagine?"

"Probably not so strange these days," said Paula. "I've received about twenty thousand spam emails offering all sorts of sexual fetishes." She shook her head, loosening a strand of hair from the clip.

"Your hair's exactly the same colour as mine," said Lili, changing the subject precipitously.

Paula held a strand of her long hair up against the screen. It did seem to be the same colour as Lili's shorter curls, and they both had grey strands just beginning to show through the dark brown.

"Are you Italian?" Paula asked.

Lili shook her head, thick curls bobbing.

"I'm Jewish--New York for two generations--from Hungary on my mother's side and Poland on my father's. Your family are Italian?"

Paula nodded. "My parents' families migrated here from Calabria in the thirties."

Lili smiled. "Not so different in some ways. Both tribal cultures with ancient traditions."

"Are you a Gemini?" asked Paula.

"No. I'm a Scorpio. Can't you tell? Obsessed with the secrets of the past!"

"My moon's in Scorpio. I know what you mean."

"I confess," said Lili. "My moon's in Gemini."

"Good," said Paula. "That makes us perfect partners in crime!"

They left it there and arranged to Skype again the following night. Paula dreamed the voice again saying, "Many are called; few are chosen."

The next night, their conversation went straight to the tablet.

"This tablet has never shown up in any of the translations," said Lili. "It could have been written by the same person who wrote the Lament for Ur. Have you read that?" She said it like someone might say, "Have you read the paper today?"

"No, I haven't," said Paula, wondering how many people had.

"The lament was most likely written by a High Priestess just before the fall of Ur. About 2000 BCE," said Lili.

Paula smiled to hear the familiar phrase. It was common parlance amongst academics, but most people still thought of BCE as Before Christ, rather than Before the Common Era. Another example of the arrogant assumptions that pissed her off; if the three faiths of the father God could only agree that this was truly the Common Era, then maybe everyone could get on with working out how to solve the global crisis.

"What are you thinking?" Lili looked at Paula curiously.

Paula told her about her chain of associations from hearing the use of BCE. "I know I sound like a fanatic, but I really do believe this prophecy's important. We have to do something to stop what's happening!"

"I love your passion," said Lili wistfully. "That's what I'm missing. I can translate the tablet, but it doesn't excite me."

"Well, you do the translating, and I'll be excited for both of us. By the way, what does it mean when you say "the sacred me"? It sounds like some New Age mystical state."

Lili smiled. "The me were symbols of power in ancient Sumer. Physical things like a crown and necklaces, although they were said to hold mysteries as well."

"Are they still around?" asked Paula.

Lili shrugged. "No one knows. My mother gave me a bracelet the other day that might be that old."

"Your mother had a bracelet that old? What's it like?"

Lili pushed her chair back and reached for a bag on the bookshelf next to her desk. She drew out a bracelet.

"Oh, shit!" Paula pushed back from the computer and stood up, hopping from foot to foot.

"What?" said Lili. "What's the matter? Has something bitten you?"

"Stay there," said Paula.

She ran to the bedroom. Where was it? She pulled open drawers, threw undies and tights, socks and bras onto the floor, felt under the bed for the document box, remembered it was in the safety deposit, and stood on a chair to reach onto the top of the wardrobe.

"Ah!" She ran back to the computer and waved a cloth bag at the screen, spilling powdery dust onto the keyboard.

"Don't tell me it's a bracelet!" said Lili, face close to the camera as if she was trying to climb through onto Paula's desk.

Paula pulled out a necklace with blue stones set in rosettes. She'd always thought it was brass.

"Unbelievable!" Lili sounded drunk.

"You can say that again."

"Where did you get it?"

"My mother. Is it real?"

"Looks real to me. It could be from the same set."

"It must be worth a fortune." Paula wiped dust from the necklace with her fingers.

"What did your mother say when she gave it to you?" asked Lili.

"Not much. It was when she had her heart attack. She gave it to me in hospital. Had it in her bag. I thought it must have been a gift from a boy back in Italy, something she kept hidden from my father. All she said was: 'From her hand to mine, from my hand to yours, from your hand to hers. The line is unbroken.' It was in dialect, but I think that's what she said. She had another heart attack a few hours later, and we never spoke again."

Lili was quiet.

"Where did she get it?" asked Paula. Had her mother brought it from Calabria? Had it come from someone back there?

"I wonder if these pieces could be linked to the *me*," said Lili.

"From the tablet? Inanna's *me*? That would be too strange!"

"Forget I said that," said Lili. "You start looking into something, and bits begin to connect up in ways that defy logic."

"I can't believe we both have this jewellery. It's weird."

"That's what my daughter said."

"I feel a bit like a teenager in an urban fantasy. How old is your daughter?"

"Mish is eighteen," said Lili absently. "I'll talk to someone at work. Miriam--my mother--didn't want me to show anyone, but I could describe the pieces and see if anyone recognises them. There's nothing in my books."

"What would my mother be doing with something from ancient Sumer?" asked Paula.

They were still discussing that two hours later when Mary woke again.

"Talk soon," said Lili, head filled with thoughts that kept her awake until dawn. Some of Paula's ideas were crazy, but Lili felt more alive than she had in years.

CHAPTER VI

The city of Urim (Ur), Ancient Sumer. c 2000BCE.

AGE OF TAURUS: FERTILITY, CONSTRUCTION, AND ABUNDANCE

+/- 4000 BCE - 2000 BCE. Located where Iraq is today, Sumer was a matriarchal agrarian economy with a financial system based on abundance and shared wealth. One of the oldest known bronze coins was the Sumerian shekel, dating from 3,200 B.C. It was inscribed with the likeness of the Goddess Inanna-Ishtar, who bestowed kingship in Sumer and was the goddess of fertility, life and death. Inanna wore the horns of a cow, the sacred animal that personified the Great Mother everywhere in ancient myth.[vi]

AGE OF ARIES: WARFARE, VIOLENCE AND CONQUEST

+/- 2000 BCE - 0 CE The Goddess Inanna was superseded as the source of supreme kingship by the male god Enlil of Nippur, and the matriarchal system of shared communal abundance was forcibly displaced by a militant patriarchal system. The cornucopia of the Horned Goddess became the bull horns of the Thunder God, representing masculine power, virility and force.[vii]

It is an honour to be chosen for the Temple. Or so Mir-ri had been told ever since she could remember. Now that she was sitting in the Temple, waiting to see the High Priestess, she wondered if her mother and aunts had been lying.

How could her mother have just handed her over like a sack of washing? How could she just walk back home and drink sweet tea, sweep the floor, go to market? If it was an honour, why did it feel so bad?

Mir-ri's bottom ached on the stone bench. "Don't move," the Priestess had said when she left her there.

Her feet stung with the cold of the tiled floor. "Wash," the Priestess had said before leading her to the bench. Didn't she know that Mir-ri had been scrubbed and preened by her mother and her mother's sisters for three whole days?

Mir-ri bit her lip and counted the brown floor tiles. Her feet itched to follow the tiles back to the door, out to the river, and away. Shivery bumps rose on her arms and legs as she scuffed her toes on the patch of dampness where her long hair had dripped, plip-plop, onto the floor.

The new shift scratched her skin. Didn't the Priestess know that the one she wore from home had been dyed by her mother? That the dye had cost a whole month's tokens? That it was her last link to home?

Mir-ri shivered. *It is an honour to be chosen for the Temple.* Back in the days before she turned nine, the women had told her that over and over again, laughing and gossiping as they cracked the emmer wheat, cooked the flatbread, and washed the clothes.

"But what about my friends? And all of you?" she had asked once, throwing the question at them as a challenge.

"You will not think of that when you are a Priestess," her

mother had replied in a dreamy voice. "Nanna is the Great One closest to the hearts and souls of women."

"Nanna is the Moon," said the women as they carried the lettuce and dates home from market.

"The Moon changes with the rhythms of women's bleeding and the fertile days," said the women, laughing away Mir-ri's questions and fears.

"Who knows?" they whispered as they bathed together. "Perhaps one day our Mir-ri will be High Priestess."

"She is marked for Inanna," they said, stroking the star-shaped birthmark on her wrist.

Mir-ri rubbed the mark. It did look like a star, the sign of Inanna, Queen of Heaven and Earth, but maybe it was just an ordinary old birthmark. She traced the eight-rayed star with her toes on the tiles, as she had traced it in the dust when she played with her cousins.

The Priestess from the bath returned. Mir-ri gripped the edges of the bench and clenched her teeth. The woman's robe swished closer.

She led Mir-ri down another corridor to a room where the morning Sun streamed in through arched window-openings to shine on murals of palm trees and birds. The Sun warmed the air and dispelled some of the dark thoughts.

A Priestess stood by the window; the High Priestess in her purple-trimmed robe! Her face was the face of Inanna, strong and radiant. Mir-ri bowed her head. Would the High Priestess know what she had been thinking? Would she send her home in disgrace? Would she turn the eyes of Death on her?

Nin-lil-la turned her attention to the child. A shiver of

premonition rippled through her body. It was her! The one she had foreseen, the one she had feared would never come . . .

"Many are called but few are chosen," she said, beginning the ancient ritual with which she welcomed every initiate.

The girl flinched like a startled gazelle. Was she flawed? Lacking courage? Too weak?

"Do you bring your feet to walk in Her Ways?"

The girl was silent.

"You must answer, child," said Nin-lil-la. "Do you bring your feet to walk in Her Ways?"

"I do," whispered the girl, raising her head, meeting Nin-lil-la's eyes.

At least she was not weak. "Do you bring your knees to kneel in Her praise?"

"I do." She knelt.

"Do you bring your sex to rejoice in Her Life-giving."

"I do," said the girl.

"Do you bring your breasts for Her abundance flowing?"

"I do."

"Do you bring your hands to do Her work?"

"I do."

"Do you bring your lips to sing Her acclaim?"

"I do."

"Do you bring your eyes to see Her presence in all?"

"I do."

"Rise, child. You are called."

She was the one, but would there be time enough for her to fulfill the vision?

Mir-ri looked up into kohl-lined eyes, dark as the

midnight sky, deep as the deepest well. The morning Sun completely filled the chamber, and the High Priestess seemed to grow taller, more luminous. She beckoned, and Mir-ri followed her through an arched doorway, along a tiled passage, up a wide stairway, along another passage, through double doors to an inner chamber set with four altars--East, North, West, and South--and a round, reed mat in the centre. Candles on each altar lit the room. Smoke rose in spirals from charcoal braziers, carrying the scent of cedar and frankincense.

"I come here to hear Her voice," said the High Priestess. "And to remember. This room is very old."

It was quiet in the room of altars. Drawn by a movement, Mir-ri turned to the East. Suspended above the altar, an alabaster carving of a dove hovered in a sunlit sea of dust motes.

"Celestial dove," said the High Priestess, her voice loud in the silence. "She bestows radiant love. We call on Her for laughter, lust, and inspiration."

Mir-ri knelt before the dove. Peace filled her body, and her fears dissolved. Warmth settled in her bones.

"She lifts us on Her golden wings." The High Priestess's voice rose as she repeated the words and lifted her arms above her head, backs of her hands meeting like wings.

Mir-ri mirrored the movements, the life of the dove filling her arms.

The High Priestess pointed to the South. Eyes of topaz glared fiercely from a statue of the Lady of Heaven in her lioness shape. The topaz eyes glowed like the gaze of Utu, Great One of the Sun.

"Lioness of battle," said the High Priestess, her voice deep.

Mir-ri trembled. There were tales told around the Enten fires of the great mother lions roaring to stop the hearts of goats, roaring to take the breath from gazelle and antelope.

"She brings strength invincible. Mighty warrior, fierce defender, She is the protector of women and children, always there." The High Priestess raised her hands to her shoulders, elbows held close to her sides. Her fingers curled outwards, forming the shape of lion's claws, tensed, ready to fight.

Mir-ri took on the posture and moved closer to the altar. The great beast blinked once. Mir-ri shook her head. Had she imagined it? Had the incense clouded her mind?

She walked back to the centre, the lioness's eyes on her back.

In the West, something moved on the altar--snakes with soft patterned scales, glittering mosaic eyes, tongues darting in and out.

"The West is home to the sacred serpent who holds the ancient wisdom. Sibyl, soothsayer and seer, She speaks Her truth that we may hear." The words slid into Mir-ri's ears, into her senses.

The High Priestess raised her hands before her forehead and moved them down and up in front of her body, palms crossing in the undulating movements of the snakes. Mir-ri let the movements take her.

When stillness returned, the High Priestess lifted one of the smaller snakes. Raising her hands slowly, Mir-ri touched it . . .

. . . and gasped with surprise at the soft smoothness of the creature. The snake's tongue darted in an out as its head swayed closer and closer to her face.

"She's beautiful," Mir-ri whispered. Its skin was soft, its tongue gentle against her lips. She placed it back on the altar before turning to the North.

In beaten copper, mounted on a base of lapis lazuli, rested

the curved horns of the crescent Moon. Mir-ri had seen the Moon appear over the horizon just like that, a boat sailing the heavens.

"The Horned One," said the High Priestess. "She brings blessed fruitfulness, the life-giving power of the womb, of women, of the Earth. Her arms are always open, from Her breasts abundance flowing."

Mir-ri knelt close to the altar that she might receive the blessings of the Queen of Earth, the Mother of all. She extended her arms out to the side, bending her elbows and opening her hands so that her palms faced up to the heavens. The sign of the Cow-eyed One came naturally, as if her arms had always known what to do.

She walked again to the centre, to the symbol woven into the mat, an eight-rayed star, the sign of Inanna, Great Lady of Heaven, the sign she had been tracing on the tiles.

"We return always to the centre," said the High Priestess. "To the formless Chaos. To the Primal Waters. To the beginning. It is from this we come and to this we return. The centre holds the Balance."

Mir-ri sank to her knees, not fully understanding the words, yet sensing the truth of them. A humming sound filled the chamber, like bees and birdsong carried on the breeze. The High Priestess strummed a harp she held on her lap; inset with lapis lazuli and shells, the sound box was beautiful. Mir-ri's sight blurred as her senses drifted with the harp's song . . .

Time itself stopped and then began again, leaving a deep calm. The High Priestess lifted Mir-ri to her feet

"Come. I will have you taken to the city Temple. There you will live and study. Soon it will be time for the Evening Rites."

Late that night, Nin-lil-la stood on the parapet of the nearly complete E-gish-shir-gal. The great, stepped Temple had been built high enough that she could look out over the rooftops to the Pars Sea.

The girl had come, but Nin-lil-la's heart was heavy. A messenger had also come: Manark had been found dead, sitting at his table, head resting on his hands as if asleep. Manark, who had been there since the beginning of her time in the Temple. Manark, who remembered the old ways and shared her fears for Urim.

All things must pass, but some endings were harder than others. Who now would share the passing of the Age of the Bull? Who else truly understood what it meant for Urim?

The Age was passing as quickly as the Sun sailed through the last moments before descending into the Underworld. But the Sun would return; Urim would fall and be covered by dust.

Again the question: Would there be time for the girl--Mir-ri--to learn all she must? Time to set her feet on the path she must walk?

Nin-lil-la stayed on the E-gish-shir-gal as the lamps went out one by one, and the crickets sang their warning to the stars.

CHAPTER VII

The city of Urim, Ancient Sumer. c 2000BCE.

Most people would define priestess as a woman who leads ritual. But there are a range of names and culturally defined meanings, including shaman, medicine woman, diviner, spirit-medium, oracle, sibyl and wisewoman.[viii]

Mir-ri stood alone in her new room, a small, square hole in the thick wall of the bottom level of the Temple of Nanna. Rolled in the corner she found a reed mat. Hanging on a hook on the brick wall was a spare shift, plain as the one she wore. There was no window opening and no lamp. At least it would stay cool! She unrolled her sleeping mat on the tiles and lay down for the first night of her new life.

Pictures danced before her eyes in the darkness: rising before dawn; bathing in the courtyard at home; dressing in the soft, blue shift; saying farewell to her family; walking with her mother through the lanes, along the river to the Temple; the Temple door closing.

Her chest hurt and her eyes stung. The image of the Horned One from the room of altars floated before her eyes, and she slept.

Mir-ri woke to an ululation echoing through the corridors. The call to rise!

Mir-ri had heard the call from the Temple all her life: as she walked with her mother to market at dawn; as she lay on her mat dreaming; as she tiptoed out with her cousins to watch the Sun return for the day.

Now the voices were summoning her.

She scrambled up and stood blinking in the dark. Two steps to the door, hands out to find the opening in the wall. The dim shapes of other girls moving in the hallway. Mir-ri smoothed her shift, combed her fingers through her hair, and stepped out. She followed the others along the corridor, up a flight of stairs, and through a tunnel to an open courtyard. As she emerged from the darkness, the first rays of Sun glowed red on the bricks. Voices swelled forth, welcoming the morning star.

"Hail to Inanna, Great Lady of Heaven

Hail to Inanna, First Daughter of the Moon."[ix]

Mir-ri found the rhythm and sang her praises to honour the Lady of Morning. Her voice was soft, but her heart sang clear and true to the morning star. Lions called from the riverbanks.

After the invocation, she followed the others to the washroom. Behind a wall she found a row of holes where the girls squatted. Accustomed to the small privy at home, she hesitated, but the others seemed unconcerned, laughing and talking as they crouched over the holes. Urns of water with long-handled ladles stood close by for washing. The water was so cold she shivered.

On the other side of the wall were more urns and bowls for washing, with soaps and oils set out on low benches. The soap was not as sweet as her mother's, but it lathered well enough.

Strangely, the other girls acted as if she was not there. They continued to talk and laugh, but not once did they speak to her or even look at her. It made her think she might be in the wrong place, that she had followed the wrong girls from her room. Should she ask someone? But no one looked her way.

The girls left through a low arched doorway. Mir-ri trailed behind them into an open-sided pavilion filled with low tables laden with bowls of dates, bunches of grapes, flatbread and honey. Goat's milk frothed in cool stone jugs, and an urn of fresh water sparkled in the morning Sun.

The others sat in groups, eating and talking, like the women did at home. Mir-ri bit her lip and wondered what her mother would be doing.

Suddenly silence flowed through the courtyard like an invisible wave. On the wave glided the High Priestess, like a bardi reed-boat on the Sea. All heads bowed respectfully, although Mir-ri couldn't help but peek.

"Today we welcome a new Acolyte," said the High Priestess. "Mir-ri, come closer."

Mir-ri jumped. Now everyone was looking at her.

"Mir-ri is from the city, but is now given to Nanna," said the High Priestess. "I charge you with her care as she is charged with yours."

Cries of welcome echoed around the pavilion. Three girls ran up.

"I'm sorry about before," said one of them.

Mir-ri turned to see a short girl with huge, round eyes.

"I'm Hedu."

Mir-ri nodded, suddenly shy.

"It is not permitted, you know."

She turned to find a serious-looking girl with a long face and neatly plaited hair.

"Ner-nin," said the girl, pointing to herself.

"To talk with a new girl until the High Priestess has spoken," said the third girl, completing the sentence. Tall and slender, she leaned down to hug Mir-ri. "I'm Anna."

Mir-ri wondered if they always spoke like that, each one following on from the others. She managed to smile; she was in the right place after all.

Living as an acolyte was much better than Mir-ri had feared. Up with the call from the Kalu priest, kneeling to the East to welcome the morning Star, singing the praises of Inanna, Queen of Heaven.

"We sing Hail! to the Holy One who appears in the Heavens

We sing Hail! to the Holy Priestess of Heaven

We sing Hail! to Inanna, Great Lady of Heaven

We sing Hail! to Inanna, first daughter of the Moon."[x]

And standing to dance, hand movements matching the words, hips swaying to the flute music of the Kalu priest and his assistants.

"Mighty, majestic, radiant,

Ever present,

To you, Inanna, we sing!"

And kneeling again to sing,
"My Lady looks down in sweet wonder from Heaven
Your Priestesses kneel before Holy Inanna
Inanna, the Lady of morning, is radiant on the horizon."

And then the rush to the washroom where the tubs were freshly filled with sweet water from the river for a laughing, splashing welcome to the day.

Anna and Hedu treated her like a sister. They showed her how to wash her own shifts and dry them on the low wall of the courtyard outside the sleeping cubicles. They helped her oil her skin. They taught her how to comb and twist her hair in the style of the Priestesses, while Ner-nin watched over them and gave advice.

The seasons changed, and the memory of Mir-ri's own family faded as she grew to love the chatter and chores, devotion and dancing. She learned the sacred songs and dances for the morning and evening rites, for the seasonal rituals, and for her own personal devotions to Nanna and his daughter Inanna, Holy Priestess of Heaven. She washed the Priestess's linen robes and emptied kitchen scraps into panniers for the asses to cart to the rich farmland given to the Temple by the King.

All the girls worked in the gardens, and Mir-ri savoured the walk through the early-morning shadows, across the city and out towards the river. She happily weeded lettuce beds, milked goats, and dug soil made rich by the floodwaters of the Buranun.

"The young need time in Nature," said the Priestesses, "for the body to grow strong and the spirit to rejoice in the Elements."

The rich, black soil smelled of life and of the Northern lands from where it was carried by the Buranun. Crumbling the soil in her fingers, Mir-ri closed her eyes, sensing the dream of the earth. *I am the womb of life. From me you come and to me you shall return. Nothing is wasted. Do not fear. The green shoot is nourished by all that has gone before. It grows and, when the season is done, it returns. Nothing is wasted.*[xi]

In the wind, she heard the song of the air. *I am the breath of life. From me come the winds of change. Nothing remains the same. Do not fear. To live you must leave the safety of the womb. To eat you must crush the wheat. Nothing remains the same.*

In their season, the rains came, followed by Sun, leaving a damp, glistening world. *I am the beginning of life. From me all things come forth. Nothing is forgotten. Do not fear. The primal vortex of destruction is also the central wellspring of creation. Nothing is forgotten.*

She found warmth in the golden light of the Emesh Sun and the glowing flames of the Enten fires. *I am the heart of life. From me comes the searing heat of desire. Nothing is unknown. Do not fear. The barley and the corn agree to live in the Sun and die in the flames to give you food. Nothing is unknown.*

Time passed. Life in the Temple of Nanna went on, and the fall of Urim moved inexorably closer.

CHAPTER VIII

Philadelphia. Updated Tue January 7th 2015 8.15am UTC

A slow-moving winter storm smacked the Northeast on Sunday, unleashing heavy snow, rain and hurricane-force winds as it knocked out power to more than a million homes and businesses and turned Maine beachfront streets into rivers. More than 1,000 flights were canceled, bus service across northern New Jersey was knocked out and roads from Ohio to West Virginia to Maine were closed. State troopers used snowmobiles to reach motorists stranded for hours on an eastern New York highway. Power failures were severe and widespread in New Hampshire - 330,000 of the state's roughly 800,000 customers. Sunday's storm made January the snowiest month ever for New Brunswick, N.J.-- 40 inches so far. And it may not be over. There is the potential for another storm to hit the East Coast next Friday, Axelrod reports.

Lili pulled the big collar of her cashmere coat up around her ears. She'd had the coat so long that wearing it was like being hugged by an old friend.

"I can't remember it being so cold," she said, rubbing her hands together to take the chill from her fingers.

"You say that every year," Mish said.

"Do I? It's worse this year. Everything's worse this year."

Mish put her arm around Lili's shoulders and pulled her close. "You're too skinny. You should stop worrying so much and eat some dairy."

"Now you sound like me. I'm the Mummy, remember!"

"Yes, but I'm the daughter of the Mummy." Mish let Lili go and pulled a zombie face, raising her hands like claws.

Lili laughed at Mish's antics. "Let's get something hot to drink."

It was warm in the café, and the smell of coffee and pastries made her mouth water. They had been shopping all day, and Mish seemed tireless. But it was her birthday.

"What's happening with the Great Tablet Mystery?" asked Mish, sipping her hot chocolate.

"I thought you'd never ask."

"I've been busy. Nineteen's an important birthday."

"Only if you're a gunslinger," said Lili. She and Mish had both loved Stephen King's Dark Tower series.

"Not me," said Mish. "Peace and love and hot chocolate for me."

Lili smiled; it was a relief to talk nonsense and think about something as mundane as a birthday.

"So?" Mish smiled over her hot chocolate. "The tablet?"

"I've traced the package to an address in Amman. It was routed through Rome, but the courier says it came from Jordan."

"Are you going?"

"Of course! I won't find who sent it by staying in Philadelphia."

"And you really believe this is important?"

"I do, although I have no idea why! Paula says we have to do something to save the World, and she's right. Time's running out. Human beings can only survive in a small range of climatic conditions, and we're stretching the outer edges that now. I want your children to have a World to inhabit, and I want to be able to tell them I did everything I could to make sure of it."

"I'd like to meet Paula! She's certainly got you going."

"I think you'd like her. She's so passionate about everything. I'd forgotten what it was like to talk all night and still have energy to get through the day."

"I'm glad. You seemed so miserable for a while."

"Mid-life crisis," said Lili. "Although Paula says I can't call it that because it diminishes the meaning of it."

"I like her more and more. I hope the trip works out."

"So do I."

"At least you'll get to spend time with Paula without having to stay up all night."

"I wonder if we'll argue less in person."

"What do you argue about?" asked Mish.

"Mostly scientific proof and the absence of it. Paula's less concerned with logic than I am."

"That wouldn't be hard," said Mish, patting Lili's arm. "You're a bit like a computer sometimes."

"Systematic is what I am. Systematic and persistent."

Mish smiled. "Do you know how many great discoveries have come through dreams or by chance?"

"Yes, but you're an artist. Artists are allowed to dream and rely on chance."

Mish pulled out a pen and doodled something on the paper napkin. She held up a line sketch of two women watching a man writing a long, complex formula on a blackboard.

"Who's the one covering her eyes?" asked Lili.

"That's Paula. She only pretends to be a scientist."

Lili picked up the drawing. "I'll show her."

"What does she really think about the prophecy?" asked Mish.

Lili sighed. "She thinks it means something important for now. I think some of her ideas are crazy, but she's got me stirred up to do something. And she believes that one person--or two-- can make a difference."

"Sounds like a true friend, or a sister," said Mish. "I wish I had a sister," she added, sounding wistful. "Although Josh isn't bad as brothers go."

They talked about him for a while, and Lili hoped fourteen wasn't too young to be leaving him for three weeks.

Mish must have read her mind. "Don't worry. Dad and I will look after him."

They chatted about other things while they finished their drinks. When they stood to leave, Mish asked, "What exactly will you do in Amman?"

"Check out the address I have, and there's a sociologist at the university of Jordan I want to see. Haleli Borro. She gave a paper at that conference I spoke at last year in New York, but I didn't get to talk to her. She may have some ideas; her paper was on the relevance of ancient texts to current social issues."

"Don't you academics all email and send papers to each other?" asked Mish.

"Usually, but apparently she's a bit of a recluse. I've tried contacting her through the University, but no luck."

"That's odd. Surely she must be accessible if she's on staff there."

"You'd think so, wouldn't you? She's either in a meeting, away on leave, or will call me back. She never has."

"Odder and odder."

"Uh-huh. My guess is she's scared."

"Of what?"

"Something there. Politics. Islamists."

They walked out into the cold. Mish linked her arm though Lili's.

"You're imagining things. You've read too much ancient history. Plots within plots. She probably just doesn't like people."

"Maybe. But now I've started imagining things, I can't stop. Like the prophecy. Like the bracelet; it's almost unbelievable that Paula's mother had a matching piece."

"I'll give you that. It's enough even to make you start imagining things!" Mish's eyes sparkled. "So, you're onto some sort of mystery. Ancient prophecies reveal truth in the twenty-first Century. Dan Brown, eat your heart out."

"Something like that," said Lili. "I'll need someone here to check records, follow up leads. Will you do it?"

Mish smiled happily. "Will you be in Jordan the whole time?"

"We'll meet there and see what happens," said Lili.

"Uh oh," said Mish. "I just remembered that *The Da Vinci Code* starts with a murder." She closed her eyes and threw up her hands. "And what about *The Curse of the Mummy?*"

Lili laughed. "I've already survived that one. Anyway, no one even knows I exist, so no one's going to murder me."

"It's not really funny, is it?" said Mish. "What if you really are onto something and it turns out to be dangerous?" She stroked Lili's arm.

"Seriously, Mish, I'm a middle-aged academic who's written a few papers about ancient history. And Paula is an environmental scientist, for Goodness sake. No one murders academics! If Haleli turns out to be just another eccentric scholar, then Paula and I will hang around in museums and see the sights. She's never been to Petra."

Mish sighed theatrically. "I suppose you'll go ahead whatever I say, so you'd better tell me what you need."

"Paula says we need to look for conspiracy theories. Anything you can find on the internet, no matter how obscure or New Age, as long as it relates to ancient Sumer, prophecies, and something that's going on now."

"Conspiracies?"

"I suppose so. I need all the help I can get to find the missing bits of this puzzle."

"What sort of theories are you looking for?"

"Anything that mentions ancient Sumer."

"So you want to know what the Order of Grand Sumerian Poobahs has to say about . . .well, about anything?"

"Not the stuff about aliens. Oh, I don't know. That's the trouble with trying to limit a search; you just don't know what leads to what. Can I leave it to you? You've read all those fantasies about prophecies and things."

"It has to start with a village boy--or girl--who doesn't know his or her true heritage as a child of power and magic."

"See? You'll know what to look for. I do feel a bit like a character in a book, with the daughters marked at birth part."

"Do you really think that's us?"

"Who knows? I always thought there was something important I was meant to be doing, but I guess lots of people feel like that."

"There is something important you're meant to be doing . . ."

"What?"

"Cooking dinner for my birthday!"

Lili laughed. Nothing like kids to bring you back to

reality.

Mish was quiet as they drove to the market. While they were buying the strawberries for the cake, she said, "Did they have strawberries in ancient Sumer? Imagine if you could talk to someone from there. I wonder what it was really like."

"So do I," said Lili.

CHAPTER IX

Urim, Ancient Sumer. c 1998BCE.

Although the Ur III period lasted only a single century . . .it is significant for two reasons. First, the influence of Ur during that time stretched from the Persian Gulf almost to the Mediterranean and was maintained by economic factors rather than by military power. Second, it is quite possible that Abraham lived in or near that city during that time.[xii]

Time passed in Urim. The crickets continued their strident chirping. In her Palace near the North Harbour, the High Priestess waited. In the House of the Great Light, the Priestesses waited for the turning of an Age. In the Temple of Enki, the Priests waited for the turning of an Age.

Away from the river, along one of the winding lanes between the Palace and the Western Harbour, a young boy waited. Abram did not know what had called him from sleep to sit on the roof and watch the heavens. Stars sprinkled the charcoal sky, as many as tadpoles swarming around the reeds at the river's edge. He smiled to think of the stars as tiny creatures swimming in the night. Then like tadpoles when a shadow falls on the water, his thoughts changed: What was in the air that had called him from sleep?

He had heard talk of the omens from the old men who gathered each day in the shade between the mud-brick houses that lined the lanes. He had squatted in the dust at their feet, listening to the greybeards wheeze and sigh about the portents that had been appearing in the sky. More than anything, he wondered what the future held for the Habiru, his own people.

They were the Wandering Ones, called robbers and worse by many. Some of the Habiru, like his own father, did skilled work that was welcome in the city, but the Habiru had still not been accepted into the councils of Urim. They lived and worked there, but they were not really of the city in the same way as those who claimed their forefathers had settled the land between the rivers at the beginning of Time.

Abram's father scoffed at the claims, saying that the fertile land between the two rivers had been invaded by tribes from East and West for generations.

"None of them can say for certain who their forefathers were," he had joked to his sons in the days when he still made jokes.

"But a wise man always knows his mother," Abram had added, remembering the response from other times.

His brothers had laughed, and his father had slapped him on the back. It was a good memory.

After his sleepless night, Abram spent the day on the Harbour wall watching the boats. The air smelled of salt and fish, and sunlight danced in the water like shiny frogs. He was tired from watching the stars, but he was restless, his mind whirling with portents and possibilities.

He stood in the same place where he had since he could first walk to watch for the great, bardi reed-boats with their curved prows and proud sails. Out of habit, he scanned the water for vessels that sat lower in the water than the others, sure sign of cargoes of marble or diorite, lapis lazuli or carnelian. There! A boat as full as a mother goat about to give birth to twins.

A year ago he would have run home, calling for his father. But now he just watched the gentle rocking of the boat and thought about change. His father still used the stone to carve plaques and votive sculptures, cylinder seals and altar bowls, but he did not need Abram to tell him there was a load of stone making its slow way into the Harbour; his father had an apprentice now, and their ready laughter always stopped when Abram appeared.

Abram sighed deeply. Perhaps he should have refused to attend the E-dub-ba, the House of Tablets, the place of learning built for the sons of Kings and Priests. It had only been a whim of Baldur's anyway; the High Priest of the Temple of Enki had been so pleased with the two great statues Terah had carved from glistening obsidian that he had granted Terah's youngest son a place in the E-dub-ba.

Terah had made it clear to Abram that he would rather have had a gift of rich, farming land near the raised banks of the Buranun, but how could a Habiru Stoneworker argue with the High Priest?

So Abram studied at the House of Tablets with Baldur's sons and the sons of King Shulgi.

Perhaps he should have begged his father to let him stay at home to work with stone, but what he was learning at the House of Tablets excited him far more. Besides, his father had said he was not blessed by the Great Ones with the gift of shaping like his brothers were.

Abram frowned at the boats. What was he blessed with?

His mother's voice reached him from their house by the Harbour.

"Come, come, Abram," she called. Her voice always dripped with honey and rosewater when she called him. Never did she call to his father or brothers the way she called him. Whenever she treated him like a Blessed One, he felt strangely shamed. When she said nothing, he craved her words. He shook his head at the mystery of women.

It was another thing again with his father. He never met his father's eyes any more, shying away from the defeat he heard in the heavy tones of his voice, the weariness in his bent back and sloping shoulders. Even the old men who told tales in the shady lanes seemed less worn down by life than Terah, the Stoneworker.

Before climbing the stairs to the rooftop, Abram washed his hands and face, smoothed his curls with water. As always, his mother served him the best portion of dried fish, filling his bowl to the brim with onion, cucumber, and goat's cheese. He smiled up at her, but his body tightened as she ruffled his hair.

"What did you learn today, little brother?" asked Haran, hurrying up for the evening meal. Six years older than Abram, Haran worked alongside their father, learning the Stoneworker's trade.

Abram shrugged. He no longer knew what they wanted to hear. Last time he had tried to talk about the Laws he learned at the House of Tablets, his father had raged and left for the Harbour.

Nachor ran up after Haran, shaking water from his hair. Younger by a year, Nachor followed Haran in all things. Terah joined them, and the men drank date wine and talked about their work until the stars showed bright against the blue-black sky. Sometimes Abram found it hard to believe that Haran and Nachor were truly his brothers.

When the men left for their sleeping mats, Abram stayed on the roof to sleep with the goat. His brothers said it was strange, but the truth was that he loved Dar-ge, the kid goat with its gangly legs and floppy ears. Loved it enough to have dripped milk from a rag into its mouth until it had learned to eat. Loved it enough to sleep out under the stars, fingers twined in the kid's coarse hair.

Just before dawn, Abram was shaken awake by yet another earth tremor. He ran down the stairs, only to hear his mother murmuring sleepily, "It is only Abram dreaming."

Terah grumbled as he rolled off the sleeping mat. "Don't be foolish, woman," he said. "It is the earth moving again. The Great Ones are restless. There was another accident at the Temple yesterday."

"But he is special, our youngest," said Amaslai, shuffling around inside. "It is true that Abram's dreams can shake the house. One day they will shake the world."

"Stop filling his head with your nonsense," said Terah, voice grating like the stone he worked. "He will toil like the rest of us and die when his time comes. There is nothing special about that."

He staggered outside to make water. Abram pulled back behind the wall. Once his father had been able to rise easily from the ground, but years of lifting and turning stone, bending over the workbench, chiselling and hammering, seemed to have taken his strength and his good humour. He was like an old date palm that had been battered by strong winds, yet still held to the earth with deep roots.

"Three sons to feed and them not yet old enough to do a

full day's work," Terah grumbled to himself. "As if that is not enough, I have a wife who imagines a special destiny for her last born." He sighed, clenching his fists as if to gather what strength was left to him.

Abram watched his father twist the coarse stands of his still-dark beard into tight, gleaming curls with thyme-scented grease. Once he would have run up for a dab of it on his forehead.

Amaslai was still humming to herself when Abram went down to eat. She came up to him and whispered one of her peculiar ideas.

"Ah," she said. "I just close my eyes and I can see the handsome face of Nanna, the benevolent gaze of Utu, shining down from the Heavens. You know you are really the son of a Great One."

Abram pretended not to hear her, but he did wonder which of the Great Ones she imagined was his father.

When Haran and Nachor left for their half day in the workshop alongside Terah, Abram collected his clay tablets, took the food his mother lovingly prepared, and set off to study. The E-dub-ba was in the Temple compound of the King's Palace, a winding walk through lanes to the heart of the Western quarter. Most of the craftsmen lived closer to the E-dub-ba, in the centre of the city, behind the walls of the main Temple compound. Carpenters, Jewellers, and Weavers worked alongside Scholars, Scribes, and Priests in the complex near the Palace of the King. But the Habiru lived close to the water in the lanes near the Western Harbour.

Abram started early and walked quickly until he began to climb to hill to the Temple. Some said Temples were always built higher than the rest of the city because the Great Ones were above ordinary men and women, but others said the custom came to Urim from the mountains in the East where the Temples all perched high in the peaks.

Abram had no fixed opinion about the elevation of Temples, but the climb to the E-dub-ba did give him pause. He stopped at the base of the hill, searching the doorways for Nemmor and his friends. Sons of wealthy merchants, they often lay in wait for him, jumping out to push and shove, breaking his tablets and scattering his food, taunting him for his father's lowly station, for living by the Harbour. Like the scavengers who prowled the river at night, the boys treated him like a stranger in their pack and tried to drive him away with snarls and threats.

Shaking his head to clear the curls from his eyes, Abram scanned the alleyways by the Temple gate. Three girls were filling their jugs at the shaduf on the opposite corner, and he walked their way. Four boys erupted out of the alley and bounded across to the shaduf to upset the girls' jugs before turning on Abram. He ran for the gate, the girls' shrieks echoing in his ears. He feared he had more in common with the girls at the shaduf than with the sons of the ruling classes.

Hamminabi, Master of Mathematics and Astronomy, stepped out through the gate just as Abram hurtled in. They collided with such force that Abram sat down abruptly, broken tablets scattered all around. So much for his meticulous lettering and painstaking calculations. Winded and even more frightened than he had been of the boys, Abram hung his head and mumbled an apology. It was only a matter of time before the Scribes discovered that he did not belong and sent him home in disgrace.

"Has someone been killed by an earth tremor? Are we attacked by the desert tribes? Is there a comet?"

From the corner of his eye, Abram glimpsed a smile on

Hamminabi's face, white teeth bright against his dark skin. He held his breath.

The Master Scribe helped him up and was dusting him down when the other boys walked through the gate, greeting both Abram and the Master politely. Hamminabi raised one eyebrow at Abram, inviting him to name his assailants, but Abram shook his head slightly and looked away. He did not particularly need friends, but neither was he seeking enemies.

Time passed, and Abram's studies gave him neither friends nor enemies. He received the gift of reading and writing, the magic of numbers, and the secrets of the Heavens. He also found Laws by which to live.

"Whoever has walked with truth generates life," said the Scribes.

"What of those who walk in untruth?" asked Abram.

"The payment for untruth is death."

It never occurred to Abram to doubt the certainty of the Laws. In him grew an insatiable desire to know the truth and right of all things.

CHAPTER X

Urim, Ancient Sumer. c 1998-1989BCE

. . .it would not surprise me to discover that the Inanna of the "Sacred Marriage" rite was actually properly named, for the goddess was using the body of a willing and devout ecstatic priestess, who was certainly not a "cult prostitute." On the contrary, she would have had extremely high status and have been deeply revered, for she was chosen of the goddess. Finally, then, the identity of the human female participant in the ritual is irrelevant. She was Inanna![xiii]

Mir-ri's time in the gardens taught her about the cycles of the seasons, the rhythms of day and night, the rising of the Sun each day. She learned about change from the waxing and waning of the Moon, the seasonal flooding of the Buranun, the months of heat, the months of windy cold.

Her own change--the sacred Moonblood--came in her twelfth year, deep red mystery connecting her to the life-giving power of women and the Earth.

By custom all acolytes attended the Room of Tablets in their twelfth year. There they stayed until they could recite the Praises, read their own names, and use the number systems of six and ten to count the passage of the days as the star of Inanna moved from morning to evening or disappeared from sight.

"It is my task to see to it that you can read your own name and count the fingers on your hands," said Ad-ilah, the ancient Scribe who greeted Mir-ri on her first day in the Room of Tablets.

Ad-ilah had hair so white there was not one strand of black left, and eyes so cloudy Mir-ri doubted she could see. Despite her age, Ad-ilah managed to calm the roomful of students without even raising her voice.

Window openings invited the Sun into the quiet room where fifteen girls sat on reed mats practising their letters and numbers. Mir-ri sat near Anna and Hedu, who had both graduated to the Room of Tablets the previous season. She bubbled with excitement to be with them again.

"What must I do?" she whispered to Hedu, who was painstakingly copying marks from a baked-clay tablet to a damp one she held cupped in her left hand.

Hedu jumped, leaving a jagged line on the clay. She scowled and smoothed the surface of her practice tablet to erase the error.

"Shhh," she said, looking across to where Ad-ilah was guiding the hand of a new student.

Mir-ri moved closer to where Ad-ilah instructed the other girl. Looking from the tablet to the stylus, she saw how the reed pen could be angled to mark the clay just so. Her fingers began to move as if she were already writing.

"You will never learn to read and write by watching," said a voice by her ear.

Ad-ilah was no taller than her, but her eyes suddenly looked like the eyes of death that Eresh-ki-gal had turned on her sister, Inanna. Mir-ri gulped.

"Over there, by the door. Fetch yourself a tablet." Ad-ilah pointed to a basket around which some of the girls were standing.

Mir-ri hurried over to join them. She watched as Ed-iba scooped a large handful of the clay, pressed it into the palm of one hand and flattened the top with the other hand. When the others had finished, Mir-ri formed her own tablet. The clay was cool on her palm and moist enough to leave brown streaks on her fingers as she smoothed the top flat. It made her skin feel softer. Ad-ilah showed her how to hold the sharpened reed between her thumb and the next finger, resting the reed on the middle finger for balance. Her first wedges went too deep or slipped off the clay, but she only had to wipe the surface with a smear of water and start again.

By the end of her first month in the Room of Tablets, she proudly showed Ad-ilah the groups of wedges she could mark perfectly.

"This is a beginning," said Ad-ilah. "Now you can learn the groups for the stories and lists."

There were thousands, but Mir-ri just smiled; she liked this even better than working in the gardens. Her fingers held the stylus as if they had done it before, her wrist moving and turning in just the way needed to form the angles and directions of the letters.

The number system also came easily. Based on 10, the fingers she had already learned to count, she discovered the magic of multiplying 10 by 6 to find 60, then 60 by 10 to find 600, and then what happened when she multiplied 600 by 6, and so on . . .[xiv]

"The number 60 has the advantage of being divisible by 2, 3, 4, 5, 6, 10, 12, 15, 20, and 30," explained Ad-ilah.

Most of the other students were content to count the days in a month, the months in a year, but Mir-ri covered her tablets with calculations. It was wondrous that a circle could be divided into 360 degrees, that one fifth of 60 gave a number that could be used to measure hours, minutes, and seconds.

She arrived early in the Room of Tablets and left late, running to do her chores or to sing praises to holy Inanna.

"You will end up a Scribe," teased Hedu, for whom numbers remained a mystery.

"Old and grey and shortsighted," said Anna, whose first love was dancing.

Mir-ri just smiled; there were worse things than becoming a Scribe.

In their fifteenth year, the students left the House of Tablets to prepare for the rites that would take them through to become fully-consecrated Priestesses of Nanna and Inanna. As they approached the time of Initiation, Anna and Hedu talked constantly about where they hoped to find a place in the life of the Temple.

"What exactly happens in the Initiation?" Mir-ri asked one day as they sat in the courtyard of the Room of Tablets.

"It is a mystery. No one speaks of it." Hedu shook her head, her eyes even more round than usual. "Not even Ner-nin would say."

Mir-ri missed Ner-nin, who was older and already wearing the pleated robes. She worked now with the Healers; her mother and her grandmother, and all their mothers back through time, had been wise in the ways of healing and childbirth. Even before her initiation, Ner-nin had spent three days each week in the street of the Physicians, apprenticed to one of the more respected Healers. At first she had returned with stories that made Mir-ri and the others writhe and groan, complaining of feeling sick. But now she rarely came.

"She's been avoiding us since she passed through," added Anna.

"Probably so she doesn't tell us anything."

"But if we don't know what to expect, how can we prepare ourselves?" A shiver of fear rippled up Mir-ri's back.

"They say that we have been preparing since we entered the Temple," said Anna. Then she laughed. "I hope we don't have to write something."

Mir-ri smiled. "What path will you choose?" She could not imagine anything more wondrous than learning, but she knew her friends would be glad to leave the Room of Tablets.

Anna and Hedu spoke together. "We want to be chosen to dance for the Emesh rites."

Mir-ri frowned. At the fertility rites, they all recited verses of the ancient lays and danced in prescribed ways while the chosen Priestess and Priest joined together as Inanna and Dumuzzi.

It was no surprise that Anna and Hedu wanted to enter more fully into the rites. Many nights Mir-ri had listened to them practising the sacred verses. Anna would take the part of Inanna: "My vulva, the horn, the Boat of Heaven, Is full of eagerness like the young moon. As for me, Inanna, who will plow my vulva? Who will plow my high field? Who will plow my wet ground? As for me, the young woman, who will plow my vulva?"

And Hedu, taking the part of Dumuzzi, would answer:

"Great Lady, the king will plow your vulva. I, Dumuzzi, the King, will plow your vulva!"

"Then plow my vulva, man of my heart! Plow my vulva!"

Then they would roll around, flushed and laughing, while Ner-nin and Mir-ri made faces at each other.

But now Ner-nin was gone, and Anna and Hedu would soon be leaving the House of Tablets.

"We've been preparing for months," said Hedu.

"To be chosen for the rites," added Anna, finishing the sentence like she had in the early days.

Mir-ri hugged them close, one arm around each of them. "You are both so lovely. Of course you will be chosen."

"When we are older, we will lie with the Priests," said Anna. "It starts with the dancing, but one day we might even be chosen as Inanna for the rites."

Mir-ri shuddered. She had no desire to be chosen for the Emesh rites, even if it was considered a great honour.

When Anna and Hedu ran off to practise their dancing, Mir-ri sat alone, wondering if there was something wrong with her for not wanting to dance the rites or lie with the Priests in the sacred marriage.

"We are all called by a different face of the holy Priestess," said Ad-ilah, sitting beside her. "East, North, West, or South

"Like the room of altars," said Mir-ri.

Ad-ilah raised her eyebrows. "Which room is that, child?"

"The High Priestess took me there when I entered the Temple. She said she goes there to hear Her voice."

"I do not know this room," said Ad-ilah. "Perhaps it was a dream."

It had seemed real. Didn't the High Priestess take everyone there? Mir-ri shivered.

"Never mind," said Ad-ilah. "A dream can be more true than what we see while awake. You know your friends are called by the Dove; laughter and lust are Her way. Your friends answer to Her."

Of course they did. Hadn't she been attracted to their laughter, inspired by their playfulness?

"If it is the Lioness," said Ad-ilah, "then a woman must follow the way of strength, training to guard the Temple, shield and protector for others.

"The Snakes guide the healers and the seers. Like your friend, Ner-nin."

Mir-ri smiled, thinking of Ner-nin's capacity to see beyond the surface to the dark underside where sickness formed.

"The Horned One calls to the mothers, the ones who give life and tend it."

Mir-ri shivered. "And me?" she asked softly. "Where will I be called?"

Ad-ilah stroked her hand, but she did not answer Mir-ri's question.

CHAPTER XI

Update March 20th 2015

6.24am   Thursday   Melbourne/3.25pm   Wednesday Philadelphia
According to current projections, the world population will expand to 9 billion by 2040, which will lead to severe shortages of food, water and energy, and dramatic increases in malnutrition and disease. Overpopulation is also expected to exacerbate other environmental problems, such as climate change, loss of wildlife habitat, deforestation, and air and water pollution. http://www.epa.gov/hero/

Paula was up before the children, thinking about beginnings and endings. She called Lili on Skype.

"Hello," said Lili. "You're up early. It must be about six there."

"Six thirty. It's the equinox and Mary's birthday. I'm always restless at this time of year."

"What time was she born?"

"At sunrise. About now. A true child of change, born on the cusp of the new season."

"Is she different from the others?"

"She's certainly more sensitive. She's still having nightmares."

"Will it be okay to leave her?"

"I'm coming, Lili! She says she'll be fine with Thom's mother for three weeks. I can call her on Skype. That reminds me, are you taking the bracelet?"

Lili's hand went to her wrist, as if she could feel it there. "I think we should take both pieces. I was planning to wear mine."

"I'd be nervous wearing it" said Paula. "But I'd worry about it if I left it here, even though it just gathered dust on top of my wardrobe for two years. I'm embarrassed to admit it, but every now and then I even think about how much someone would pay me for it."

Lili nodded. "That's one of the first things you have to get over as an archaeologist, like medical students have to stop imagining they have every illness. I just don't think of something this ancient as really being mine."

"I'll try that," said Paula, although the idea of wearing the necklace through the airport scanners made her palms sweat. "Any luck with contacting your sociologist?"

Lili shook her head. "As elusive as ever. If we can't find her, and there's nothing at the address, we'll start somewhere else."

"Where?" asked Paula. She didn't want to tell Lili, but every now and then she felt sick at the thought of looking for ancient treasures in the Middle East. Didn't they shoot people who stole their artifacts?

"It will work out," said Lili, as if she had sensed her thoughts. "All we have to do is start." That part of it was easy; she had been on digs all over the World.

The part that bothered her was how much Paula was investing in following the prophecy, finding the *me*, and saving the World. It was exciting, but what did they really have to go on? A cuneiform poem on a clay tablet, two bits of antique jewellery, and Paula's intuition . . .

"Penny for your thoughts," said Paula.

"You wouldn't want to know," said Lili.

By the time they hung up, Lili felt enthusiastic again. After all, hadn't it been the idea of taking action that had made her agree to meet Paula in Jordan in the first place? It had to be better than moping around feeling sorry for herself!

Paula happily prepared for the trip. She had completed her PhD, the bound copies signed and submitted for marking the week before; the children were organised; even Thom had given his blessings. No one could predict what would happen when they got there; all they could do was try. It wasn't as if they had to write a thesis about it!

CHAPTER XII

Urim, Ancient Sumer. c 1993 BCE

From the great heaven she set her mind on the great below. From the great heaven the goddess set her mind on the great below. From the great heaven Inanna set her mind on the great below. My mistress abandoned heaven, abandoned earth, and descended to the underworld. Inanna abandoned heaven, abandoned earth, and descended to the underworld.
xv

Nin-lil-la bided her time as Mir-ri grew from child to woman. Only seven years had passed, but Time was flowing away faster then the floodwaters of the Buranun. She made her plans as she walked the corridors of the Palace, as she led the cycles of morning and evening invocations, as she lay sleepless on her mat at night. When Mir-ri emerged as a consecrated Priestess, she would be ready.

The Mistress of Initiations came for Mir-ri at the end of a

day when clouds moved lazily above the trees and herons called from the river. They walked together, in silence, to the House of Initiation.

The flat-roofed House sat on a low hill overlooking the river. The plain walls were made from mud bricks like the Temple but with no pillars or arches. The small, single gate of precious cedarwood opened to reveal walls covered in inscriptions, running in columns from top to bottom. Would she have time to read them all?

The Mistress did not speak as she led Mir-ri to a chamber with bare walls and no window. The tiled floor was cool. A sleeping mat waited in the centre of the room. Mir-ri lay in the dark, pictures dancing before her eyes as they had on her very first night in the Temple, seven years earlier. She no longer yearned for her family, but it was strange to be alone after living so close to others. Only the crickets disturbed the stillness of the night.

As she settled towards sleep, she considered the paths open to a Priestess: the way of the Dove that called Anna and Hedu; the way of the Warrior, those strong women who bore arms; the way of the Serpent that Ner-nin walked as Healer; the way of the Mother, cow-eyed one whose arms are open . . .

After the morning invocation, the Mistress led Mir-ri to a room of altars. It was simpler than the room Nin-lil-la had shown her, but the faces of Inanna were there: the dove for laughter, lust and inspiration; the lioness for strength; the serpent for wisdom; the cow-eyed one with Her horns for abundance.

She sat where the Mistress indicated, in the centre of the room, the tiles hard through her shift. The Mistress sat facing her, legs crossed, back straight.

"You have heard that Inanna was the favourite of An, how she came to womanhood in his Palace." Her deep voice seemed to come from all four altars at once. "You know how she won the sacred measures from Enki, Great One of Wisdom. How they drank beer together, toasted and challenged each other. How Enki said, 'In the name of my power! In the name of my holy shrine! To my daughter Inanna I shall give The high priesthood! Godship! The noble, enduring crown! The throne of kingship!'

"And how Inanna said, 'I take them!'

Mir-ri nodded. She knew all the stories told in the Temple, all the stories scribed in the Room of Tablets.

"You know that Enki gave to Inanna Truth! Descent into the Underworld! Ascent from the Underworld! The art of lovemaking! The kissing of the phallus!

"And that Inanna said, 'I take them!'

"You know the story of the courtship of Inanna and Dumuzzi. How the holy Priestess chose the Shepherd who was conceived on the sacred marriage throne."

Again Mir-ri nodded, remembering Anna and Hedu reciting the verses.

"You know the story of Inanna's descent to the Underworld," said the Mistress.

Mir-ri nodded.

"Tell me," said the Mistress.

Mir-ri took a deep breath and spoke the story as she had learned it, pacing her voice to the steady rhythm of the sacred verses. "Inanna, holy Priestess of Heaven, turned her thoughts to the Great Below.

"From her seven Holy Temples she gathered the seven Holy Measures and prepared herself.

"She placed the Crown on her head.

"She tied the single strand of Beads around her neck.

"She let the Double Strand of Beads fall to her breast.

"She wrapped the Royal Robe round her body.

"She bound the Breastplate around her chest.

"She slipped the Gold Ring over her wrist.

"She took the Measuring Rod and Line in her hand.

"Inanna told Ninshubur to watch for her, and if she did not return, to go to the Great Ones, so that the holy Priestess of Heaven not be lost in the Underworld."

The hairs on her arms moved, as if ants were crawling on her skin. Was this to be her Initiation?

"When Inanna arrived at the outer gates of the Underworld, She knocked loudly.

"She called for the door to be opened.

"Neti, the Gatekeeper, left Inanna on the doorstep to speak with the Queen of the Underworld.

"Eresh-ki-gal told the Gatekeeper to bolt the seven gates of the Underworld. They would be opened one by one, just wide enough for Inanna to enter.

"And so it came to pass that at each gate Inanna had to surrender one of the Sacred Measures. Only then, naked and bowed low, could She face the Holy, Dark and Eternal Eresh-ki-gal."

Mir-ri's stomach tightened, her head throbbed. Would she have to face Eresh-ki-gal? She glanced at the door. It was open. She could run out of the room, out of the House of Initiation, past the palm orchard to the river. But what of Inanna? Who would sing Her praises? Who would walk in Her ways? She licked her dry lips and spoke the rest of the verse.

"Inanna faced the Annunaki and was judged.

"Eresh-ki-gal turned the eyes of Death on Inanna."

The breath left Mir-ri's body as if it were she who hung in the Underworld, condemned by Eresh-ki-gal. Spots danced before her eyes like nemes from the swamps.

"After three days and three nights, Inanna had not

returned.

"Ninshubur sought help from the Great Ones, so that the holy Priestess of Heaven not be lost in the Underworld.

"Father Enki sent help, and Inanna returned as Queen of Heaven and Earth. Eresh-ki-gal remained as Queen of the Underworld. What is above is like that which is below, and what is below is like that which is above. Balance was restored."

Mir-ri let her breath out in a long sigh. Could a flesh and blood person really walk in the steps of Inanna? Could she go to the Underworld and return?

The Mistress spoke, her voice slow, as if reciting another verse. "You will make the seven Measures, using only what is offered by the Great Ones in the gardens. Speak no words. Await me."

Mir-ri sat in her chamber for two days and nights. Her thoughts were of the Underworld realm of Eresh-ki-gal. Strange images haunted her: darkness, piercing eyes, dead bodies.

Dreadful sounds assaulted her: moans, shrieks, mad laughter.

Terrible feelings assailed her: pain, tremors, paralysing fear.

Water and fruit appeared outside the doorway at dusk. She ate and drank and walked to the washroom. Had it only been two days?

At dawn on the third day, the Mistress led her to the orchard of date palms bordering the Temple gardens. After the shadows of her chamber, Mir-ri's eyes burned in the brightness.

"First you must make the Shugurra, Crown of the Land," said the Mistress.

Mindful of speaking no words, Mir-ri moved away from the Mistress. It was cooler under the date palms, the gentle swishing of the fronds like women whispering as they worked.

A crown fit to offer Eresh-ki-gal, Dark and Eternal Eresh-ki-gal, whose face was hidden. Mir-ri shivered. She moved deeper into the grove where the palms grew taller, reaching to the sky, rooted in the Land. Her head tingled, as if a crown already rested there, but she felt only the softness of her hair.

Gripping long strands, she pulled hard. Tears filled her eyes as the hair ripped from her scalp. The blue-black strands looked almost purple as she wove them with long grass stems into a plaited rope. When the ends were joined, the garland rested lightly on her head, the grass rasping on her forehead. Was it too simple? Would it be acceptable?

Mir-ri sat in the House of Initiation for two days and nights, her Crown resting on a mat before her.

"Let it speak," said the Mistress of Initiations. "Listen for the voice of the Shugurra."

Mir-ri listened. The silence of the House echoed. Faint, far-away sounds of life beckoned. Her own breath hissed in and out. When Time had ceased to matter, a deep, thundering voice resonated in her body, as if the Land itself were speaking: *That which is above is the same as that which is below; That which is below is the same as that which is above.*

The Crown glowed with silvery light.

At dawn on the fifth day, the Mistress led her back to the date orchard. "You will seek a single strand to wear around your neck."

In the temple gardens beyond the palms, the younger girls called to each other as they worked. Mir-ri remembered her days working the rich, black soil, crumbling it in her fingers, sensing the dream of the earth: *I am the womb of life. From me you come and to me you shall return. Nothing is wasted. Do not fear.*

The memory lingered as she walked between the palms. It was peaceful there, like walking between the pillars of the Temple where the Priestesses wore lapis lazuli and carnelian, gold and malachite. But there were no precious stones under the palms. How could she make a strand of beads beautiful enough for an offering?

At the edges of the palms, flax grew wild and thick, the blue flowers like beads against the green. The leaves scratched against her legs, and she kicked at the bush. Her foot disturbed a nest, spilling fragments of blue eggshell onto the dried grass like shards of fine pottery. She picked them up and carried them with her, cradled in her palm.

She spotted the feathery leaves of the glue plant and knew what to do: she dug the root and chewed it into sticky balls to hold the bits of eggshell on a strand of woven grass. As the necklace dried in the Sun, she wondered about its voice.

She sat in the House of Initiation for two days and nights, listening, sensing, waiting. The single strand whispered of possibility, hinted at seeing through the visible world. Lapis-colored lights danced before her eyes.

At dawn on the eighth day, the Mistress led her to the edge of the Temple gardens to make another necklace, a double strand.

Mir-ri walked up and down between the garden beds. Lettuce sprouted, soft and green, sweetened by the waters of the

Buranun. As she neared the palm orchards, she remembered the taste of dates, sweet and sticky. Pierced with a stick, the fresh dates made perfect beads to string on a rope of twisted grass. She licked the stickiness from her fingers and persisted until the strand hung twice around her neck.

Two days passed in the House of Initiation. Two nights passed in the House of Initiation. Mir-ri slept and woke as she watched over the double strand. She heard the sacred verses in her mind and beheld the power of naming. The double strand shone with a soft blue light.

The Mistress led her to the gardens at dawn on the tenth day. "The fourth offering is to be a breastplate that covers your heart, your breasts, your belly, and your sex."

Walking alone under the palms, Mir-ri wondered what she could use. Inanna in her lioness form was the mighty warrior, fierce protector of women and children, and her breastplate must be strong. Mir-ri stroked the front of her body where it would rest: breasts, belly, sex. Perhaps the strength of the breastplate was not in covering but in revealing . . .

She bound flax leaves a finger-width apart in a small ladder to hang from a cord around her neck. To the bottom she attached red berries from the bushes by the river.

For two days and nights she sat beside the Breastplate as the berries withered and the leaves wilted. It seemed to protect and beckon at the same time: "Come, man, come!" it called. Thick curls and warm eyes promised long nights of love, blessed by the evening star. The Breastplate emanated a green glow.

The Mistress led her out at dawn on the twelfth day and instructed her to make a band of gold to wear around her arm.

Mir-ri hurried through the palm grove, past the garden beds, to the fields where rippling waves of golden grain moved to an invisible tide. She waded into the emmer sea up to her waist, skimming the surface with her hands. A long way in, she sank beneath the waves, surrendering to the enormity of Earth and Sky.

When she emerged, she wore a woven strand of golden stalks around her arm. She wore it through the two days and two nights of vigil, absorbing the power that comes from Sun and Earth. *I am the heart of life. From me comes the searing heat of desire. Nothing is unknown. Do not fear. The barley and the corn agree to live in the Sun and die in the flames, to give you food. Nothing is unknown.*

At dawn on the fourteenth day, the Mistress explained the sixth offering: a measuring rod and line.

Was it like the short, gnarled staff Ad-ilah carried as she walked through the Temple? Or like the measuring rod used by the Overseer at the E-gish-shir-gal? Perhaps her staff must be made to measure time or distance, or something else she could not even imagine . . .

Mir-ri searched through the fallen fronds along the rows of the palm orchard. She walked to the edge of the palms. There, on the ground before her, lay a snakeskin, long and sinuous and empty. It moved slightly in the breeze, rustling like dry leaves. The snake would have basked on the Sun-warmed earth, shed its skin, and slithered away fresh and gleaming. The skin came up in one piece, surprisingly light, yet strong like the dried skin of a kid goat.

Drawn by the sound of water and the cries of the boatmen, Mir-ri climbed the embankment to the Buranun. A branch thinner than her wrist bobbed on the current, half-submerged, as if just surfacing after a long journey. With a final turn, it came to rest where she stood, its tip pointing at her feet. She pulled it from the river, wondering if it might be from a Huluppu tree, like the one planted by Enki and pulled from the river by Inanna. The slippery wood fitted her hand perfectly. She draped the snakeskin over the forked end, as if the snake were basking in the branch.

As she sat with her measuring rod for two days and two nights, Mir-ri thought about snakes. They lived in the gardens, drank from the canals, rested in the Sun, moved in circles and spirals. Sybil, soothsayer, seer, the serpent represented wisdom. Wisdom was not gained by following a straight path but from moving through the twists and turns of life. The measuring rod pulsed with orange light.

At dawn on the sixteenth day, the Mistress did not lead Mir-ri out to the gardens but brought her a bundle of cloth, a basket of sewing tools, and an oil lamp for light. Mir-ri unfolded the cloth, feeling the texture of the fine, blue linen. She gasped, tears filling her eyes. Neatly folded was the shift she had worn to the Temple the day her Mother had given her to the Priestesses. She lifted it to her face, breathing in the smell of Cassia oil, inhaling the scent of her mother's soap, touching the softness of her mother's hair . . .

She let the memory go. She did not need the Mistress to tell her that she must remake the cloth of her childhood into a garment fit for Initiation; she had been working towards this for seven years. She loosened the threads and unstitched her mother's sewing. From the pieces, she fashioned a robe, adding the other lengths of cloth that had come in the bundle.

For two days and two nights she stitched, turning each seam with care. Drops of blood seeped from her fingers, staining the cloth. The cloth of her own becoming, red with the blood of life.

Finally all seven offerings lay on the reed mat in the altar room. Mir-ri sat alone with them for three days and three nights. She ate nothing. She drank only water.

Strange images haunted her: darkness, hooded eyes, dead bodies.

Dreadful sounds assaulted her: moans, shrieks, mad laughter.

Terrible feelings assailed her: pain, tremors, abject fear.

Eresh-ki-gal awaited with Her eyes of Death.

Mir-ri's heart beat slowly, heavy as a lump of clay. Her skin prickled as if ants were biting her arms, her legs, her belly. Surely no one ever died in the House of Initiation.

Did they?

On the fourth night, when the Moon was dark, and even the crickets had fallen silent, the Mistress beat once on a gong. Mir-ri walked to the courtyard, shed her shift, and washed. Cold water sluiced away the doubts, though fear remained.

The sound of the second gong made her jump, but the implacable demand took her back to her room. She lifted the

Robe and slipped it over her head. The panels of her old, linen shift rubbed softly against her skin.

She hung the Breastplate from her neck and arranged the dried leaves across her chest.

She placed the Double Strand over the Breastplate, the Single Strand over the Double.

She fitted the Gold Band over her wrist and lifted the Crown onto her head.

She took up the Measuring Rod.

Was she really going to walk to the Underworld, towards Eresh-ki-gal? Until the threshold is crossed there is still the possibility of refusal.

The sound of the third gong throbbed in her body, a summons, a warning, an invocation.

She left the small chamber. The silent, robed Mistress led her along a corridor, down two flights of stairs, along another passage, and through a small doorway into a courtyard Mir-ri had never seen before. The stars were bright overhead, the air cool. The Mistress pointed to a rough stairway descending into the earth.

Mir-ri spoke the ritual words. "If I am not returned when three days and nights have passed, seek help to secure my return." She knew there would be no reply.

The threshold lay two steps before her, Eresh-ki-gal beyond that. Sweat, acrid with fear, dampened her underarms and inner thighs. The air seemed thicker, harder to draw in, harder to expel. A bird called from the river.

With a final look at the night sky, Mir-ri turned and began the descent.

Bare feet touched bricks, the steps wide and worn in the middle. Others had walked this walk.

Breathe.

Hands brushed the sides of the tunnel, the brick smoothed by the hands of others who had passed this way.

Breathe.

The steps ended in a room of earth with a low ceiling. The walls glowed in the light of coals smouldering in a bowl on the floor. Smoke rose from the coals, redolent with incense. The next threshold lay three steps ahead. A heavy stillness in Mir-ri's body cautioned against movement.

Breathe.

The coals died. The room darkened. Three steps to the threshold. She moved one foot. Moved the other. Stepped to the door. Her head was thick with incense, but she remembered that she must knock. Her knuckles barely made a sound on the wood. She pushed against it. Nothing moved. As the last glow faded, she hammered at the door with her fists, like a child begging to come in from the dark.

"Who seeks entry to the Otherworld?" asked a voice like a dark-Moon night.

Mir-ri's lips stuck together, mouth too dry to speak. She licked her lips and swallowed.

"I, Mir-ri, seek entry," she whispered.

"Wait," said the voice.

Cold seeped from the walls.

"You may enter," said the voice.

The door moved to make an opening lit by the glow of a single candle held by a dark-robed figure. Mir-ri strained to see beneath the hood, but there were only shadows.

She entered. The door slammed shut behind her.

Hands reached for the Crown, pulled it free from her hair.

"What is this?" she cried, the ritual words torn from her throat.

"Quiet, Mir-ri. The Ways of the Underworld are perfect

and may not be questioned."

Her legs trembled. She bit her lip and thought of the Crown: *That which is above is the same as that which is below; That which is below is the same as that which is above.*

From above, the weight of soil pushed down. From below, pressed that which waited. Mir-ri felt herself crushed, cracked like a piece of grain between grinding stones. Her bones snapped like twigs, and she fell into blackness.

Her thoughts returned to an absence of pressure. She shivered in the cold darkness. Had she slept? Had she fainted?

She pressed her hands against the floor. The soil was hard packed, smooth and dry. It smelled musky, full of life. The Crown was gone, but the Land was solid beneath her hands. She picked up the measuring rod and stood. The ceiling of the chamber was hard-packed, smooth and dry. *That which is above is the same as that which is below; That which is below is the same as that which is above.*

How long had she been there? There was no way to tell. She remembered that she was meant to knock and reached out to find the door.

She beat loudly on the wood with her fists. The door opened. She walked through. Hands took the Single Strand from her neck. The eggshells tinkled.

"What is this?" she asked, her teeth chattering.

"Quiet, Mir-ri. The Ways of the Underworld are perfect and may not be questioned."

Her head spun as if she had been turning in circles. Why was this so difficult when she already knew the story? Dots of light flashed like stars, becoming brighter, bigger. One rushed at her and exploded against her forehead.

She was on the ground again, head pulsing with pain like stabbing knives. Was it meant to hurt like this? Was she doing something wrong?

She stood on shaking legs to reach for the next door. Her hands met empty space ahead but found walls to both sides and a ceiling above. She found her measuring rod and walked forwards into the chill.

Her feet told her that the path sloped downwards, but her other senses were baffled. She could not tell how long she walked before meeting the next door. Surprised at the trembling in her body, the fearful thoughts in her mind, she hit her hands against the wood. The slapping sound and the stinging of her palms reminded her that she was alive.

The door opened. She walked through. Hands took the Double Strand. The ritual words burst forth: "What is this?"

"Quiet, Mir-ri. The Ways of the Underworld are perfect and may not be questioned."

A fight welled up inside her; like fire and wind all at once, it raged in her chest, her arms. A cry burst forth, leaving a wound in her throat.

Why was it so hard? Surely this was what she wanted? What she had prepared for. She sat in the darkness, heat coursing through her body.

When the fire and wind stopped raging, she rose and walked on. It was so dark she could not even see her fingers when she held them close to her eyes. The air shifted as she moved her hands, but she saw only blackness. If not for the glimpse of light at each door, she might think the Gatekeeper had taken her eyes as well. She felt for them then, scrabbling with her fingers, breath coming in gasps.

Her eyes were still there.

She knocked on the next door. It opened. She walked through.

Hands grasped the Breastplate, lifted it over her head.

"What is this?" she asked, her voice unfamiliar to her.

"Quiet, Mir-ri. The Ways of the Underworld are perfect and may not be questioned."

This time she stood quietly as the dim light disappeared. There was no sound except the slow beating of her own heart. Crossing her arms over her chest, she imagined the Breastplate, sensing it as part of her body, something that could never be taken.

She moved more certainly to the next door and knocked on the smooth wood. The Golden Band of wheat was taken from her arm. Strangely, the skin was taken also, leaving her arm flayed and bleeding.

"What is this?" she asked.

"Quiet, Mir-ri. The ways of the Underworld are perfect and may not be questioned."

Blood dripped onto the ground, falling onto her feet as if eager to leave her body. The candlelight began to flicker, dissolving into blackness as her eyes lost focus. She fell.

When awareness returned, it brought pain. Her head hurt. Spots danced behind her eyelids. Her arm throbbed as if it had been scraped raw, but she felt only unbroken flesh with her fingers. Had it been fear alone that had weakened her?

Water dripped from the low stone ceiling, falling onto her face with a small, wet sound. It reminded her of thirst, of her body struggling to live despite being buried in timelessness. A rush of warmth filled her chest, love for the life that pulsed in her body. She moved to catch the drips of water on her tongue. It tasted of metal and earth.

Truly, she reasoned, no one had done her any harm. Fear

alone had overwhelmed her. Perhaps that was what she must learn: to overcome the power of fear to rob her of will and life.

She rolled to the side and stumbled to her feet. She was still tempted to cradle her left arm in front of her but refused the image of flayed skin and dripping blood. The illusion left like a sigh.

She picked up the measuring rod and moved steadily through the darkness until she found the next door. She knocked against the wood. The door opened. She walked through.

Nothing. She peered into the faint light. Nothing. Then the measuring rod was taken.

"What is this?" she asked, feeling like the Huluppu branch, tossed to and fro by currents beyond her control.

The voice of night answered. "Quiet, Mir-ri. The Ways of the Underworld are perfect and may not be questioned."

To reach her, the branch had travelled far, with no measurements or calculations; it had come simply by letting the Elements carry it.

She walked to the final door and waited. She could not tell if it was moments or days that she stood, wondering at the path, at the crossings that brought her to this place, wondering if this final door had been waiting for her all the days of her life. The silence deepened, as if the walls, too, were waiting.

She reached out and knocked. Could she have chosen not to?

The door opened. She passed through.

The Gatekeeper took the Robe, leaving her naked.

"What is this?" she whispered.

"Quiet, Mir-ri. The Ways of the Underworld are perfect and may not be questioned."

She must walk now, naked and bowed low, to meet Eresh-ki-gal.

Queen of the Underworld.

Holy, Dark and Eternal Eresh-ki-gal.

Mir-ri's cheeks flushed, like a child caught at something shameful. It was not the lack of clothing; she had always bathed and dressed with others. It was the sense of being seen by eyes that would reveal all her secrets, even those she did not know she held . . .

She walked, naked and bowed low, to meet Eresh-ki-gal.

Have you ever woken from a nightmare and found it real?

The corpses stink the baby's dead not breathing darkness bloodied and beaten she screams for help six of them hold her down heads on stakes put out their eyes burn her stone her skin him alive . . .

I am only the secrets of your own dark heart, your lust, your greed, your anger, your flesh . . . I am the living power of water, the cry that catches in the throat, the sob that shatters stone
    xvi
. . .

Have you the courage to lift up my veil?

If you stand only on the safety of the banks spearing fish, how can you know the depths of the river? Can you fathom the darkness under a ledge of rock or understand the life of the fish writhing on your spear? You mistake the teeth of the crocodile as the edge of the abyss, but the chasm is more terrible than teeth, and certain . . . I fulfill the law and the law demands your blood.

Have you the wisdom to hear beyond my wail? I am . . . the catastrophe, the devourer, the necessity. Impaled on my teeth, you shall be blessed for you will glimpse truth. Have you the courage to welcome my voice? Have you the wisdom to embrace the choice?

Three days and three nights passed in the Underworld . . .
Holy Eresh-ki-gal, great is your renown.

Stripped of all illusion, Mir-ri turned her ear back to the
upper world.

She came first to the seventh gate. Her Robe, folded,
awaited her. She shook it out and dropped it over her head. It
settled softly on her body, imbuing a deep inner security and
stability, a warm solidness, bestowed as a blessing on those who
walk with courage and integrity. She stood tall, prepared to face
whatever might come in her life as Priestess.

The sixth gate opened. Mir-ri found the measuring rod, the
river-washed branch with the snakeskin banner: twin symbols of
earth joined to hold desire and intimacy, bonding and
commitment. Gone now the fear and rage, helplessness and
despair. Restored, opened, changed, she fully accepted the path
her feet walked, moving with a grace never known before, as if
moving through light rather than air.

She came to the fifth gate. It opened. She passed through.
She raised her left hand to receive the Band of Gold. It shone with
a soft glow in the pale light. She knew the certainty of who she
was and her purpose in walking this sacred road. Where there had
been chattering doubts, there was now silence deep as Time.

She walked to the fourth gate. It opened. Hands replaced
the Breastplate. Peace filled her, arising from her heart's capacity
to feel both love and grief, to open to the fullness of life and
death, constancy and change.

She walked to the third gate. The way opened. She passed
through. She was not surprised by the hands that restored the

110

Double Strand of golden beads to her neck, but her mouth released an unexpected sound that vibrated in her throat, opening her to every nuance of life. Even the vibration of the Gatekeeper was known to her.

She found the next gate very close, the path fully revealed now, as if she had been walking it all her life. She stepped through. Hands placed the Strand of blue eggshell over her head, settled it around her neck. With a sudden sharp pain, the centre of her forehead opened to a vista of light that existed beyond the horizons of time and space, revealing her own deep wisdom.

The Gatekeeper moved aside. Mir-ri walked on, guided now by light.

She passed through the last gate, the first, and hands placed the Crown back on her head. In that moment, she knew the meaning of the Shugurra, felt the simultaneous absolute simplicity and complexity of knowing each and every person to be unique and separate and yet all one. She experienced the helplessness of being able to control nothing at all, and knew that everything was unfolding as it should. She moved in the limitless, boundless nothingness that encompasses everything, at the same time feeling the solid earth surrounding her. She understood the complex interconnections between self, others, and all living things.

With a bow of acknowledgement to the Gatekeeper, Mir-ri emerged into the light of a new morning. The sky was clear, and herons called from the river.

CHAPTER XIII

Amman, Jordan. Update May 4th 2015 3.24pm UTC

About 5:00 pm last night, a magnitude 7.9 earthquake struck just offshore of the town of Padang in Sumatra, Indonesia. The quake toppled buildings and started landslides, smashing homes and swallowing up entire villages. This is the fourth major quake in 5 years to strike the area. Over 1,000 people are known to have died, an additional 3,000 still missing.

Paula staggered off the plane at Queen Alia airport, clutching her passport and visas, bleary-eyed and irritable after twenty-one hours flying. She followed the other passengers towards a bustling crowd negotiating immigration. Blessing Thom for his foresight in organising her visas, Paula made for the short queue under the visa sign. A burly man in a uniform held up his hand to stop her.

"Transit," he said, pointing in the opposite direction.

"No," said Paula, shaking her head. "Visa."

"Transit," repeated the man.

Not bloody likely, thought Paula, never wanting to see another transit lounge in her life. She tried to explain, but apparently "transit" was the only English word the man knew, and he was determined to practise it on her.

Paula gave up on him and turned away to join the visa queue. The man ran around to stop her, flapping his arms as if she were a stray chicken.

"Transit."

"I HAVE A VISA!" yelled Paula, waving her passport in his face. That got his attention.

He studied the passport for so long Paula thought he might have fallen asleep, but then he looked up, smiled, and ushered her to the head of the visa queue.

Then she was through.

Mysteriously, her bag was the very last on the carousel, but she had dropped into a sort of neutral zone where that seemed quite normal. It might just have been sheer exhaustion, but Paula indulged herself with imagining the blissful state as some sort of air travel enlightenment.

As if to make up for the delayed luggage, Customs just waved her through, and Paula finally stood in the airport terminal. She changed some money and dragged her wheeled suitcase out through the front doors into the night air of Amman. It was cool, just as the travel agent had said. In Paula's imagination, the Arab countries basked under a red-gold sun all year round. In reality, it was about fifteen degrees, and the travel agent had told her to pack warm clothes for the evenings. So much for dreams of balmy, star-studded nights.

Paula found a taxi and directed the driver to the Hillside Hotel. He said something about the fare, waving his hands about for emphasis, but Paula just pointed at the meter as the guidebook recommended, and he turned it on without another word. Funny how taxi drivers were the same all over the world. And funny how taxis were so often yellow . . . Paula's mind drifted tiredly as the city lights flashed past.

Forty minutes later, she stood outside the Hillside Hotel and wondered if she was in the right place. The tall building looked more like a hospital than a hotel. The internet had said it was close to the University of Jordan, but it was hard to tell at night. Paula just hoped there was a bed with clean sheets.

Inside it looked more like a hotel, and the man at the desk was friendly. He called for a younger man to carry her bag up three flights of stairs to a small room at end of a long corridor. Paula wasn't sure she knew the way back out, but that didn't seem to matter as much as the neat, single beds, covers turned back to reveal clean, white pillows.

The young man left, and Paula sighed with relief. Then she sneezed. And sneezed again. What was the smell? Stale cigarette smoke seeped out of the walls, tickling her nose. She made a mental note to buy air freshener and went to look at the bathroom.

A bold sign announced in broken English that, due to the small circumference of sewer pipes, toilet paper was not to be placed in toilets in Amman. A red arrow pointed to a small container placed to one side of the toilet for used paper.

"Oh well, when in Rome . . ." Paula used the toilet, placed the paper in the bin, and took a shower. Exhausted beyond thought, she lay on top of the bedcovers wrapped in the towel and closed her eyes.

The door opened with a bang.

Paula leapt up, heart pounding.

The towel dropped to the floor.

Naked, Paula grabbed for her phone. What was the emergency number in Jordan?

Silhouetted in the doorway stood a tiny woman with a large suitcase.

"Lili?"

The woman dropped the suitcase on her foot.

"Aargh! Oh, Paula. Hi! They didn't tell me you were here."

Paula grabbed the towel to cover herself and went to help Lili with the case. They stood for a moment--strangers meeting for the first time--then threw their arms around each other.

"It's so good"--"It's really you"--"to see you."

They laughed and sat on the beds facing each other.

"You're so tiny," said Paula. "You look bigger on Skype."

"You're not so tall yourself."

"But I'm rounder. Italian, remember."

"Mish is always telling me to eat more."

"Will I order room service?"

Lili went to shower. Paula phoned for dips and bread and fruit. She changed into her old, red pajamas and unpacked the rest of her clothes. Lili came out dressed in leopard print pajamas, and they sat cross-legged on one bed, eating and talking.

"It's like a sleepover," said Lili. "At last we're here!"

"And none too soon," said Paula. "Did you see the latest reports about the sea levels? They're building sea walls on every seaboard in the World."

"Where they can afford them," said Lili.

Before they settled for the night, their talk came around to the tablet and the address from the courier company.

"Any news on who lives there?" asked Paula.

Lili shook her head and looked glum. "It's just a warehouse and a depot for couriers. They couldn't trace the parcel. I'm hoping Haleli Borro knows something about the local antiquities dealers or can point us in the right direction."

"Do you think she'll be at the University?"

"We'll find her," said Lili. "I've been thinking about that paper she gave in New York. Did I tell you it was about the relevance of ancient texts to current social issues? I think she'll know something about the tablet."

"You think it was her who sent it? You never said that before."

"Mish tells me I'm developing a vivid imagination since meeting you. I've been trying to keep it in check, but the long flight got me going."

Paula smiled. "Well, Mish isn't here, so you can imagine all you like. Sounds like she bosses you around."

"Isn't that what daughters do?"

"And I have three!"

They settled down to sleep, although Paula had a headache from the cigarette smell and was missing the children. They loved their Gran, and Mary could sleep with her. And Rinna was there . . .

Paula sat up in bed. Daylight showed around the edges of the curtains, and someone was yelling loudly enough to wake the dead. A fire? A bomb? A terrorist attack?

"The call to prayer," said Lili, sitting in bed with her laptop open.

"Oh. Of course." Paula stood and stretched. Her body felt bruised all over.

They breakfasted in the dining room on ample carbohydrates and disappointing coffee.

"There'll be good coffee at the University," said Lili hopefully.

The sun shone just as Paula had imagined, although billowing clouds hovered at the edges of the hills on which Amman rested like a white crown.

"They call it the White City," said Lili, pointing at the mosaic jumble of stone houses and faded minarets.

"Like Gondor in Lord of the Rings," said Paula.

"Let's hope there aren't any Orcs," said Lili, laughing. "Do you know that there was a city here around the time of Christ? It was called Philadelphia."

"You're making that up!"

"I am not. Where do you think the name comes from? There was enough rainfall then for a number of cities out here to survive by producing and raising cattle."

"I know! They chopped down all the trees and the rain dried up," said Paula. It had happened all over the Mediterranean and Middle East.

"Ah, Gilgamesh and the cedars!" Lili shaded her eyes and looked out over the city.

The modern metropolis of Amman lay before them like a postcard picture. Paula looked through half-closed eyes, trying to imagine the city with flat-roofed houses and ancient temples.

"What are you doing?" asked Lili.

"Seeing into the past," said Paula. "It feels very close here."

The past was lost to them as they entered the grounds of the University. It was like a small, modern city, with local and international students hurrying between classes or chatting on the lawns. They followed signs to the Sociology department.

In the foyer, they found Dr. Borro's room number and photo on the staff notice board: a dark-eyed woman with an aquiline nose, high cheekbones, and glossy black hair.

"She's beautiful," said Paula. "Like a queen."

Lili jumped. "The Queen's gift?"

Paula shrugged. As they climbed the stairs to her office, she was sure they would find the office unoccupied.

On the closed door was a handwritten note in both Arabic and English: Dr Borro is away until further notice. Please direct enquiries to the front desk.

"I knew it!"

"Let's see what they have to say at the front desk," said Lili.

Paula sighed and followed her down the stairs.

Apparently Haleli had not left a number with the front desk, and they were not expecting her back for another ten days. Lili wrote out a message and left it with the bored-looking woman behind the desk.

"What now?" asked Paula.

"You have to see the Old City," said Lili. "But first we find some decent coffee."

"Lead on."

They drank half-decent coffee at the cafeteria and then walked back through the University. The sun beat down, and the air was full of unfamiliar smells. Lili pulled a crumpled white hat from her bag and tucked it over her curls. Paula rubbed sunscreen on her nose, and they set out downhill for the city.

"Are you a romantic?" asked Paula.

"Of course," said Lili, laughing. "Would I be here chasing after an ancient prophecy and a will-o'-the-wisp sociologist otherwise? Why do you ask?"

118

"I was just thinking that there must be a love story tied up in this somewhere."

"Why on earth would you think that?" asked Lili, looking puzzled.

"Because there's supposed to be some sort of lineage--daughters marked at birth--and a lineage has to begin somewhere. Probably with a man and a woman and at least one child."

Lili wrinkled her forehead and bit her lip, her characteristic thinking pose. "I suppose so," she said. "I hadn't thought of it like that, but it's a nice idea. Although lineages can begin in other ways, like rape, subjugation, casual sex."

"See, you're not a romantic," said Paula, punching her arm. "Besides," she added, widening her eyes and raising her eyebrows in mock outrage, "did people have casual sex four thousand years ago?"

"I don't know, but they worshipped Inanna in Sumer, and she certainly wasn't a shy virgin. The poetry of her love life said things like, 'Come plow my vulva, man of my dreams.'"

"Echoes of the Song of Songs: Let him kiss me with the kisses of his mouth . . ."

"I think it began in Sumer," said Lili. "And maybe Saba to the south, and it went from there to Jerusalem in Solomon's time." Her eyes took on the faraway look that signalled a temporary excursion to the ancient world.

"Oh, to have been a fly on the wall when it all began," said Paula.

"Or better still, an initiate in the Temple of Inanna!" said Lili.

They wandered the streets of Amman, asking directions to the souk, the market in the old part of the city. The locals shouted their directions over the noise of hammers and construction machinery, over loudspeakers broadcasting the call to prayer or hawking anything and everything from bread to washing machines, and over the incessant roar of traffic. They took a bus and finally a yellow taxi to reach the heart of the city. They ate spiced lamb and rice from roadside stalls, drank sugary lemon drinks, and browsed the market as if they really were tourists. Paula bought small souvenirs for the children, although she suspected they wouldn't seem as exotic back in Melbourne.

That night, footsore and weary, they ate at a small restaurant close to their hotel. The décor was basic, but the food smelled good. Paula had just refilled their glasses with iced tea when a woman sat at the next table. With a sharp intake of breath, Lili flung her arm out to grab Paula's hand. She knocked a glass, spilling iced tea over the table. She leapt up, mouthing, "Haleli Borro."

Unbelievable. The queenly woman from the photograph sat quietly, reading the menu, apparently oblivious to them.

"Told you so," whispered Lili, dancing out of the way of the dripping tea.

Paula signalled for the waitress. Lili nudged her and walked over to Haleli, who was still reading the menu despite the fuss over the tea.

"Hi."

"Good evening," said Haleli, as if she had just noticed them.

"I'm Lili Frenkel, University of Philadelphia, and this is Paula Matthews, University of Melbourne. I saw you at the conference in New York last August. We called in to see you at the University, but you were out."

Haleli nodded. The hairs on Paula's neck tickled; here they were, in a strange city, with someone she didn't know, playing out some sort of cloak and dagger drama. Talk about weird.

"May we sit here?" asked Lili. "We seem to have ruined our table."

Haleli looked across to where the waitress was bundling up the soggy tablecloth. She smiled, a blaze of sunshine that lit her face from within.

"Of course. I would be delighted."

Paula sat on the edge of a chair on Haleli's left. Lili sat opposite, warning her with her eyes. Paula nodded slightly; she would go along with the charade.

Lili and Haleli spoke briefly of the conference and their work. Lili talked about some of the ancient sites they planned to visit. Haleli said very little. After dinner, as they exchanged their work details, Haleli invited them to meet with her at the University the following morning. She made it sound like a casual offer, one they might easily refuse. With a quick look at each other, Paula and Lili agreed to be at Haleli's office at ten.

As Haleli walked away, Paula whispered, "Either she's paranoid, or there's really something going on here."

Lili shrugged. "We'll see soon enough."

They hadn't mentioned the tablet.

They arrived at Haleli's office to find the door ajar, Haleli at her desk. She greeted them formally and invited them in. She closed the door, and the formality dropped away, replaced by a smile that lit her face.

"I am so glad you have come." She indicated two chairs by the bookcase and pulled her own chair close. "We can talk here."

Lili nodded, her eyebrows raised in question. "It's not safe elsewhere?"

Haleli frowned. "Nowhere is truly safe, but here we will not be overheard."

"Is that why you couldn't talk in New York?" asked Lili. "Were you being watched?"

"Probably," said Haleli, shrugging. "There was too much at stake then to risk contact, but now we must talk." She looked intently at Lili. "Daughters will come marked at birth," she said slowly.

Lili dropped her bag on her foot.

"What does that mean?" asked Paula, grabbing Lili's arm. "Isn't it from the tablet?"

"You have read the prophecy?" asked Haleli. "I arranged for the tablet to go to Philadelphia."

Paula tensed at the tone of self-congratulation in Haleli's voice.

"Go on," said Lili. She sounded eager, her eyes bright with excitement.

"I am sure the prophecy points to this new millennium," said Haleli. "It is four thousand years since it was written, but the time for it to be read is now."

Lili gasped. That's exactly what Paula had said.

Haleli leaned towards Lili. "I started to dream you. Glimpses at first. Your face. Your home. It took me ten years to find you."

Huh? Lili shook her head. What on Earth did Haleli mean? Was she crazy?

"I found you and waited for an opportunity to make contact. I hoped you'd come." Haleli's face softened, her dark eyes asking something.

Paula leaned forward. "You dreamed Lili?"

"The mark drew me."

"The what?"

Lili held up her left arm and pointed to a small black mark on her wrist. Was it a tattoo? A secret mark? What the hell? Paula looked more closely and gasped. The mark was like a star or a flower, just like the birthmark on Mary's thigh. She told them.

"Ah. This is good," said Haleli.

"Good?" said Paula. "My mother called it 'voglie'. She said it was there because of the unfulfilled wishes of the mother. I always felt a bit guilty." She shivered at the thought of Mary's dreams, how small she looked, sitting up in bed, hugging her old teddy.

"My mother and Mish both have one, too," said Lili.

"Daughters will come marked at birth!" said Paula. "Why didn't you tell me about it?"

"Sorry"--Lili shrugged--"I was embarrassed. I thought you'd think I was being stupid to imagine it might be about me." Her cheeks flushed, making her look like a girl caught out at something.

"I don't like not knowing things," said Paula, promising herself a Skype call home to check on Mary as soon as it was morning in Melbourne.

"There is much we do not know," said Haleli.

You can say that again, thought Paula. "Do you think the birthmarks mean we're related? A common ancestor or something?"

"It is possible," said Haleli. "Many are descended from the people of ancient Sumer."

"Do you have the mark, too?" asked Paula, feeling a bit dizzy with the idea.

"Not that I know of," said Haleli. "But many things change over four thousand years. I was drawn to the mark, so it may be that there is a link."

"A link? How exactly did you dream Lili? What do you mean?"

"It is a gift from my mother and her mother before her. There have always been dreamers among the Bedu."

Lili nodded. "I've read about it. There are stories from the Hebrew tribes about it, too."

"Of course," said Haleli. "So I found you, and you are here."

Paula was impressed; Haleli spoke with such authority.

"Now what?" asked Lili.

"Now you must find the *me*. Follow the prophecy. Restore the Balance." Haleli looked at them as if they were students to whom she had just given the topic for the next term paper.

Paula was bouncing in her chair. She caught Lili's eye and then touched her fingers to her throat. Will we? she asked silently.

Lili nodded.

The atmosphere changed as Lili spoke of the necklace and bracelet. Haleli looked at jewellery briefly, but she seemed withdrawn.

"This is surprising," she said, as if she were offended by the revelation.

"What do you mean?" asked Lili

"I, too, have a token from my mother, but I thought it had nothing to do with this. I did not dream it."

"This is not just your dream," said Paula, irritated again with Haleli's self-absorption.

Uncertainty flickered across Haleli's face. "You are right," she said in her precise English. "I have been alone with this for so long, I forget that others have their part."

"Are you all right?" asked Lili, leaning towards her.

Haleli nodded. "What we speak of here is very large. I have been preparing for twenty years. I do not like to be taken by surprise."

"Who does?" said Paula.

Haleli frowned. "There is more to this than you know. The prophecy is a warning. Global warming, degradation of freshwater systems, food-producing systems; do you think this is all natural? Our world is being destroyed by greed, and we call it climate change!"

Paula's head was spinning. She agreed that cutting down trees and burning fossil fuels was an environmental disaster, but was Haleli suggesting that the juggernaut of global consumerism was part of a conspiracy? How could any right-thinking academic believe in conspiracy theories?

Haleli turned to her computer. She entered a series of passwords that opened a virtual storage cache. Encrypted material appeared. More passwords. She moved the screen so they could see: lines of data, names, dates, documentation of meetings, correspondence, financial transactions.

"I have collected evidence."

"I don't understand," said Lili.

"There are those who would erode the environment to the point of global collapse. The world will be saved by the same ones who destroy it, and they will have the power to do with it as they want. What do they care if millions die?"

Paula sighed. Conspiracy theories were always flawed: why did the richest people in the world need to invent elaborate schemes to have more?

"Wealth is nothing but a construct," said Haleli as if she anticipated Paula's objections. She spoke slowly, emphasising each word, as if talking to children. "A useful construct to disempower entire populaces. But I am not talking about a global coup. The same ones who would be capable of such a thing could not trust each other long enough to bring it about. No, I am talking about the misinformation and deliberate disregard that has allowed the situation to deteriorate to the point of no return; governments, multi-national companies, and thousands of smaller operators all benefit from it."

Lili was biting her lip, her face pale.

Haleli sighed. "Let me show you one of the things I found." She opened more files on her computer. "This is HAARP, the High Frequency Active Auroral Research Program."

An emerald green cloud illuminated a field of huge antennae.

"What is it?' asked Lili.

"It's part of the Strategic Defence Initiative. Star Wars, some people call it. HAARP was constructed to investigate the ionosphere and establish whether some of its properties could be used for communication or surveillance purposes, but we now know it has the ability to trigger floods, droughts, hurricanes and earthquakes."

"How?"

"HAARP intensively bombards the atmosphere with high-frequency rays. Low frequency electromagnetic waves then bounce back onto earth and penetrate matter. These waves modify the World's electro-magnetic field, affecting everything from people's brains to tectonic movements."

Lili whistled through her teeth. Paula sucked in air as if she had been winded.

"It's like a gigantic heater," said Haleli. "It slices away the protective layer of the ionosphere."

"Can't it be stopped?" asked Paula.

Haleli shook her head. "It has been presented to the public as a program of scientific and academic research. People believe what they are told."

"But it's a weapon!" said Paula.

"We only call them weapons when they are aimed at us," said Haleli. "When they belong to us we call them protection or defense, or research."

"What can it do as a weapon?"

"It can target laser beams of enormous power anywhere in the World. It can selectively destabilise agricultural and ecological systems of entire regions. It can trigger earthquakes and tsunamis and change weather patterns."

Lili sighed deeply. "I would never have thought it, being the child of a Holocaust survivor, but my life seems sheltered all of a sudden. What are a few academic papers compared with this?"

Paula shook her head. Was Lili buying the conspiracy theory?

"In my family there are missing bits: people, places, memories from before the Holocaust. My mother was ten when she lost her family. I've tried, but I can't imagine what that would be like." Lili looked intently at Haleli. "But I think you might know."

Haleli met her look. The silence became intense. When she spoke, it was like listening to a storyteller. "I was twelve when I left my family, but they were not at risk like your family during the War in Europe. It was I who would have been at risk if I had stayed.

"The women in my family, like women throughout the Mediterranean and the Arab countries, lived and died at the sufferance of the men who owned them." She stated it as a fact, no emotion apparent in her voice or face.

Paula winced at the pain she guessed was there. Her own heritage was full of child brides and slave labour in the name of marriage, but she rarely thought of it. Her father had not been like that . . .or had he? She thought of the smallness of her mother's world, the day-to-day toil of it.

"You were both born into different cultures," said Haleli. "You escaped the worst of it, and you are here. Unlike your mothers or their mothers, you have a voice." Her own voice sounded tired.

"What happened when you were twelve?" asked Paula.

Haleli looked startled, the whites of her eyes showing like a frightened horse. "I do not speak of it."

"I'm sorry," said Paula. "It's the sort of thing women would talk about back home. I'm a bit out of my depth here."

"Please do not apologise," said Haleli softly. "This is a time of great change. Much will be asked of us. Perhaps it is fitting you should know my story.

"My sister, Huna, was three years older . . . There! I am speaking of her in the past. In my mind I keep her alive. Perhaps that is why I do not talk about it." She was quiet for a moment, her eyes closed.

Paula held her breath. Would Haleli change her mind about telling them?

Haleli stood and paced the small room. "Huna had been married for two years to a man the age of our father. It was a good marriage for our father but a nightmare for her. She was her husband's slave in every way; he only allowed her to visit us for an hour or two on feast days. She had miscarried twice--

much to her shame--and I tried to help her by carrying her water as well as our own, by taking meat to her when she had none. At first I was afraid; soon I would be married, and who would help me?

"Then something happened. The brother of her husband came to stay and, when Huna was alone, he forced himself on her. She was terrified. If her husband found out, she would be blamed, although a more modest, downcast woman you would never see. Of course her husband did find out, and my father was petitioned to return the bride price and punish his daughter. Huna was kept in a tent for three days while the men haggled.

"I listened to them talk, although I would have been thrown in with Huna if they knew I was hiding there. They spoke of bride goods and punishment, but never once of rape--I had no word for it then, either--and justice. I stopped being afraid, and anger started to burn in my body. Then the men in my family agreed that Huna must die to maintain their honour. The honour of men! Huna's husband agreed, but he did not want to lose the abundance that seemed to follow the women in our mother line, so they offered me as a wife to him. I would rather have died.

That night I cut through Huna's tent to take her away with me, but she was too frightened. Then the men came."

Haleli's eyes darkened. "I ran from them. I took a horse, and I ran. I left her to die."

"But they would have killed you, too," said Lili quietly.

Haleli shrugged. "I heard Huna screaming as I rode away."

"How far did you ride?" asked Paula, although there were other things she could have said.

"Through the night to the tents of my uncle, my father's brother." She spoke in a matter of fact voice now, as if giving directions to the nearest marketplace.

"Why him?" asked Paula, her heart thudding like the hooves of a fleeing horse.

"He had told me to come to him if there was trouble. I was hoping this was what he meant. He was more moderate than my father, and they had argued many times about the Laws. His own sister was killed for honour when he was a boy. I thought he might help, but I could not be sure."

"You were twelve!" said Paula, thinking of Hayley, Rinna, and Mary. And imagining Jon sitting on a council to decide whether his sisters should live or die. She shuddered.

Haleli shrugged, a gesture they were coming to know as hers. "My mother was twelve when she had Huna. It is not so young in the desert."

"Did they follow you?" asked Lili.

Haleli nodded. "But I had learned the way of the desert from my brothers. I rode so well when I was young, I think they forgot I was a girl. It was not hard to keep ahead of them." A shadow crossed her face.

Paula was still thinking of her own daughters, safe in Australia, where women weren't stoned to death. Another shiver ran up her spine. She was feeling increasingly strange, as if the enormity of what Haleli was telling them was crushing her.

"Some water?" Haleli offered her a cup filled from the cooler in the corner.

Paula took it and held it between her hands, not sure what to do with it. "Thank you. I think I just had a glimpse of how big this really is. I came here to make a difference, but it was still a bit of a game to me. I expected to do something and go back to Australia the same as when I left."

Haleli and Lili were quiet.

"Thank you for telling us," said Lili, nodding to Haleli. "But they must know where you are now."

"They do, but my uncle sent the story to newspapers around the world. He is a very rich man and has many friends. Suddenly everyone was interested in the plight of Bedu women." Haleli made a mocking sound deep in her throat. "The spokesmen for the tribes denied it all and used me as an example of their liberated views; a girl sent to Amman for education! They never mentioned my sister, and my uncle thought it prudent to leave well-enough alone, as he said. So, I am a liberated, Bedu woman, and Huna is dead."

"I'm so sorry," said Paula, breathing out some of the fear from her body. "Is it the Bedu who watch you?"

Haleli shrugged again. "Perhaps. There are others who do not like my liberal views. Some among the Bedu are more moderate than they were thirty-five years ago. There are other girls who have been educated and who have not followed tradition. But now there are Islamists everywhere who want to take us back seventeen hundred years. Who knows?"

"I saw a man at the conference last year when you gave your paper," said Lili. "Tall, dark, wearing sun-glasses. He followed you out."

Haleli smiled, the fleeting ray of sunshine that so changed her features. "Ah! An Islamist for sure!"

Paula had a strange feeling in her chest, like bubbles rising. It really had been a game until now: she had lived her life in a safe, Australian city, working as an academic in a respected University; she was married, had healthy children and expected to die of old age in the distant future. Alongside Haleli, she was playing at make-believe.

Lili and Haleli were quiet.

Paula shook her head. "It's all so new to me: conspiracies, honour killings. I feel like a child."

"Me too," said Lili, placing a hand on her arm.

"There is no shame in that," said Haleli. "Children often see more clearly than adults. I think your task is to see like children and let the prophecy lead you."

"To the *me?*" asked Paula.

Haleli nodded. "Perhaps we already have some." She touched her neck.

"Do you really think they could be from the sacred vestments of Inanna?" asked Lili.

"You talk as if Inanna was real, as if she really lived," said Paula. "I thought she was a goddess, a myth."

"How do you think the myths were formed?" asked Haleli. "It denies their power to say they are just stories. Whether or not Inanna actually walked the Earth, there was a time when people were certain she did. The *me* come from that time, and hold the power of ritual and magic, the power of the old Gods and Goddesses."

Paula groaned and held her head in her hands.

Lili stood behind her, hands on her shoulders. "How can we find the *me?* And what have they got to do with the global power games?"

"Let me worry about the power games, as you call them," said Haleli. "If you can find the *me*, I believe it will help. Some of them were almost certainly in the museum in Baghdad. Where they are now?" She shrugged.

"But where do we start?" Lili's question echoed around the office.

Paula just wanted to go back to the hotel and pull the bedcovers over her head.

"Be like children," said Haleli. "See the sights of Jordan. Go to Jerusalem. Follow the old trade roads as far as is safe. It makes little sense, but I am sure the time is right for them to be found." Once again, she sounded like a storyteller or a prophetess. "How they fit with the rest . . ." She shrugged again. "It is one part of a puzzle I have been working on for a long time."

Her voice changed to the crisp tones of a businesswoman. "How long do you have here?"

"Three weeks," said Lili.

"It will have to be enough," said Haleli.

"Will you come with us?" asked Paula.

Haleli shook her head. "I cannot be seen to help you, for all the reasons we have discussed. I will arrange help, and you can contact me."

She gave them a cell phone number and a system for contacting her: phone her cell phone, hang up after two rings, wait one minute, call again. If it was safe, she would answer it. If the number changed, she would let them know.

"Phew! It really is like a mystery novel," said Lili.

"An ancient mystery novel," said Haleli.

It took Paula a few moments to realise that Haleli intended that as another joke. She couldn't even smile. Lili laughed, but it sounded a bit hysterical.

They left Haleli's office ten minutes later, Lili exclaiming loudly with promises to keep in touch from their respective universities. It seemed like two months rather than two hours since they had arrived. The midday light was bright after the shadowy office, and they were both quiet until they reached the gates of the University.

"It's strange," said Paula. "I knew the first time we spoke that you and I could be friends, but I'm not sure about Haleli.

Even after she told us that extraordinary story about her sister, I still feel distant. Maybe it's just that I'm not convinced about everything she says."

"I don't imagine friendship has been a big part of her life," said Lili, linking her arm though Paula's.

"What makes you say that?"

"Imagine how it must be to have every move watched from when you're twelve years old." Lili looked around and lowered her voice. "Imagine the pressure she's lived under."

"I'm not sure I can. I'm still stuck on what happened to her sister. And all that stuff about a conspiracy. I don't know, Lili, I've heard that sort of thing before. It's right out there, even for me."

Lili sighed. "I'm not feeling so sure of anything, either, but this is exactly what we wanted, isn't it? We dreamed of finding the *me*! The rest of it might all be Haleli's imagination, but at least she believes the tablet is important."

Paula tucked Lili's arm tighter against her. "I wonder if the person who wrote on that tablet had any idea what a fuss it would cause."

"Nothing about ancient Sumer would surprise me now," said Lili. "Let's go get some lunch."

CHAPTER XIV

Basra, Iraq. May 5th 2015CE 10.43pm

The supreme martyrdom is only conferred on those who slay or are slain in the way of God. As death is inevitable and can happen only once, partaking in jihad is profitable in this world and the next. Five Tracts of Hasan al-Banna (1906-1949): A Selection from the Majmu'at Rasa'il al-Imam al-Shahid, 1978.

The lights flickered and went out. With a string of muttered oaths, one of the uniformed men left his post by the door to light the candles sitting in glasses on the table. His companion moved to the curtained window to check the street. What he saw made him cross quickly back to the door, nodding curtly to a third man who was clearly in charge. Older than the guards, the third man wore a white robe as was the custom.

At the signal, he closed the laptop and placed it on the floor. Their visitor knocked in the correct sequence and was admitted. He ignored the two guards and walked across to sit opposite the robed man, bowing his head in greeting.

An old woman, face hidden behind a dark headscarf,

served tea in gold-leaf glasses, and the two men drank in silence. When the glasses were empty, the robed man spoke in a deep, cultured voice.

"So, Ahmed, my friend, what have you seen?"

The newcomer removed his dark glasses. "She met with two academics, one from America and one from Australia. It seems to have been a chance meeting."

The robed man made a sound in his throat that suggested doubt. "Has she had contact with these academics before?"

"She attended a conference in New York last year where the American gave a paper. They did not meet."

"Remind me about the conference."

"She travelled alone, stayed one night at the University, delivered a meaningless paper about ancient texts, attended a lecture by the American academic who spoke the usual obscenities, and then flew home. She asked a question at the lecture but spoke to no one else."

"The topic of the American's lecture?"

"May I be forgiven for repeating it: Giving women power because they produce life from their bodies." The armed guards stirred at their posts. The older man raised his hands in front of him, fingers steepled, and looked thoughtful.

"And the question?"

"She asked if the birth control Pill were part of the problem of which the American spoke."

"And the answer?"

"It was long but in the affirmative. There was some dissent in the audience."

"So, she is careful."

"Always," said the man called Ahmed. "The whore knows she is watched."

"As long as she is watched, she can do no harm where she

is. It lulls the moderates to see her so free."

"What of the American?" asked Ahmed.

"She is nobody," said the robed man. "Forget her."

"She spoke words of evil," said Ahmed, spitting out the words as if they tasted bitter.

"America is full of evil words. Would you silence them all?" The older man's voice was mild.

Ahmed nodded and smiled, a thin, mean expression that made him look like a predator.

"Patience, Ahmed. One step at a time. Watch Haleli. If she deviates from being the perfect academic--lectures, tutorials, conferences--we will act. Either she is what she seems and is harmless, or she is more cunning even than her Grandfather."

Ahmed inclined his head; he would do his duty.

Like a benevolent master tossing his dog a bone, the older man called after him as he was leaving the room. "If the American has further contact with Haleli, let me know. You may need to do something, after all."

CHAPTER XV

The city of Urim, Ancient Sumer. c 1993 BCE

The union . . .in the sacred marriage signifies, expresses and effects the meeting of the male-female axis of the world.[xvii] Possibly, then, the "Sacred Marriage" rite was not originally concerned with king-making at all, but rather with "goddess-making"; perhaps it was a ritual for, as it were, "activating," making fertile a "Goddess on Earth."[xviii]

"I have a special task for you," said Nin-lil-la.

Mir-ri looked into the deep eyes of the High Priestess and shivered. She stood in the room of altars--that first visit had not been a dream, after all. Was this the reckoning that followed the descent and return? In the first story, Inanna had to send someone to Eresh-ki-gal in her place. Inanna refused to send her faithful companions, but she found her consort, Dumuzzi, indulging himself with no regard for his kingship. Inanna turned the eyes of death on Dumuzzi, and he was taken to Eresh-ki-gal .

Mir-ri sighed deeply and turned to the centre of the small room: mighty vortex of destruction; central wellspring of creation. What in her must be sent to Eresh-ki-gal for transformation?

Very little remained of the girl who drew eight-rayed stars in the dust. There had been many crossings since the first visit to the room of altars, and Mir-ri now stood as tall as the High Priestess, her hair coiled high.

Mir-ri walked to the centre and inclined her head towards each altar in turn. Familiar now with the elements of life--Air, Fire, Water, Earth--she greeted them as intimates. She then turned again to face the High Priestess to learn what was being asked.

"You have been instructed in the Temple by Ad-ilah." The High Priestess's voice was formal.

Mir-ri nodded. She had learned to read and write, to use the sacred units of measure, to look to the Heavens for the movement of the fixed bodies, and to recite the King lists, the lists of Priests and Priestesses, and the names of all the cities of Ki-en-gir. She was, in fact, one of the most educated and informed young women in Urim.

"It is exactly as I wished," said Nin-lil-la. "Now it is time for you to attend the E-dub-ba."

She might as well have said: "Now it is time for you to go with the ass traders to Kemet." Mir-ri's heart beat like a drum against her ribs.

"The House of Tablets. Me?" So it was pride that must be banished. At the Temple she was the most learned, the most skilled, Ad-ilah's best student.

"Yes." The High Priestess sounded strong and sure, speaking with the voice of Aarua, the lioness of battle. "Who else but you?"

Despite her fears, Mir-ri shook with excitement The E-dub-ba was a place of learning for the sons of Priests and

Scribes, and even the sons of the King. She had watched the young men in the courtyards from the high walls of the E-gish-shir-gal. Now she would be attending classes with them.

"You shall attend as daughter of the Holy Priestess of Heaven, daughter Herself of Nanna, Father of Urim. None will challenge your right."

Inside a walled compound on the Eastern side of the King's Palace, stood the House of Tablets. Decorated with the faded mosaics of another Age, the walls of the E-dub-ba had stood in the Sun and rain long before the House of Tablets grew around them.

Interested in everything he saw, Abram had asked his Father about the mosaics.

"The Old Ones made them," his father had answered, looking into the distance.

Abram had waited, knowing that his Father would speak or not, depending on his mood. Terah's eyes had taken on a faraway look, as if he were seeing into the past, watching the craftsmen work.

"This work is no longer done, but my father told me the way of it. The potters gathered clay from the riverbank to shape small cones, rounded on top. About so long." He had held his thumb and middle finger stretched wide apart to show Abram the size of the cones. "They painted the tops with crushed diorite, lapis lazuli and other stones mixed with sand. When they baked them in the fire pits, the patterns hardened. The finished cones were pressed into a thick layer of wet clay, with only the tops showing."

Just when Abram thought there would be no more, Terah had sighed. "I have seen the mosaics. It is fine work. All things must pass, but at least the first people have left something that endures."

Abram had nodded, wondering at the long-ago clay workers who decorated the walls that ran through the E-dub-ba.

That had been in the early days, when he still asked his father questions and listened to the answers. In the eight years he had studied at the E-dub-ba, Abram had turned from the wisdom of his own people. He looked instead to the Scribes and to the tablets stored on shelves in the thick-walled rooms surrounding the courtyard of the House of Tablets.

Now he wore his dark, curly hair tied back in a tight bun as suited his position as Tutor. He sat atop one of the decorated walls, speaking eloquently of the city's history to nine boys sitting cross-legged on the tiled floor of the courtyard. He spoke of the city of Urim, but his talk was not of mosaics; he spoke of Kings and warriors, of lands won and lost. He thought often about Time, and the passing of things. He, too, wanted to make something that would last, something to be wondered at by those who followed.

"Men take lands only to have them taken in turn. It is the way of men." Abram modulated his voice to sound like the older Scribes, and his audience listened in awe as he recited the King lists of Urim and Eridu, Uruk and Kish.

"But enough of men and their achievements. No matter how long the rule of a King, sooner or later the rule will pass to another." He changed his voice, leading the rapt boys away from King lists to a topic closer to his own heart.

"Do you think the tribes of the desert make offerings to the Great Ones of Urim?" he asked.

The boys looked puzzled. "Are not the Great Ones the same everywhere?"

"There are many Great Ones, as there are many lands," said Abram, leading to the thoughts that had been troubling him of late. "If the men of different lands honour different Great Ones, which are the true ones?" he asked.

His audience stirred uneasily, exchanging frowns and raising their eyebrows. Such questions were not usually asked in the E-dub-ba.

"Are they all true?" continued Abram, not expecting answers. "In the North there are tribes who honour one Great One only, One who cannot be named."

There, he had said it. No sooner had he heard of the Northern practice from one of the Eastern, spice traders than he had wondered about the One who cannot be named, finding something irresistible in the mystery of it. His reverie was interrupted by the clear, ringing tones of a question.

"If this Great One of the Northern tribes has no name, how do the people give praise?"

Abram looked up to see dark eyes in a face more beautiful than the visions that had been coming to him at night. He gasped. The voice belonged to a young woman! A woman in the E-dub-ba!

"Perhaps you are lost," he said coldly, dismissing her question. "I will summon an attendant."

"Perhaps I am invited," replied the woman calmly. "Can you answer my question?"

"Impossible!" said several voices at once. The young men around Abram scrambled to their feet to defend their inner sanctum.

"You name that which is in front of your eyes 'impossible', yet you listen in wonder to tales from lands so far away you will never see them." The woman's voice held just a hint of contempt.

"You do not belong here," said Abram, standing on the wall to assert his leadership.

"Perhaps you are correct," said the woman, smiling slightly. "Yet this is where I am."

Abram scowled. Heat rose into his chest, and an unaccustomed agitation filled his mind and body. How dare this woman enter the E-dub-ba, let alone presume to talk back to him? He glared at her, considering his next words.

The students backed away from the confrontation. "Perhaps," they mumbled to each other, "the Great Ones have taken exception to Abram's talk of the Northern practices. Perhaps the Priestess has been sent to investigate." They watched the newcomer with frightened eyes.

Abram continued to glare at the woman, as if his look could hold her at bay. She looked back calmly, continuing to smile slightly.

As they stood there, locked in their first encounter, something new entered the E-dub-ba, hovering in the air between them. Later, some of the students were heard to comment that it was as if Time stood still, like the water near the mouth of the Buranun at the moment of the turning of the tides. None of them could ever say with any certainty how long Abram and the Priestess stood there looking at each other. It was very quiet.

Hamminabi hurried into the courtyard, huffing and puffing. He would have been there sooner to introduce the new student had he not been interrupted by a strange commotion over by the gate. It seemed that one of the old washerwomen was demanding entrance to the E-dub-ba, claiming to have seen a vision in the water. Hamminabi, late already for the appointed meeting with the Priestess, had been tempted to ignore the grandmother's shrill cries, but something in the garbled words caught his ear.

"A child will come where none is named. A child, I tell you. There will be a child." Her cracked voice had sounded like the harsh screeching of the black mountain birds that flew across the city in the season of floods, and Hamminabi had crossed to the gate.

What he heard from the woman was still ringing in his ears when he walked into the courtyard to find Abram and the new student locked in an engagement that crackled the very air. For a moment, Hamminabi's sight blurred, and he saw a picture of the two of them locked like that forever, Time notwithstanding. He shook his head and took a deep breath to calm his racing heart. The vision fled.

"Now. Now," he said. "This will not do." He moved to stand between them. "Abram, this is Mir-ri, Priestess of the Temple of Nanna. She is to study here. Mir-ri, this is Abram, one of our older students."

Abram scowled.

Hamminabi smiled apologetically at Mir-ri. "I am afraid that his knowledge outstrips his wisdom at this stage." He frowned at Abram, gesturing for him to come down from the wall.

With a shrug, Abram jumped down. Ignoring Mir-ri, he addressed Hamminabi. "If she is to study here, surely she should be with the boys in the lower House."

Hamminabi shook his head, his long grey beard moving from side to side. "More knowledge than wisdom," he said sadly, still frowning at Abram.

Not deterred, Abram opened his mouth to speak again.

"Enough, Abram," commanded Hamminabi.

Abram shut his mouth and pursed his lips.

"Come, Mir-ri. I will show you where we work."

The Priestess, head held high, followed Hamminabi into one of the square rooms surrounding the courtyard.

Abram frowned at her straight back and swaying walk. It took him some time to gather his scattered thoughts and resume the lecture. If the students sitting at his feet seemed less overawed, Abram did not notice.

As Hamminabi led Mir-ri through the storerooms and halls of the E-dub-ba, Nin-lil-la stood alone on the balcony outside her sleeping chamber. She had told Mir-ri some of what she had planned, but not all. She had told her of the unrest in the East, of the warring tribes who were destined to overrun Urim, changing forever the ways of Nanna and Inanna. She had spoken of the mountain people, fierce warriors from the Zagros mountains to the North East, and of the desert tribes from the West. Between them, she knew from her visions, the invaders would divide Urim, and Ki-en-gir would change forever.

"All things must pass," she whispered, shivering in the warm air. The words, as old as the city, as old as the land, came easily to her after long practice. It was their message of doom for all she held sacred that caused Nin-lil-la to shiver.

CHAPTER XVI

The city of Urim, Ancient Sumer. c 1992 BC

The king goes with lifted head to the holy lap, goes with lifted head to the holy lap of Inanna, [Dumuzzi] beds with her, he delights in her pure lap. (Sefati, 1998: 105). The "Sacred Marriage" was "joyously and rapturously" celebrated in the ancient eastern Mediterranean for over two thousand years (Kramer, 1969: 49).[xix]

Days passed, becoming weeks that passed into months. Through two complete cycles of Emesh and Enten, Mir-ri studied in the House of Tablets, instructed by Astronomers and Mathematicians. It was as if she had learned to swim in one of the irrigation canals that watered the gardens around the city, and now suddenly she found herself in the great river with currents and eddies carrying her into unfamiliar territory. It was as if she had been concerned only with the emmer wheat and oats, barley and rye, olives, dates and grapes that grew in the gardens, and now her attention had turned to the affairs of the whole land and to the orbs and gyres of the planets in the heavens.

She was pleased to find that her previous learning kept her from drowning in the new, swirling waters. As it was, she not only managed to keep afloat, but found that she could swim with the best of them. And that, of course, meant Abram.

Abram had grudgingly accepted that even the Acolytes in the Temple needed trained Scribes to teach them, and that the E-dub-ba was the obvious place to receive the necessary instruction, even if the student was a woman. He never did, however, become comfortable with Mir-ri's presence in his place of learning, his new home.

Indeed, the E-dub-ba had become more his home than the small house by the Harbour. Nachor and Haran were now well-established as Stoneworkers in their own right, accepting commissions from the Priests, as well as from householders who could afford to purchase personal seals. So popular had the seals become that there were now many who saved tokens, or found something worthwhile to trade, in order to have their family symbols carved in stone. Terah had never fully accepted Abram's calling, but that no longer concerned Abram; his life revolved around study.

Abram never fully accepted the presence of a woman in his domain, and he mostly managed to avoid the Priestess, leaving the courtyard as soon as she entered, suddenly remembering the obscure calculations he needed to complete if she joined a debate or entered quietly to listen to him lecture. It was his desire to avoid her that prompted him to visit Terah after an absence of many months. He found his father pacing to and fro in front of the small shed that served as workshop and storefront.

"Greetings, Father," he began, noticing how much older Terah seemed.

"Ah, Abram. A visit." Terah stopped his pacing to look at his son, eyes moving up and down from Abram's sleek hair to his rope sandals.

Abram looked back, suddenly conscious of his clean-shaven face and soft hands. He waited, a small knot of unease in his stomach.

"I have to go to the Harbour, but Banlir is off on an errand, and I am expecting a customer. Do you have time to mind the shop while I go?" Terah looked expectantly at Abram. "Perhaps we can share some food when I return," he added.

Abram shrugged. "I will wait here."

He half-listened to Terah's mumbled instructions and found himself a comfortable seat on a bench just inside the entrance. Dappled Sun played across his face as he closed his eyes and settled contentedly for an hour of quiet contemplation.

A loud banging noise made him leap from the bench. He stumbled over a slab of granite and fell forwards. A statue of Enki toppled into twin pillars carved with eight-rayed stars. The pillars crashed against a bench, overturning a tray of smaller pieces.

When the dust settled and all was still again, Abram lay in the midst of quite spectacular breakage, shards of stone scattered through the workshop.

"Many pardons, young man. Many pardons," said an old man brandishing a cane.

Abram scowled. The old fool must have banged the cane on the wall.

Surprisingly strong for his age, the man lifted Abram back onto the bench and set about tending the cuts and grazes on his arms and face.

"Never fear. I am a Physician," he announced as he filled a bowl with water from the urn by the door.

Abram watched in bemusement as the old fellow shuffled around, placed the bowl on the workbench, and rummaged in the deep sleeves of his robe. He produced a small flask of dark-coloured glass, pulled a twist of rag from the top, and sniffed the contents. He sneezed so loudly, Abram jumped; pain pierced his head, and his eyes blurred.

The pain in his head was just like the headache he had given himself as a child when he stole the special date wine his father stored in clay amphora in the small cellar. Abram had broken the wax seal and sipped the sweet brew until he could no longer lift the jug, but he had laughed for hours. His head now hurt at least as much as it had after the date wine, but he didn't feel at all like laughing.

Abram groaned and frowned at the old man. If that bottle held some sort of potion, he was not going to drink it, even if the stranger were the finest Physician in Urim. He was about to say as much when the greybeard nodded to himself and upended the bottle over the bowl of water. The water turned milky-white, hissing and swirling as if stirred from within.

Despite the pain throbbing in his head, Abram stood to leave.

The walls moved strangely, and the floor rippled like waves on the Sea. He sat back down, holding his head in both hands and moaning. On his forehead was a lump as big as a duck's egg.

He sagged against the wall, blinking rapidly in an attempt to focus his eyes. There seemed to be three old men now, muttering over the potion. Abram opened his mouth to order them to leave, but no words would come.

"It is only a mixture to clean the dirt from your scratches," said the old man. "It will prevent swelling and redness." His voice was low and rhythmic, like the tone used by a mother to soothe a frightened child.

Abram's vision cleared. There was only one old man, but he seemed determined to treat Abram's wounds.

The Physician pulled a clean square of cloth from his hidden pockets and began to clean the cuts on Abram's arms. When he had extracted all the splinters of stone and washed out the dirt, the old man straightened and began searching his robe again.

Finally, after emptying his pockets of an assortment of seedpods, four bundles of dried herbs, three more bottles, a wooden miniature of a snake, and a stone amulet carved in the shape of a goat-fish, he extracted several thin strips of cloth with which he wrapped Abram's arms.

"The Great Ones have taken their revenge," he joked as he finished his ministrations and returned his treasures to their pockets. "Perhaps you offended them."

"They are just rocks," said Abram, feeling sorry for himself.

"Are they indeed?" The old man turned from where he was emptying the bowl to look at Abram.

"They are nothing more than people make them." Abram glared at the broken statues.

"Or nothing less," said the old man quietly.

"What do you mean?" asked Abram. The old fellow spoke with an authority that reminded him of the Master Scribes at the E-dub-ba.

"Ah, some curiosity befitting a scholar." The Physician raised one eyebrow. "The Great Ones do not live in the rock any more or less than they live in you or me. The rock is part of the life of this world, just as you and I are. The Great Ones are part of the life of this world. In that way, they are in the rock, and they are in you and in me."

Abram considered the man's words. "But the common people, even the Priests, worship the rocks themselves."

"That is how it seems," agreed the old man. "They are, of course, both wrong and right."

"How can they be both wrong and right?" demanded Abram, master of Logic and Astronomy and Mathematics. Master of the Laws, written and unwritten.

"They are wrong because the rock, as you say, is just a rock. And they are right because the Great Ones are everywhere. They can as well be worshipped in the rock as in the stars or in the sweet water of the Buranun."

"But," said Abram, warming to the debate, "people believe the rocks *are* the Great Ones. They place them on altars and build Temples for them." This was a subject he had turned round and round, worrying at it from all angles.

The old man laughed. "The Great Ones do not mind. They know what they are."

Abram shook his head, blinking at the sudden sharp pain behind his eyes. "But it is wrong!"

"You are, perhaps, too interested in wrong and right, young man." The old man was no longer smiling.

"Is that not the task of all learned men?" asked Abram.

The old man shook his head. "It seems my seal is not ready. I will come back when your father is here."

Abram watched the Physician walk away. He had not even asked his name. With a shrug, he turned back to the workshop. At least five of the statues were broken, and a box of smaller pieces smashed. Holding his bandaged arms, he stood frowning at the shapes littering the floor.

When Terah returned, Abram was sitting on a low wall outside the shop, eyes closed. If his father noticed the bandages, he made no comment. He did, however, comment on the ruined statues, bellowing in rage when he saw the pieces lying on the floor.

"What have you done?" he cried to Abram.

Abram shrugged his shoulders carelessly. "Me? I did nothing. Ask the Great Ones. They must have fought among themselves."

"Do not be more bullheaded than usual," said Terah. "These are blocks of stone, not Great Ones! They could no more do this to themselves than the lettuce could pull up roots and attack the barley."

Abram allowed himself a small smile of satisfaction. "You admit it, then. These are false idols."

"I did not say that," Terah said. "Ever since you went as a child to the E-dub-ba, you have come home only to argue with your Father, to argue with all of the Fathers, if truth be told. Sometimes I wonder if the Great Ones are punishing me for my pride."

"You said they are just blocks of stone," said Abram, more interested in the logic of his argument than his Father's fuming.

"Of course they are," agreed Terah. "But things are not just this or that, like you say. The statues are blocks of stone, and they also remind people of the Great Ones. They remind them to honour the Great Ones. There has to be somewhere to leave the offerings."

Abram shook his head. It was not his Father's fault that he was blind to the truth. Terah had not, after all, had the opportunity to speak with scholars from the North, to hear tales of Habiru who worshipped a Nameless One, One who dwelt beyond the understanding of ordinary men and women.

"You are more like a man of Ki-en-gir than a Habiru," said Abram contemptuously as he turned to leave, all thoughts of a shared meal forgotten.

"If a Habiru man shows such little respect for his Father, then perhaps you are right," said Terah. "The land of Ki-en-gir has been good to us." He stooped to pick up the broken pieces of stone.

Abram strode back to the House of Tablets, muttering to himself about false idols and stubborn old men. His thoughts turned to leaving Urim, to travelling North to find the Nameless One of whom the travellers spoke.

Mir-ri was sitting in the courtyard of the E-dub-ba, calculating the cycles of Ninanna, the star of morning and evening, against the movement of one of the fixed bodies in the Heavens. She was biting her lower lip, a habit she had developed when young. Her skin was warm from the Sun, and her hair had begun to slip from the tight coil on top of her head, the curling strands falling over her eyes. Impatiently, she brushed her hair back and straightened from her task to stretch. As she arched her back and flexed her arms above her head, her shift pulled tight, showing her breasts through the linen.

Abram walked into the courtyard. He saw Mir-ri stretching in the dappled light. Suddenly his blood was boiling.

Sweat stung his eyes, and his gish, the tree of life between his legs, began swelling uncomfortably.

Mir-ri turned to look at him.

Who can say whether Nin-lil-la had foreseen this moment, or whether she simply hoped that it would happen? Perhaps there had been spells and rituals calling on Inanna to intercede. It is not known, and truly it matters not. The young man destined for greatness, just as his mother said, and the young woman whose name was omitted from the tablets, came together in the timelessness reserved for all great unions. Just as Ki and An, empty Earth and formless Sky, had embraced in the beginning of all things, with no Time to measure their coming together, Abram and Mir-ri found each other and moved together in the timelessness of love. Just as Ki was filled with An's seed, forming the Annunaki, the first born of the Great Ones, so new life would form in the moist, red darkness of Mir-ri's womb.

Mir-ri was not thinking of Ki and An when she rose and walked slowly across to Abram. She leaned close and whispered in his ear.

"Tonight, by the Moon's light, meet me by the river. The willow by the Palace steps."

She left the E-dub-ba in a daze. How could she have said that? Surely she was possessed by Hedu and Anna, taken over by the laughter and lust of the celestial Dove! How could that be?

The doubts clamoured for attention, but it was the warmth in her belly and the longing in her heart that called most strongly.

The Sun sailed into the West, and the night was dark. Guided by the light of an oil lamp, Mir-ri left the Temple, her body burning with a heat she had never felt before. All was quiet, the others sleeping in the arms of Enki and his granddaughter, Inanna. Who, it seemed, was smiling on the Priestess as she slipped quietly down the stairs, shrouded by the night. Inanna, holy Priestess of love in all its forms, smiled.

Mir-ri was not thinking of Inanna. She who had always loved the daylight, the rising of the Sun, was thinking that the night suddenly seemed more welcoming than the dawn. Every cell in her body sensed the darkness and the mystery waiting for her. Frogs sang and night birds called, telling an old tale of young love, forbidden love. The crickets chirped faster and faster.

Mir-ri felt Abram before she saw him, heat emanating from his body like the Sun's warmth glowing in the bricks. Brushing through the leafy tendrils of the willow, she reached for him and was pulled close. She laid her face on his chest and sighed.

There, by the Temple wall, they came together, the Habiru scholar and the Ki-en-gir Priestess. The wind caressed them, and the long night covered them. Finally Mir-ri's thoughts turned to Inanna. In the susurration of the air in the leaves, she heard the words sung by the Kalu Priest and the High Priestess for the sacred Emesh rites of Inanna's union with Dumuzzi.

"As for me, Inanna,
Who will plough my vulva?
Who will plough my high field?
Who will plough my wet ground?"

"Great Lady, the king will plough your vulva.

I Dumuzzi the King, will plough your vulva."

"Then plough my vulva, man of my heart!
Plough my vulva!"

Abram heard only the soft sighs of their lovemaking and was content. Even the crickets had grown silent, exhausted, perhaps, by the intensity.

"You seem distracted," said Hamminabi, as Abram's mind wandered yet again from the discussion. "The Tribes from the East are gaining in power. The time will soon come when they challenge the strength of Urim."

Abram nodded, whether to the first or second comment Hamminabi could not be sure. He had hoped that Abram would join him in formulating a plan to hide the sacred tablets, but the usually serious scholar was not interested. The old Scribe scratched his chin and wondered if Abram could be in love. He concluded that it was unlikely in the extreme, so conservative was the Stoneworker's son that Hamminabi had begun to fear that he would lose him to the Akkadian Scribes in Uruk.

For the first time ever, Mir-ri slept through the morning ritual. Nothing happened. That was unusual enough to make her suspect that she must, in some way she did not understand, be doing exactly what the High priestess wanted. But why would the High Priestess favour the unlikely union of a Ki-en-gir priestess and Habiru scholar?

Mir-ri did not think for one moment that the High Priestess's forbearance arose from tenderness or sympathy. What, then, was happening?

It was as if the Laws had been silenced. Unable to find an answer, she pushed her misgivings aside and continued to meet with Abram beneath the willow . . .

Mir-ri ran her hands through Abram's unbound hair, rubbed her cheek against the unshaven bristles on his chin. The tiny red spots of roughness on her face were a secret delight as she walked through her days.

Abram buried his face in Mir-ri's long soft hair, breathing in her smell. Later her scent would return to claim him in the middle of a sentence, and he would pause, a gentle smile on his face.

In the days and nights of Urim, there had been songs sung about the sacred union of man and woman for a thousand years and a thousand more. The ancient bards knew exactly what they were doing when they sang of sweet-smelling amber, when they crooned of cream and milk smoothing the black boat, quickening the narrow boat, when they chanted of planting the sweet, honey-covered seed.

Is it possible to live a lifetime in forty nights?

Sometimes that is all that is granted. Who can say if it is enough?

CHAPTER XVII

The city of Urim, Ancient Sumer. c 1992 BCE

For the gods have abandoned us, like migrating birds they have gone. Ur is destroyed, bitter is its lament. [xx]

Forty-one mornings after the first meeting under the willow, Mir-ri was again summoned to the small chamber of the altars in the Palace by the Northern Harbour.

Certain that, at last, she was to be chastised for the clandestine meetings, she took a deep breath as she ducked her head to enter the room. She expected to see the High Priestess looking stern, but Nin-lil-la was smiling.

Mir-ri hesitated; she had faced the eyes of death in the Underworld, but this was something different. She waited, barely breathing.

"It has been noted that you, of all the Priestesses, walk truly in Her ways," said the High Priestess in her formal, ritual tones. She did not meet Mir-ri's eyes. "You have been accorded a great honour. On the night of the Emesh Rites you will walk in the footsteps of the Lady of Heaven. You will wear the robes of holy Inanna."

Mir-ri's ears started ringing, loud warning noises of danger. Her heart joined the clamour, pounding in her chest. On the outskirts of the city, the farmers kept gongs, discs of beaten metal, hanging from frames, early warning if Urim was attacked. Long had it been since the gongs had been rung, but Mir-ri heard them now, clanging in the cells of her body. *Run,* they said. *Run for your life.*

Shaking her head against the insistent warning, Mir-ri tried to understand what the High Priestess was saying. She had heard the words, but she could not believe them.

"I have a confession to make." The High Priestess's voice sounded distant, like waves breaking near the Western Harbour.

The gongs were quiet now.

"Look at me, Mir-ri. I know about your shepherd, your Dumuzzi. It has been sanctioned. There is a reason."

Mir-ri gasped, sucking in air. "But . . .?" She wanted to ask why. Why had it been sanctioned? Why had she been chosen to consummate the sacred fertility rite when she was training to be a Scribe? What of the others like Hedu and Anna who had trained for the honour of wearing the robes of Inanna? The questions stuck in her throat as she realised that this, too, must be part of the High Priestess's plan. She wanted to scream and lash out, run from there. Yet it was her duty to serve the Temple, to do the bidding of the High Priestess. Her arms and legs ached, but she resisted their demands to fight, to flee.

"Why?" she asked finally. "Why?"

"Because the Elamite army is moving. Soon the Habiru will leave Urim. The one who leads them will leave the Great Ones behind," said the High Priestess.

Once again Mir-ri was caught in the strange inbetween world where she could hear the words but could find no meaning. Gongs sounded in the distance.

"Elamite. Habiru. Great Ones?" she repeated.

The High Priestess nodded. "I have seen the fall of Urim."

Mir-ri had heard this before.

"I have seen change."

This, too, was familiar. The next words, however, she had never heard before.

"I have seen that Abram, Terah's son, will lead his people out of Urim before the city falls. He will become the first of the children of the Nameless One." She spoke slowly, as if to a child.

Indeed, Mir-ri felt very much like a child. Abram leaving? Surely he would come for her?

"He will not come when he learns that you are chosen for the Emesh Rites."

"I refuse the Rites." Mir-ri glared at the High Priestess. "I am trained as a Scribe."

"You cannot refuse. You are a Priestess in the Temple of Nanna. You must walk in Her ways."

"I will not do it." Even as she spoke, Mir-ri knew she sounded more like the girls at the shaduf than a Priestess of the Temple. She didn't care.

"Nevertheless, Abram will hear of it, and he will leave."

Mir-ri hated Nin-lil-la's implacable voice, loathing and rejection welling up in her like the muddy floodwaters of the Buranun. She turned away. Then she heard the gongs again and decided, at last, to run. Find Abram. Leave Urim. The thoughts tumbled over each other.

As Mir-ri reached the door, the High Priestess spoke. "You asked me why."

Everything in Mir-ri screamed for her to keep moving, yet she turned, body braced as if for a killing blow.

The High Priestess's voice took on the familiar tones of ritual. "The way of Nanna, father of Urim will be lost. The way of Inanna, Queen of Heaven and Earth, will be lost. All this will turn to dust, and those who walk in Her ways will be forgotten. The world is changing. I have tasted it in the sweet waters of the Buranun. I have seen it in the flames. I have heard it in the wind. I have felt in the earth beneath my feet. The world is changing."

Moved despite herself, Mir-ri whispered, "All things must pass."

Nin-lil-la nodded. "So it is said. Yet I cannot let all this pass without setting something in place for the times of dust and forgetfulness."

Mir-ri frowned. How did that concern her? It was then, as if in answer to her own question, that she felt a tightening in her lower belly and remembered that her bleeding had not come with the dark of the Moon as it had every cycle since she became a woman. She placed her hands over her womb.

The High Priestess met Mir-ri's gaze and nodded.

"This is what you have set in place?"

The High Priestess nodded again. "This child is not recorded on the tablets. It is unexpected."

Mir-ri could, at least, agree with that. She leaned against the doorpost. She had walked the corridors to this room basking in the sweetness of her love for the dark-eyed man of her heart. She was leaving with a taste in her mouth more bitter than the saltwater at the mouth of the Buranun.

If, that is, she could bring her feet to carry her away at all. Away from the vows she had taken, the promises she had made to the holy Priestess of Heaven and Earth. Wrapping her arms around her chest, she moaned.

"Why?" she asked again.

"Abram is the one foreseen. The one who brings change. He will father a line of sons that will change the world. Now there is also a daughter to carry the line of the Mother." She paused, as if considering whether to say more. "You can run from the vows you have made. You can leave them, but they will never leave you." Whether a curse or a blessing, the words rang with truth.

Mir-ri did leave then, running from the truth. She ran along the tiled corridor, through the patterned archways, down the steps, across the courtyard, and out of the Palace. She brushed past the hanging branches of the willow, running for her life and the life of the child she carried. She ran through the city to the E-dub-ba, to the courtyard where she had stretched and been seen, had turned and been taken up by the Great Ones for their own unfolding purpose. Only yesterday it seemed.

Abram was not there.

Mir-ri ran back through the city, along the winding lanes to the Stoneworker's house she had never seen. Running and running in her Priestess linen, hair uncoiling from her head to fly around her face like the snakes at the water altar in the West. Gasping for breath, she stopped only long enough to ask the way to Terah's house. Soon she had drawn a crowd, eager for the news she surely carried; it must be dire indeed for a Priestess to run through the streets like a wild one from the Zagros mountains. Word spread through the quarter. By the time Mir-ri arrived outside Abram's house, the lane was packed.

Alerted by the noise, Amaslai climbed down from where she had been preparing the evening meal on the rooftop. No sooner did she see the bedraggled Priestess than she began to wail. Something must have happened to Abram for someone from the Temple to run all the way to the Harbour!

Mir-ri stared at the sobbing woman. Obviously Abram was not there. She turned to leave and felt a strong hand on her arm.

"What news, Holy One?" demanded a man, fingers bruising her.

Suddenly Mir-ri saw her peril. Alone among the Habiru, she could hardly tell them her news. She gathered herself, shook off the man's hand, and schooled her face into the imperious lines of a Priestess.

"I was coming with a commission for the Stoneworker. I was . . .uh . . .chased." She closed her eyes and calmed her breath.

"Chased?" repeated the man. "A Priestess chased in Urim? Why did you run for the Harbour rather than the Temple?" Clearly he did not believe her.

"I was frightened. This was closer." She looked the man in the eyes, daring him to contradict a holy one.

He shrugged. "If you say so." He sniggered, making a crude joke that was uncomfortably close to the truth.

The crowd dispersed. Amaslai stopped wailing. "It is not my son?" she asked, her eyes begging Mir-ri to reassure her.

"Nothing has happened to your son," said Mir-ri wearily. Even as she said it, she wondered if it was true.

She replayed the silent withdrawal of the students at the E-dub-ba. With a shiver, she began to suspect that the High Priestess had already let it be known that she was chosen for the Rites. What would Abram do? Abram, with his pure logic and implacable reasoning. Abram, with his ideas of right and wrong, his love of the Laws. Abram, with his contempt for women and women's business, be it cleaning or singing praises to Inanna. Mir-ri shivered. She began the long walk back to the Temple.

The news of Mir-ri's participation in the rites had been whispered to one of the students by the acolyte he met behind the cookhouse. Before long, the whole E-dub-ba knew that Mir-ri would stand for Inanna in the rites.

Abram was dreaming of the silky softness of Mir-ri's hair and the fragrance of her skin when Imbinuk, one of the younger students, ran up to tell him. Feigning disinterest, Abram shook his head and turned back to the tablet lying in his lap. Had the boy seen his sudden tears or the flush that burned his cheeks?

How could he have forgotten that she was a Priestess of the Temple, a worshipper of statues and plaques? How could he have been so stupid? Of course she would go willingly to the obscene Rites, her Great Lady of Heaven was a Harlot too! His thoughts raced away as he sat perfectly still on the stone bench where, a lifetime ago, he had seen Mir-ri stretching. To tempt him, he now supposed.

Even as all his dark thoughts and rigid thinking constructed the case against her, a small voice pleaded for the love in Mir-ri's eyes when she looked at him, and for the huskiness in her voice when she spoke his name.

With an abrupt movement, Abram stood, shaking off the memories, hardening himself against the feelings. By the time Mir-ri ran in looking for him, he had left to find his father and brothers to talk about leaving Urim. For all his education, he had never heard Inanna's love song to Dumuzzi, or the shepherd's answering words.

The sense of coming doom was strong in Nin-lil-la. She would regret the necessity that had compelled her betrayal of Mir-ri all the days of her life. She would never admit it to anyone, saw no purpose in declaring it, yet she knew that she had grown to love Mir-ri as much as she loved any one person. But, she reminded herself sternly more than once, love was not enough to save Urim, not enough to stop the changes sweeping Ki-en-gir.

She knew, as surely as she had ever known anything, that the way of the ever-changing Moon and His daughter, Inanna, would be lost if not for the child in Mir-ri's womb. If asked to explain that in the language of logic used in the House of Tablets, Nin-lil-la would fail. If asked to show how she had read it in the stars, she would be unable to do so. Yet she knew it for the deepest truth: If not for the child growing in Mir-ri's womb, the blessed fruitfulness of the Holy Priestess would be lost. No longer would She be present for women as sybil, soothsayer, seer. No more would She answer the call of women and children as fierce protector. No more would She bring laughter, inspiration, and the delights of love. And if the Holy Priestess were forgotten, then women, too, would suffer through all the Ages of the world.

It was the Balance, Nin-lil-la decided, the Balance of a child conceived in love by the man who would walk away from Ki-en-gir to found a new line in which there would be too little respect for the life-giving power of the Mother.

Nin-lil-la stood atop the E-gish-shir-gal and looked out across the city. It seemed too much to entrust to an unborn child, yet it was the vision she had been sent. It was the Balance.

CHAPTER XVIII

The city of Urim, Ancient Sumer. c 1992 BCE

If you stand only on the safety of the banks spearing fish, how can you know the depths of the river?[xxi]

Mir-ri sat on the Palace steps all that first night, waiting. Abram did not come to her beneath the willow tree.

Sometime before the lions began to call, she stopped sobbing and accepted that she was alone. It was not just that Abram had deserted her; it was a deep realisation that no other could walk the walk of her life, no other bear the burdens that were hers to bear, no other receive what blessings might come.

That night, under the stars, by the flowing waters of the Buranun, Mir-ri became a woman more surely than when she began to bleed, or when she had opened herself to Abram under the willow. A woman who, once touched by the Great Ones, would truly walk in their ways all her life.

As the first glow of the new day softened the edges of the world, she bathed in the river. The sweet water flowed as it had since the beginning of time, on and on endlessly, rushing to the

Sea. She imagined herself floating, being carried until she, too, dissolved, her bitterness absorbed by the salt Sea.

It was a fleeting fantasy, one her body would not countenance, not with the child growing in her womb. She dived beneath the surface, letting the current carry her to the deeper water.

Midway between the banks she surfaced and saw the crocodile. Unusual so close to the city, it was old and large, gliding lazily among the reeds, ancient eyes watching her. Mir-ri became still. She had seen those eyes before, the eyes of Death . . .

If you stand only on the safety of the banks spearing fish, how can you know the depths of the river? Can you fathom the darkness under a ledge of rock or understand the life of the fish writhing on your spear? You mistake the teeth of the crocodile as the edge of the abyss, but the chasm is more terrible than teeth, and certain . . .I fulfill the law and the law demands your blood. I am Sebak the crocodile, the catastrophe, the devourer, the necessity. Impaled on my teeth, you shall be blessed for you will glimpse truth. I am only the secrets of your own dark heart, your lust, your greed, your anger, your flesh . . .I am the living power of water, the cry that catches in the throat, the sob that shatters stone . . .I weep with the loss, but you do not believe. Such destruction is madness you say. You do not understand. Is it madness to cut the wheat so that bread can be made? When you were born into this bright land, did you not weep for the lost dark of the womb? Whether or not you understand the law, you exist because of it. [xxii]

Surely the crocodile was sent by Eresh-ki-gal to remind her of necessity. To remind her of the immutable laws of change. She closed her eyes, hearing fragments of the verse again. When she opened them, the crocodile was gone.

She left the river, dressed in her Priestess linen, and walked slowly up the stairs and along the corridors she had come to know so well. She walked past the bench where she had sat alone waiting to meet the High Priestess on that first day in the Temple.

She found the High Priestess in the room of altars. Had Nin-lil-la spent the night there in a vigil of her own?

"I am glad you have come here before you go," said the High Priestess.

Mir-ri nodded. Some things had become very clear to her since she had run from this same room less than a day ago. She recognised the necessity, yet she also sensed the catastrophe. Could she really carry all that Nin-lil-la asked of her?

"Who else but you," said the High Priestess.

Mir-ri stood in the centre of the small room and turned slowly from East to South to West to North, accepting the task that had been set for her. She would carry the Balance into the future.

Finally, she crossed to the High Priestess and took the older woman's hands between her own. Nin-lil-la's hands were very cold.

"I will do all you ask," said Mir-ri, knowing that these were the words that mattered most. She brought Nin-lil-la's hands to her lips and kissed them once before leaving the room of altars forever.

Eight days after her night by the river, Mir-ri left Urim, no longer wearing the pleated folds of a Priestess. She left with her family, who had been warned by one of the market traders, who had heard from the son of the ass-herder, that the Elamite army was moving and would not stop until Urim fell.

Mir-ri's mother had wept with relief when her daughter appeared the same morning as the warning. She promptly set her to work packing the family's belongings into panniers for the three asses and into bulging packs for their own backs. Mir-ri's aunts may have suspected that she was with child, or else fleeing from some indiscretion, but not one question was asked. It took considerable concentration to uproot eighteen people, three asses, eleven goats, and Lelu, the rat catcher. Mir-ri's father had wanted to leave the cat behind, but the women had fashioned a reed basket with a lid, and Mir-ri agreed to carry it. Grateful for the distraction, she worked alongside the others, gladly doing the hardest tasks.

The family left early one morning, walking away from their mud-brick house without a backward glance. As she neared the city gate, determined to keep her feet walking away from Urim, away from Abram, Mir-ri felt a hand on her arm. She froze, daring for moment to hope.

She turned to find Ner-nin looking at her. They had not spoken since Mir-ri had run from the High Priestess.

"Nin-lil-la sent me," said Ner-nin, her brown eyes soft. She carried a small bag over one shoulder.

For a moment, Mir-ri did not understand. Then she saw it: Ner-nin was gifted in the way of birthing, something she had from her mother even before her time in the Temple. The High Priestess had done what she had to, and now she had also done this. Mir-ri considered refusing, but then she thought of the time ahead, and there was an easing of the pain that had lodged in her heart. She nodded and took Ner-nin by the hand, leading her after the others.

Abram and his family left Urim twenty days after Mir-ri. They had delayed long enough for Abram to take as wife the daughter of his Mother's sister. It had been Amaslai's idea, her way to keep him close. He had agreed, desperate to be rid of the haunting memories of Mir-ri, memories that filled his dreams: Mir-ri, skin glowing in the Moon's light; Mir-ri laughing at something he said; Mir-ri calling his name over and over. He was so fraught by the time his Mother proposed the match with his cousin that he probably would have married the blind daughter of the gravedigger if someone had suggested it. Not that Sarai was in any way undesirable. With her downcast eyes and soft voice, she was, in fact, a very suitable wife. Abram had no idea what she thought of the match.

Sarai and he had spent an awkward wedding night that proved her a virgin. He had known Sarai all his life, and it did not seem strange to share a sleeping mat with her, but nor was it particularly exciting. In the morning, Sarai sat combing out her long hair, watching him dress. She was young and comely enough, but Abram was distracted by the plans for leaving.

"Do you remember your Father?" he asked, more to make conversation than from any real interest. Sarai and her mother had always been there, part of the family; he understood that her father had been killed in one of the battles that Terah and the other young men of his time had fought to keep the desert tribes and the mountain people from overrunning Urim. So many had died then, but Abram had been a heedless child, and the memories were dim.

"My father and your father are one," Sarai said in her soft voice.

"I know," said Abram patiently, thinking she referred to Terah's kindness in supporting her mother over the years. "Did you know your real father?"

Sarai looked up, eyes wide with fear. "My father and your father are one," she repeated, flinching as she spoke.

Abram sucked in his breath with a gasp, suddenly remembering the nights when Terah did not share the sleeping mat with Amaslai, the nights she cried herself to sleep. He had thought his father was behind the worker's huts, drinking and playing games. As if a door had opened, scenes replayed themselves: Terah and Anu embracing; Amaslai and Anu not speaking, not even looking at each other; Sarai always so quiet, so humble around her three cousins.

Abram turned away in disgust. His own sister! Surely he was cursed: first a harlot from the Temple and now his sister. With a bitter look at his wife, he left the room, silently vowing to avoid women for the rest of his life.

Amaslai was there waiting, a satisfied smile on her face. Abram pushed past her to leave the house.

"Do not worry, my Son," she called after him. "It will improve with time."

Abram hunched his shoulders and walked faster. What was she talking about? Did she think he needed advice from his Mother about his wedding night? He clenched his fists and walked to the river.

Before he realised where he was, he found himself beneath the huge, old willow that grew by the Palace of the High Priestess. Had he really stood there waiting for a woman? Had he really held her in his arms and felt the weight of her head on his chest? Had he truly lain with her, skin to skin, heart to heart, as if she were his wife? Abram shook his head. What had happened to him? Just sixty days ago he had been a respected scholar at the E-dub-ba and had known right from wrong. What was it the old Physician had said?

"You are, perhaps, too interested in wrong and right, young man."

Not the words. The old man's tone. Abram stopped walking to recall the Physician's voice. What had the old man been saying? That it is possible to be too interested in right and wrong? He shook his head. Perhaps the old fool had poisoned him with his potion. At least now his head was clear, and once again he could be sure about right and wrong. Only a fool would sacrifice pure, idealistic thought for the chaos of desire.

CHAPTER XIX

The last days of the city of Urim, Ancient Sumer. c 1991 BCE

In time, all Nin-lil-la had foreseen came to pass. The city of Urim was overrun, the Temples destroyed. In time, the bitter waters of the Pars Sea receded, the sweet waters of the Buranun turned to the East, and the once great city sank beneath the sands.

In another Age, four thousand years after the fall of Urim, archaeologists came to the desert looking for the lost city they now called Ur. Visionaries and dreamers, they scoured the sands for signs of the life that once filled the air with song.

The songs were silent, and the river no longer flowed, but in the sand the archaeologists found fragments of the wonder that had been. They found poems and songs, written by hand on clay tablets baked to a hardness that had endured for two millennia.

Found also was a single verse on a stone tablet, another poem perhaps, or a prophecy. The stone tablet was taken from the ruins of Ur to rest in a labelled box in the basement of the

Baghdad museum. Colourless, with no gold to attract looters, the tablet survived the destruction of the years of violence and bloodshed in Iraq. The prophecy awaited the turning of the Age . . .

CHAPTER XX

Amman, Jordan. Update Wed May 7th 2015 4.23 pm UTC

The Middle East and Central Asia regions are currently in the grip of one of the worst droughts in recent history. Widespread failure of rain-fed grain crops have occurred since 2008/09, as well as sizable declines in irrigated crop area and yield. Food grain production has dropped to the lowest levels in a century, increasing grain export bans and resulting in abnormally large region-wide grain imports. The drought poses substantial threats to internal security in countries like Iraq, Afghanistan, and Pakistan.

Paula sat opposite Lili in the same restaurant where they had eaten dinner the previous evening. The events of the last eighteen hours--Haleli appearing, the time in her office--seemed like a dream. They ordered lunch, shwarma and mansaf, and sipped lemon iced tea.

"Where do we begin?" asked Paula. "It's all very well for Haleli to say 'be like children'. Children get hurt in countries where people are fighting." But not her children! She sent a silent prayer to the Protectors of Children to keep Mary and the others safe.

Lili frowned at her drink. "We have to suspend our normal thinking, or we'd never do this at all, but we do need a plan. If this all began in Sumer, where did it go from there? How did the *me* leave Sumer? And if the whole daughters marked at birth thing is true, how did our ancestors get to Hungary and Italy?"

"Ah, logic!" said Paula, "I'm too overwhelmed to think about plans; I'm still trying to get my head around your birthmark! Why don't I have a birthmark? Or my other girls?"

"It could be under your hair, I guess," said Lili, shrugging. "Or maybe it skips a generation. Or maybe it's a bizarre coincidence, and that's not what the words mean at all. Translations can be way off sometimes."

"I hope so in a way," said Paula. "I don't like to think of Mary caught up in this. But then we don't really know if any of the words mean anything today, do we?"

"Let's do what we know best and go to the library," suggested Lili. "But not until we've eaten!"

Sustained by flat bread, rice, and lamb, as well as two coffees each, they returned to the hotel for Paula to Skype home before the children went to bed. She found them all well, loving their holiday with Thom's parents. Mary was even sleeping through the night.

"Maybe it was me causing her nightmares," said Paula, as they walked back to the University.

"I don't think so," said Lili. "Maybe it was the necklace. If she starts when you get back, you will have to sell it."

Paula stopped walking. "Huh?"

"Just joking. Everyone says I have a warped sense of humour."

They found the library, where an eager librarian beamed over their credentials and led them to the Reserve section. They spent a scholarly afternoon typing notes onto their laptops from old texts about the fall of Ur, patterns of ancient migration, and the discovery of Sumerian artifacts.

"What do we have?" asked Lili over dinner.

Paula scrolled down the information she had saved. "From clay tablets to laptops; I wonder if we're any better off for it?"

"It would have taken us a lot longer to gather all this. Imagine marking it all in wet clay." Lili drew imaginary cuneiform letters in the air.

"No thanks!" said Paula, pulling a face. "But listen to this. It's a Sumerian proverb: 'What became of the Black people of Sumer?' the traveller asked the old man. 'What happened to them?' 'Ah,' the old man sighed. 'They lost their history, so they died.' What do you think?"

"Sounds like the time we're interested in. The fall of Ur, the change from the old Gods to Marduk." Lili leaned over to read from Paula's notes. "He slew Tiamat, you know. The old Goddess vanquished by the Warrior God."

"Sounds gruesome. Were the Sumerians really black?" asked Paula.

"Oh, of course," said Lili. "Didn't you know?"

Paula laughed. "How amazing. Even after all the papers I've read about not imposing our values on other cultures, I never imagined the Sumerians as anything but Arabic in appearance. When I tried to picture a High Priestess from Ur, I saw a cross between a Minoan bull-dancer and Elizabeth Taylor as Cleopatra. I was way off."

"Don't worry," said Lili. "Most Iraqis don't even know there were ancient Sumerians, let alone the colour of their skin."

"Did they really lose their history?" asked Paula. "Is that why the Iraqis don't know about them?"

"That's more recent, I think. A combination of twentieth century religion and politics," said Lili, rolling her eyes to show what she thought of that. "But my guess is the proverb refers to something that happened about four-thousand years ago. The lands of Sumer were lost to other tribes, and the Sumerians were either killed, enslaved, or fled to the North."

"Do you think they took the *me* with them?" asked Paula.

Lili frowned. "Who knows? It's so long ago. Even if they did, anything could have happened to them after that."

"So you don't think we need to go to Iraq?"

"If only we could! But even Haleli can't be expecting us to do that. It's marginally safer than it was five years ago, but it'll be a while yet before they let tourists into the ruins of Ur."

"Are the ruins still there?" asked Paula.

"They certainly are. In a place called Tell el-Mukayyar, near the city of Nasiriyah, south of Baghdad. There's even a local legend that says it's unsafe for Arabic men to walk alone in certain parts of the ruins. Apparently there are lions and other wild beasts waiting to tear them to pieces." Lili's face lit up with amusement.

"Wasn't the lioness one of Inanna's creatures?" asked Paula, remembering an image from the day's research.

"One of her forms, more like. Lioness of battle, they called her. Mighty warrior, fierce defender. A bit like Sekmet in ancient Egypt."

"Wow! So they still believe she's lurking in the ruins?"

"They probably don't think of it as Inanna, but, according to some Iraqi men I've spoken to, they still avoid that part of the ruins."

"What does the prophecy say? *Hidden in stone soaked in sweetness, Riding the wind burnished bright.* Where can we find a stone soaked in sweetness?"

"The Sumerians called the waters of the Euphrates 'sweet'. Perhaps it refers to a place, although there wasn't much stone there. It was mostly mud and sand."

"What about *riding the wind burnished bright*?"

"Maybe a high place where there was temple or something that shone in the sun. Perhaps the great, stepped temple that was built in Ur just before the fall. But anything hidden there would be long gone."

"I wonder what happened to the Sumerians?" said Paula, feeling wistful.

"And did we have an ancestor among them?" asked Lili, frowning at the computer.

The waiter brought dinner, and they packed away the computers. Their talk turned to the challenges of marriage and their hopes and fears for their children. They both slept better that night, although Paula woke twice thinking there was someone standing over her bed. She was startled but not frightened, as if someone familiar had come unexpectedly to tell her something important.

CHAPTER XXI

Arabkha, Northern Mesopotamia. c 1991 BCE

Arrapha . . . was an ancient Assyrian city that existed in what is today the city of Kirkuk, Iraq. The city was founded around 2000 BC and derived its name from the old Assyrian word, Arabkha, which was later changed to Arrapha.[xxiii]

Mir-ri first heard the lament for Urim as she sat with Ner-nin under a cedar tree in the North. There were many from Urim there now, wandering in the aftermath of the Elamite invasion. The lament had been carried by the Kalu priests, trained since boyhood to remember the praises and the songs. In the words of the lament, Mir-ri heard Nin-lil-la's voice, naming that which cannot be named, that which she had foreseen.

"How did she bear it?" she asked, looking back the way they had walked.

Ner-nin shook her head. "It is the task of a High Priestess to bear that which others cannot."

"That is no answer," said Mir-ri. "Nin-lil-la was a woman, too."

Ner-nin shrugged. "I send her blessings every day."

Mir-ri remembered the message Ner-nin had carried from Urim for Mir-ri and Mir-ri's daughter:

To the daughters of Ki-en-gir, from Nin-lil-la, High Priestess of Urim in the time of Nanna and Inanna, to you I give blessings. You carry the wisdom of the past and the hope of the future. In you flows the blood of history and the promise of Balance. A time will come when all memory is lost, when the Queen of Heaven and Earth is forgotten. You carry the memory. Guard it well. It is the time of Kings who do not honour the life-giving Mother. Without Her, the Earth will die. Without Her, there will be no future. By the mixing of the blood, there is hope. It flows in your body. Carry it into the future that the Earth may live.

Mir-ri sighed. "I am not sure I can bear that burden."

"Who else but you," said Ner-nin.

They had taken longer than expected to reach the North, stopping for some time in both Nippur and in Uhaimir. But the threat of the Elamite armies hung over those cities, too, and everywhere on the road there were rumours of attack from the desert tribes.

"We must remember that Nippur is Enlil's city, and we know what he did to Urim," said the men, deciding to move further North.

As they crossed the empty lands to Arabkha, they encountered others wandering in the aftermath of the Elamite invasion, and thirty weeks after leaving Urim, they reached the northern city. At last they were safe.

The men said that the rich lands in the South would hold the attention of the Elamites and leave the North in peace. Mir-ri thought it might be because the Queen of Heaven was honoured in the North as the Warrior. Everywhere she looked she found statues of the Lioness, defending the city. The name they gave her in the North was Ishtar.

Mir-ri's small tribe consisted of her mother, Nama, her father, Ekur, her two brothers, her three aunts, sisters of her mother, their husbands and nine children. With Ner-nin, they numbered nineteen, a smaller group than some who had fled the Southern lands, yet large enough to form their own small camp on the outskirts of Arabkha.

They settled near the banks of the River Hasa that flowed from the Zagros mountains. It was not as great as the Buranun, nor were its waters as sweet, but it gave them water to drink and mud for making bricks.

At first Nama grumbled constantly, saying to anyone who would listen that everything in Urim was better.

"We cannot live our lives comparing everything we find to what we have lost," said Mir-ri, as much to herself as to her mother. "That which we have lost will only grow more perfect, and nothing will ever be as good."

Nama stopped voicing her complaints, and Mir-ri was grateful. She was also grateful for her mother's easy acceptance of the child growing in her womb. She had wondered at that, but thought that perhaps Nama assumed it had come through a holy rite in the Temple. Or perhaps her mother sensed the grief in her heart and decided not to ask, although Nama was not known for her reticence. Perhaps, Mir-ri finally concluded, Nama felt guilty for leaving her only daughter there at the Palace by the Harbour, and she was just glad to have her back, baby notwithstanding.

Three days after arriving in Arabkha, Mir-ri's family gathered around the cookfire for the evening meal. As well as flatbread and soup, there was also precious goat meat to share, traded at the market for the neatly tied bunches of herbs Ner-nin had gathered and dried as they walked. There were more travellers on the roads than there had been in centuries, and sickness was spreading faster than the magic workers and physicians could conjure up medicines and spells. Many a woman, far from home, was pleased to pay for healing herbs from the South.

Mir-ri was chewing her first mouthful of the juicy meat when a ripple of pain moved across her lower back. She paused and sucked in a deep breath. The second time it happened, she looked to Ner-nin, who had described exactly this as the signal that the birth was beginning. As if they had been waiting, all the women stopped eating and rose to prepare the birthing tent.

They moved a tent away from the others and hung it with green, trailing vines to celebrate life reaching from the dark for Utu, the Sun. Then they plied Mir-ri with drinks and advice until Ner-nin sent them all away to make offerings to the Mother, the Cow-eyed One whose arms are open.

"Call on Her," repeated Ner-nin for the tenth time in as many minutes.

Obediently, Mir-ri mumbled to Inanna between the intense, rhythmic tightening of her belly. She sipped the water Ner-nin had prepared with herbs. Would the pains ever end?

For hours she breathed and cursed, sang and called to Inanna, all the while sensing her daughter moving down. She knew it was a girl because all the women said so, and because Nin-lil-la had seen a daughter to carry the sacred life-giving power of Inanna forward in time. But all of that was too much to think about as the intensity of the waves in her belly and back increased.

Mir-ri could not tell if it was the light of sunset or dawn she could see as she felt her daughter's head stretch her wide open. Had a whole day passed while she gave birth eternally in the tent? Before she could answer that, a slippery, red creature was in her arms, and she was laughing and crying and falling in love. And the world was too full for thoughts of past or future.

Two days later, Mir-ri once again sat with Ner-nin under the cedar tree. Her baby lay at her breast, making the small, grunting sounds that had become as familiar as her own breath. As she smiled down at her daughter, she felt humbled by Nin-lil-la's trust in her and not at all certain how this tiny creature in her arms could keep alive the way of Nanna and Inanna. She could not, after all, even keep herself alive yet. Mir-ri adjusted the cloth sling in which Inna happily rode, and she stroked the birthmark, identical to her own, on Inna's wrist: the eight-rayed star of Inanna.

In the early days in Arabkha, Mir-ri's family continued to gather around the fire each evening. Her father and uncles spoke about selling their goods and providing for the family.

"Some of those from Ki-en-gir are entering service in the city," said her father, Ekur, when the evening meal was finished, and the women were cleaning the bowls. The other three men nodded.

"It is the Habiru who are selling themselves." Amar spat on the ground with disgust at the thought of trading his freedom for food and shelter. "They think only of today, but what of tomorrow when they have not saved enough tokens to buy their freedom?"

Mir-ri paused in her work when she heard mention of the Habiru. Could Abram be in Arabkha? She had not sensed him near for many Moon cycles, but that may be because he had closed himself to her so completely.

Nama exchanged a knowing look with her younger sister, Pu-abi, wife to Amar. Mir-ri knew the women suspected that the father of her child might be Habiru; she had looked long enough at each of the Habiru families as they wandered North along the Idigna, swift twin of the Buranun.

"But it is not slavery," said Ishme, husband to Nama's older sister. "Nan-Teshup, the potter from the Harbour, has entered into service here. I met him at the market. He has not sold himself or his wife or his children. Just the work they do for food and shelter and clothing."

"Of course not. But if he wishes to leave he has to find tokens for the whole family, or find others who can do the work instead," said Amar, spitting into the fire. "I would not like to be bound that way."

"Let us hope it does not come to that," agreed Ekur. "Although a man might do things he never thought possible to feed his wife and children."

"And grandchildren," added Ishme, nodding towards where Mir-ri worked with Inna in the sling.

"If we cannot find what we seek here, we will move again," said Ekur, looking past the fire into the cobalt night. "Tomorrow we will see."

The men planned to take the mats and the herbs to the market early the next morning, rising with the Sun. Ekur, one of the few workers of metal among the Ki-en-gir, was sitting with the tools he had carried from his workshop in Urim, turning them over and over in his hands. He voiced his uncertainty about whether his skills would be wanted by the Northerners. With metal ore more readily available than in the South, they probably had their own metal workers. Most people in the South had used sharpened stone knife-blades, and only the craftsmen had needed adzes and chisels of bronze. The King's guards had carried great double-bladed axes, but Ekur had never made one of those, although he had the skill to melt the ores and pour the molten metal into the clay moulds, calling on Nin-agal for guidance.

"I wonder if Nin-agal will hear me here in the North, so far from Ki-en-gir," he said to the night.

The other men were silent.

Nin-agal and the other Great Ones must have heard them, because Ekur's tools, Ner-nin's dried herbs, and the men's woven mats were eagerly taken up by the people of Arabkha. The family found a suitable place to build a house from the clay of the River Hasa.

Months passed, and Inna grew out of her mother's arms to crawl and walk between the square, windowless houses of her extended family. Soon she was joined by the children of Mir-ri's cousins who found husbands from among the other Ki-en-gir who had fled to the North. The families all lived together, and the cluster of houses spread. Only Mir-ri's cousin, Enananta, took an Arabkhan husband and moved to live within the city walls.

Mir-ri did not look for a husband; she still had the husband of her heart. She dreamed of him at night, waking with tears on her cheeks.

One morning, about a year after settling in Arabkha, Mir-ri woke to feel Inna's small fingers stroking away the dampness on her cheeks. It was time to put her grief to rest.

Instead of retiring early to her room, Mir-ri forced herself to sit with the others by the evening fire, reliving the events of the day. They spoke of the day's trading or of news from the South.

They were joined by travellers from other lands, proud-looking men and women from the East, their children tough and wild. They had only the common language of those who wander far from home, but that was enough. It mattered not whether the journey had been one whole cycle of seasons or three, they were all beginning a new life.

When Mir-ri found herself seated next to one of the Eastern men for the third night in a row, she began to suspect that her cousins had decided it was past time for her to find a husband. The women sat together on the other side of the fire, laughing and whispering, rolling their eyes and sending her encouraging looks. Mir-ri smiled at their antics. The young man from the East took that as encouragement and moved closer. He spoke in a language that sounded like frogs on the Buranun. Mir-ri understood nothing except his enthusiasm, but she found herself smiling more often. Her cousins whispered and giggled about her companion's handsome features, clear eyes, and full lips.

"He will kiss like Dumuzzi, little cousin," said Enheddu, tickling Mir-ri under the arms.

Mir-ri blushed. The kisses she had shared with Abram had been so secret, so forbidden, that she could not share her cousin's easy way of talking about the delights of lovemaking.

The young man from the East let it be known that he found Mir-ri beautiful, with her long shining hair and heavy-lidded eyes, and the way she held her baby so close. He practised saying her name over and over again, but it always sounded like a frog calling in the night: "Meeree."

His name was "Daroo", and he told her with stumbling words and eloquent hand signals that he had walked away from the ruins of an Eastern city with only his mother and one of his sisters. Muddy, swirling floodwaters had taken his father, three brothers, and a younger sister. He wept when he spoke of his lost family and of the drowned city.

"The whole world is walking," he said to Mir-ri. "Looking for a safe place."

Mir-ri thought he might be right. There were Habiru from the South, Akkadians from the North, as well as tribesmen from the Mountains and the sandy deserts. Daroo said her people reminded him of his own home, lost now to Time and the floodwaters of the Sindhu. He moved his tent of deerskin closer.

Time passed in Arabkha, and the city grew to surround the family compound of small square houses Ekur and the other men made for their families. Mir-ri and Daroo lived together as husband and wife, and Inna soon had a sister and brother.

CHAPTER XXII

Urim to Aleppo. c 1991 BCE

It is hoary Aleppo legend, both Jewish and Muslim, that the patriarch Abraham had settled for a period in Aleppo in his wanderings from his native Ur. He is believed to have milked his cows there. Halab, the Arabic name for Aleppo, is the Aramaic, Hebrew, and Arabic for 'milked.'[xxiv]

Abram walked in Mir-ri's footsteps as he and his family moved North from Urim. He was not, however, thinking of Mir-ri. He was studiously thinking of the Habiru living in the North West and of the lands beyond Ki-en-gir. The roads were now packed with people fleeing the Elamite invasion. Most were on foot, the fortunate few pulling asses burdened with a lifetime's collection of goods.

Occasionally the asses were used as mounts, carrying the riders past those toiling on foot. Once or twice a cart trundled past, stirring up even more dust to cover the weary travellers. It was one of these carts that brought such grief to Abram's family that that they spoke of turning back to take their chances with the Elamites who were, after all, more like the Habiru than the people of Ki-en-gir had even been. What could be worse than dying slowly, body broken beneath the wheels of an overloaded cart?

Nachor had been lagging behind, worried by a bruise on the sole of his foot. All of them had strips of cloth tied round their feet, scant protection from sharp rocks and shards of pottery littering the road. Fragments of Urim were being left by those who fled, much like the old tale from the East of children leaving grains of wheat as they walked deeper and deeper into the forest. And everyone knew how that tale ended.

In the last light of day, Nachor had paused to retie the cloth on his foot. He bent down just as the Sun dipped below the horizon, sending indigo shadows slanting across the road. The cart driver may have been half asleep, lulled by the rhythm of the wheels, or he may have turned to stare at the three sisters walking with their parents just behind Abram's family. Whatever the reason, the ass veered aside to miss the man who suddenly loomed up from the shadows.

Nachor stumbled.

The ass's shoulder struck him on the back.

He fell and slid under the cart as if it were a beast hungry to be fed.

Amaslai screamed, the high-pitched sound of an animal in great pain and terror, and the world slowed into the strange twilight region where nothing seemed quite real.

Abram saw his brother's body emerge behind the cart, limp and bloodied. He closed his eyes. He knew that Time would not stop or turn back, no matter how desperately he wanted it, but he did not want to see what was left of Nachor, did not want to walk the twenty paces to kneel at his brother's side as the blood ran from his lips and his eyes glazed over.

He had, however, done all those things, calling on the detachment that had had served him before. He blocked his ears to his mother's cries and carried his brother's body from the road. When the Great Ones had been called to take Nachor safely to the Judges who waited just the other side of Death, the family camped there, sitting around the grave in silence. Abram sat a little apart, staring up into the night sky. The stars looked back, unperturbed by death.

Abram wondered if the stars were the constant, Nameless One worshipped by the wandering tribes in the North. Yet the stars faded when the Sun returned. There must be One greater than the stars.

The Moon rose, round and golden in the East. Perhaps they had been right in Urim: the Moon was the Supreme One. But the Moon also vanished before the night was done.

When the Sun found Abram still awake, he wondered blearily if the Sun could be worshipped as the One: Utu, golden one. Then he remembered that the Sun also went down, leaving travellers alone on the darkened road.

He stood and paced back and forth. There must, then, be One beyond the stars, beyond the Moon, beyond the Sun. This must be the Nameless One of the Northern tribes: the One who created the Heavens, who told the Moon when to rise, who called forth the very stars. A calm settled on his mind, and he resolved to continue the journey North.

He knew better than to share his revelations with his father, and Haran was busy consoling his wife, pregnant with their first child. Amaslai and Anu held each other and wept. Why was he not moved to join them? He reasoned that he had hardly known his brother, six years older and working by the time Abram went to the E-dub-ba. No use seeking grief when it comes so often unbidden.

He turned to find his wife, Sarai, watching him, a strange look in her eyes.

"What is it?" he asked. "What do you want?"

She shook her head and went to join the others.

The next morning, they left the grave of Nachor and followed the Buranun into the North. Abram walked alone, meditating on the revelations of the night. He walked along a dusty road, away from the mistakes of his youth and into the pages of history.

As Amaslai predicted, the name of her youngest son would, indeed, echo down the ages. Abram. Abraham. Ibrahim. Father of a line of sons that would be remembered.

CHAPTER XXIII

Amman, Jordan. Updated Sun May 10th 2015 8.53am UTC

More than 50 million people in southwestern China are being affected by the worst drought in 70 years. State media says the drought has left more than 20 million people without adequate access to drinking water. The provinces of Yunnan and Guizhou have experienced the most severe conditions.

Paula and Lili had been immersed in their research for two days, spending their time between the Library and an internet café near the University. Lili had sent some tasks home to Mish, who was only too happy to follow obscure leads on the internet.

"If we have an ancestor among those who left Sumer, my guess is she ended up in the north, possibly Arabkha," said Lili, sitting back and stretching her arms above her head.

"She?" Paula was puzzled. "What makes you think it was a she?"

"A fancy. I'd like to think that if we have a common

ancestor, she was a priestess or at least an acolyte from the Temple of Inanna."

Paula smiled. "So be it, then. A priestess she is."

Lili looked pleased. "She would have gone North with the other refugees and set up home there. Her descendants probably lived there for hundreds of years. And then . . ."

"And then?" asked Paula, staring over Lili's shoulder.

"What are you looking at?" asked Lili, turning to look.

"I think that man was here yesterday and the day before."

Lili gasped.

"What?" asked Paula.

"It's the man from the conference."

"Are you sure?" The hair on Paula's arms rippled.

Lili stood and pushed back her chair.

"What are you doing?" Paula's anxiety flared into panic. "He must be following us. These people are dangerous."

"Which people?" asked Lili sharply. "The Bedu? The Islamists? Another descendant of the Sumerians we're trying to trace? Be reasonable, Paula. Other than our visit to Haleli--or even including that, unless someone was hiding under the desk-- we are just two academics researching a trivial bit of ancient history. What's there to follow?"

Paula felt stupid. "I know. You're right. But he must be watching us."

"Why would he be doing that?" asked Lili, reaching out to squeeze Paula's hand.

Paula shrugged. "I don't know. Sometimes I feel so lost here. We're going to have to do something soon, and I have no idea what. What if someone doesn't want us to do it?"

"Whatever it is," said Lili, raising her eyebrows.

"Well, there could be people who don't want us trying to find the artefacts, presuming we ever decide where to start."

Lili nodded. "Perhaps. But how would they know that's what we're doing?"

Paula didn't have an answer for that. It was impossible to make sense of how scared she felt. "I know it sounds crazy, but I'm really spooked."

"I can see that," said Lili, sounding more sympathetic. "Maybe I'm too blasé, having grown up in New York."

"Maybe you're too logical, using your thinking to stop feelings," said Paula, her fear making her irritable.

"Maybe," said Lili quietly. "But I don't like being out of control. Ever."

Paula nodded. Not really her business. Her business was to manage her feelings. How had excitement turned to fear so quickly?

They turned to look at the man, but he had gone.

"Tell me if you see him again," said Lili. "And we'll find out what's going on."

Paula reached for her coffee.

A shadow fell over their table.

She shrieked and jumped, knocking her coffee over. She snatched her laptop away from the coffee spreading like an inkblot across the table.

A man in dark glasses raised his hands in apology and smiled, teeth gleaming white against his olive skin.

Paula's breath caught in her throat.

"Excuse my intrusion," said the stranger, speaking slowly, as if English were not his first language. "I overheard your conversation. I, too, am in Jordan seeking lost treasure. Perhaps we could work together? My name is Peter Moneghi. I am from Cairo."

Lili's face had lost colour, and even she seemed to be having trouble finding a response.

"What exactly did you overhear?" asked Paula, clutching her laptop like a shield.

"You were speaking of artefacts and of danger. In this part of the World these things go together. I thought perhaps we could help each other."

He looked from Paula to Lili, one eyebrow raised as he waited for them to answer.

"We don't know you," said Lili. "And how could we possibly help you? Clearly we're amateurs."

Peter smiled. "Children often see more clearly than adults with all our prejudices and expectations."

Paula shivered. He had just repeated Haleli's words from their meeting. Was this the help she had organised for them?

With a mutual glance for confirmation, Lili and Paula welcomed Peter with smiles that almost matched his. Paula placed her laptop out of reach of the coffee spill and extended a hand in greeting.

"We are new here, and I'm nervous, as you heard. My name is Paula Matthews."

Peter held her hand in a warm, strong grip and shook it gently. He looked amused.

Lili shook his hand and introduced herself.

Paula invited Peter to sit and offered to order him a drink.

"Mineral water," he said, smiling his thanks. He really did have extraordinarily white teeth.

"How exactly can we help each other?" asked Lili.

"I deal in antiquities," said Peter. "Some of them are listed in whatever records each country keeps of such things. Others come to me on . . .what do you call it? . . .a grapevine. Many of these are clever imitations, but sometimes there is a genuine piece. It is for these that I stay in the game."

Paula heard him say "game" and frowned as she waved

over the waiter to order his mineral water and another black coffee for herself.

They sipped their drinks and spoke mostly of Peter's adventures. After a while, Lili excused herself to go to the toilet, to phone Haleli, no doubt. Paula listened to Peter's stories and stored away anecdotes for the children; they all loved the old Indiana Jones movies.

Lili returned, communicating with furtive nods and winks that Haleli had just confirmed that Peter was a friend. Paula laughed at Peter's heroic attempt to pretend Lili was acting perfectly normal.

"Did I say something funny?" asked Peter.

Paula shook her head. "Please keep talking. It's fascinating to hear all this first hand."

Peter shrugged and continued telling tales about the business of finding lost treasures. "There is danger in it. Although it is usually the various governments who do not appreciate losing their national treasures to the black market. I once spent five days in an Egyptian prison for meeting a dealer behind a bar in Cairo."

"Fair enough, I suppose," said Lili.

"I was only relieving my bladder," said Peter, clearly enjoying the exchange. "And they do not feed you in Egyptian prisons. If you have no money or no relatives, you starve."

"I didn't mean it was fair that you went to prison," said Lili. "I meant it was fair enough for governments to protect their treasures."

"In that case, perhaps I deserved to starve for a few days," said Peter, laughing.

His easy good humour helped Paula to forget her fears.

Then he asked, "What exactly is it you seek?"

Paula's breath caught, and her heart started racing.

"Five or six sacred objects from Ancient Sumer," said Lili. "We have no idea where they are."

Peter looked thoughtful. "Only five or six?" he asked.

Paula wasn't sure if he meant: "Why not seven?" or if he was being facetious, as in, "Oh, is that all?"

Lili asked. "How many do you think there should be?"

"Seven, of course," answered Peter promptly. "All ancient treasures come in multiples of seven or three." He looked quite serious.

Paula still wasn't sure how much he knew, but she was content to let it be. Enough that Haleli had sent someone to help them. And, she hoped, to protect them.

Peter looked over their research.

"Your best approach is to gather local folklore. Treasures like the ones you seek have long since been forgotten, but they can sometimes be found in the stories passed down through the centuries. Like fairytales about pearls and gemstones falling from a girl's mouth, or glass slippers worn by a slave girl, or a ball gown made of stars. These all have their origins in the ancient past and tell of objects and events that would otherwise have been lost to us."

Lili asked more about the sort of tales they should be seeking, and Peter made further suggestions. He really did seem to know his way around the Middle East and the world of antiquities.

About an hour later, Peter stood to leave, arranging to meet them at their hotel the next morning. Lili, cheeks glowing with excitement, took charge of the new search. She sent an email to Mish, asking her to find folktales from northern Mesopotamia and all across the North to Syria. She appointed Paula to search for tales from Lebanon, Palestine and Israel, and set herself to search for stories from Jordan, Egypt, and the old trade roads to the East.

"It would be better to be there in all these places and ask people," said Lili. "On the digs the best information always came from local farmers or children."

"That might work if we left our jobs and our families for years!" said Paula. "It's a bit of a wild-goose chase at the moment."

"A wild-goose chase," said Lili. "I read somewhere that the Celtic Christians took the wild goose as the symbol of the Holy Spirit."

"Maybe what we're seeking can't be found in the normal ways," said Paula. "Like the spirit of whatever we call God, or Goddess."

"Maybe it can't," said Lili. "But we have to start somewhere."

"Oh, Lili. Can we really do this? I feel like a schoolgirl playing at finding the lost Ark or something."

"But now we have Indiana Jones," said Lili.

CHAPTER XXIV

Amman, Jordan. Updated May 15th 2015 9.52pm UTC

Ecofeminism argues that there is a connection between women and nature that comes from their shared history of oppression by a patriarchal society; this connection also comes from the positive identification of women with nature. This relationship can be argued from an essentialist position, attributing it to biological factors, or from a position that explains it as a social construct. Vandana Shiva claims that women have a special connection to the environment through their daily interactions with it that has been ignored. "Women in subsistence economies, producing and reproducing wealth in partnership with nature, have been experts in their own right of holistic and ecological knowledge of nature's processes. But these alternative modes of knowing, which are oriented to the social benefits and sustenance needs are not recognised by the capitalist reductionist paradigm, because it fails to perceive the interconnectedness of nature, or the connection of women's lives, work and knowledge with the creation of wealth."[xxv]

"Women will die," said Ghali, his voice mournful.

The other eleven men gathered in the small tutorial room at the University of Jordan waited silently for their leader's response. Some shifted uneasily on the straight-backed chairs. Some sat still as statues and as inscrutable. All looked to the slender, dark-eyed woman sitting at the front of the room.

Haleli nodded. "Women always die in war."

With an impatient flick of her hand, she tucked back a loose strand of hair, still midnight-black and glossy, like the manes of the desert horses she had ridden as a child. She looked in turn at each man in the room.

Her gaze was direct, but her mind wandered. These men had never ridden with the desert wind under indigo skies, had not imbibed the ancient Laws with their mothers' milk. They knew nothing of the old ways that still lay at heart of the desert tribes: "I against my brothers, I and my brothers against my cousins, I and my brothers and my cousins against the world".

It was from that she had fled on one of the desert horses, leaving behind a lineage so ancient her father claimed direct descent from Father Ibrahim. The familiar, dull ache pulsed in her chest.

With an effort, Haleli brought her attention back to the task before her. The single, overhead light etched austere lines on the faces of her companions, robbing them of their youth. They may not be Bedu, but they were fully committed to her desperate, impossible plan to change the World. They may not know all the details--like how a university lecturer accessed such vast amounts of money, or why this was more important to her than breathing--but they knew enough to make this work. If all went well.

"We can save some of them," she said. "We have enough money to resettle women and children from major cities, and there are safe houses set up in most areas."

Ghali sighed. Alongside him Fatin scowled, the only look Haleli had seen on his face since he joined them five years before. She spread her hands wide.

"We cannot protect everyone. What we are doing is a chance for change. Does anyone want to stop now?"

She resorted to that question when she felt them wavering, when the endless days and nights of planning sapped their will and crushed their spirit. She understood their exhaustion; she was even more tired than she had been when she fled across the desert. But, like then, she would not give up. Not now, so close to a real beginning. Not ever, while the Earth was in the hands of those who were destroying it.

As one, the men stood to pledge their allegiance to the project. Hands on their hearts, they signalled their commitment by nodding, by speaking words of loyalty and devotion to the cause that had become their lives.

"So it begins."

Haleli acknowledged their pledge with a handclasp as each man left the room.

She closed the door, turned off the light, and sat alone in the dark, her mind returning to the paths that had led her from the desert to the halls of academia and her determination to change the World; there were some things that drove people so far beyond themselves that they no longer lived by the rules that bound others.

CHAPTER XXV

Arabkha, Northern Mesopotamia. c 1980 BCE

A woman's personal altar evokes her particular--her intimate--relationship to the divine, human, and natural realms. There she assembles a highly condensed, symbolic model of connection by bringing together sacred images and ritual objects, pictures, mementos, natural materials, and decorative effects which represent different realms of meaning and experience--heaven and earth, family and deities, nature and culture, Self and Other. By actively engaging the Divine at the self-created sacred place, she makes her altar a living instrument of communication, a channeling device for integration, reconciliation, and creative transformation.[xxvi]

"Less light," said Nama, moving her head from side to side on the reed mat. She lay under a canopy on the roof of the house Ekur had built for her in the first year after they arrived from Urim.

"What about the light?" asked Inna.

Nama mumbled again. With a sigh, Inna left the grain she had been rolling and turned to her grandmother. She poured a bowl of fresh water and helped Nama lift her head to sip at the bowl. Nama's skin had become almost transparent, and Inna knew it would not be long before she left this life.

"Less light here than in Urim," said Nama, staring at the sky.

Inna knew her grandmother was not really seeing the gathering clouds of the Northern sky; her sight had returned to the endless blue of the heavens above Urim.

Inna had never seen Urim, but Nama had spoken of the great city whenever she thought they were alone. Inna nodded now, wondering if Urim really had been as wondrous as Nama said. Murmuring endearments, she lifted the bowl to Nama's lips again. Her grandmother pushed the bowl away and sat up, staring into the distance.

"I see him," she said.

"Who?" asked Inna, looking around.

"Nanna, Great One of the Moon, protector of women." Her old eyes were shining bright as a girl's. "Never forget, my child. You were born to remember Nanna. And Inanna."

"I will not forget." Inna settled Nama back onto the mat and turned back to the grinding stone. Nama grabbed her arm. Her hand was bony and wrinkled, but she gripped hard enough to make Inna gasp.

"Know your Father, child." Nama's voice cracked with the effort.

"Daroo has been good to me," said Inna, nodding at her grandmother.

"Not Daroo! Your Father. There was a reason you were born."

Inna went very still. Her mother had told her this, but something in Nama's voice made her hear it differently. She had seen the tablet from the High Priestess, but it was like a story from another time. Perhaps she should ask to see it again now she was older. She bent her head closer to Nama, wrinkling her nose at the stale, sweet smell of sickness.

"Tell me more, Nama. More."

"A child was born to carry the Balance. To remember the life-giving power of the Mother. A child who should not have been born. To keep the Balance. It is you, Inna." Nama closed her eyes.

Inna took Nama's hand between her own. "Who was my Father?" she whispered.

For twenty breaths there was no answer. Even the birds stopped calling from the cedar trees lining the streets. Finally, Nama shook her head.

"I know not his name. He walked from Urim to begin something new. I know that Nin-lil-la, High Priestess of Nanna, saw you in the future. 'Balance,' she said to me. You, Inna, are the Balance."

"You knew the High Priestess?" asked Inna.

Nama nodded. "She spoke to me once. Each year, on the same day a daughter left to enter the Temple, she returned home to work alongside her mother again, remembering those who lived to serve Nanna by bearing children, making bread and nurturing the family. Mir-ri was shy the first year, but she came every year after that, running to see me. But one year she did not come, and I went to ask at the Temple."

Why had Nama never told her this story before?

"I was taken to the High Priestess, Nin-lil-la, she was called. She told me that Mir-ri was to bear a child for Nanna and Inanna, a child to hold the Balance. I was glad in my heart that Mir-ri would soon return to us, but I was troubled that she had been noticed by the Great Ones."

"Why, Nama?" asked Inna.

"Honour the Great Ones but do nothing to catch their eyes," said Nama. "That is what the old folk said, but my sweet, bright Mir-ri had been seen by Nanna himself. But you are a blessing, child, never forget that. A blessing."

Nama's hands had grown cold. Inna covered her with the goatswool blanket. A breath of cool air passed over the rooftop, and she shivered. She felt the eyes of the Great Ones on her and was afraid.

"What am I to do?" she asked, as much to the air and the trees as to Nama.

A cloud passed across the face of the Sun, and the city fell into shadow. Inna looked up, half expecting to see Nanna or Inanna blocking the light. As if from far away, she heard a humming sound, like bees buzzing and birdsong carried on the breeze. A woman spoke.

"Many are called but few are chosen." Deeply resonant, the woman's voice intoned the ancient words of initiation.

Inna gasped and looked around. She knew the words from her mother's lessons, but there was no one on the rooftop except her and Nama.

"Do you bring your feet to walk in Her Ways?" asked the voice.

A warmth rose up from the clay of the rooftop, lapping at Inna's feet. She nodded.

"You must answer, child," said the voice, not unkindly. "Do you bring your feet to walk in Her Ways?"

"I do," whispered Inna, shaking all over. She looked around again for the Priestess who must surely be there somewhere.

"Do you bring your knees to kneel in Her praise?"

"I do." Inna lowered her head, absorbed now in the strange visitation.

"Do you bring your sex to rejoice in Her Life-giving?"

"I do," stammered Inna, blushing.

"Do you bring your breasts for Her abundance flowing?"

"I do."

"Do you bring your hands to do Her work?"

"I do." Inna rubbed her hands together, hoping that the dirt under her nails would not be seen.

"Do you bring your lips to sing Her acclaim?"

"I do." She smiled as she remembered the songs her mother sang.

"Do you bring your eyes to see Her presence in all?"

"I do."

"Rise, child. You are chosen."

Inna stumbled to her feet, sure now that the woman who had spoken the ritual words would appear from the stairs. She crossed to the edge of the roof. There was only Shuba walking slowly up the lane, holding her granddaughter's hand and waving her other hand in the air as she told one of her stories.

Inna sighed; she had just received a story and more than a story, a blessing, from the High Priestess. Perhaps this was what Nama has been trying to say.

She turned back to where her grandmother lay, but the old lady's chest was still. On her lips lingered the traces of a smile.

Wiser than she had been an hour before, Inna bent to kiss Nama farewell, giving thanks that the sacred words had been spoken before her grandmother breathed her last so far from home.

Nama was buried wrapped in her reed sleeping-mat with a bowl of grain and an urn of water beside her. From grain and water came life, taught the Great Ones. From death came new life, just as the seasons followed each other, and light followed dark, an eternal cycle. Inna knew the ritual words and songs, knew the promise of eternal return, yet she keenly felt the absence of her grandmother.

Time passed, and she found herself listening for the voice of the Priestess. What had Nama called her? *Nin-lil-la.*

Nin-lil-la came to Inna in her dreams and in the quiet moments of her life. The High Priestess came to Inna as she lay halfway between waking and sleeping on her wedding night, her husband warm alongside her. She came as Inna held her first born, a daughter, to her breast and listened to her small, contented murmurs. Nin-lil-la came to Inna as she watched the Moon rise round and glowing, or small and curved like the horns of the water cows who pulled the plows, like the curved prows of the tiny bardi reed-boats her grandfather had fashioned for her when she was young.

One day, not long after Nama's passing, Inna found Ner-nin and Mir-ri sitting in the shade of a huge old banyan tree. The tendrils of the aerial roots trailed in the breeze like long flowing hair, glowing pink in the Sunlight.

"Will you teach me more about walking in Her ways?" she asked them. They had taught her to write and to use numbers to tally the tokens taken at market and to calculate the number of bricks needed for a new house. They had also taught her to watch the heavens, to know when Inanna would shine in the morning and when in the evening, to calculate the movement of the planets. There were songs Inna knew also, songs of praise for the Queen of Heaven and earth, Holy Inanna. But now she wanted more . . .

The two women looked up, startled out of their conversation.

"We were just speaking of our days in the Temple in Urim," said Mir-ri. "We were remembering the morning and

evening songs and the lessons. And our friends, all lost now."
Mir-ri smiled up at her daughter. "Of course we will teach you
more. We will teach you everything."

They began daily observances in the old ways Mir-ri and
Ner-nin had learned in the Temple of Nanna in Urim. Inna
joined with them to greet the dawn, singing the praises of holy
Inanna. Farida, Mir-ri's second daughter, sang alongside Inna,
and gradually the other women came, drawn by the songs and
the sense of reverence and joy.

Ner-nin, always there for women in childbirth, and in the
sicknesses that came more often in the Northern heat, taught
Inna the ways of healing. She showed her which herbs to pick
for fever and which to pick to ease the pain of childbirth:
calamus and hellebore, mentha, myrrh, and thymus. Inna
watched Ner-nin's ways as she gathered and dried the herbs,
mixed them into medicines, and dispensed from a small tent in
the market. She learned when to pick the herbs and how to
always leave enough for the plants to continue growing.

Daroo also had wisdom passed down from his mother,
who had been a healer in the Eastern city where he had been
born. He showed Inna how to use the tall, feathery plants
growing along the roadside--vagharni, he called them. Together
they dug up the roots and collected the resin, replanting the roots
for next season.

"Good for the stomach," said Daroo, offering Inna a stem
to chew.

"It is good," said Inna, eyes watering at the sharp taste.

Ner-nin laughed, and Inna wondered why such a beautiful
woman had never found a husband. When Daroo left them
alone, Inna tried to find a way to ask Ner-nin about it.

"Daroo is a good man," she said.

Ner-nin nodded and put aside the herbs she was tying in bundles for drying. "So you are wondering why I do not have a man," she said softly.

Inna nodded, cheeks hot with embarrassment; perhaps it was not for her to ask such a thing.

"It is good you ask," said Ner-nin, reaching out to squeeze Inna's hand. "Soon you will be looking at the young men yourself, and you need to think about these things."

Inna blushed even more. She had already noticed the laughing eyes of one of the boys from the stall next to theirs at the market, and she secretly admired the strong thighs of the water sellers as they carried the panniers through the streets.

"I like men well enough, but there has never been one for me." Ner-nin looked into the distance, as if there were a memory she was seeking.

Inna nodded. "Who was my Father?" she asked, surprising herself.

Ner-nin sighed. "Truly I do not know. I believe he studied at the E-dub-ba with Mir-ri, but she has never named him. Perhaps you should ask her."

Inna shrugged. Many times she had been about to ask her mother, but something stopped the words.

"Perhaps I will."

By the next season, Ner-nin had found a husband: Muldim, a physician of Arabkha. She met him as they worked with the sickness that came with the rains, and soon they were inseparable. Their reputation for healing grew, and they moved to a room near the House of Scribes, where even the wealthy came to them for healing.

On the day of the wedding ceremony, Mir-ri and Inna walked with Ner-nin to deliver her to Muldim. It was not the custom, but there was no one from Ner-nin's family in the North. Muldim, a tall, serious-looking man, nervously lifted the veil he had been clutching in sweating hands and managed to drape it over Ner-nin's head.

"She is my wife," he announced solemnly to a cacophony of cheering and good wishes.

The ceremony was simple, but the feasting lasted all night, with music and dancing. Inna sat with her mother and Ner-nin as people sang and danced around them.

"You look beautiful," Mir-ri whispered to her friend, admiring the gold bracelet Muldim had given her as his wedding gift.

Ner-nin looked in wonder at the bracelet, turning it this way and that to catch the light.

"I'm not sure about beautiful," she said. "But I am content."

Some time later, when Ner-nin was dancing with her new husband, Inna sat alone with her mother. Mir-ri opened her arms for Inna to sit close.

"She looks happy," murmured Inna.

"Mmmm," agreed Mir-ri.

With a deep breath, Inna turned to her mother. "Who was my Father?"

Mir-ri stiffened. She had thought the old pain long gone, but there it was, as if her frantic run through Urim had only happened yesterday. She moved a little away from Inna, reaching for the words to answer the one person who had a right to know.

"His name was Abram," she said quietly. "I have never told anyone that."

Inna nodded, reaching for her mother's hands, stroking them and holding them between her own. She waited.

"I was the age you are now," said Mir-ri. "Something brought us together, a wind, a promise, a dream."

Inna nodded. "Nama told me again about Nin-lil-la. About the Balance."

Mir-ri gasped. "She knew?"

"She told me the day she died. Then something came."

"How did she know?" asked Mir-ri, as much to the air as to Inna.

"She said Nin-lil-la spoke with her."

Mir-ri shook her head. "Imagine Nama keeping a secret like that all her days. You can know someone all your life, and still they can surprise you."

"Where is he now?" asked Inna. It was the question she had been longing to ask.

"I believe he left Urim before the fall, but I do not know where he is," said Mir-ri. "He was Habiru and wanted to find a Northern tribe who honour a Great One who has no name."

"No name? If this Great One of the Northern tribes has no name how do the people give praise?" asked Inna.

Mir-ri laughed. "That, my dearest Inna, is a very good question."

They sat quietly for a few moments. Then Mir-ri turned to Inna. "You said something came?"

"I think it was Nin-lil-la, the High Priestess. She said, 'Many are called but few are chosen'."

Mir-ri grabbed Inna's arm. "You heard her voice?"

Inna nodded. "She asked me if I would walk in Her ways."

Mir-ri laughed out loud then, throwing her arms around Inna. "Nin-lil-la was right! The way of Inanna lives. You carry the Balance."

Inna shrugged. Perhaps she did carry the Balance, but she had no idea what to do with it. She was seventeen years old.

Mir-ri found peace in the North, watching her children grow, teaching her daughters the ways of the holy Priestess of Heaven and Earth. She and Ner-nin often sat together at the end of the day, remembering Urim. After her conversation with Inna, Mir-ri spoke more freely of Abram and of Nin-lil-la's prophecy.

To Ner-nin she said, "I have been thinking of Inna and the Balance. We know the truth of what Nin-lil-la began, but how do we keep the truth alive when we're gone?"

"You do not think it enough for us to teach our daughters?" said Ner-nin, suckling her own firstborn. "To teach Inna and her daughters and the daughters who follow?"

Mir-ri shook her head. "There must be some way for them to know who they are, what they carry. Although I am not sure exactly what it is Inna carries." She sighed deeply. "And I was there at the beginning."

"We know it is Balance she carries," said Ner-nin, sounding for a moment like Nin-lil-la. "She holds the Balance against the ways that deny the life-giving power of the Mother."

"Of course," said Mir-ri. "But what exactly is it? And what will it mean in a hundred years when you and I are gone? When Inna is gone?"

"I have no answers," Ner-nin said quietly. "But I am sure that Nin-lil-la saw further than one hundred years. We must find a way for the daughters to remember, for a hundred years and a thousand years."

They invited Inna to join them, the three of them pondering a future they could barely imagine.

"We must tell the story," said Inna, as if it were obvious. "Write it down, make it into a song, teach it to all the children." Already she imagined her children's children hearing the story of Mir-ri and Abram, and of their daughter, Inna.

"Begin it by saying: 'Your grandmothers want you to do something for them'," suggested Ner-nin, making the others smile.

Together they formed a story to be told to every daughter of Mir-ri's line. Leaving nothing to chance, they wrote the story in the old way on thin clay tablets. It was from these that the children learned to read and write and to calculate the movement of planets. From the tablets they also had stories of Mir-ri and the treasure she carried from Urim.

Time passed. Life in Arabkha continued season by season. The city grew as more travellers arrived from the East and the South, the time of the Ram bringing change just as Nin-lil-la had predicted.

Mir-ri and her family were more prosperous than some of their neighbours, but they were still considered newcomers by the Arabkhans. Her cousin Enananta, who had married an Arabkan, encouraged her husband, a trader in livestock, to sponsor the men into the market guilds, paving the way for more acceptance than was usually granted to refugees from Ki-en-gir.

Inna married Zage, whose family were also from the South. He reminded her of Daroo, with his teasing humour and eager affection. Late at night, when the cookfires had burned down and all were sleeping, she lay beside her husband and wondered about her real Father. Had Abram looked at Mir-ri with soft eyes like Zage looked at her? Was it always the same between a man and a woman?

Her nighttime thoughts changed when she gave birth to her daughter, Alika; now she lay awake wondering how to pass on the inheritance entrusted to her. If only Nin-lil-la were there to say more about what she wanted.

After Alika came two sons--Emmul and Hanish--bright-eyed like their father. Finally, another daughter, Etana, who bore the birthmark on her wrist and looked at the world through dark, serious eyes.

Alika and Etana learned from their mother and grandmother to honour the holy Priestess of Heaven. To them she was still Inanna, although the Arabkhans worshipped her as Ishtar. Grandmother Mir-ri taught them the morning and evening praises and showed them the cycles of the star named for the holy Priestess of Heaven and Earth. In the North, there were no Temples to Inanna, so they learned to build altars to celebrate her many faces: Mother, Priestess, Warrior, Beloved.

They placed altars for Air In the East, adding feathers, bones of birds, and images of wings and flight drawn by Etana, who had a gift for etching lines in the clay tablets Daroo made for her.

"Hail! Lady of the Morning. We invoke you and call you. Radiant One of the dawn, Winged One of the morning Sun, Come! Bestow on us your laughter, love and inspiration. Lift us on your wings so golden."

In the South, they made altars for Fire, with candles lit each day at the midday meal, scenting the home with sweet fragrances made from oils of thyme and rosemary. They decorated the Fire altars with carved statues of four-legged creatures, the fierce ones who hunted and protected.

"Hail! Lady of the Daylight. We invoke and call you. Fiery One of the midday heat. Mighty warrior, fierce protector, be our shield and our defender."

In the West they honoured the element of Water with bowls filled fresh each day, snake skins for the serpents of the watery depths and carvings of frogs and fish.

When the evening star shone by the Moon, they called to Inanna. "Hail! Lady of the Evening. We invoke you and call you. Flowing One of the Watery Depths, Twilight One. Sibyl, soothsayer, seer, speak your truth that we may hear."

The altars to the North were for Earth, the cornerstone of life. Here they placed stones of all shapes and sizes: crystal, amethyst, and garnet found in the foothills, as well as river-washed pebbles. Fruit and flowers adorned these altars throughout the year, alongside statues of the mother, arms wide open to hold and nurture her children.

As they settled for the night, the women lit oil lamps scented with essences of thyme, rosemary, and geranium to hold out the dark. They called to the Lady of Night for protection. "Hail! Lady of Night. We invoke and call you. Black One of the Midnight Hour, Stone, Mountain, Life Giving Soil, Cow-eyed one whose arms are open, be with us through the night."

Alika and Etana imagined themselves Priestesses in the Temple Mir-ri and Ner-nin described to them. They braided each other's hair and stole Inna's precious linen to practise the folds and pleats of the robes worn by the priestesses. When Inna found them parading in the lane beside the house, the linen dragging in the dust, she did not have the heart to scold too loudly. Better they remember to walk in Her ways, she thought, eyes filling with tears as she watched the girls.

For two hundred years life in Arabkha went on in the same way. The unification that had begun with Sargon continued with a succession of Akkadian rulers. As long as the new settlers worked and respected the laws, they prospered alongside the Northerners. Alika and Etana both married men from Arabkha, further strengthening their family's position in the city. They gave birth to seven children, and Inna rejoiced that she was there to deliver the babies. She held the daughters especially close, calling on Inanna to bless them. She also loved her grandsons, fine, strong boys who ran and tumbled in the lanes, jumped yelling from the flat rooftops, and grew to be men who lived easily with women.

Inna loved them all and taught them to read and write and to use the number systems she had learned from Mir-ri. The girls all sang the morning and evening praises and told and retold the story of grandmother Mir-ri and Urim. Inna sensed Mir-ri close by as she told the old stories and sang the old songs. It still caught her sometimes, the absence of her mother, bringing tears to her eyes as she watched her granddaughters sleeping, as she sat with her daughters and the other women tying herbs, preparing meals, talking about the day.

By the time of Inna's passing, there were three more girls in the line of Balance from Abram and Mir-ri: Farah, Hanife, and the youngest, named for her great grandmother Mir-ri. They, in turn, married, and gave birth to daughters. The daughters of Hanife and Mir-ri were called Nama, Safi, and Rashida, a name from Daroo's family. Farah had one daughter whom she called Inna, after her grandmother, although she was lost to her before she could walk. The daughters of Hanife and Mir-ri called one of their daughters Inna, and she grew to bear daughters of her own. So the names of Mir-ri, Inna, and Nama returned again and again, carrying echoes of the early days.

And always the stories, the songs, and the lessons, reminding them of the past, and of the future . . .

CHAPTER XXVI

Amman, Jordan. Updated Tues May 15th 2015 3.11pm UTC

Hundreds of fires are raging across America's heartland to its west coast. Worse even than the tragic fires of 2000, the unfolding disaster is the culmination of the worst drought season on record. Firefighters from around the world have joined 4000 soldiers and marines to battle hundreds of fires burning throughout 11 States, from the Canadian to the Mexican border and West from California across to the Rocky Mountains.

Paula and Lili rose early to sift through stories from Iraq to Israel, Ethiopia to Egypt. Mish's emails arrived with her finds and, by the time Peter came to meet them at the café, they had both drunk too much coffee and had accumulated more tales than they could ever hope to make sense of.

"And these are only a fraction of what's on the Internet," said Paula, exasperated.

"Story is how human beings have maintained community, continuity, and meaning since the first people sat around fires at night," said Peter, reading some of the old tales over Paula's shoulder. "We are still no different, really."

Lili focused on her computer screen, sifting through the information. Peter ordered them all more coffee and some pastries he recommended.

Forty minutes later, Paula called excitedly, "Look at this!"

"Read it to me," said Lili, sitting back and closing her eyes.

Peter sat next to Paula, reading the story as she spoke.

"It's an old tale from northern Iraq, from the area around Arabkha: In the old days, in the very old days, the black people of Sumer walked from their homes in the South to settle in the North. With them walked a Priestess of Inanna. She carried a treasure from their great city in the South. This she hid in the walls of a house in Arabkha, and there it stayed for countless generations. Many searched, but it was no ordinary treasure. It chose the time when it would be found and the hands that would find it. In the time of Hammurabi, the descendants of the people of Sumer fled the armies and went into the West. Not wanting to be left behind, the treasure revealed itself to a daughter of the house. So it travelled from the land of the two rivers to a new home in the West. And there it remained until it was once again time for it to be revealed."

Lili sat up, her eyes bright. "That sounds close."

"Do you really think that could be it?" asked Paula. "The me?"

"I can't imagine the treasure was left in Ur for the Elamites, so it was probably taken out of the city by someone travelling North. This could be it."

"When was the time of Hammurabi?" asked Paula.

"About seventeen hundred and fifty years before the common era," said Peter.

"I wonder where they went in the West," said Lili eagerly.

Peter answered, almost as if he were reading the information from a book. "By Hammurabi's time, the Sumerians had inter-married with Arabkhans and other refugees from northern India. They maintained their religion; the northern Gods were not so different, although they worshipped Ishtar instead of Inanna. When they moved, they settled all across the north: Kahlu, the northern plains, Harran, Carchemish, Khalpe-- modern day Halab. Their descendants are still there today, although most have no idea their ancestors hailed from Sumer."

"Who are you?" asked Lili, sounding impressed.

"As I said, a dealer in antiquities," replied Peter. "It pays to be well-informed in this business."

"Let's check through what Mish has sent us," suggested Paula. "Isn't Halab in the area she was covering?"

CHAPTER XXVII

Arabkha to Khalpe, Northern Mesopotamia. c 1750BCE.

Only when we have considered the whole scope of the basic feminine functions - the giving of life, nourishment, warmth, and protection - can we understand why the Feminine occupies so central a position in human symbolism and from the very beginning bears the character of "greatness." The Feminine appears as great because that which is contained, sheltered, nourished, is dependent on it and utterly at its mercy. Nowhere perhaps is it so evident that a human being must be experienced as "great" as in the case of the mother. A glance at the infant or child confirms her position as Great Mother[xxvii].

Afsana--the nine-times great-granddaughter of Mir-ri--sat on a low stool, suckling her baby daughter in the shade of a lemon tree. She had named the child Mir-ri, for the long-ago ancestor who carried a treasure from Urim. The story was legend in the family, passed down by her mother and her mother's mother, and all the mothers whose ancestors had come from Urim in the South.

"The history of Urim was lost," said the old men, generation after generation, as if that was the only truth they could name with any certainty.

Afsana looked down at her daughter and called on the blessings of her many times great-grandmother who was said to have saved something of great value, carrying it from the great Southern city in the days before the Elamite invasion. Baby Mir-ri had also been born into a time of unrest, and Afsana hoped the name would give her strength. Although, truth be told, no one really knew the full story of the first Mir-ri.

Afsana had talked long into the night with the other children of the family about just what Grandmother Mir-ri might have saved from Urim. And what she might have done with it. Like previous generations, they tapped on the walls and listened for the hollow echo of hiding spaces. For it was said that the original house of Mir-ri and those who travelled North with her was right there in the middle of the huge sprawling compound that now housed six families in Arabkha.

When they were younger, it had been Afsana's older brother, Kiral, who led the search.

"We must test the walls with water," he had announced one day.

"Water?" said the others.

Kiral had explained his intention to swab sections of the walls to reveal the underlying bricks, thereby locating the original house where Mir-ri's treasure might be hidden.

Afsana had been dubious. "Mother just had it painted with gypsum, remember?"

"Don't worry. It won't show."

Of course it did show, and their mother had noticed almost immediately. The search for Mir-ri's treasure was stopped before it had really started. Over the years, Kiral and

Afsana still tapped the walls with their knuckles as they walked from one part of the compound to another, but it was more from habit than any expectation of truly finding anything.

As Afsana sat under the lemon tree with the baby snuffling and grunting between contented bouts of sucking, she found herself thinking of Mir-ri's treasure. Her lips brushed the soft down on the baby's head, and warmth filled her body; new life was so precious. With a certainty that had nothing to do with logic, she knew that Mir-ri had left Urim carrying a baby.

Afsana closed her eyes, imagining a young woman, tall and dark like all the women in the family, bundling her belongings into a reed basket and walking away from Urim with her precious treasure. Afsana wondered how it would be to leave her home, her friends, and follow the river North. She shivered. Just for a moment the Sun dimmed, and she looked up, expecting to see someone standing nearby.

She heard a distant humming and a woman's voice, speaking softly but clearly. "Many are called but few are chosen."

Afsana looked around for the one who had spoken, but she was alone with the sleeping baby. The house seemed strangely silent.

"Do you bring your feet to walk in Her Ways?" asked the voice.

Afsana jumped, earning a grumble from young Mir-ri. Looking around again, she wondered what she was meant to say in reply.

"You must answer, child," said the voice, not unkindly. "Do you bring your feet to walk in Her Ways?"

"I do," whispered Afsana, trembling despite the warmth of the day.

"Do you bring your knees to kneel in Her praise?"

"I do." Afsana closed her eyes again, absorbed now in the ritual.

"Do you bring your sex to rejoice in Her Life-giving?"

"I do," said Afsana, remembering her thoughts of moments before about Mir-ri's treasure.

"Do you bring your breasts for Her abundance flowing?"

"I do," said Afsana as milk started to leak from her nipples.

"Do you bring your hands to do Her work?"

"I do."

"Do you bring your lips to sing Her acclaim?"

"I do." She thought of the songs sung by the women at the altars and nodded.

"Do you bring your eyes to see Her presence in all?"

"I do."

"Rise, child. You are chosen."

Afsana lifted her head and prepared to rise.

Noise erupted from the house. Her husband, Itamar, came running out.

"It has happened!" he cried. "Hammurabi has taken Ashur." Face flushed with running from the market, he looked older than his twenty-two years. Was there fear in his voice?

"So it has come," said Afsana, holding Mir-ri close.

Long had they discussed the threat from the great city of Bab-Ilu, old even before their parents were born. Itamar and his friends feared that Hammurabi had finally gathered enough strength to take the North, and he and Afsana had often talked about it at night while the others slept. He had convinced her that they must leave Arabkha if Hammurabi's army came North, but Afsana had prayed that it not happen in her lifetime. It seemed that her prayers had not been accompanied by enough offerings.

"It is time," said Itamar. "We must leave. I will gather the others." He no longer sounded frightened.

Perhaps it had been her own fear all along.

She had lived all her life in this house, the house where Mir-ri had first brought the treasure from Urim. What would happen to it if they left? She was gripped by a moment's frantic need to break down the walls, to tear the house to pieces before abandoning it. Just then little Mir-ri stirred in her arms and looked up with deep, trusting eyes. Afsana shook her head. Here was her treasure in her arms. What was she thinking?

The family gathered in the main courtyard, almost filling the open space between the wall and the house. Most knew of Itamar's plans, and there had been months of talk about what they would do. Itamar's own family, Arabkhans whose ancestors had settled the city, had agreed to leave for the West if the uneasy balance of power shifted to Bab-Ilu; the fabled justice of Hammurabi did not extend to those he conquered.

Long did they debate that afternoon in the courtyard, calling out suggestions about when they should leave, where they should go, and how much to take with them.

Itamar's voice rose above the others. "I have talked with travellers and traders from the West. Some of you know Nizam of Khalpe, who buys our mats. He told me that in Khalpe they have a Great One of the weather, Teshub they call him. He is no different from the Great Ones of war who are now honoured here, but his consort is called Shaushka, and she is like our own Ishtar, holy Priestess of both love and battle. I think we could make a home there."

Afsana's mother rose to stand by Itamar, raising her eyebrows for permission to speak. Itamar nodded and sat down.

"You all know that I am Nama, mother of Afsana and Kiral. I was named for one of the first mothers, and I have lived here in this house all my life. My mother also lived here all the days of her life. It is said that all the mothers have lived here right back to Mir-ri, who walked from Urim before the fall. Our family is here because mother Mir-ri left Urim before the armies came. It seems that we have always been here, but there was a time when this house did not stand. The Banyan was not even here when Mir-ri came." She pointed to the huge tree that overshadowed the house, dark green leaves glistening in the Sun, pink aerial roots dancing in the breeze.

All eyes turned to the Banyan as if it might hold the answers they were seeking.

"What we have built, we can build again, as long as we are alive to do it. Khalpe sounds as good a place as any." Nama sat down, face flushed.

Her words had been strong and brave, but Afsana wondered how her mother would be able to walk away from all she had ever known. She shook her head. Of course she knew; Nama would be walking with her children and the daughter of her daughter. Wasn't that enough?

By the time the lanterns were lit, and the women had made food to share, most of those gathered under the tree had decided to leave for Khalpe.

"We must be gone in a week. No later," said Itamar, as people left for their own homes or found their way to their rooms in the huge, sprawling house that had sheltered the family for four centuries.

It was a long walk from Arabkha to Khalpe. Afsana listened to the travellers' tales of a rich country nestled between the Sea and a great river. The only great river she knew was the

Buranun, the river that flowed through her family's dreams. Would they find the Buranun as they walked into the West?

They left Arabkha to walk North and then West, following the path of the setting Sun. Afsana walked with the other mothers, Mir-ri in a sling tied across one shoulder. They slowed for the toddlers, took time to feed the babies, and arrived last into the camp at the end of the day. The tents were already up, the fires lit, the evening meal cooking. To do her share of the work, Afsana cleaned up after the meal, banked the fire, and took the scraps away to keep wild creatures from the camp at night. Alone under the stars, she felt closer to the Great Ones who guided their journey.

They reached Kahlu, the trade city on the Eastern bank of the river, one afternoon just as the Sun settled into the West. That night they camped amongst a long line of travellers waiting to pass through the great gate of Kahlu in order to cross the Idigna.

"Will the city be like Urim of my ancestors?" Afsana asked Itamar that night as they lay on their sleeping mat

"Perhaps," said Itamar thoughtfully. "Although I never think of Urim as being so noisy."

The city of Kahlu was certainly full of noise: asses braying, hawkers calling out their goods, great gongs announcing the hours of the day.

Itamar shook his head. "It may be foolish, but I always see Urim as clean and bright in the golden light of the Sun. Sort of glowing."

Afsana laughed. "Of course you do! After being around our family, how could you see anything else? We speak of Urim like some speak of the golden halls of the Great Ones. Perhaps that is always the way when your home has been lost to time and change. One day Arabkha may seem like that to us, too."

They spoke long into the night. Mir-ri woke to feed, the Moon sailed across the Heavens, and still they spoke softly of the past and of the future. Crossing the Idigna would take them into unknown territory, another step towards their new home. What would it be like? Would Mir-ri be safe there?

The day of their crossing was fine, blue skies heralding the beginning of the dry season.

"Not the best time to be crossing the Plains," said the ferryman.

Afsana frowned at him. They had paid him to pole them across with his gnarled hands, not give them unasked-for advice. He would scare Pinar, wife of Itamar's brother, who was full of complaints about the heat, the cold, the dampness, the dryness.

"Hotter than the kilns of Gibil before the month passes." The ferryman shook his head as if to say that only fools planned to cross the Plains now.

Afsana tried to distract Pinar by pointing to the other ferries pushing through the swirling waters. A water bird dived for fish, and the children's excited cries drowned out the talk of burning deserts.

That night Afsana asked Itamar if they should, after all, go further North rather than risk the Plains.

"It is hard to say. I have spoken to travellers who say it is still possible to cross the Plains. And we must hurry; Hammurabi's armies are already in Ashur."

From Kahlu they travelled West, keeping South of the rolling hills, the natural boundary for the settlements between the Idigna and the middle reaches of the Buranun. They learned to travel in the early hours of the day and again in the evening, taking shelter in the hottest hours from the Sun that was, as the ferryman had promised, more scorching than the kilns of the Great Ones.

Mir-ri grew round and strong, squiggling and squirming in Afsana's arms, straining for the ground. In the middle of the day, the dried stubble was too hot for bare skin, so she took her to the open-sided tent where the livestock sheltered. There Mir-ri crawled round and round, under and between the hooves of goats and asses, finding her feet by balancing on the horns of the gentle mother goat who had two young of her own to watch over.

Afsana smiled to see the animals play with Mir-ri, nibbling and snuffling her hair. By the time they reached the Habur river, Mir-ri was walking and running like a kid goat. She talked in a language that was at least half-goat, although Afsana understood her perfectly.

On the Plains they found small settlements where travellers had stopped to build houses of packed earth, to scratch their livelihood from the dry soil. How would it be to live there forever, so far from water? Afsana shuddered at the thought of it.

They shared nights around communal fires and moved on, heading for a city on the Buranun, gateway to the lands beyond. Traders from the West called the great river by another name: the Fererehat, 'wide flowing water' in their tongue.

By the time they reached the high-walled city of Harran, their food and water were almost at an end, and Afsana was grateful to rest outside the city while the men exchanged woven mats and dried herbs for flour and wine. Mir-ri chattered like a bird as she helped gather firewood and milk the goats.

The weather changed from scorching heat to pelting rains, and Pinar pleaded for a delay to wait out the wet season. She was carrying her third child, and she longed to spend the time before the birth in the one place.

"It is not our way to decide for others," said Itamar. "If Pinar needs to stop, then so be it."

Pinar sagged with relief.

"Yet," said Itamar, "we are only ten days or so from the Buranun, and I, for one, have waited long to see the sweet waters of which I have heard so much. Afsana and I will go on."

"But the dust will have turned to mud, and the roads will be washed away," said his brother, Hassan.

"Nevertheless, we will be leaving soon."

Hassan talked to the others, convincing many to stay in Harran. In the end Itamar, Afsana, and Mir-ri left with Nama and three other families, including Afsana's brother, Kiral, and his wife and two children.

As the day of leaving approached, the farewells became so intense that Afsana wondered if it boded ill for their journey. Surely it was only a matter of a few Moon cycles before the others would follow?

They left Harran on one of the clear, cold days when there was no sign of rain. The bitter wind sliced through robes and blankets, carrying away their words of farewell.

"In ten days we will be beside the Buranun," whispered Itamar to Mir-ri, who rode on his back like a bundle of furs. Wrapped and rewrapped in goatskins, her little head turned to peer back at the receding faces of her aunts and uncles, cousins and neighbours.

In the end it took them fifteen days of rain and mud to reach the Buranun, even with five clear days and only one truly wild storm in which they had huddled together beside the sturdy bodies of the asses as the wind howled and the sky rained pellets of ice. Mir-ri had been the warmest of them all, snuggled against Afsana's skin inside layers of wool and fur.

When they did reach the river, Afsana was surprised to find Carchemish, the city of merchants, on the Western bank of the Buranun. She had always pictured it as another gateway, like Kahlu, but Carchemish was a silhouette against the setting Sun, the city walls spaced with towers as if prepared for battle.

"Now there's a city for you," said Itamar, whistling through his teeth.

Afsana nodded. Mir-ri peered around her father's head, staring wide-eyed across the river.

They camped there on the Eastern bank, refilling their water jars with the sweet water none of them had ever tasted. If anyone found it disappointingly like the water from other rivers, not a word was said about it. Each received the first sip like a sacrament, both a fulfillment and a promise.

This crossing felt different from the Idigna, more sombre. Afsana wondered if it was because the Buranun was so much a part of the family stories, the great river that flowed all the way to the old city of Urim. They loaded the ferry and set off as the Sun rose behind them. Afsana sat on top of their bedding, Mir-ri in her lap, watching the towers of Carchemish grow bigger.

"An eel!" cried Jabbaar, Kiral's youngest son. "Look at the eel!" He leaned over the side.

With a cry, he fell, feet kicking the side of the ferry in a flurry. Then silence.

People yelled and pushed, trying to reach him.

Dilshad lunged past Afsana.

She fell backwards.

The sky tilted as she fell, arms straining to keep Mir-ri from toppling over the side.

Mir-ri cried out.

Afsana's head hit the side of the ferry with a noise like breaking wood. A wave of sleepy blackness washed over her.

Mir-ri heard her mother's head hit the wood. She felt her die; there one moment, then gone. Her mother's arms still held her safe from the water, but she squirmed out of her grasp and crawled up to sit by her head. She placed one hand on her mother's forehead and whispered a prayer.

Dilshad sent up a mighty splash as she lunged overboard after Jabbaar. Kiral cried out like a water bird and dived in after them. He came up, face wild, sucking in air, and dived again.

Surface. Breathe. Dive.

He kept doing it. Didn't he know they were gone?

Mir-ri's father sat beside her and held her close.

Kiral came up again, spitting water. The boatman hooked him and pulled him in. The eel was still swimming in circles around the ferry.

Mir-ri looked down at her mother. "Many are called but few are chosen," she whispered. "Many are called but few are chosen."

Her mother was safe in the arms of the Great Mother.

Mir-ri stood with her father by the river for the burial. Nama sang to Ishtar and to the dark Mother who was holding Afsana in her arms now. Mir-ri sang the words she knew and hummed the rest.

"Mother of Life and Death, be with us in our sorrow. Great Weaver of Life and Death, we call on you to mend what has been torn. Father Nanna, we ask you to guide those who are lost. Mother, we ask you to bring them home to your halls."

Her father chanted in a voice croaky with tears. "Powers of Air, we call on you to receive the last breaths of those who have died, to send soft breezes to blow under clear skies. Powers of Earth, receive the bodies of our loved ones when they come to you, earth returning to earth. Powers of fire, we call on you to take the fire that was their life back to the Source. Powers of water, hungry and cruel, we call on you to carry those you have taken to the Sea."

Mir-ri was carried around the city all that day by her father, and she wondered what her mother would have thought of the lion statues and the carvings of wild boars. She wanted to touch them, to climb up and stroke their faces.

"Let her go, Itamar," said Nama finally. "You have to do your grieving without her."

Mir-ri felt sorry for him, but she was glad to walk and run again.

"Tell me what you were saying to Afsana in the ferry," said Nama.

Mir-ri told her and also told her about the voice that spoke the words to her at night.

Nama stroked her head. "I will miss Afsana always, but I give thanks that you are safe, little one."

When the others came from Harran, Mir-ri went with them to market to sell the woven mats. It was a magical place with hanging cloth dyed all colours of the rainbow, jewellery of beaten gold and silver fit for a Queen, and spices so strong they made her nose itch just passing by the stalls where they were displayed in tiny wooden boxes with hinged lids.

Mir-ri's uncles gave her tokens to buy small reed baskets of flower petals from the old women near the market gates. They held her up to place them on the carved stone shrines to Shauska, the Mother, giving thanks for those who had survived the crossings and asking blessings for those who suffered. She asked extra blessings for her father, who never laughed any more.

CHAPTER XXVIII

Khalpe (modern day Halab). c 1748-1000BCE.

The ancient city of Aleppo/Khalpe (Halab), Syria's second city after Damascus, nestles in a depression on the bleak, arid Central Plains around 30 miles from the Turkish border . . . The earliest mention of the city was recorded on stone tablets, dating from 2000 BCE, found at Mari, an ancient Mesopotamian city sited on the west bank of the River Euphrates.[xxviii]

As the nights grew longer and the air drier, Mir-ri's family left the city of Carchemish and travelled south through a long descending valley the local people called the Bekka, womb of Shaushka.

"It is good the people honour the life-giving power of the Mother," said Nama, holding Mir-ri's hand as they walked to Khalpe.

Mir-ri was disappointed to find that Khalpe not as grand as Carchemish.

"Is it a good city?" she asked her father.

Itamar seemed surprised by the question. "I was thinking about Harran," he said.

"Was that a good city?" she asked.

He nodded. "You mother liked it."

Mir-ri stroked his hand and wondered if he would learn to smile again in Khalpe. Built around a central hill, the city teemed with life, even if it was less grand than Carchemish.

The people of Khalpe bought the woven mats made by Mir-ri's family, and soon a new house started to sprawl like the one Nama remembered from Arabkha. They heard that the old city had fallen to Hammurabi, and many people praised Itamar for his foresight. He still didn't smile.

"At least the journey was not made for nothing," said Nama.

When Mir-ri was seventeen, she married a man from Khalpe. By the time she was twenty, she had two daughters: Afsana and Inna, who were the only ones in that generation to bear daughters of their own. Afsana and Inna taught their four daughters the mysterious songs passed down to them from their mother and their great-grandmother. They told the story of Mir-ri of Urim and the treasure she carried with her.

Generations passed, and the true nature of Mir-ri's treasure was lost and found many times. The daughters of the daughters of Mir-ri bore daughters of their own. Life continued much as it had for centuries: families living together in the ever-spreading mudbrick house; cooking on the rooftop or under the verandah in the rainy times; sleeping on mats woven by the men, who learned the art from their fathers and their father's fathers.

The women continued the skill of healing, holding to each other through the birthing times, passing the wisdom from mother to daughter, grandmother to granddaughter, aunt to niece. They still sang the morning and evening songs to the great Queen of Heaven, although her name became a distant memory. They learned to read and write, even when it was not customary for girls to do so. And always they told the stories of their ancestors.

War came to Khalpe in the time of Mir-ri's great, great-great-great granddaughters and continued off and on for centuries. Although Khalpe was in the path of the armies, the family stayed in their house and survived. They lost sons to battle and other children to sickness, yet the household continued to grow.

The rulership of Khalpe changed many times, and the family adapted. The men stopped weaving mats and took up leatherwork, tanning hides to craft bridles and saddles for war horses, boots for fighting men, and waterskins that became so popular they employed apprentices to meet the demand. The women shared their gift of healing with those around them, and the ongoing battles did little to alter the daily life of Mir-ri's descendants for five hundred years . . .

Khalpe--Halab--c1000BCE

At the midpoint of the Age of the Ram, there were six daughters in the household: Inna and Mehtap, and their cousins Nama, Afsana, Alika, and Etana . . .

Mehtap ran into the courtyard to find her older sister. Inna would be sewing or reading, hiding away from the noise and bustle of too many cousins and more mothers than anyone needed.

Not there.

Mehtap dashed up the stairs to the flat roof.

"Inna?" she called, looking for the telltale sign of her sister's red shawl hanging out of an alcove or trailing from behind the storage jars in the corner. "Mir-ri has a story."

Inna crawled out from under the grape vine that had taken over one corner of the rooftop. Mehtap waved to her and ran ahead down the stairs and behind the garden wall.

Mir-ri had already started to talk.

Mehtap squeezed between Nama and Afsana and settled down to listen.

"They took the power of the holy Priestess and gave it to the men. Now they make offerings to Shamash for conquest. Such is the way of the Ram." Mehtap looked over her shoulder. If any of the boys heard, they would tell the men, and Mir-ri would be forbidden to tell her stories. Not that Mir-ri would stop, but already it was hard to find a time when all the men were out, the boys chasing each other through someone else's courtyard.

"They say that Shamash knows everything, sees everything, understands everything," said Mir-ri. "And, what's more, they say he can prune a tree as easily as split open a mountain. Do you know what that means?" She looked intently at Mehtap. Alongside Mehtap, Afsana and Nama shook their heads.

"Er . . .that he uses the same thing for all his deeds?" said Alika.

"Perhaps, my child. Perhaps." Mir-ri smiled her gummy smile. "Some men are like that."

"It means that he has forgotten the Law of change," said Mehtap.

Mir-ri nodded. "Go on."

"He makes all certain and permanent, forgetting the cycles of Nature, the cycles of death and birth, birth and death," said Mehtap, pleased with herself.

"They even say he controls the seasons of the year," said Alika, who did not like anyone knowing more than she did.

"And that, my beauties, is obviously not true," said Mir-ri, sending them all off to finish their chores.

Mehtap helped Mir-ri up from the low wall and followed her to the kitchen. It was the best place to be because she could keep whispering questions as she stoked the fire, ground the nuts, cracked the wheat, and mixed the filling for the vegetables. And Mir-ri could whisper the answers to her questions as they made kebab, kibbe, and muhammara, Mir-ri's special paste of hot pepper, pomegranate juice, and ground walnuts. Inna joined them, with questions of her own. They were safe there: the boys would never come close enough to the kitchen to hear the answers Mir-ri whispered to them.

In the kitchen they learned to name the fixed stars and recite the King lists. They learned the words of the morning and evening praises sung to the great Queen of Heaven by the women in their family since the oldest days. Women in Halab might have power--managing the family business, directing workers and slaves--but it was still Shamash they honoured, consort of the God rather than the Queen of Heaven.

When the food was ready, Mehtap and Inna piled a cloth with bread, meat, and stuffed vegetables. They tied the ends and filled a water skin with Mir-ri's lemon drink.

"Remember, Inna," said Mir-ri, "the dealers of Halab can . . ."

"I know," said Inna. "They can even sell dried donkey skins to the ass traders."

"Well, you only know because I've told you," said Mir-ri, patting Inna's arm.

Mehtap kissed Mir-ri's soft cheek and hurried after Inna through the gate and down the winding lane past the other houses. They called to their friends, who called back in the language of Sindhu in the far East and the tongue of Kemet in the South. Temu, the water-carrier's son, ran alongside them to the end of the lane, teaching Mehtap more words from Kemet: nebu (gold); sesen (lotus flower); heka (magic).

The market was still busy at midday, even noisier than the house when all the boys were home. Mehtap's nose tickled with the smells of spices and frying meat, ass dung and incense. She followed Inna through narrow aisles stacked with baskets of red beans and golden grain, mounds of walnuts, and piles of sticky dates.

Baba sat with his waterskins under a woven awning at the East end of the market square. He kissed them both, took his lunch, and left them to watch the stall while he ate with the other men, squatting in a circle under the trees. Women laden with baskets of vegetables stopped to run their hands over the waterskins and haggle over the prices. Inna hung back, but Mehtap stroked the leather and told them how hard her Baba worked to produce such fine quality goods, and how strong the skins were. When her Baba returned, she proudly counted silver tokens for two skins into his hand.

CHAPTER XXIX

Amman, Jordan. Updated Friday May 16th 2015 6.18pm UTC

KABUL, 12 May 2015 (IRIN) - Air pollution in Kabul may be hastening the death of over 3,000 people every year, according to the Ministry of Public Health (MoPH). Epidemiological studies by the MoPH indicate cardiovascular and respiratory diseases resulting from air pollution in Kabul are increasing the country's crude mortality rate by four percent a year. "If we apply the four percent increase in mortality due to air pollution to the population of Kabul, then an extra 3,060 persons may be losing their lives due to air pollution per year," the MoPH said in a statement.

Lili and Paula spent all that day at their computers, following internet pathways through museums, ancient sacred teachings, and myriad references to Abraham. Peter had left after an hour, to do some business, he said, in the souk.

"Do you trust him?" asked Paula. Silly question, really; how could Lili tell any more than she could?

Lili shrugged. "It feels better having him with us," she said. "He reminds me of some of the grad. students who are still in love with the work."

"Aren't you still in love with your work?" asked Paula.

"Since I received the tablet and met you, it's become less of love affair and more of an obsession."

"My fault, is it?" Paula sighed. "But aren't all great love affairs like that?"

"I suppose so, but don't most of them end tragically? That's the problem with obsession; you don't know where it's taking you, and you don't really care."

There wasn't really an answer to that, so Paula went back to scrolling through a remarkable online gallery of Sumerian artifacts.

When the sun dropped low enough that passers-by cast long, moving shadows over the table, they packed up their computers. It was surprisingly tiring searching through the accumulated information of two millennia of human history. They ate at their usual restaurant and went back to their room to Skype home, go over the notes from the day, and eventually settle into dream-filled sleep.

The next morning, Paula's head ached, and pictures moved behind her eyes like almost-images of forgotten dreams. Lili mumbled something about the curse of the Mummy, so she must have had a bad night, too.

They ate breakfast in silence, and left early for the café, carrying their laptops and notes in shoulder bags. Across the road from the café, Paula gasped and grabbed Lili's arm.

"It's him again!" Paula pointed to a dark-haired man in sunglasses, walking slowly past their café.

They watched him until he turned the next corner.

"He could just be a local out for a morning walk," said Lili.

"Sure. And he could be watching us, too."

They crossed to the café, to find Peter already there, reading The Jordan Times and sipping a black coffee. Paula told him about the man.

"Perhaps he lives here," said Peter.

"And follows tourists?" asked Paula.

"Can you really be so sure it was him?" asked Peter.

Lili was unpacking her notes, but she paused to listen.

"I'm sure," said Paula. "It's the same man, and he's watching us."

"Then he will have nothing of interest to report, will he?" said Peter in a calm voice. "Two foreign academics taking up with a known treasure-hunter to look for ancient artifacts. Nothing to suggest anything else. The most that will happen is that some government officials may want to search your luggage before you leave."

Paula gasped, and Lili began busily organising her papers. Peter frowned at them both, but he said nothing.

Ahmed smiled his predator's smile. Long had he watched this Moneghi, the treasure-hunter. Long had he waited for signs of the subversive activity he knew was there. Perhaps now the jackal would reveal himself . . .

Mish's search found countless tales of Abraham, or Father Ibrahim, as he was known in the Arabic world. Apparently the Father of the three faiths had travelled much the same road as the later migrations from northern Mesopotamia.

"Not another Abraham story," said Paula, scrolling through Mish's finds.

"Did you know he was supposed to have been born in Ur?" asked Lili.

"Abraham, as in the Old Testament?" asked Paula, surprised. "Was he Sumerian?"

Lili laughed. "Please! He was Habiru, from the wandering tribes who may have been the forefathers of the Hebrews."

"May have been?" Paula was puzzled. "Don't they know? You'd think with all that emphasis on patriarchal descent, they'd know exactly where the Hebrews came from."

"Yes, but the idea of a chosen people only arose with Jacob, Abraham's grandson. If we believe the stories, the Hebrews were just another tribe before they claimed their special relationship with God. It's hard to sort the facts from the stories that have grown up around it all."

Paula nodded, considering the nearly impossible task of finding out what really happened even a hundred years ago.

"Some accounts say Abraham was born in Ur about four thousand years ago," said Lili. "Like our hypothetical, great-great, a thousand times great, grandmother."

Paula went very still. "You don't suppose . . .?"

"No," said Lili emphatically. "It's all conjecture, anyway. The Abraham of the three faiths was probably just a story arising out of a time of change. It was another new millennium, remember. There might have been a man of that name--although it probably would have been Abram in those days--but most likely the legend of Abraham arose as a focus for the new religion. Abraham's early life became another lesson, a moral tale: being human is not being safe or comfortable, but rather uncertain, like the wandering of the tribes from place to place. All of that sets him up to question, to yearn, to desperately seek answers that the old religions apparently didn't offer. Hence, he was on his way to God all along. It seems more likely that he was a metaphor rather than a man."

Paula persisted with weaving a fantasy about their long-ago ancestors in Ur. "But what if there was a real man, and he had a child with . . ."

"No one would believe you," said Lili. "It's we Jews who are the true descendants of Abraham. We are the Chosen Ones. It would turn Judaism on its head if we discovered that he had fathered yet another line of descendants."

"But don't the Muslims call him Father as well?" asked Paula, wishing she'd paid more attention to the articles on Islam in the media over the years.

Lili nodded. "When Abraham's wife, Sarah, couldn't conceive, she gave him--that's the biblical expression--to her maidservant, an Egyptian woman called Hagar. Hagar had a son, Ishmael, who became the father of the Arab nations. When Sarah finally had a child, that was Isaac, father of Jacob, the line of David and Solomon etcetera."

"Too complicated for me," said Paula. "I still want to know why this lineage we're trying to find couldn't have come from Abraham, whoever he was. It would make sense. The prophecy's about balance. Imagine the balance of a child of Abraham's, metaphor or not, whose descendants didn't go on to develop one of the three faiths."

Lili frowned. "What difference would that make?"

"What if there were daughters?" asked Paula, bubbling with inner excitement.

"But there were daughters, Paula, or at least grand-daughters. Haven't you read *The Red Tent?*" Lili frowned at her, shaking her head. "It's a great idea, but there's nothing to suggest the women carried anything special. The Red Tent is all about the loss of power of the feminine."

Paula nodded; she had read the book when it came out. "Maybe not those daughters, then. What about before Abraham left Ur?"

Lili shrugged. "Maybe. But, as I said, he might not even have been a real person."

Paula pulled a face and returned to her reading, although her fantasy persisted as she read the stories of Abraham's life. Why not daughters as well as sons? Daughters of a mother from ancient Sumer . . .

CHAPTER XXX

Halab to Jerusalem. c 950BCE.

According to the Hebrew Bible, Solomon's Temple, also known as the First Temple, was constructed by Solomon, king of the ancient Israelites, on mount Moriah in Jerusalem. It housed the Ark of the Covenant and functioned as a religious focal point in ancient Judaism for the worship of YHWH.[xxix]

Mehtap and the others were all in the kitchen when Yasuf rushed in from the street.

"Have you heard what they're saying in the lanes?"

Nama and Inna were sitting on the floor, grinding walnuts with the heavy, rolling stone. Mehtap held up the knife with which she had been chopping parsley.

"This had better not be one of your tricks."

Yasuf looked indignant, pouting and rolling his eyes. "Well, there could have been a comet last night."

"But there wasn't," said Mehtap. "And someone might have been hurt running around like that in the dark."

He turned to leave.

"Well, what are they saying in the lanes?" asked Mehtap. Why were little brothers so difficult?

Yasuf spun around, smiling. "The King of Ursalimmu is calling for workers to build his new Temple. It will be the greatest building ever made."

"What does that have to do with us?" asked Inna.

"We are not even his people," said Mehtap, running through the King lists in her head. The ruler of Canaan was not mentioned.

"That is true, little one," said her Baba from the doorway. "But Yasuf has the right of it. The great Sulaman has invited skilled workers from Halab and the Northern cities to come to Ursalimmu. There are riches to be had."

He made way for the other men, all three of them aglow with excitement. The women hurried in from the storeroom.

"But you are not builders." Enananta and Ashura spoke together, echoing each other's thoughts as twins often did. "We cannot go to Ursalimmu. What do you say, Harika?"

Mehtap turned to her mother. Would she agree with her sisters?

Her mother was looking thoughtfully at Baba.

"We could make enough in one season to double the flock," he said.

"What would you do there?" asked Ashura. "None of you are skilled at carpentry or masonry."

"Water will be needed, and waterskins. Look at the size of the purse carried by Temu's father."

Everyone spoke at once, and the room became as rowdy as the market place. Mir-ri reached out for Mehtap's hand.

"You mother will do what is right," she whispered.

Mehtap squeezed her grandmother's hand as the arguments flew around the room. Would life in Ursalimmu be as good as life in Halab?

By the time the family sat down to eat that night, the men had planned how they would be spending the silver they would earn in Ursalimmu. The women were still arguing, but now it was about which one of them would go with the men to see that they were fed and their clothes mended.

Mehtap stopped breathing when her mother said she would go.

"My children are older," she said. "They will travel more easily."

Mehtap sucked in a breath of air. Tingles rushed up her arms. Never had she been further than the villages on the outskirts of Halab, and now she would be seeing Ursalimmu. Inna and Yasuf ran over, laughing.

"Teach us to speak like Temu," said Yasuf. "We are going to the South."

"But Ursalimmu is not in Kemet," said Mehtap, who had once seen a map drawn in the sand.

"It is not," said Baba. "But the trade road runs to Kemet, and I have heard that the market at Ursalimmu is a wonder."

Mehtap's excitement dimmed some nights later when her aunts, Enananta and Asuhra, called the family together for a meeting on the rooftop. With three courtyards, the rooftop was seldom used, and Grandmother Mir-ri grumbled about the size of the grape vine and the dried leaves that had piled up.

Enananta spoke first, in the serious voice she used when she was certain that she knew better than her sisters. She spoke directly to Mehtap's mother.

"The children will be better here in Halab with us. You and Azhar will have enough to do without caring for them."

Mehtap grabbed Inna's arm. They were perched with all the other children in the spreading branches of the acacia that grew alongside the rambling house. The leaves rustled, but only Grandmother Mir-ri looked up.

Mehtap glared down at Enananta. How dare she tell their mother what to do.

One branch over, Yasuf snorted in disgust. It sounded enough like a tree frog that no one seemed to notice.

"They are mine to protect," said Mehtap's mother. "And you know this."

Mehtap wanted to hug her. Her father stood quietly with Dekel and Feroz, neither of whom would dare speak against their wives.

"But it will be dangerous on the road," said Ashura. Enananta nodded in agreement.

Mehtap's mother raised her voice. "The children come with us."

Before Enananta could speak again, Mir-ri stepped forward.

"Enough, my daughters. Never have the women in our family left their children while they live and breathe. You know this. It is a sacred task to bear children and tend them. Let it be, Enananta. The children will travel with Harika."

Enananta looked to her husband for support, but he was carefully engrossed in a conversation with Baba and Feroz. She threw up her hands and left. Ashura followed her.

Mehtap smiled across at Inna. Yasuf grabbed her foot and shook it so hard the leaves rustled like cicada wings.

They left through the South gate with five asses and a cart pulled by another two. Grandmother Mir-ri rode proudly in the cart, waving to everyone she passed. Some waved back, although it seemed that half the city was also on the move. Word of Sulaman's wealth had set Halab buzzing like a hive.

Mehtap took turns with Inna and Yasuf to sit in the cart with their grandmother. As the days turned into weeks, they all learned to hold the reins and manage the asses. Not that the asses needed any real tending, plodding obediently along behind the riders.

So eager were the men to arrive that they bypassed Kadesh, making straight for the coast.

Never having seen the Sea, Mehtap didn't know what to expect. By the time they reached Hamath on the Axius river, they had told and retold all the old tales.

"It is said to be bitter like tears," said Mehtap. "Perhaps it will be a sad place."

"It is only salt," said Yasuf.

"It reaches all the way into the West," said Inna. "To the land of the Dead."

"Well, that is sad then," said Mehtap, remembering the death of grandfather Kivil only last season. She had been the one who sat by his side, singing him songs and telling him stories when he became too weak to leave the house.

"The Sea is the birthplace of life," said Grandmother Mir-ri, in the voice she used for storytelling. "In the oldest of old tales, life began in the waters. It was in the Abzu, the ancient Sea, that Nammu, the mother, gave birth to An, the Sky, and Ki, the Earth. Once, long, long ago, at the beginning of time, An and Ki were one. Together they moved in the Sea. Together they would have remained for all time but for the Chance that lives in Chaos. From Chaos comes the night, from the boundless empty space comes the power of Nature."

Mehtap was entranced by her grandmother's words, intrigued by the story that seemed even older than the ancient tales she usually told them.

"From the empty space came a spark that gave rise to a wind that blew between An and Ki, driving them apart. Curling into a sphere, Ki formed the solid matter on which we stand. Spreading wide, An formed the vault of the Sky above. The space between they filled with their children, first the Annunaki, the beloved of the above and the below."

"Are they the Great Ones?" asked Mehtap, never having heard of Annunaki before.

"They are indeed." Mir-ri nodded her head. "My grandmother told me the same story I am telling you." She was quiet for a moment. "I wonder what she would say to see me on my way to the land of Canaan."

From Hamath they turned towards the coast, crossing the rolling hills to the road that would take them South. It also took them away from the road to Damaski, home of warrior-princes and rich merchants.

"Why can't we go to Damaski?" asked Yasuf, who had heard the ass traders talking about the city. They said it rose suddenly from the desert, beckoning like a bejeweled woman. Yasuf thought that a wonder worth seeing.

"We are not going to Damaski," said Baba, "because it is too easy to spend silver there."

The coast road took the easiest way South, revealing only a few glimpses of the Sea, winding mostly between low, rolling hills before veering inland to Ursalimmu. One night they camped close enough to the shore to hear the constant murmuring of the waves, and Mehtap heard sirens singing in the darkest hours before dawn. When she told the others, Yasuf just rolled his eyes, but Inna looked thoughtful.

Sulaman's great city of Ursalimmu lay three days from the Sea and did not appear like a jewel in the desert. It sat atop a rise in the rocky plateau with no easy road to the gates.

"It would have been better to follow the trade road," said Feroz, grumbling as he helped Baba and Dekel push the cart up yet another hill.

"This is the old way," said Baba, stopping to wipe sweat from his eyes. "Ursalimmu wasn't always on the trade road. If not for Sulaman's father, there would be no city here, just a few houses."

"Tell us, Baba. Tell us," said Mehtap.

Baba smiled. "Once, not one hundred years past, Ursalimmu was a town with only ten houses and a small wall."

Mehtap leaned against Inna as Baba's voice settled into the rhythm of storytelling.

"Far from the trade road, Ursalimmu slumbered. Children were born, grew to have children of their own, and died old and happy. Nothing changed for a very long time. The Kings of Kemet collected tribute from the town, but the Habiru wanted it as their own."

"Why?" asked Mehtap and Yasuf.

Baba shrugged. "I have not heard why they wanted it. Perhaps we shall see."

"It is very hilly," said Yasuf, who had been given the task of pulling the lead reins when the asses balked at climbing a slope.

"Go on, Baba," said Mehtap.

"Perhaps it was the spring. In the valley below the city is a spring that never runs dry. The water is said to be sweeter than the Buranun."

"No!" said everyone.

"Well, it would explain why Sulaman's father took the town and built himself a palace."

"How did he take it?" asked Yasuf.

"Is that the palace they are building now?" asked Mehtap.

"How far now?" asked Inna.

Baba laughed. "I have heard that he entered the city through the channel that ran from the spring. It was a wonder in itself, running up from the valley so the townsfolk did not have to leave the walls to fill their jugs. And it is a different palace; the son must build something that outshines the father. You will see for yourselves by nightfall."

Yasuf let out a mighty hurrah that spurred the asses on to the top of the hill. Inna and Mehtap clasped hands and danced around and around, laughing and singing an old song about journey's end. Their mother looked happy as she gave them food for the last league to Ursalimmu.

Baba had spoken true: as the Sun settled in the West, they crested the final hill. By the time they reached the city walls, they were jostled by crowds of newcomers. Inna, Mehtap and Yasuf rode on the wagon with Grandmother Mir-ri. The cart was moving so slowly that the asses did not even notice the extra load. Their long ears twitched and their nostrils flared at the sounds and smells. Some of the travellers looked hungry and dirty, and everywhere animals milled around. Even Yasuf wrinkled his nose.

"Why did they bring their goats?" asked Inna, staring around.

"For milk and food," said Mir-ri. "Not all are assured of work. Be thankful that your Baba and your uncles carry their own work with them."

Then they were through the gate, and all thoughts of goats vanished. At that moment the Sun, in a last blaze of radiance for the day, illuminated the topmost columns of the palace crowning the hill ahead of them. Every man, woman and child in the square looked up. And forgot to take the next breath as the palace glowed golden.

Mehtap was certain that it was a sign, although of what she had no idea.

They finally found an empty place between two buildings to cook the evening meal and lay out their sleeping mats.

"What is that smell?" said Yasuf

"Which one?" said Mehtap. "I have smelled more things since we arrived than in my whole life. I was just trying to count them."

"It is the tannery," said their uncle Dekel. "They use milk, eggs, and urine to work the skins."

They all turned to stare at him. "I smelled it once before. Up North. They use it to cure the skin like we do at home. Just more of it."

"Er . . .whose urine is it?" asked Yasuf.

"Why don't you go in and ask them in the morning," suggested Baba.

Mehtap and Inna giggled. They really were in Ursalimmu.

The stars shone down into the alley where they lay on their mats for their first night.

CHAPTER XXXI

Amman, Jordan. Updated May 17th 2015 3.23am UTC

A massive earthquake in the Indian Ocean has triggered sea surges and the deaths of thousands of people.

By the fourth day of their research, Paula and Lili were both restless. They knew considerably more about the migration patterns of the Sumerians and their descendants and, thanks to Mish, they had gathered an impressive collection of myths, legends, and folktales. Unfortunately, none of it--other than Paula's find from Arabkha--helped them directly.

Peter had also made enquiries about the *me* using his usual contacts, but there had been no response.

"It's too soon to know," he said, in answer to Lili's questions. "Sometimes I have waited years for a lead. I have let the usual suspects know there is a buyer interested in the Sumerian artifacts. We may hear nothing, or we may receive some interesting offers. You never know."

256

Lili scowled and went back to her computer. She checked her emails from Mish and returned to the stories from Jerusalem. She was up to around 1000BCE.

"Eureka!" she cried, making Peter jump.

"What?" asked Paula, peering over her shoulder.

"A story from Jerusalem. And it's about the Queen of Sheba."

"You're kidding," said Paula.

"It says the Queen came to visit Solomon bearing treasures from the ancient world. Gold and precious stones, stone carvings and . . .wait for it . . .sacred measures.".

"Huh?" said Paula, completely lost.

Peter looked confused.

"Sacred measures. Sacred *me*," said Lili, bouncing up and down with excitement

"Did you just make that up?" asked Paula, frowning at her.

"I did not," said Lili. "It's another name for the *me*. You see it in the literature all the time."

"Sounds familiar," said Peter, scratching his chin.

"It might be the Queen, Lili. Your mother's Queen. It might be her gift."

"I think I might be missing something here," said Peter, frowning suspiciously at them both.

CHAPTER XXXII
Saba to Ursalimmu. c950 BCE.

In a brief, unelaborated, and enigmatic passage, the Hebrew Bible describes how the fame of Solomon's wisdom and wealth spread far and wide, so much so that the queen of Sheba decided that she should meet him. The queen is described as visiting with a number of gifts including gold and rare jewels to decorate the temple, and also bringing with her a number of riddles. When Solomon gave her "all her desire, whatsoever she asked," she left satisfied (1 Kings 10:10).

Makeda, the Shebu, shaded her eyes with a jewel-laden hand that glinted in the afternoon Sun. She wore the rings to symbolise obedience to the four elements of Air, Fire, Water, and Earth, to the four directions of East, West, North, and South, and to the Sun and Moon.

Gold threads in her silk robes also caught the light, adding an even brighter aura to the nimbus of power surrounding her. She loosened the cloth from her head, shaking out her hair.

Coiled all day, the curling strands leapt around her face and snaked down her back, as if rejoicing in their freedom. As Makeda stretched, a deep sigh escaped her lips despite her intention to show none of her fatigue to the everpresent retinue. She wondered why she had thought it a splendid thing to ride the length of the Sea to meet the Northern King. It had been his reputation for wisdom that had lured her away from the cool fountains and sweet songbirds of her Southern home, but that seemed a small thing after so long on the road.

As if sensing her tiredness, a horn sounded the end of the day's ride. Seven hundred and ninety-seven mules, camels, and asses slowed to a shuffle. The size of the caravan befitted a Queen and also made it possible for a significant number of Makeda's people to have made this momentous journey with her. She may have been seeking wisdom, but the people of Saba were expecting their Queen to make yet another conquest.

Strung together by ropes of goat hair, even the camels were becoming weary. The mother camels moved slowly to nuzzle their babies. Born along the way, the babies were carried on the back of the camel ahead to assure the mothers of their wellbeing.

Carried aloft by twelve asses, a large white-draped palanquin swayed gently to rest. Unlikely boat of the desert, the palanquin housed Makeda's handmaidens and her two daughters. Children of different fathers, men chosen by the Shebu for a night or a season as was the custom, the girls, nine and six years old, had not yet shown any of their mother's inclination to ride camels and ruin their fine skin in the Sun and wind.

Alesha, older and therefore superior, nudged her sister awake as the palanquin stopped. Chanu grumbled, tucking her head further under the cushions where she had sought shelter from the incessant chatter of the women moaning about the sand-laden winds.

When they thought both girls asleep, the serving women complained about the Shebu's vision that had them tossed to and fro all day rather than living in the comfort of the Palace. If Alesha had heard them, she would have scolded and threatened to report them to her mother. Chanu, who did hear them, merely noted who said what and wondered at the need for comfort that drove most people. She was more like her mother than anyone had yet realised.

Makeda was different from other women. Beloved of her people, she was revered for her courage and spirit; that she refused to spend her days swathed in the finest silk was no more than they expected of the Shebu. Even the complaining handmaidens expected no less as they nibbled dates and sipped sweet drinks. That Makeda rode free on her distinctive white camel gladdened the hearts of her people, lifting their spirits on this endless journey.

The caravan halted in swirling clouds of golden desert sand. Makeda smiled the secret, soft smile that had inspired thirteen poems and five songs in the season before she left on the journey to which Astarte had called her.

Astarte, called Shayba in the old tongue, watched over women. She was the Moon, everchanging, looking down from the Heavens as maiden, mother, and old woman. She held the mysteries of life and death with her consort, Ilmukah, who rode a crescent moonboat across the sky, dispersing evil and darkness, sending dreams and prophecies. Makeda's dreams, however, always came from Astarte. Giver and destroyer of life, Astarte was Mother of all. Arriving from heaven as a ball of fire and accompanied by a lioness, she always appeared to Makeda with the crescent moon above her forehead.

Touching the ring she wore to honour Astarte, the Shebu motioned for her camel to lower her to the ground.

Asses milled around seeking food. Bedecked with wooden saddles covered in bright cloth sewn with lapis lazuli and malachite, dripping with silver bells and medallions, the camels shone in the last of the Sun's light, even as they would tinkle and chime in the dark of night. The asses were less resplendent; filled with the indignity of their inferior stature, they brayed and whickered, kicked and nipped.

As the tents were being pitched on a rise overlooking a valley that promised easier riding, Makeda walked among her people, greeting many by name, asking after their health and the health of their camels and children. That children travelled with them was a sign that they came to Ursalimmu in peace, a sign of goodwill that Makeda hoped the great King Sulaman could not ignore. She had heard from Tamrin, leader of her trade caravans, and now leader of this expedition winding along the shore of the Sea, that the great King was renown for wisdom and justice.

Makeda had first heard Tamrin speak of Sulaman one night as she sat sipping the sweet wine he had brought from the North along with silk and medicines traded for the spices, precious stones, and woven cloth of Saba. Tamrin was not only the leader of her trade caravans, he was friend to the Shebu. Which is why he had tried to dissuade her from making the journey North.

Tamrin knew the Shebu's pride and curiosity, her intelligence and her courage; had she not brought all of the tribes under one rule? Had she not faced down the enemy herself, winning him to her cause with the power of her will? Had she not written new laws for the whole land? Had she not asked him for tablets and papyri from the whole world for her library? Philosophy and medicine, astronomy and mathematics, King lists and Priest lists. And the questions! Endless questions about his travels on the trade roads, about the markets and the other traders, about the rulers of each city, the disposition of their armies, and the thickness of their walls. Questions befitting a ruler of men. But he did not believe that the Northern King had anything to offer, despite his reputation for wisdom. Tamrin had lived too long under the rule of a truly wise leader, and had seen too much of Ursalimmu to believe it would benefit Makeda to travel North. Yet she had dreamed it. If not for the women and children who travelled with them, Tamrin might believe she was going North for conquest.

As it happened, that is exactly what Makeda intended, although not with strength of arms. As was often said about her, she ruled with the head and hands of a man but the heart of a woman. The Shebu was seeking a father for her next child. Had she not spurned over forty suitors this last year alone? She longed to find a man with at least as much pride, curiosity, intelligence, and courage as herself. The trader's tales from the North promised as much in the Sulaman, even if the great King was said to be beloved of the One supreme being, all knowing, all powerful, and present in all. Makeda smiled her secret smile at the thought of such delusions.

Days and nights passed, and the whole caravan moved slowly Northward like a giant snake woken from a mythic slumber to stir up dust and draw the winds from the desert. The swaying walk of her camel soothed Makeda, reminding her of the dreams that had called her to the trade roads. Power and riches could not satisfy her soul; it was truth and wisdom she desired above all else.[xxx]

When Makeda roused from the reverie, she thought about where she was going, what she was seeking. Golden walls and a dark-eyed man with a handsome face and generous mouth. This she had seen in her dreams. And a child. Not the son she already knew she would make with the Northern king, but a girl, no older than her own daughters. Tousle-haired and lively, intelligence shining from her eyes, the girl ran and skipped through Makeda's dreams.

What did she need with this dream girl? Already there were two daughters to carry on the unbroken line of mothers and daughters that sustained the land of Saba, her fields, her people, her wide, blue skies. Makeda shrugged. It was not for her to know all the mysteries; the girl would come or she wouldn't, and then she would see.

There was no such uncertainty about the son she had foreseen. How could her time with the Northern king not bring a son? Sulaman was a son of Kings, fathers and sons carrying power bestowed, they claimed, from a supreme being. Makeda smiled. How men postured and proclaimed, how they desired sovereignty, when it was the mother from whom all life came, and the mother whose arms received Her children when life was done. Makeda shook her head, her black, oiled hair heavy in the brooding heat. Women were the life-givers, and so men like the Northern king claimed all else. Well, soon she would see this King for herself.

Six months after leaving her home, Makeda entered Ursalimmu through the Southern gate just as Inna, Mehtap and Yasuf arrived with their family from the North. While the children slept in the malodorous lane, Makeda slept in a carved bed surrounded by the wonders of Sulaman's palace. She had not yet seen the King, but she had been made welcome by the

High Priest even while the long line of camels and asses was still entering the city.

CHAPTER XXXIII

Ursalimmu. c 950 BCE.

Sheba (Ar. Sabā') was the most important kingdom in ancient southern Arabia with its capital Mārib (in inscriptions: Mayrab, east of San'a), the largest city in that area. This kingdom existed from the beginning of South Arabian civilization, and the oldest stone inscription dates back to the eighth century BCE . . .Owing to the frankincense and many other spices exported to ancient lands, Sheba was quite known in the classical world, and its country was called Arabia Felix.[xxxi]

Ursalimmu was strangely quiet for a thriving city. Apart from the steady stream of new arrivals, the streets were almost empty, except for a few people hurrying to the South walls.

"What is it, Baba?" asked Mehtap. "Where are they going?"

Her father shrugged and asked a man in the street.

The man answered as he hurried away. "The biggest caravan you've ever seen, still coming in from the South."

"Good for us, then," said Baba. "Everyone will be on the South wall for hours."

"Will we see it, Baba?" asked Yasuf, jumping up and down.

Baba shook his head. "Better we find a place to stay while the streets are quiet."

They did not see the caravan, but they heard the echoes of speculation that filled the city. Who had arrived amid so much wealth? Had anyone seen who rode in the palanquin? Was it one of the conquered rulers come to make tribute? Was it a wife for the King?

The family left the lane where they had camped for the night, and Mehtap and Yasuf ran ahead. Would they see someone from the mysterious caravan?

They were headed for the marketplace in the Eastern quarter, where they hoped to find others from Halab. The tannery smells gave way to market smells: ass dung, cooked meat, spices, and sweat. Baba led the way to a small lane between two squat storage sheds.

"Stay here and watch the asses," said Harika firmly, looking each of the children in the eye to ensure obedience.

They all nodded, meeting their mother's eyes. They had no intention of leaving the lane that sheltered them from the crush of asses and people laden with market goods; they had already been jostled and bumped by bunches of dates, trampled by goats, hissed at by geese, and pecked by ducks. And the deafening cacophony of bleating, squawking, and yelling made their heads spin.

Nor would they have left the lane except that Mehtap spotted something on the ground, kicked to and fro by heedless, rushing feet. It sparkled in the sunlight, flashing red and blue. Yasuf saw it as well, and the two of them set off together to retrieve the bauble. Inna yelled for them to stop, but her cries were lost in the hubbub around them.

Not to be beaten to her prize, Mehtap pushed Yasuf aside and ran out of the lane like a whirlwind . . .

. . .straight into someone tall, thin, and wrapped in a long robe.

Mehtap and the robed figure wobbled, spun around, and fell to the ground in a tangle of fabric and limbs, Mehtap waving her arms in the air like a trapped bug. The hapless figure underneath her moaned and heaved like an ass trying to throw its rider.

Yasuf, a step behind, leapt over the heaving mass. He nearly cleared the jumble of arms and legs, but his foot caught on Mehtap's arm, and he fell heavily onto the hard-packed earth.

He scrambled to his feet, both hands over his nose. Blood seeped through his fingers, dripped down the front of his tunic, and landed like liquid rubies on the white robe of the person still struggling under Mehtap.

Inna grabbed Mehtap's leg and pulled her off the unfortunate stranger. The stranger sat up gracefully and looked at them.

Mehtap, sitting on the ground by Inna's feet, was shocked to see a face darker even than Temu's, her friend from Kemet. Then the stranger lunged forward and grabbed her arm. Mehtap shrieked and scrabbled back behind Inna.

"You!" cried the stranger, reaching again for Mehtap.

Inna tapped Mehtap on the head. "Apologise!"

"I . . .I am very sorry for running into you," said Mehtap. "And for pushing you over. And for landing on you."

The stranger rose from the ground in one sinuous movement. She was tall, with black hair cascading down her back like snakes. On her fingers were more rings than Mehtap had ever seen on one person.

"Are you hurt, child?" asked the woman, voice resonant with strange music.

Mehtap shook her head. Her left ankle ached where Inna had pulled her, and she had grazed her right elbow, but she wasn't about to tell that to the tall woman.

"And your brother?" asked the woman, extending a hand to Yasuf, whose nose seemed to be intact despite the slow ooze of blood.

Yasuf stared at the woman's hand if it were a snake coiled to strike. Inna grabbed Yasuf's collar and dragged him out of harm's way. He hid behind her and peered out from under her arm.

Inna glared at the woman. "They meant no harm," she said, licking her lips. "They are children and new to the city."

Mehtap squeezed Inna's hand; no one ever had a braver sister.

The woman smiled. "I, too, am new to this city," she said. "I am not hurt, but I would like to sit and rest."

Inna gestured towards the pile of baskets in the lane.

The woman nodded regally and glided past the asses to sit straight-backed on the most solid basket.

"Will you have a drink?" Inna offered the water jug. "It is only water."

The woman took the jug and sipped the water. "You are kind."

Mehtap stayed behind Inna, Yasuf beside her, watching their visitor.

The woman spoke oddly, but she held herself proudly, and her robes, ruined now by dust and blood, were of the finest silk.

"My name is Makeda," said the woman. "I am from the South."

"The caravan!" said Yasuf, curiosity overcoming his fear.

Makeda nodded.

"But you are here in the city alone," said Inna.

Makeda smiled again. "I wished to see the great city of Ursalimmu before I met the King."

Mehtap wondered what Makeda thought of the back lanes of the city, so different from the Palace.

"But you must be staying in the Palace," said Yasuf, as if he had just noticed the stranger's jewellery and fine clothes.

Makeda nodded. "Indeed. It is a fine Palace. But a King is only as great as the least of his people. Or so it is taught in the South."

"Are you a King?" asked Yasuf.

"I am a Queen. Shebu in my land."

Inna and Mehtap gasped. A Queen!

"I am still only a person. A person who is interested in how people live in the lands of Sulaman."

"But you could take us as slaves or kill us," said Jasuf.

"Why would I do that?" Makeda raised her eyebrows as if surprised.

"Many have been taken as slaves to build the Temple in Ursalimmu, even some from the North," said Inna. "They are taken if they have debts or there is other trouble. Our father says the Elders are angry at the taxes. Many are hungry."

Makeda nodded, frowning. "Your family?" she asked, concern in her voice.

Inna shook her head. "Our father sells waterskins. He is here to earn silver. We are not slaves."

"I am pleased that is so," said Makeda, as if it really mattered to her.

By the time Harika and Mir-ri hurried into the lane, Inna, Mehtap and Yasuf were sitting cross-legged on the ground listening to tales from the Southern lands.

Harika ran up to the children, her face creased with worry. She stopped when she saw their faces and the manner of the stranger.

Mehtap helped her sister explain the chance meeting with their wondrous guest.

"You are welcome," said Harika to Makeda, as if the lane were the courtyard of her home with lamps lit for the afternoon. The words were the age-old words said to guests, and she was not one to hold them back because she had no home.

Makeda smiled. "I thank you."

Mir-ri set up the cooking frame, using the last of the dried dung they had carried as fuel. She heated a clay pot of tea and handed the first bowl to their guest.

Cupping the bowl, Makeda inhaled the steam. "What do you call this?"

"It is tea from the mountains in the East. Good for new beginnings," Mir-ri answered. She went on to explain the other virtues of the hot drink.

Mehtap smiled; her grandmother could talk endlessly about tea, food, and medicinal herbs.

"You do not have tea in the South?" asked Harika.

"We drink bunna," said Makeda. "Do you know it?"

They all shook their heads.

"Then I shall invite you all for bunna," announced Makeda, as if it was natural for a Queen to befriend homeless travellers. "I have not yet seen the King. He will see me soon, but I will always have time for friends."

By the time the men returned with heavier purses and a lighter load of waterskins, the visit had been arranged.

Makeda was thoughtful as she left the lane. That she had found the child from her dreams did not surprise her, familiar as she was with portents and magic. She did, however, wonder what it might mean. Mehtap . . .a name from Kemet.

The meaning would either be revealed or it would not.

Makeda turned her thoughts to Ursalimmu. She was glad to have seen the city beyond the Palace.

"Learn from your people," her mother, Isemenie, Shebu before her, had taught. "Walk among them. Speak with them. Listen. Look. Feel them in your bones."

Her mother's wisdom had always served her well, yet Makeda feared that it may not suffice for this meeting with Sulaman. What did the Great Ones want by calling her to Ursalimmu? What could she gain from meeting with a man who took slaves, who divided his land for the sake of a temple?

She entered the Palace as she had left, slipping through the courtyards and the small side door like a serving woman, head bent, hurrying about her tasks. She would have regained the guest rooms with no one knowing of her excursion had not a man stepped through a doorway directly in her path.

If he had lingered a moment longer with the woman who lay sleeping amidst scattered pillows and silken bedcovers, he would not have met the woman hurrying in from the courtyard. If she had walked more slowly or more swiftly from the lane, she would not have seen him leaving his afternoon pleasure.

Makeda's nostrils flared at the familiar smell of sweat and sex, and she moved to brush past, looking only at the man's sandalled feet.

A strong arm blocked her way. "Why are you wandering here?"

The voice was deep, with nuances that should have warned her, but Makeda was not accustomed to being questioned. With a movement quicker than a snake striking, she drew a slender blade from her sleeve and held it to the man's throat.

His heavy-lidded eyes widened, but his arm held firm.

"You are a stranger here."

Now Makeda heard the cultured tones, the command in the voice. Her hand held steady.

"I am a guest. Is it customary for guests to be accosted here?"

"It is not customary for guests to roam these hallways."

"I am not a customary guest." Makeda spoke very slowly, pausing between each word.

He frowned. The lines added a pensive beauty to his sensuous features. He searched her face as if she was a puzzle for which he had no answer.

"Your name," he asked courteously, moving his head slightly as if to reassure her. His dark curls fell forward to frame liquid eyes, a strong hooked nose, and lips still swollen from kissing and biting.

Makeda's body began to hum, a deep vibration in her very bones. Suddenly she knew who this must be. A smile tugged at the corners of her mouth. This was not the way she had foreseen their meeting; in her dreams, sleeping and waking, they met in a great hall with stone columns and crimson floor coverings. He sat on a dais flanked by golden lions, and peacocks fanned the air with luminous tails. Lutes played and smoke from incense curled lazily in the air. In her vision, he stood as he saw her, body trembling with desire, and she mounted the dais to stand beside him.

With a shrug at her own folly, Makeda let the smile blossom into fullness and looked into the King's eyes.

Time, ever fascinated by the random encounters of men and women, slowed. Breath slowed, as if the air, too, were enchanted. A muscle twitched on his cheek. It was so quiet that it seemed the whole Palace had fallen into Time's trap.

Even while Makeda drank in the face before her, she remembered a tale told by her grandmother.

Beshu, one of the Great Ones, one of the very first great Ones, watched over the land. He watched over men and women, flowers, birds, and lions. While Beshu watched, Shebu, his sister-wife, grew big with new life. In Time she gave birth to the Great Ones who inhabited every living thing: sand and trees and wind, animals and birds and reptiles. At the beginning of Time, Beshu and Shebu had laughed together, dancing across the land, making love. Now Beshu turned more and more to his watching, to contemplation of all they had made. Less and less did he laugh and dance and make love with Shebu. She spoke with him, reminding him of the thousand, thousand years of their lovemaking. He nodded once before returning to his contemplation. She sighed, kissed his forehead and left. Shebu wandered, seeking something in the waters, on the wind, in the bright light of the Sun. After a thousand years, as she walked by the shore of the Great Sea, a man appeared. It seemed to Shebu that he appeared at that moment, as if he had never existed before. The man, whose name is not told, knew his moments in Time. He walked by the Sea to calm the agitation that, even in the beginning, was the torment of mortals. Their eyes met. Time slowed, paused, waiting. He saw such beauty and grace shining from Shebu's eyes that his heart opened to receive her. Shebu saw the companion for whom she longed, and her heart opened to receive him. Thus did she learn the true nature of mortal life, with joys intense and fleeting, sorrows deep and lasting. Thus did she become the very first Shebu of the land of Saba.

Makeda sent a silent prayer to her many times great grandmother as she felt her heart open to receive the man standing before her.

Sulaman, fresh from the sweet pleasures of lovemaking, was surprised to feel his body stirring again with desire. He was even more surprised to feel his heart open to receive the woman standing before him. He had long since stopped seeking more than momentary pleasure with women, and even that was frowned upon by the Priests. Man's true home, they taught, was not here in the mortal body, but in the Heavenly realm with El. Was he not building a Temple in recognition of this? Was he not honouring El, all-powerful, all-knowing, ever-present? Was he not making the most magnificent, most golden Temple ever built? Yet Sulaman still felt the desires, the joys and sorrows of his bodily existence. He may have been the son of great men, of men beloved of El 'Loam, but he knew in his heart of hearts that he had failed them. Perhaps the Temple would redeem him in the eyes of his forefathers, the eyes of El 'Elyon. Perhaps.

Or perhaps he could lose himself in the black eyes of the remarkable woman before him.

"My name is Makeda," she said in a voice from his dreams. "I am Shebu of Saba in the far South. It is my caravan that has entered your city. It is I who come to meet Sulaman."

The formal meeting of Sulaman and Makeda came about much as she had imagined.

He received her in his colonnaded hall, complete with golden lions, strutting peacocks, and lute music. She made her way slowly through three large, pillared halls, built of cedar and cypress, ornamented with carved ivory, gold, and sandalwood, hung with draperies of crimson and purple silk. Sulaman sat on his great ivory throne with golden armrests and golden embroidery. She mounted the steps to stand before him. He rose and took her hand, greeting her as an equal.

Thus it was remembered by those who saw the spectacle and recorded it for posterity in word and image. No one knew that the King and the Shebu had met three days earlier in the hallway, had come together that night and the night after and the night after that. No one knew that their son had been conceived in those early days.

Only the Priests dared object to the Southern Queen, and Sulaman was building them a Temple.

"Come," said Sulaman once they had satisfied the formalities. "I will show you the resting place of my forefather, Ibrahim, he who was beloved of El 'Elyon." He smiled, his eyes alight with newfound enthusiasm.

Makeda returned his smile, truly feeling a love for this man despite the misgivings she had about his kingship. These she had not yet spoken to him, but she knew the time must come when she named her truth. She did not know what he would do. They had played with words, with riddles and conundrums, testing each other's minds as they tested each other's bodies, yet she did not know how this son of illustrious fathers would respond to rebuke.

They walked together with ten of his people and six of hers through the gardens to the cave upon the hill, the burial place holy to the people of Ursalimmu. Mindful of the sacred wherever she found it, Makeda bowed low with Sulaman and knelt in prayer, although this El was not one of the Great Ones of her people.

"I kneel before father Ibrahim. To him spoke El 'Loam, the Everlasting One. To him spoke El 'Elyon, the One most High. To him spoke El Shaddai, the One of the Mountains. To him spoke El Ro'i, the One of Vision." Sulaman spoke the sacred words and then was quiet, head bowed, hands clasped before his chest.

Makeda watched him from the corner of her eye, mirroring his movements. She wondered if this El was like Beshu, absorbed in contemplation, so quiet were the prayers offered up by the devout.

Finally Sulaman rose, the signal for the others to straighten aching legs and stretch cramped muscles. He took Makeda's arm and showed her the view of the city from the hill of the cave.

"From Ibrahim we have duration, power, and knowledge. He was the friend of the almighty One, and he alone received the promise, the Covenant, sealed by sacrifice." Sulaman looked into the distance as he spoke, chest swelling with the pride of his heritage.

Makeda was quiet. She knew of sacrifice. In the days of her own ancestors, there had been sacrifices to the Serpent of Time, the great snake who circled the world, who existed before the world began and who would rise to signal the end. If she had lived a thousand years earlier it may have been her Fate to meet the Serpent. But now Fate had brought her to meet a King.

As they walked back to the palace, Makeda spoke quietly to Sulaman. "Is this El male or female?"

Sulaman frowned. "El just is."

"All the Great Ones hold either the male or female principles," insisted Makeda, remembering her study in the Temples of her homeland. "We are their children."

"El is beyond the Great Ones." Sulaman spoke the words of the Priests, the words of his father and the fathers before him.

Makeda pursed her lips. She was a visitor in this city, but all her life she had spoken truth.

"There is great presumption in claiming sovereignty over all."

Sulaman stopped walking. "I am not sure I heard you correctly," he murmured, not meeting her eyes.

"Perhaps you wish you had not heard me," she suggested.

Sulaman walked on.

They spoke of other things as they walked back through the gardens where Sulaman had planted olive, spice and nut trees. He showed Makeda the well-ordered vineyards and picked grapes himself for her to eat. At the Palace, they were greeted by a retinue of officials waiting to consult the King. Sulaman excused himself to attend to the endless task of administering the city. Makeda watched his purple robes disappear through an arched doorway. She noted that all the officials had been men.

That night she tested Sulaman. Armed with philosophy, mathematics, astronomy, and a woman's heart, she tested him with questions about peace and war, the meaning of life, about his thoughts on evil, the secrets of death and immortality, the relationship between spirit and body, sexuality, male/female differences, the role of women, the reliability of paternity as a basis for an economic system, the cycles of the moon and tides, and the name and nature of that which is greater than mortal men and women. She posed riddles and conundrums set by her own teachers, and some she had devised herself as her camel carried her Northward. She asked and he answered until both paused for breath. All the while, the scribes wrote, the letters forming across the scroll from right to left, like the tracks of exotic creatures with inky feet.

Makeda wondered how the questions and answers would sound in a hundred years, or a thousand.

In the morning, she left for her rooms to prepare for her guests; the children from the lane were coming for bunna.

As her attendants lit the brazier and plumped the cushions, they repeated stories they had heard of Sulaman's justice. The Palace servants were still talking about the time two of the harem women both claimed the right to a robust baby boy, said to be the King's own son.

"How could motherhood be so uncertain?" asked Makeda.

In her world, a baby always knew its own mother, and a mother, her child. Was this another of the claims of Sulaman's Kingship, to preside over motherhood? She was not impressed with the King's solution to cut the child in half. Of course the mother would cry out in horror, but what if the baby had belonged to a third woman? Would Sulaman have carried out his test? She resolved to tell him that there were other ways to determine mother right.

Sulaman sent a messenger inviting Makeda to visit the new Temple. She made an excuse, but the truth was that the sight of so many slaves sickened her, and her guests were coming.

She dressed in a white robe like the one she had been wearing when she met the children in the lane. She walked slowly to the Palace gate to await their arrival, certain that a Northern working family would not otherwise be admitted by the guards.

CHAPTER XXXIV

Ursalimmu. c 950BCE.

And she came to Jerusalem with a very great train, with camels that bore spices, and very much gold, and precious stones: and when she was come to Solomon, she communed with him of all that was in her heart. And King Solomon gave unto the Queen of Sheba all her desire, whatsoever she asked, beside that which Solomon gave her of his royal bounty. So she turned and went to her own country, she and her servants. (I Kings 10 v.1-13)

Mehtap ran ahead as they left their new home, an outbuilding behind one of the city inns. Harika called her back.

"Stay close," she said. "The city is too full for children to be running."

"Remember, child, the first Mir-ri was a princess," said Mir-ri. "Daughters of a princess do not run like street children to meet a Queen."

Mehtap was not sure she believed the story about their ancestor being a princess, but she dutifully fell into step beside Inna and Yasuf.

The lanes were soon too crowded for running: carts bearing cedar and sandalwood for the temple, asses laden with trade goods for the market, dark-faced stone workers from Kemet, and broad-shouldered carpenters from the North, all vying for right of way. A lone child could become lost forever.

Nevertheless, Mehtap wanted to run and skip all the way to the Palace. The noise, the colours, the smells of the city made her heart race and her mind whirl. They were on their way to see a Queen!

As they climbed the rise to the Palace, the crowd thinned, and the lane opened into a broad road lined with leafy acacias.

"These trees are sacred to Isis, the Queen of Kemet," announced Mehtap, drawing on her store of wisdom from Temu.

"Isis is sister to Ishtar, Queen of Heaven and Earth," said Mir-ri, looking up into the leaves. "These are holy trees in Urim also, if the tales are true." She spoke of the ancient city as if it still stood in the land of the two rivers.

Then Mehtap saw Makeda waiting by the Palace gate, a tall, still figure draped in white. She ran forward eagerly, hair flying, forgetting all about being dutiful and the descendant of a princess.

She slid to a stop a few steps before the Queen.

"Come, child, you are welcome here." Makeda's voice was deep and low, soothing as warm goat's milk and honey.

Mehtap walked forward slowly, strangely compelled by the woman to whom she felt so linked.

Makeda took her hand.

The others approached more slowly.

Makeda made them welcome and led them into the Palace. The guards eyed them warily, but no questions were asked as she led them through lush gardens and past colonnaded pavilions to the guest rooms.

Mehtap wrinkled her nose at the spicy smell and looked enquiringly at Makeda.

"It is bunna." Makeda pointed to a brass pot heating over a brazier in the centre of the room.

When they had all entered, she gestured for them to sit on silk cushions--red and green and gold--arranged in an alcove. She served them herself, pouring the steamy, dark drink into brightly-patterned bowls.

Mehtap sipped and gasped at the bitterness.

Makeda laughed.

"Here is milk and honey for you to use. Add as much as you need to make the bunna sweet."

Mehtap leant forward eagerly to sweeten and dilute the drink with milk and dollops of honey. Inna and Yasuf did the same, but Grandmother Mir-ri watched Makeda and drank hers as the Queen did, dark and thick as it came straight from the pot. Harika added milk and sipped delicately.

When everyone had settled back onto the cushions, bowls cupped in their hands, Makeda spoke to Harika. "Have you found a home in Ursalimmu?"

Harika nodded. "We have a room. It is not like home, but it will suffice."

"It's just an outbuilding," said Yasuf, looking around at the splendour of the Palace.

"Nevertheless," said Harika, with a warning glance at him.

Makeda nodded. "I have seen the city. It is no small thing for a family from afar to have found a home so soon. Not all who come to Ursalimmu fare as well." Her face invited comment, eyebrows raised, eyes waiting.

Harika and Mir-ri exchanged a glance.

"It seems there are many who are called to Ursalimmu," said Harika.

"But few, perhaps, who find what they seek," added Mir-ri, watching Makeda closely.

"Ah," sighed Makeda. "Your words are strangely familiar to me. Like ritual words I have heard spoken in the temple of Astarte." She looked from Harika to Mir-ri, and then to Mehtap and Inna. "Is this also the way of women in the North?"

The question hovered in the room.

Yasuf had moved to the window opening, where he hung out to watch the washerwomen at work with their vats of water and wooden paddles.

Mehtap sensed the new mood that had entered and moved closer to Inna.

Grandmother Mir-ri shook her head, white hair falling free of the blue cloth she used to wrap it for the day. "Once it was so, in Urim, the city of our ancestors. But now the words are almost lost."

"But not quite," added Makeda, looking thoughtful.

"Not quite," said Mir-ri. "The Great Lady of Heaven and Earth still speaks to her daughters."

"We know her as Astarte in the South," said Makeda. "She is Isis in Kemet," she added.

Mehtap nudged Inna with her elbow and opened her mouth to speak.

Makeda continued. "She has a thousand names and is nameless."

Mehtap closed her mouth.

Harika and Mir-ri were nodding, and Inna had become very still.

Never had Mehtap felt her mother and grandmother quite like this, although Mir-ri often spoke of the old ways.

"I know of this Urim of which you speak," said Makeda, breaking the spell. "It is the birthplace of Sulaman's ancestor, the one who was beloved of their El, the Great One they worship here in Ursalimmu."

"I did not know that this line of Kings began in Urim," whispered Grandmother Mir-ri. "Long have I wondered at the tales of the first Mir-ri, who left Urim carrying a treasure. I am sure that her treasure was the child she carried, but I have never understood what made the child precious enough for the tale to be told, mother to daughter, for a thousand years. Now you have given me an idea." She laughed then, eyes shining.

Harika stared at her mother, the bunna bowl resting forgotten in her lap. She opened her mouth to speak, but Mir-ri raised a hand.

"Tell me," she said, turning to Makeda. "Do you know when Sulaman's ancestor left Urim?"

Makeda frowned. "I think it was not long before the fall of the old city, if the tales tell true."

Grandmother Mir-ri nodded knowingly. "It is the same in our tales: the first mother, Mir-ri, left Urim not long before the Fall."

Then Harika laughed. "I see it, too." Shaking her head in wonder, she looked at Inna and Mehtap.

Mehtap was trying to understand, but their words seemed like nonsense, although heat flushed her cheeks, as if her body knew what this was about.

"What do you see?" she asked her mother. "What is it?"

Makeda looked questioningly at Harika and Mir-ri.

They looked to each other and nodded.

Mehtap and Inna leaned forward.

Grandmother Mir-ri spoke solemnly, like when reciting a teaching story. "Before the fall of Urim, the first Mir-ri, for whom I am named, left the city with her family. We know she carried a treasure, although no sign of it has ever been found. She carried a child, a daughter if I see truly, a daughter to balance the line of sons that came from Sulaman's ancestor. A daughter to carry the way of women through the ages, to ensure all is not lost to the way of men and their Great One."

Makeda nodded. "I have heard of this in the old tales from Ki-en-gir. Through this line of daughters the way of the Queen of Heaven lives, to remind us that El is not all present, all powerful, all knowing as Sulaman and his Priests would have us believe." She spoke softly, looking at Mehtap. "I have seen you in my dreams, but I did not understand."

"That means it's us, me and Inna," cried Mehtap. "But what can we do?"

"It is not what you do," said Makeda. "It is who you are. It is the lineage you carry, and why you have been running through my dreams; the way of the Mother, the deep reverence for the life-giving power must not be lost. I rode my camel for half a year to see for myself this King who is beloved of El, the Supreme One. Sulaman claims dominion over life and death in the name of El. He claims that the way of El is the only way."

Just when Mehtap thought she had finished, Makeda began speaking again, her voice soft. "I have seen a King great in the ways of men. He rules with power. He conquers all who resist, and he takes slaves and women for tribute. He builds a glorious Temple for this El. He answers the riddles of the philosophers and knows the patterns of the stars." She paused as if remembering something. "He is strong and powerful, with the head, hands, and loins of a King."

"And?" asked Mir-ri.

"He forgets the power of women. For him they are another conquest." She shook her head, eyes shadowed.

"The world forgets," agreed Mir-ri sadly. "In my lifetime I have seen the way of the Mother fade before the might of the Fathers of Sky and Light. It is like the old tales of Marduk slaying Tiamat for dominion over the Earth."

"But all is not lost," said Makeda loudly. "We remember."

Yasuf turned from the window.

Grandmother Mir-ri nodded. "While there are daughters who remember, the Mother will not be lost."

Makeda smiled. "I am thinking of my own daughters, of the unbroken line of mothers and daughters stretching back to the beginning of Time. It takes such a small time for a man to plant his seed in a woman's womb, just a few heartbeats. It takes so much longer for a woman to grow the new life, bring it forth and tend it until the child can stand alone. It takes so much more time for a woman to become a mother. How can this be forgotten? How can this new way of worship forget that all life, even that of Kings and Priests, comes forth from woman?"

"Perhaps," said Grandmother Mir-ri, "that is why Sulaman builds a golden Temple, to forget."

They were silent then, until Makeda clapped her hands for the attendants to bring trays of honey cakes and fruit.

Yasuf joined them for the food, sitting between his sisters. It was very quiet in the room while they ate.

"Do you really think we are of the line of Kings?" asked Inna after some time, looking from her mother to her grandmother, and across to Makeda.

Yasuf stopped chewing to stare at his sister.

"We are of the line of Ki-en-gir," answered Harika. "The blood of Sulaman's ancestor might flow in our veins, but we are of Ki-en-gir."

"Me too?" asked Yasuf, looking pleased with himself.

Inna, Mehtap, and Yasuf never forgot the seasons in Ursalimmu. Twice more they met with Makeda in the Palace, drinking bunna, talking of prophecy and fate. Makeda gave Inna and Mehtap scrolls filled with words of power, and she instructed them in ways of thinking and attending that would guide them on the path they must walk.

The morning before she left for her Southern home, Makeda came to the outbuilding Harika and Mir-ri had brightened with woven cloth and small altars. She entered the cleanly swept courtyard with only one attendant, dressed like any other traveller in the great city. The Queen stood quietly, watching Mehtap scoop the last of the ass dung into a large woven basket.

"Can I help you with that?" asked Makeda, smiling at the girl who had run through her dreams.

Mehtap jumped. She had not heard Makeda enter. She had been lost in a dream of her own as she worked. In the dream she had been standing high atop a stepped temple in a great walled city, bordered by water North and West. The Sun had been rising in the East, and voices rose in song to greet the dawn.

Mehtap smiled up at Makeda. "It is not work for a Queen," she said, shaking her head.

"There is no work too humble for a Queen," answered Makeda, hoping this child would remember her lessons, the lessons of Makeda's own mother, and all the mothers back through time.

"Yasuf will come soon. He will carry it with me," said Mehtap. No matter what Makeda said, Mehtap knew that Grandmother Mir-ri would scold her if she let the Queen carry dung.

Inna emerged from the flat-roofed building that had become their home. She rested the palm broom against the doorpost, smoothed her clothes, and walked sedately across to greet their visitor.

They brewed tea from the herbs Mir-ri had sent the children to gather in the valleys surrounding Ursalimmu. Makeda sat on a low stool, sipping her tea and listening to the girls talk about their new life. When they fell silent, she told them she would be leaving. She also said she had gifts for them, and one for Yasuf who had still not returned from scrambling up and down the gullies behind the inn.

"For you, Inna, I leave this bracelet. It is an unbroken circle, like the endless line of mothers and daughters that leads back always to the First Mother."

Inna held the bracelet in both hands. It was made of linked circles of gold, with eight blue stones equally spaced in small rosettes of gold. She slipped it over her hand and settled it on her wrist. Tears sprang to her eyes as she thanked Makeda. Her words were formal, as if from a ritual.

"I will treasure it. It will pass to my daughter, and her daughter and all the daughters to come. We will remember." Then she jumped up to hug Makeda, all formality forgotten.

"For you, child of my dreams, I have a strand of blue and gold," whispered Makeda as she took from her own neck a necklace of lapis lazuli set in gold.

Mehtap felt the necklace settle around her neck, resting down over her heart. She met Makeda's eyes and smiled.

"This is your birthright, daughter of my dreams. Made from gold found deep in Saba and from Lapis found in the East, it holds the secret of the life-giving power of She who is Mother of all. It is said to be the necklace worn to the Underworld by the Queen of Heaven. I believe it came from the city of Urim, like your ancestors. Perhaps one of them carried it out. May it serve as a symbol when Time erases all memory of Her power."

Yasuf appeared then, dirty and dishevelled from his adventures.

"Greetings, Makeda," he said casually, as if she visited everyday. He was still more interested in finding caves and hidden treasure than in women's business, even if one of the women was a Queen. "Look what I found." He held out a chipped tile, the blue pattern faded from lying in the Sun.

Makeda took the tile and turned it over and over in her hands. "This tile has travelled to Ursalimmu from afar, even as I have, even as you have." She handed it back to Yasuf. "I will return to my home, but it may be that you, or your children, or your children's children, will travel like this tile. May they find loving hands like yours to hold them."

Yasuf frowned as if not quite sure what to make of the Queen's words. He studied the tile in his hands.

"I have something for you." Makeda held out a small pouch to Yasuf. Inside he found the pair to the piece Mehtap and he had spotted that day from the lane. Part of the saddle decoration of one of Makeda's camels, the silver half circle glittered with red and blue stones. Silver bells hung from the rounded section, tinkling as Yasuf moved.

Makeda had identified the original piece on that first day, laughing to think that someone from Ursalimmu had found it in the wake of the caravan, only to lose it again in front of the lane, ensuring that Mehtap and she would have their fateful encounter.

"Stay alert to small signs, and you will always walk the path set out for you by the Great Ones," said Makeda.

When Harika and Mir-ri saw the Shebu's gifts, they became very quiet.

"These are things of great value," said Harika, looking at each of her children. "Selling even one would bring more silver than your father will carry back to Halab."

"But we can never sell them," cried Mehtap, clasping her necklace.

"Your mother knows that, little one," said Grandmother Mir-ri. "She is just worried about what it will mean to carry such things." She looked at Harika as if to say, "What can we do?"

"We could hide them," said Yasuf, thinking of the pouch Makeda had given him. "I could make pouches like this from the scraps of goatskin."

Reluctantly the girls agreed to carry their treasures in pouches, but only if they could hang them on thongs around their necks. By the time the men arrived for the evening meal, Yasuf had fashioned two more small bags, and all three of them wore the Shebu's gifts close to their hearts.

The story of the great Queen from the South became one of the family myths, told along with the legend of Mir-ri and her treasure, the wonders of the ancient city of Urim, and the stories of Inanna, Queen of Heaven and Earth. The gifts also became part of the legend, passed down through the generations with the tales.

That night Makeda told Sulaman she would be leaving Ursalimmu, returning South to her own land. Their lovemaking was fierce and tender in turn, as if they were both absorbing the best of each other.

Makeda knew that Sulaman truly believed Ursalimmu to be the centre of the world, the city chosen of El, beloved of El. She knew that if she had chosen to ask him about the slaves, the women taken unwilling to the harem, the poor who survived or not on scraps from the Palace kitchens, he would have paused for a moment, seeking a response from the vast storehouse of wisdom for which he was renown. He would have woven an answer that left his world intact, and it would not have satisfied her at all. She did not ask. She had learned to seek only what it is possible for a person to offer. She, therefore, spent the last nights with the father of her next child, giving and receiving pleasure, enjoying his strong body and kingly stamina. When the songbirds announced the dawn, Makeda kissed Sulaman once, wrapped her robe about her, and turned to leave.

"Makeda." He seldom used her name.

She turned. He held a ring in his outstretched hand, a golden circlet, plain but for a single emerald.

"For my son. So I shall know him when he comes to me."

Makeda took the ring and tied it in a corner of her robe. "You shall know him when he comes."

The camels, asses, and mules left Ursalimmu as laden as when they arrived, so rich were the gifts Sulaman bestowed on Makeda. At his feet she had laid spices, precious stones, woven cloth, and bunna. He reciprocated with gold and cedar, jewellery and inlaid furniture, scrolls from the East and papyri from Kemet. The caravan wound as slowly out of the city as it had entered, the people of Ursalimmu lining the walls to watch the Queen leave.

Tales were told and retold of the great Shebu who had come to test Sulaman's wisdom and who had left satisfied in more ways than one. The stories grew and changed with Time, embellished deliberately and by accident, until the "Queen of Sheba" had become a convert, renouncing the idols of her homeland for the religion of El, the Supreme One.

Makeda cared not what was said; she knew the truth of her life. She arrived home in Saba in time to birth her son in the Palace. She held him to her breast as she called on Shams to make him strong and on Astarte to teach him true wisdom. Sometimes she remembered the nights with Sulaman, and she was content that she had chosen a strong father for her son.

She thought often of Mehtap and the lineage carried by the daughters of Mir-ri. She prayed that it would be enough to hold the Balance through the Ages to come. There was also a secret she carried out of Ursalimmu that she only ever shared with one person--Tamrin, her old friend and leader of her trading caravan.

"I have only one regret," said Tamrin as he lay dying from a flux ten years after the Northern expedition. Half of those who had accompanied him on his last journey to Kemet had succumbed, and even the camels had suffered.

Makeda held her friend's hand, noting the grey tinge of his skin and the stench of his breath. She was truly sorry to lose him.

"What, my friend, do you regret?"

Tamrin sighed deeply. "I have accrued great riches as the leader of your trading caravan. I have a wife whom I have loved and who has loved me in return. I have five sons, any of whom can take my place on the trade routes. I have had the friendship of the great Shebu, more precious than riches. I have been blessed." He closed his eyes. "But I would have liked to discover the source of Sulaman's gold," he whispered through cracked lips.

Makeda smiled. Well she knew it was not for lack of trying that Tamrin had failed to discover the fabled mines from which the King took the gold that lined Ursalimmu. She leaned closer and whispered the words her old friend longed to hear. A slow, sweet smile replaced the grimace of pain, and Tamrin died content.

Makeda rose from her seat at his side to make way for his family. She was not ashamed of the tears that flowed freely at the loss of her friend.

The secret she whispered only to Tamrin as he died was that the gold came not from a mine hidden in the desert sands, nor from a mine in the Eastern mountains; the gold came from the tombs of the Pharaohs of Kemet, plundered for the glory of the Northern King in desecration of all that was sacred in the Redlands and the Blacklands. Tamrin was one who would have recognised the irony of robbing the Neters of Kemet for the glory of El.

Makeda lived to see the children of her children rule Saba in the traditional way. Much was made of her son, Menelek, when he travelled North with two of Tamrin's sons to visit his father. Makeda could imagine the Scribes proclaiming him the true son of his father, ruling as a man should in woman-bound Saba. The truth was that Menelek ruled alongside his sisters, the sacred mother-right deeply respected.

In time, Makeda heard that Sulaman had fallen foul of the Priests, accused of decadence and debauchery despite the magnificence of the Temple he built for the glory of El. The line of Kings was, however, strong, and son followed father for many generations.

CHAPTER XXXV

Halab. c 950 BCE.

Ever since the 3rd millennium BC, Aleppo (Halab) has been a flourishing city, with a unique strategic position. This position gave the city a distinctive role from the days of the Akkadians and Amorite kingdoms until modern times. It was the meeting point of several important commercial roads in the north. This enabled Aleppo to be the link in trade between Mesopotamia, the Fertile Crescent and Egypt.[xxxii]

The remaining three months of Mehtap's time in Ursalimmu passed without any more fateful encounters. She, Inna, and Yasuf did their daily chores, visited the teeming marketplace, and explored the gullies that surrounded the city on three sides.

Their father and uncles continued to make and sell waterskins, adding each day to the bag of silver tokens hidden in a hole in the earthen floor of their dwelling. Harika and Mir-ri found the best sources of water, grains, and vegetables to cook for the family, the innkeeper, and eventually his customers. The reputation of the inn grew during that season and the next, keeping Harika and Mir-ri busy, and leaving the children free to roam the hillsides.

The first time his sisters followed him down the incline behind the inn, Yasuf spoke eagerly of the friends they would meet, the treasures they would find.

"What sort of friends?" asked Inna, remembering Mir-ri's words about watching over the others.

"What sort of treasure?" asked Mehtap.

"Come and see," called Yasuf, scrambling ahead of his sisters.

Inna and Mehtap hurried after Yasuf down into a winding culvert that ran with water in the rainy season, but teemed with children, dogs, and rubbish in the hot months. They soon learned to sort through the debris scattered down the steep hillsides, finding scraps of cloth they tied around their heads, shards of pottery they used to scrape their names in the dusty ground, and enough palm fronds and scraps of building materials to make a house of their own hidden in the boulders lying in the bottom of the ravine. There were two girls whom Mehtap and Inna befriended, children of stoneworkers who had travelled from Kemet for a share of Sulaman's silver.

Mehtap practised the words she had learned from Temu, finding a way to ask the questions that still intrigued her, questions about the Great Ones of Kemet: Isis, Osiris, Nephthys, Set, and Horus.

By the time they left for home, Inna, Mehtap, and Yasuf could understand at least four languages and speak well enough in three of them. There were many friends to farewell.

Azhar, Feroz, and Dekel decided to return to Halab through Damaski, curious to see the city they had missed on the way to Ursalimmu. They approached Damaski late one day as the sun was sinking in the west, and the city did appear out of the desert like a jewelled wonder. Other than that spectacular sight, however, Damaski proved no more wondrous than Ursalimmu, and they decided not to linger.

"Perhaps we have seen enough of great cities," said Azhar quietly as the family walked through the marketplace of Damaski.

The smells and noise were familiar from Ursalimmu, and none of them wanted to spend their hard-earned silver on market goods. They left the next day, eager to be home. It had been six months since Feroz and Dekel had last seen their families.

There were times in the years to come when Harika wondered if she had been right to take her children with her to Ursalimmu. Inna, Mehtap, and Yasuf were different when they returned, both more restless and more thoughtful. They seldom spoke of their meetings with the Southern Queen, but she knew it had marked them, setting them apart from their cousins. Mehtap and Inna studied the scrolls and practised the rituals Makeda had taught them, and Yasuf became something of a philosopher, debating the meaning of life with anyone who dared.

Harika gave thanks when Inna married a man from Halab, the son of the town's most prosperous weaver. She saw a bright future for her first born, even if Mustaf's family no longer honoured the ways of the Queen of Heaven. In time, Inna and Mustaf had a daughter and three sons, much to the delight of their extended families. Mustaf was especially proud of his sons. Inna named her daughter Nama, and taught her the old songs and stories and the wisdom she had learned from Makeda. Her husband was content to follow tradition and live in the home of his wife's family, although his sons followed him as weavers.

Mehtap grew into a woman both beautiful and strong, her dark curls framing large, almond-shaped eyes, high cheekbones, and a dazzling smile. Young men began bringing her gifts and promises almost as soon as she returned from Ursalimmu, but she ignored them all. More often than not, she could be found talking with Temu, or practising the new form of writing she had learned in Ursalimmu. When she finally announced that she had met a suitable husband, Harika and Azhar were not surprised to learn that he was the son of a Kemet trader. They gave their blessings to Mehtap and Naram, although Harika spoke often with Azhar about the changes.

"For the first time in a thousand years, a daughter of the family is not bringing her husband home to live in the house of the mothers," she said late at night when the others were sleeping. "Mehtap will not give birth here, with the women of her family."

Azhar just nodded, filled with his own grief at parting with the bright-eyed girl whose destiny had called her away.

As well as Harika's late night musings, there were many open discussions and many tears. Mehtap listened to the fears and grief of her mother, her sister, her cousins, and her aunts, but she was certain of her path. Sometimes, when she was alone, she wondered at the enormity of what she was doing.

The simple wedding took place in Halab, in time for Mehtap to join the homeward journey of Haram's caravan. They would be travelling South along the trade route to Kemet, and Mehtap was almost as excited about the places she would see and the people she would meet as she was about the man she had married. Haram knew that he had married a rare jewel of a woman; grandmother Mir-ri had told him so often enough. He could, however, see that for himself.

As it happened, Mehtap's journey became more common over the next years as a new prosperity in trade and commerce quickened the trade routes. Where people had married only into families living in the same town, they now found husbands and wives in the marketplace, not for sale like goats and asses, but trading their goods, tending the livestock, and counting the tokens. Like Mehtap, the young men and women encountered travellers from faraway lands, and it suddenly seemed less strange to make a new life in another town or city.

Mehtap made her new life in Thebes, where Haram's family had lived for generation after generation in a flat-roofed, mud-brick house. From the rooftop, Mehtap could see the river; she watched as the strip of land on the riverbanks turned from green to black, and back to green again as the river watered the crops, flooded, and watered the next season's crops.

She fulfilled her dream of learning about Kemet, accumulating her own collection of papyri from the market. She came to know the Scribes who copied the ancient texts and the sacred images from the temples, and she learned the secret art of khemia, practices based on the ancient wisdom of Kemet. It was already familiar to her from the songs and stories of her family, but now she learned it in numbers and images. Haram was proud of his wife's ability to tally the profits and read the ancient spells, and Mehtap became a valued member of the family, travelling the length and breadth of the trade routes each year. It was the life she had dreamt of as a child, learning new languages and meeting people from distant lands.

She returned often to Halab with the trade caravan, and she even persuaded Yasuf to return with her to Kemet for a season. She saw Inna's first child before he walked and was present for the birth of her niece two years later.

Her own children she birthed easily, finding women in Kemet who practised the old arts of healing, calling on Hathor as Mother. The curved horns of the Great One seemed strangely familiar to Mehtap as she gave thanks in the Temple and joined in the seasonal rituals of the Black Lands.

Named for the dark, rich silt washed down from the mountains, the Black Lands were filled with ancient magic, just as Mehtap had suspected when she was young. She learned much from the Scribes and from the old woman who cooked for Haram's family. Grey-haired and toothless, Pu-abi had been with the family since before the birth of Haram's father.

Mehtap made it her business to be in the courtyard as Pu-abi bustled around preparing the evening meal. So engrossed was the old woman in her work that Mehtap soon realised she would have to ask questions if she wanted Pu-abi to speak. Strangely, for one who was always so full of questions, she could not think of one to ask the old woman. Finally she decided to begin at the beginning. After all, she had not been formally introduced to Pu-abi.

"I am Mehtap, wife to Haram."

Pu-abi grunted without looking up from the bowl in which she was grinding wheat.

Mehtap tried again. "Can I help you prepare the food?" she asked, reaching for a bowl of dates that clearly needed to be pitted.

Pu-abi swatted her hand away, like she might a wasp.

Frustrated, Mehtap glared at Pu-abi, thinking thoughts best left unsaid. She was just about to leave when the old woman spoke.

"This is no place for a daughter of Ki-en-gir. Long has your land been ruled by others. Long is it since you left your true home. You will not find what you seek in Kemet." She said the words like a litany, her voice a monotone.

"It has been a thousand years since my people left Urim," said Mehtap, wondering how Pu-abi knew of it.

"Nevertheless. The blood runs true." Pu-abi looked up, her eyes milky with age.

"What do you see?" asked Mehtap, uneasy under Pu-abi's scrutiny.

"I was sent to the Temple of Hathor as a girl. Hathor and her seven sisters watch over Kemet."

Mehtap nodded. She had come to love Hathor, the Great One who sometimes appeared as a beautiful woman, sometimes with the head of a cow. There was a story about that, and Mehtap had been hoping to hear Pu-abi's telling of it. In Halab, it had been the old women who knew all the stories and had the time to tell them.

Pu-abi finally relented and began to talk as she worked. "It is the oldest of old stories, the one of the great Queen. Do you know the story?"

Mehtap shook her head and held her breath, hoping Pu-abi would go on.

"When the ass-headed one, Seth, fought with Horus, the falcon-headed one, the battle lasted eight hundred years. It was a battle between the old and the new. Seth blinded Horus and, by the eight Gods' grace, his sight was restored. Horus wounded Seth and, by the eight Gods' grace, he was restored. So it went on. Finally, Horus overcame Seth and drew his blade to behead him. Hathor stepped between them and it was her head that was severed. In its place grew the head of a cow, with the horns of the crescent Moon. From the love of the Mother came renewal. Seth no longer brought destruction. Horus no longer sought revenge. The opposing forces worked together for Balance."

Mehtap sighed deeply. A tale of the Balance held by the Mother, just like the stories she had heard from grandmother Mir-ri. She felt the weight of the necklace that hung always around her neck, a reminder of the sacred trust she carried.

"Why did you leave the Temple?" she asked Pu-abi.

"Ah. That is another story." She turned away as if it was not one she intended to tell.

"Do you miss it?" asked Mehtap, wondering how it would be to serve just one family after tending the altars in the Temple.

Pu-abi smiled, her old gums pink as a baby's. "This has been my work. I can walk in Her ways wherever I am."

Mehtap went very still. The words echoed the ancient words of initiation that had come to her three nights after her arrival in Kemet. At first she had thought she was dreaming when she was called from sleep by something she couldn't quite name, a deep humming like bees and music like birdsong. It was as she stood alone in the garden, looking at the stars, that the voice had spoken.

"Do you bring your feet to walk in Her ways?" The words had been new to Mehtap, yet they were familiar also. At the end, the voice had said, "You are chosen."

Mehtap sighed again and smiled at the old woman.

By the time Mehtap's three daughters had daughters of their own, Mehtap was the old woman telling tales. She told of her childhood in Halab, of her brother and sister whose children lived still in the North. She told of the journey to Ursalimmu when they had met Makeda, Queen of Saba. She told of her own life travelling the trade routes with her husband. When she sat with her daughters, and all the tales were told, she would bring out the goatskin bag from around her neck and take out the necklace of lapis and gold.

In time, the necklace passed to Mara, Mehtap's oldest daughter. Mara passed it to her oldest daughter, called Inna for her grandmother's sister, whom she had never met.

In Halab, Inna's daughter, Afsana, had two daughters of her own, named Mir-ri for their great grandmother, and Mehtap for the sister Inna missed every day of her life. Mir-ri and Mehtap both had three daughters, four of whom lived to have daughters of their own. Again the names continued down the centuries: Mir-ri, Inna, Nama, Afsana.

CHAPTER XXXVI
1000BCE to the Age of Pisces.

For one thousand years, Kings died and were followed by more Kings, sometimes so often that people had only just learned the name of one before another rose to take his place.

As with all of those who survived the momentous changes of the times, the descendants of the first Mir-ri learned to change when change was called for and to build when they could. As cities were destroyed and rebuilt, workers from Halab and other northern towns once again travelled the trade roads to work for more than could be earned at home. Some of the families built homes and settled in Ursalimmu, slowly becoming absorbed into the life of the Habiru.

In the time of Mehtap's nine-times great-granddaughters, King Jeroboam II died, and the Northern kingdom of Israel had five new kings in the next ten years. Soon after that, Sargon II conquered the northern lands, an echo of his namesake's conquests over one thousand years earlier. It was a time of ongoing bloodshed and war, exactly as Nin-lil-la had foreseen for the Age of the Ram.

When the great Assyrian army invaded the southern kingdom of Judah in 701 BCE, King Sennacherib had the defeated generals impaled on poles around the city. The smell was terrible, lingering in the air as the bodies rotted in the heat. The Habiru King was imprisoned, and thousands left the city.

One hundred years later, Nebupolassar, King of Babylon, crushed the Assyrians, paving the way for Nebuchadnezzar to destroy Ursalimmu. The Habiru, among them daughters of the daughters of the original Mir-ri, were sent East to Babylonia, or fled south to the delta lands of Kemet.

In the old lands to the East, the Habiru settled on the banks of the canals carrying water from the Buranun, although they did not remember the ways their ancestors had practised in those lands. During their time there, the Habiru banished all the Great Ones who had been worshipped before, and turned to YHWEH as the only one.

There were other Habiru, those who made their homes in Kemet in the south, who turned to Ishtar, restoring her rites in their temples. Long had Ishtar been honoured as Isis and Hathor in Dendera, Thebes, and the other cities of Kemet.

When Cyrus, King of Persia, conquered the Babylonian empire, the Habiru who had settled by the Buranun returned to Judah. There they built a Temple to YHWEH, and the old story of Abraham became enshrined in Habiru lore; the story of Abram, who became Abraham, father of a multitude, was told in the Temples. No one, however, told the tale of the Priestess and her daughter.

Empires rose to span old borders, allowing people to finally settle in one place rather than moving as Mir-ri had from Urim seventeen hundred years earlier. There were still wars fought for land and power; Nin-lil-la would have said that the Great Ones of might and wrath had finally conquered the Queen of Heaven who once brought life and abundance.

Kingdoms rose and fell, and rose again. In the old lands between the rivers, the great city of Bab-Ilu fell to the Assyrians.

Half way through the last millennium of the Age of Aries, daughters in the line of Mir-ri lived in the new Jerusalem, honouring YHWEH alongside the old Gods passed down through the mother line. It had been over a hundred years since King Josiah had smashed the statues of Asherah in the temples, destroying the fertility symbols, but the women still practised their rituals at home. Their neighbours paid them no mind; it was the Kings and their priests who were intent on destroying practices that differed from their own.

Three hundred years before the end of the Age of Aries, Darius of Persia was defeated by Alexander of Macedonia, and the first signs of a new Age were seen across the known World, from India to Persia, through the old land of Ki-en-gir, across the sands to Assyria and Judah, and south to Kemet. New city states arose down the coast of the Sea, from Tyre to Gaza, and a great centre of trade and culture came into being at the mouth of the Nile.

Named for the young man who had conquered the known World, Alexandria housed the finest library and philosophers. Alexander and his people were impressed by YHWEH, calling this new Great One "IAO" in their tongue, although the Old Gods were not abandoned.

As the Age of Pisces approached, the philosophy of Alexandria engaged the Habiru traditions, giving rise to treatises such as The Wisdom of Solomon, written by a Habiru scholar calling for resistance to the new culture of the invaders. The Romans in Egypt and the northern lands merged their culture, philosophy, and deities with those of Alexander and his followers.

Fearing Habiru insurrection, Emperor Vespasian conquered Jerusalem and burned the Temple in response to rebellion by Habiru zealots. Communities of Pharisees were founded in Palestine, Babylonia, and Jabneh near Jerusalem.

By the time of the new millennium, daughters in the line of Mir-ri and Abraham lived in Alexandria, Jerusalem, and between the rivers in Babylonia. Once again, it was a time of change . . .

CHAPTER XXXVII

Amman to Jerusalem. Updated May 18th 2015 5.43pm UTC

Officials in northeastern Brazil say over 200 people are dead and some 300,000 others are now homeless following the area's worst flooding in recent memory. The severe weather has isolated communities, flooded highways and hampered efforts to get emergency aid to trapped, fleeing and displaced residents. In the hard-hit state of Maranhao, officials expected to begin distributing tons of food, medicine and other supplies airlifted in by military planes. They report that the bad weather is a sign of climate change. Places that are normally dry are receiving rainfall, while the opposite is happening in other areas.

"So you have jewellery that might have belonged to the Queen of Sheba?" said Peter quietly. The subdued tone of his voice was testimony to his wonder at their revelations. "Do you have any idea what that would be worth?"

Paula shook her head, and Lili shrugged.

"Not really," said Lili. "But it's not for sale."

"So I gathered," said Peter, hands trembling at the impossibility of such a treasure.

"We have to go to Jerusalem," announced Lili, closing her laptop. "We only have a week left."

"But it all happened three thousand years ago," said Paula, head spinning with the sheer improbability of it. "What could we possibly find there now?"

"Like children," said Lili. "We'll be like children, following our noses."

Paula nodded. "Might as well be there as here, I suppose."

"Besides which," added Lili, "you've never been, and everyone should visit Jerusalem at least once."

Paula shook her head and smiled; with four children and only one salary for at least half her married life, Jerusalem had not been at the top of her travel wish list.

Paula may not have planned to visit Jerusalem, but she instantly fell in love with the kaleidoscope of ancient and modern that made up the city.

"I've heard of Jerusalem all my life, but I never imagined it would be so . . .I'm not sure what it is, but it hums with it. I can imagine the Queen of Sheba here."

Lili laughed. "She's not who people usually think of when they come here."

"Who do they think of?" asked Paula, as the taxi took them past yet another holy site.

"Well, the Jews claim it as their own; they have the longest history with David and Solomon and the temples. And the Christians have Jesus Christ and the Church of the Holy Sepulchre where his body was washed and entombed. And the

Muslims have the gold-domed mosque of the Haram-al-Sharif. Don't forget that they call Abraham and Jesus Christ prophets, so they can lay claim to all of it. Anyway, the Queen of Sheba tends to get lost amongst all that."

"I suppose she would," said Paula. Then she laughed. "I don't suppose anyone's ever started a holy war to claim Israel for the Queen of Sheba."

The taxi driver, who must have had enough English to understand, scowled at them in the rear-vision mirror. He seemed relieved to leave them at the hotel Lili named.

They checked in and left their bags in another shared room.

"Where to first?" asked Paula.

Lili led her through old alleyways to a small, open plaza. Paula realised where she was and started to cry. It was not that the Church of the Holy Sepulchre filled her with the immanence of Christ or any particularly spiritual experience, but she could imagine her mother's joy in approaching the very place where her beloved Jesu had suffered, died, and risen again. Although there was nothing impressive or overwhelming about the building from street level, Paula knew her mother would have trembled with awe to walk in the footsteps of Christ.

She paused at the doors, wondering how an event that was so commonplace two thousand years earlier could have begun a whole new religion. She had studied enough ancient history to know that crucifixion was the preferred method for the Romans to deal with insurrection in Jerusalem and the surrounding territories; thousands had died on the Roman crosses. What made this particular crucifixion so remarkable?

Then she was inside. It was very dark, and the modern world fell away as if she had stepped through a time warp. Ahead was the stone where Christ's body had lain. Up a stairway to the right, a huge, steel cross dominated the space where the wooden cross of Golgotha would have stood. To her mother it would have been a miracle, but Paula shuddered at the thought of someone being nailed to the crossbeam and suspended in the air to slowly suffocate.

Then she remembered something she had read about the nailing being considered a kindness: when someone was merely tied to the crossbeam, it was initially less painful, but they might take six days to die instead of two. Feeling nauseous, she hurried back down to the Stone of Unction.

She tried to imagine the place two thousand years earlier: no church, no roof overhead, grieving women preparing the body for burial . . .

But the press of visitors was too much for her powers of visualisation. She followed Lili to the tomb where the body had been placed, and from where Christ was said to have risen on the third day. So many claims for one small part of the world.

They walked back slowly through the lanes.

"Who knows what really happened here two-thousand years ago," said Paula.

Lili nodded. "No doubt something happened. By all accounts, it was a time of prophets and prophecies. Another new millennium."

That night Paula had her first Jerusalem dream. She was watching something move slowly up a hill towards her in the pre-dawn light. At first she thought it was a big dog or a donkey. Then she saw that it was a man, his white robe stained brown from mud and blood. No sooner did she see the mud than she noticed the rain falling steadily from a grey sky.

"She weeps for us," said the man. He spoke a language Paula didn't know, yet she understood him. She also understood his meaning and nodded to him as he passed.

He continued on up the hill. When she turned to follow his path, she saw a cross, outlined in the sun's first light. She woke, calling out a warning to the man.

Her cry woke Lili, who jumped out of bed, picked up the bedside lamp, turned it on, and held it in front of her like a laser gun.

"It was a dream," said Paula. "Sorry."

Lili looked confused. "I thought it was your man again." She put the lamp back on the bedside table.

"I think I dreamt about Christ going to the cross," said Paula.

"Not so strange after the places we visited today." Lili sat on Paula's bed. "Are you okay?"

Paula nodded, still half in the dream. "He said, 'She weeps for us'. It was raining, but he meant the Goddess, the Great Mother."

Lili smiled. "They say he was the first feminist."

"I wish the Church had remembered that!" said Paula.

They settled back into their beds.

"I wonder what he was really like," said Paula.

"If he existed at all," said Lili.

CHAPTER XXXVIII

Ursalimmu (Jerusalem). c 30CE.

For wisdom is better than rubies; and all the things that may be desired are not to be compared unto her. Proverbs 8:11

The swallow soared and dipped like a playful child. Miri-amne lay on her back on the parapet of the roof-top, spread her arms, and sent her soul flying with the bird. There, on the roof, was the only place she could be truly free.

Quick as a flash of lightning, a hawk swooped from the clouds and caught the swallow in its talons. Feathers floated down on the breeze.

Miri-amne sat up, shivering as if someone had walked on her grave. Even a fool could interpret an omen like that, and she was certainly no fool: she spoke Greek, Aramaic, and Hebrew; she had read the works of Greek philosophers, the verses of Persian mystics, and the words of the Hebrew scholars from Alexandria. She knew an omen when she saw one. The hawk was cousin to the eagle, and the eagle signified only one thing:

Rome. The smaller birds might ride the wind, but it was from Rome that the wind blew.

Miri-amne sighed, and it came out as a groan. What good was all her learning if she were not free to soar and dip as she chose? If she were not free to ride on the back of the wind to wherever it might take her? Her father was more liberal than the fathers of her friends, but even he must obey the Law, and the Law was clear: women were subject to the control of men at all times. And she was of an age where the control must soon pass from father to husband.

She left the rooftop and walked listlessly around the courtyard where scholars came to eat and drink and talk with her Father. The potted palms whispered secrets, and the water bubbled merrily in the pond. A square yard with a circular fountain in the centre represented the font of all wisdom bounded by the four elements of air, fire, water, and earth, or so said the ancient wisdom of the Magi; her Father had based it on sketches he had from Persia. It probably contravened one of the Laws, but he would have an argument to justify it.

Miri-amne sat on the edge of the pool and trailed her fingers in the water. Fish chased each other through the bubbles and nibbled gently at her fingertips. Were they pleased to see her?

"How foolish I have become," she whispered to herself. "Seeking the favour of fish!"

Shaking the water from her fingers, she left the pond and walked to the gate. Now that she was old enough to marry, she was not allowed to leave her father's house unless accompanied by a gaggle of women and at least one trustworthy male, and she was not permitted to leave the house at all when her monthly blood flowed.

But the death of the swallow had made her restless.

She slid the wooden bar free of the bracket and opened one panel of the carved gate. The lane was empty, everyone at the Temple. The men would be making sacrifices for good weather, better trading, the birth of sons, and whatever else they desired. The women would be sweltering on their side of the Temple, whispering and gossiping and waiting for the men to finish. A few of the women would be quietly at home like she was, unclean and exiled from life.

"Why do men call the bleeding unclean?" she had asked Bubba Afsana.

"Because they are afraid," answered her grandmother. "Think about it, my child. We bleed with no wound and produce life from within our bodies; no man can do that. They know we are more powerful, but, of course, there can be nothing more powerful than a man." She had laughed heartily at that, but her eyes had been serious.

"But, Bubba, they are more powerful! They make the Laws, they are beloved of El, they . . ."

"Enough, Miri!" Bubba Afsana had stopped laughing. "Those things are only the trappings of power that men have taken for themselves because they cannot produce life from their bodies. They deal death--to the animals for sacrifice; to each other in battle--but they cannot give new life. Thus they fear us and make Laws to control us. Never forget this!"

Bubba Afsana was full of wisdom, and it was her stories that made Miri-amne dream of flying. She told stories of a time when G-d looked on them with the face of the Mother as well as the Father, a time when women walked with their heads held high and sang praises to the daughter of the Moon.

Miri-amne hummed one of the old songs defiantly as she left the courtyard and walked down the deserted lane. The other unclean women must be behind their gates, cracking wheat, marinating lamb, and baking bread. But not her.

Miri-amne held her head high and strode towards the hill where the swallows nested. Perhaps there would be eggs, or even hatchlings; it had been weeks since she had been there, and the cycles of life and death moved quickly for the birds. No wonder they made such a fuss when the Sun set each day, twittering and swooping in the fading light.

At the hill, she kicked off her sandals and climbed the rocky outcrop she had been scaling since she was old enough to walk there alone. From the top she could see along the ridge, past the rooftops, down the gullies on either side, and into the heart of the city. But not today; today she stopped at the nest halfway up. The mother bird stared at her with round, unblinking eyes. Were there eggs? Had they hatched? The bird fluffed out her feathers and raised her sharp beak.

Miri-amne leaned closer.

"Many are called but few are chosen," said the bird, in a voice from a dream.

Miri-amne jerked backwards.

Her feet slipped.

She lost her grip and slid down the rock face, twisting to protect her face.

She landed on her back in the dust, chest burning, ears ringing. Her palms stung and her back was bruised. But worst of all, her shift was torn.

"Do you bring your feet to walk in Her Ways?" asked the bird.

Miri-amne groaned and covered her ears. Had she lost her mind? Was someone playing a trick on her?

She scrambled to her feet. There was no one there. But it couldn't be the bird . . .

"You must answer, child," said the voice. "Do you bring

your feet to walk in Her Ways?"

It must be a dream, a waking dream. Bubba Afsana said that dreams were like a journey: you had to keep going to come out the other side.

"Do you bring your feet to walk in Her Ways?"

"I do," whispered Miri-amne. Someone was playing a lyre in the distance.

"Do you bring your knees to kneel in Her praise?"

"I do." She rolled over and came to her knees.

"Do you bring your sex to rejoice in Her Life-giving?"

"I do." Her cheeks flushed.

"Do you bring your breasts for Her abundance flowing?"

"I do."

"Do you bring your hands to do Her work?"

"I do." Miri-amne rubbed her hands on her shift, leaving trails of blood from the grazes.

"Do you bring your lips to sing Her acclaim?"

"I do." Bubba Afsana's songs echoed on the breeze.

"Do you bring your eyes to see Her presence in all?"

"I do."

"Rise, child. You are chosen."

A deep stillness settled on Miri-amne. She stood slowly, filled with such sweetness that even death seemed welcome. The vast dome of sky went on forever . . .

Then the light changed.

A cloud of smoke drifted overhead, casting a shadow on the cliff. A terrible premonition made Miri-amne climb again, ignoring her torn hands.

Smoke rose in billowing clouds over the city. Birds wheeled, calling warnings to each other. No, it wasn't the birds. People were screaming, their cries carrying to the hills.

Miri-amne's skin went cold. She climbed down and ran

back towards her home. Others were in the lane now, heedless of custom. Some called down from the rooftops.

"The Temple is burning!"

"Can you see anyone?"

"Are there soldiers?"

But there were no answers until the first of the Temple-goers trudged up the road. Miri-amne ran to her Father.

"What happened, Abba? Is there a fire? Was anyone hurt? Where's Bubba? Where's Mama?"

For the first time in her life, he did not answer her questions. He looked through her with empty eyes, stepped into their courtyard, and fell to his knees on the paving stones.

Was this her Abba? The same Abba who had left home that morning, laughing and talking with his wife, calling farewell to his daughter?

Miri-amne went to stand beside him, her legs shaking, fear crawling over her skin like ants. When Abba began to pray, she knelt with him. The courtyard filled with people, kneeling and praying to a G-d who seemed to have abandoned them.

Yesh-ua from next door tugged at her shift and rolled his eyes towards the gate. They sat on the step, and he told her how the zealots had thrown stones at the Roman soldiers, how the soldiers had ridden their horses into the Temple, how people had panicked, how terrible it has been. He sobbed as he told her how someone had thrown a flaming brand onto the palm fronds decorating the pillars, and someone else had thrown an oil lamp. And how the soldiers had withdrawn, letting the Temple burn.

By the time Yesh-ua had run out of words, Miri-amne's father had stopped praying and disappeared into the house. Most of the neighbours had gone home.

"Mama and Bubba?" she asked. Please let them be safe. Please.

Yesh-ua shrugged. "I didn't see them. Have you asked your Father?"

"He didn't answer me."

"It was terrible, Miri. Terrible. People fell beneath the horses. They were screaming for help, but we were too far away. Then everyone was running and pushing, and more people went down . . ." He started to cry again, great gulping sobs that shook his whole body.

Miri-amne put her arm around him and listened for footsteps coming up the hill.

When Miri-amne climbed the hill in search of the swallow's nest, it had been a thousand years since a girl called Inna had travelled from Halab to Ursalimmu with her family and met a Queen there. Miri-amne did not know the story, although there was a family myth about a Queen's gift. She was Inna's many-times great-granddaughter, through forty generations of mothers and daughters. Miri-amne was born Ivri, or Hebrew, and she was the first daughter in the line of Mir-ri to hear the High Priestess for three generations.

"The Romans are calling him 'King'," said Miri-amne's Father to the men gathered in the courtyard.

Miri-amne poured wine and pretended not to listen to the talk about the troublemakers, but her heart beat faster at the thought of seeing the old prophecies fulfilled. Maybe then the Ivri could fly free of the eagle. After all, she had reason to hate the Romans, two huge, unforgivable reasons. Mama and Bubba had never returned from the terrible day at the Temple, nor had Abba been allowed to search for their bodies among the broken columns and charred pillars. They were gone, their bodies lost amidst the blood and shattered dreams.

It had taken Miri-amne three cycles of the Moon to accept what Abba had known the day he climbed the hill alone: Mama and Bubba would never climb the hill again. She missed them every day, when she sang the morning songs, when she gathered wood on the hillside, when she lit the fire . . .

Some of the men with Abba talked excitedly about the promise of a King, but others shook their heads fearfully.

"A moment's freedom followed by more persecution. Already the roads are rank with the smell of death. If they have to crucify every dissident in Jerusalem, the Romans will do it." Hamman was older than Abba, and his words carried weight with the men.

Miri-amne left them to their debate and retreated to the open-sided kitchen area at the back of the house. She was almost happy standing there at the bench, chopping almonds. The rhythmic movement of her arm on the knife led her into a daydream . . .

. . .Bubba in the lane, talking with the other grandmothers about long-lost friends and dead husbands. Soon she will come in to sit on the step to sip her mint tea and rub ointment into the swollen joints on her fingers, and the smell of camphor and wintergreen will fill the air. Mama will appear any moment from the house to tell her to chop the nuts more finely. She will take the knife and show her how to do it . . .

A breeze from the valley rustled the leaves like mice in the wheat husks . . .

. . .Mama will sprinkle dried mint and say spells to banish the mice, but she will do it quietly, when Abba won't hear her chanting the words she learned from Bubba.

Miri-amne wrinkled her nose. What was that smell?

A shiver ran up her spine, dissolving the daydream. The smell was of decaying flesh, bodies rotting on the crosses, like Hamman said. Miri-amne gagged and covered her nose. Her hand smelled of the bitter hearts of almonds.

The back gate flew open with a crash.

Two men ran in, eyes wild, chests heaving.

Strangers.

Fear prickled Miri-amne's skin like nettles. She held up the knife and stepped back behind the bench, spilling the nuts to the ground.

Her foot caught the flour bin.

The lid clattered to the paving stones.

Had Abba heard? Would he come to check?

One of the men closed the gate. The other pointed at Miri-amne.

"Ah. A virtuous woman. See how she defends herself."

Miri-amne flinched at the harshness in his voice. His dark hair hung down like rope, knotted and twisted in long strands, and his mouth curved down like a sickle.

"More precious than rubies," said the other man, in a softer voice. His hair was also long, in the style of the dissidents, but tied back in a plait.

"What do you want?" Miri-amne pointed the knife at them. Could they see her hand shaking?

"Freedom from persecution," said the one with the ropy hair, spitting the words out like venom.

"A place to hide from Roman soldiers," said the soft-voiced one.

Miri-amne shuddered. If the soldiers caught them they would be nailed to crosses, and the stink of their rotting flesh would ride on the wind for days. She pointed to the woodshed.

The men crawled into the shadows between the shed and the wall.

The gate flew open again.

Three Roman soldiers strode into the garden, spears held ready to attack.

Miri-amne stumbled back, fell over the flour bin, and landed on her back, screaming.

Abba ran out, robes flapping around his legs.

"What is the meaning of this? What have you done to my daughter?" He pulled Miri-amne to her feet and pushed her behind him.

She buried her face in his robe so she would not stare at the woodshed.

"We seek two men. Dissidents," said one of the soldiers, in the rough accent of the Romans.

"Clearly we have no dissidents here," said Abba. "Myself, my daughter, and some friends in the courtyard. That is all."

"We will see these friends," said the soldier, striding into the house. His companions followed, the last one elbowing Abba aside.

With a warning look at Miri-amne, Abba straightened his robe and hurried after them. Would they catch the guests speaking of the Ivri King?

The strangers scrambled out from behind the shed and ran to the gate. The softly spoken one turned and smiled; he looked younger when he smiled, but his eyes held unbearable sadness.

Miri-amne was still staring at the gate, heart hammering, when the soldiers returned to search the yard. She quickly bent to scoop up the scattered nuts.

When the soldiers left, her father propped a sturdy beam against the gate so it could no longer be opened from the lane.

"Did they harm you?" he asked.

She shook her head but didn't trust herself to speak. Her heart was still racing as if it were she the soldiers had been chasing, she who might become a rotting corpse on a wooden cross.

Days passed, and Miri-amne heard more talk of the King who had come to fulfill the prophecy. Could it be one of the men in the garden? Which one? When she closed her eyes, she saw the sad eyes of the man who had smiled at her. What had he said? *A price above rubies . . .*

It was hard to sleep. The whole city was humming with stories of the Essenes who gathered under the stars to listen to the one they followed. Would the Ivri be free of Rome at last? Or would there be more bodies rotting in the Sun?

Miri-amne climbed to the rooftop to listen to the secret sounds of the night.

A movement caught her eye. Yesh-ua was awake also, walking softly across the nextdoor rooftop. He wore dark-coloured clothes and held his sandals in his hand. Wherever was he going in the middle of the night?

Miri-amne followed him down to the lane. Later, she would remember the way her heart leapt with excitement, the way her legs moved of their own accord, as if they already knew where they were headed.

She followed Yesh-ua past the houses, through the shadows, to a garden near the hill where her swallows nested. She hovered behind a tree as he greeted people by name and joined a group of men sitting on the ground in a rough circle.

One of them was talking excitedly.

Miri-amne gasped; it was the man with the rope-like hair.

"Welcome, sister," said a man behind her.

She turned to find two men watching her, one as old as Abba, one as young as Yesh-ua. Their long hair marked them as dissidents, and they both held wickedly curved knives. They seemed to be waiting for something.

"Shalom alacheim," she said, trying to smile.

"Come," said the older man, pulling her towards the group on the ground.

She pulled against him, but his grip was strong, his fingers bruising her arm. He led her to the man with the ropy hair and said something she did not understand. He called the man Simeon.

Simeon looked up. "Ah, the virtuous woman. What brings you here?"

Miri-amne shrugged; she truly did not know why she was there.

"She must have followed me," said Yesh-ua, standing to take her arm. "She knows not what we do here."

"Yet she is sympathetic to our cause," said another man from across the circle. Miri-amne recognised his soft voice.

"How do we know?" asked another, his tone challenging.

"She hid us from Roman soldiers," said Simeon.

Yesh-ua looked at her in amazement.

"But she does not have the word," said the man who had pulled her there.

"Baraka," said the softly spoken man. "Now she has the word. Leave her be."

As quickly as they had turned to stare at her, the others resumed their discussion.

Yesh-ua took her gently by the hand and led her to a small mound under an acacia tree. They sat there, away from the others, while Miri-amne told him the story of the soldiers, and he explained the gathering.

"They are dissidents. They follow the Law, but some of them teach that we must fight the Romans. And they welcome women in their councils."

"How long have you been coming here?" asked Miri-amne.

"Since the Temple burned," said Yesh-ua quietly.

Of course; so much had changed that day.

"The two who hid in your garden are the leaders here, although they often argue. Simeon would have us fight to the death, but the other is slower to anger. It is as if he knows something the rest of us have not yet seen, but he has trouble finding the words to tell us. It is for him I come."

Yes. There was something about the sad-eyed man that held one's attention. "What is his name?" she asked.

"He is Yesh-ua, like me."

CHAPTER XXXIX

Alexandria, Egypt[xxxiii]. c 30CE.

Unlike almost all ancient cities, Alexandria was planned, designed and built within a century and thus its broad, open avenues and grid-like city planning made it unique in the ancient world. Two main streets, lined with colonnades and said to have been each about 60 meters (200 feet) wide, intersected in the centre of the city, close to the point where rose the great Sema (or Soma) of Alexander, the glittering tomb built to house his remains. For centuries, his body lay in state in a catafalque of solid gold - later, the Ptolemies allegedly melted down the gold and replaced the coffin with one of cut crystal, permitting Romans like Julius Caesar and Pompey to gaze upon the preserved body of the conquerer even more famous than they. The Heptastadion (seven stades long) was a marching walkway built to connect the Island of the great Pharos - Alexandria's world-famous lighthouse - with the city itself.[xxxiv]

As Miri-amne sat on the hillside with Yesh-ua, another

daughter in the line of Mir-ri dreamt of sailing ships. In the street of the Magi, in the great city of Alexandria, Meh-tan dreamt of sailing ships . . .

She woke early, still seeing the red sail of her father's ship billowing in the wind. With a glad cry, she jumped up from her sleeping mat. A dream so clear it must be true: her father, Josephus, would be home before nightfall.

She pulled on her crumpled shift from the day before and let herself out through the back gate. Her bare feet were quieter than the wind as she ran down the paved lanes to the Harbour. The air was thick with humidity, as if the Neters were all having steam baths. Meh-tan wiped sweat from her face and slowed down; Josephus would not arrive until the Sun sailed into the West. She walked sedately past the salty old men gathering on the porticos to smoke and play towla. Their wives, fine-grained like the sand, poured coffee and chattered like birds.

"Perhaps," said the women, "Meh-tan would not be running to the Harbour like a slave-girl if she had a mother."

"Perhaps she would not be reading all day rather than learning to sew."

"Perhaps she would not be debating philosophy with the men rather than washing lettuce and chopping meat."

Perhaps, thought Meh-tan, the old women would not be saying the same things year after year if they had more to think about. Then she reached the harbour. The fishy tang of the Sea stung her nostrils, and sails waved like banners in the breeze, urging the ships to ride the wind. If she were a ship, she would close her eyes and let the wind take her wherever it blew. But not today; today Josephus was returning from Athens.

By the time the Sun had risen high enough to dance on the waves, Meh-tan had settled on the Harbour wall, shaded by two whispering palms. She sat with her knees pulled up to her chin, her black hair falling down to cover her bare feet. The Sun reflected like a beacon off the white marble of the Pharos, the great tower built to guide ships to the Harbour.

All day Meh-tan sat, as still as one of the pillars lining the road to the heart of the city. She only moved to drink water from the public fountain and to empty her bladder. All day the dock workers sweated in the Sun, loading ships bound for Rome and Athens with trade goods from Kemet: amphorae of wine and oil, bales of wool and cotton, baskets of jars and bowls from the kilns.

She was still waiting when the Sun became a red disc on the western horizon, sliding down to the Underworld. Then a sail appeared, black against the red, and she stood on the Harbour wall to wave. Josephus, home at last!

By the time the ship pulled up at the wharf, Meh-tan was curled up on the wall, asleep. Josephus saw her as soon as he disembarked, and immediately he looked for faithful Inri. The old attendant waved from the doorway of a storehouse. Grey hair plaited in the style of the Greeks, Inri had been there all Meh-tan's life, helping Josephus be both mother and father to the child whose mother had died birthing her. Josephus nodded to Inri and looked down at Meh-tan. His heart ached with joy to find her there to greet him, even if she was wild and reckless-- and asleep.

He left his bags for Inri and carried Meh-tan himself, along the lanes from the Harbour to the wider, tree-lined streets of the Philosophers, Mathematicians, Priests, and Astronomers. Behind the high walls the people of Alexandria sipped chilled wine, spooned ice sorbet, and spoke of the great mysteries of the World. Josephus sighed; he had missed the debates in the forum, the long evenings of discussion in his own courtyard. The Romans might proclaim Rome the centre of the World, but it was Alexandria that shone like the Sun. He turned onto the Lane of Magi, carrying Meh-tan home.

Two evenings later, Josephus invited his Ivri friends to share a meal and discuss the reports of a King in Ursalimmu. Meh-tan was not present at the table, but she listened to the greybeards from behind the carved screen where servants bustled to and fro with platters of spiced lamb and roasted vegetables, cheeses and fruit. To the Ivri, a woman at the table was an invitation for licentiousness, even if she was only twelve years old. Josephus did not share their prudishness, but still Meh-tan listened from behind the screen when the Ivri came to talk.

"The Ivri have their customs, even as we have ours," Josephus had said. "We would only make it impossible for them to dine here if you sat at the table, and then neither of us would hear what they have to say."

Meh-tan did not mind. She lay on cushions behind the screen, and the servants gave her food. But it was better when their own people came, and she could sit at the table and join the debates; women were not feared by those who honoured Isis as sister-wife of Osiris.

When the greybeards had gone, Josephus called Meh-tan into the dining room.

"What did you hear?" he asked, testing her.

"The astronomers and soothsayers predict change," she said. "And the Ivri are resurrecting the old prophecies about a Messiah who will be their King, to free them from Rome and restore the Temple."

Josephus nodded.

"What do you think?" she asked. "Will their Messiah come from Alexandria or Ursalimmu? Or from the East like the Persian kings in the old tales?"

"If the time is right, the people will create a Messiah, so it will probably be in Ursalimmu. Perhaps he will even free them from Rome. At the very least, it will be interesting; a true prophet rarely obeys the Laws. The greybeards may be in for a surprise."

"How do they know their Messiah will be a King?" asked Meh-tan. "Why not a Queen?"

Josephus laughed. "Because, my dear, they cannot think any other way. For them it is the bloodline of Abraham through which they claim a special covenant with their One God. Therefore, it is the male seed that bestows the right to be considered Hebrew. That is why they guard their wives--and their daughters--more closely than their herds."

"But Abraham must have had daughters, too. What of their children?" She was truly puzzled; was not the life-giving power of Isis revered above all?

Josephus shook his head. "Still they need to know which man's seed has quickened the new life. What if the woman lay with a man not of the chosen line?" He winked at her, to let her know what he thought of the Laws.

Meh-tan was silent, thinking of how it might be to live under the control of father and husband, even when it came to determining the men she chose as lovers. She shivered. "I'm glad we're not Ivri, Abba."

Josephus shrugged. "We probably come from the same tribes, but do not say that to the greybeards."

That would be easy; there was little chance of her being in the same room as the Ivri men, let alone speaking with them.

As she waited for sleep that night, Meh-tan wondered how it would be to live like an Ivri woman. The men seemed so serious compared with the men of Kemet, who honoured women for their beauty and passion. As a daughter of Isis, it was her choice with whom she lay and with whom she made new life. It may be the man she called husband but not always and, as long as there was enough to eat, a child would always be welcomed as a gift from Isis.

CHAPTER XL

Babillu (Babylon). c 30CE.

While no one is certain as to the origin of the name, many believe that Babylon is derived from Babillu, a very old word which can be broken down into Bâb or gate and ili or gods, roughly translated as "The Gate of Gods" or "The Gateway of Gods".[xxxv]

As Meh-tap listened to the Ivri greybeards, a young woman called Inna paced the courtyard of a flat-roofed house in a small Habiru settlement in Babillu, the city they called Gate of the Gods[xxxvi].

Inna was named for her ancestor, who had once met a Queen in Ursalimmu.

It was market day, and Inna was home alone. She had begun to have her monthly bleeding, and that changed everything: no longer could she run barefoot with her friends in the lanes; now she must cover herself from neck to ankles in a robe, even when the Sun made the clay walls too hot to touch;

now she must not look a man in the eyes, even if it was Harif whom she had known all her life. Suddenly she had become dangerous and precious all at once.

She hated it.

She should not leave the garden at all, but the Sun was shining, and she needed to smell the air from the river. She would only walk to the end of the lane and back, and no one would see her . . .

As she passed a high wall, the wind changed. A robe hanging on a rooftop flapped like a boat's sail in a storm. Inna looked up.

The pole holding up the washing-line fell. It struck a pot of marjoram, balanced precariously on the edge of the rooftop.

The pot toppled off the roof.

Inna saw the movement and ducked down, covering her head with her hands. The pot hit the wall and bounced onto her head. She fell to the ground, her soul soaring towards the Sun.

When consciousness returned, there was nothing but the memory of flying. Despite the throbbing pain in her head, she laughed out loud.

A young man, chasing after the falling pot, stared in amazement at the crazy woman covered in soil. Blood trickled down her face, and marjoram poked from her robe as if growing from her breasts.

Jerem looked around. His family was new in the village, and he did not wish to lay hands on a woman in violation of the Law. But what could he do? His mother and sisters had not yet arrived from the South, and his neighbours were at market.

The woman on the ground stopped laughing and started to cry.

With another look over his shoulder, Jerem stooped to help the woman to her feet, saying a silent prayer that she not be in her unclean time. No sooner had he lifted her than she swooned against him, her body warm and heavy in his arms. Flustered beyond the fact of it having been his family's marjoram pot that fell on her, Jerem stumbled with his burden back through the gates of his father's house. He lay the woman on the ground and fetched water in a bowl. Then he sat by her side, waiting for her to open her eyes again. They had been remarkable eyes: blue like the sky on a clear day when the Sea sent strong breezes and the vines on the trellis in the courtyard reached for the Sun.

Jerem shook his head, his dark curls falling forward into his eyes. He flicked the hair back. His father wanted him to cut it short as befitted a worker in stone, but he wanted to wear it long like the wandering zealots who preached freedom and rebellion. He was sure his father and his brother had not guessed the real reason he refused to cut his hair.

Where were his father and brothers?

Soon enough, they returned from market.

"What have you done?" cried his father, Joseph, dropping the dates he had brought for supper.

"Who is she?" cried Haran, squatting beside his brother to stare at the woman.

"Why do you always assume I have done something, Father?" said Jerem. "All I have done is see that no one knows it was our marjoram pot that fell on this woman as she passed our gate."

Joseph scowled. "Perhaps I always assume the worst because you style yourself after the rabble who roam the land calling for change. Troublemakers." He went on mumbling as he leaned over the unconscious woman for a closer look.

"Was she alone?" he asked.

Jerem nodded. He hadn't thought of that. What was a

respectable woman doing alone in the street? He looked across at Haran, whose mouth was twitching with laughter.

"Do you think she is a . . .?" For all his thoughts of insurrection and freedom, Jerem couldn't quite bring himself to say the word.

". . .harlot," said his brother, finishing Jerem's sentence, as he usually did.

Joseph shrugged. "The cloth of her robe is very fine, and she wears no kohl around her eyes. Perhaps we should not be too hasty in our judgement. We will have Matthias bring the cart and take her to the Physician."

"What if she is not a harlot?" asked Jerem, who had noticed his father's hesitation.

Joseph sighed. "If there is a question to be asked, you are bound to ask it, Jerem. If she is not, then she will be known by the Physician, and he will see to it."

Haran was sent for the cart, and Jerem watched over the woman while Joseph went inside to find silver to pay for her treatment.

Inna regained consciousness the second time to find a man stroking her arm. He was vaguely familiar, but as if from a dream. Her brothers had mentioned a new family from the South, but why would he be touching her if he was Habiru? She expected him to stop now she was awake, but then she saw that he had his eyes closed, as if inhaling a precious scent. Rather than disturb his meditation, she half-closed her eyes and waited. When he showed no sign of stirring, she groaned as if just awakening. He snatched his hand away.

She looked up into deep, brown eyes that glowed as if lit from within. With an effort, she lifted herself up onto her elbows. A flood of thoughts came, the most insistent being the dishonour she brought upon her father by lying on the ground with a strange man by her side. Inna took a deep breath and began to speak.

"My name is Inna. I live on the Street of Marduk with my family. I was out without my father's permission. He is a good father who holds to the Law."

"Why?" asked the brown-eyed man.

Inna thought she saw his lips twitch as if with humour, but she could not be sure. It was more likely to be disapproval or condemnation. What had she been thinking?

"I was restless and longed to smell the wind. I thought I could walk in the shadow of the walls and be home before my father came back. I was foolish."

The man's full lips curved into a smile. "The desire for freedom is never foolish. Do you think you can walk? If we hurry, you may be able to return to your home before anyone learns your name."

The young man helped Inna to her feet and saw her safely to the corner of the lane. She smiled at him, suddenly shy despite him having touched her twice. Or perhaps because of that. With a nod, she walked away, staying close to the wall. Her head hurt as if she had been too long in the Sun.

She was home in time to wash her face and change her robe before her parents returned from market. Her mother spotted the lump on her head as soon as Inna bent down to help with the bags.

"What have you done to your head?"

"I slipped on the stairs. It is nothing." The first lie she had ever told; it burned like sour milk in her throat, but it opened up a secret place in her thoughts.

Her father gave her a lecture about taking more care of herself. What would he have done if her excursion had been discovered? He would never have disowned her like Sarai's father did when she met the ass trader's son at night. Nor would he have had her beaten; her mother would not allow it. Perhaps he would have sent her to their distant relatives in Ursalimmu, where the Laws were upheld by Priests in a Temple bigger than their whole village.

Inna slept poorly for a few nights and then dared to hope her transgression would not be discovered. In the space between sleeping and waking, she occasionally glimpsed warm, brown eyes in the place where she kept her most precious secrets.

CHAPTER XLI

Amman, Jordan. May 18th 2015.

LYSISTRATA: Then I will out with it at last, my mighty secret! Oh! sister women, if we would compel our husbands to make peace, we must refrain...

CLEONICE: Refrain from what? Tell us, tell us!

LYSISTRATA: But will you do it?

MYRRHINE: We will, we will, though we should die of it.

LYSISTRATA: We must refrain from the male altogether.... Nay, why do you turn your backs on me? Where are you going? So, you bite your lips, and shake your heads, eh? Why these pale, sad looks? why these tears? Come, will you do it-yes or no? Do you hesitate?

Aristophanes, 410 BCE

Alone in her apartment, Haleli sat cross-legged on the floor of her small loungeroom, dressed in a soft orange jalabiya, her hair loose on her shoulders. In her lap rested a pendant of lapis lazuli set in gold. It was very old and carried secrets . . .

With a deep sigh, Haleli placed the pendant gently on her desk, left behind the dreams of magic, mystery and ancient secrets, and turned on her computer.

She opened a folder named *Lysistrata,* scrolled down to a file named *Sesame,* and set in motion the plan she had been working on for a decade. Tomorrow, her message would be sent to almost every sex worker in the World . . .

Pereira, Colombia. May 19th 2015.

Maria tiptoed into the old terrace house and eased the door closed. If she were lucky, no one would notice she was late again.

Pausing in the dimly-lit hallway, she pulled her top down to show more cleavage and ran her fingers through her hair, spreading it like a black cape over her shoulders. She flicked open her pocket mirror, examined her face, straightened her eyebrows, and pinched her cheeks for colour. With a resigned sigh, she braced herself for another night's work. For sure she would be sent to the back room for her third late start, forced to take the disgusting jobs no one else wanted. Head held high, she entered the parlour.

It was empty.

Curious, her stomach tight with anxiety, Maria climbed the stairs to the small room on the first floor where Mercedes sat managing the affairs of the brothel, like a big, black spider in the centre of her web, sensing every movement.

Maria's heart thumped harder, as if she had run up the stairs instead of creeping like a mouse. Why would everyone be up there with Mercedes? Had someone died?

She wiped her damp palms on her skirt. If she couldn't work, Miguel wouldn't be happy, and pleasing him had become as necessary as making money to feed the children. A shiver rippled up her back.

Mercedes' room was full of women and tension. A smell of fear vied with the cloud of cheap perfume. Mercedes presided over the gathering from behind her desk, a real antique from Bogota. So absorbed was she in reading the pamphlet in her hands, she had broken her own taboo and placed a coffee cup straight onto the wooden desktop.

She read aloud, her voice deep and slow. " . . .will reimburse every woman and child a sum equivalent to his or her regular earnings. This does not include moneys paid to managers, pimps, boyfriends etcetera. Arrangements can be made to relocate women and children, and there is a safe house in most areas, but this project is not without risk to the workers."

Mercedes looked up from her reading, eyeing them all like a spider with a web full of squirming insects. Her chest heaved and her breasts wobbled with barely suppressed rage. Maria had seen that look before.

Everyone was very quiet.

"What's happening?" whispered Maria to Angie. They were cousins, but looked more like sisters, to the delight of some of their regular customers.

Angie looked frightened. "Someone wants to pay us to stop work."

"What?" said Maria, loudly enough to catch Mercedes' attention.

"There has been an offer," said Mercedes, spitting in her fury. "An outrageous offer to stop work. Someone wants to shut me down and give you money for nothing."

"A man gave the letter to us all outside," said Angie. "He said not to tell anyone, but she always knows." She nodded towards Mercedes.

"Money for everyone?" asked Maria. "Even Miguel?"

"No money for pimps," said Angie, looking frightened.

Mercedes sent them to work with harsh warnings of what would happen if they even thought of taking the money.

Of course the women spoke of nothing else, between jobs, on the way home, at market the next day.

"I could go home," said Claudia. "Back to Santa Rosa de Cabal."

"Jorge would find you there," said Leidy, shaking her head.

"So what?" said Claudia with a defiant toss of her red hair. "I can't help it if there's no one at work."

"Do you think all the workers got a letter?" asked Bibiana. "Everywhere?"

Angie nodded. "It says so here." She reached into her bra and produced a pamphlet. "This offer has been delivered to every sex work establishment in the world."

Claudia whistled, something she did when surprised or excited. "La huelga de las piernas cruzadas," she said wonderingly.

"The crossed-legs strike," said Bibiana. "But what for?"

Maria had wondered the same thing. The crossed-legs strike some years back was well known in Pereira; some of the women had started a sex strike to persuade their men to give up violence. Everyone knew the story, but no one seemed to know if it had worked.

"That, Bibiana, is a good question," said Maria, biting her bottom lip. "If we stop work, the whole system will go to hell. And when things go to hell, it's the women who get hurt. We need to know more."

Everyone nodded. The letter gave them an email address and a number to call, but was it safe?

"One more thing," said Claudia. "Not a word of this to anyone. Swear it!"

Dutifully, each woman swore on that which she held most precious: children, God, the Virgin, their mothers. Not one of them swore on the men who watched over them and sent them to work.

CHAPTER XLII

Jerusalem. Updated May 19th 2015 11.52am UTC

Global sex strike. In a shocking move, sex workers closed shop in major cities across Europe overnight. An unknown organisation claiming responsibility for the strike has said the strike will spread around the World over the next few weeks. The organisation is demanding global action by governments to free women, children and nature from domination and oppression. Authorities report an upsurge in violence.

On their third day in Jerusalem, Lili and Paula were waiting for Peter in a small café near their hotel, their laptops open ready for work. Paula scanned emails while Lili read the online news reports.

Lili gasped and went very still.

"Haleli," she whispered. "It has to be."

"Haleli?" Paula's heart leapt, in fear or excitement, she couldn't tell. "What?"

Lili angled the computer so Paula could read the news report.

"A sex work strike? Why do you think it has anything to do with Haleli?"

"Because she was up to something big, and this makes sense."

"Huh?"

"Disrupting the sex trade will make the media take notice. It's going on all the time--women and children bought and sold with no regard for human rights--but governments won't act. Remember when Haleli said that the way the World treats women reflects the way we treat Nature?"

"So this is her idea of a wake-up call?"

"It's getting people's attention."

"It's crazy! How on earth did she do it?"

Peter overheard the last part as he sat down at the table. "That woman is amazing. No one else would even think of it, and she makes it happen."

"It must be costing a fortune," said Lili. "Where's the money coming from?"

Peter ignored the question and signalled the waiter.

"But will it work?" asked Paula. "Will people understand what it's about?"

"They will if the media do their job," said Peter. "And there's the internet: online organising, electronic advocacy, E-campaigning, internet activism."

"As long as it motivates action," said Lili. "It must have taken years to set this up. What a crazy, wonderful idea!"

"Haleli's a crazy, wonderful person," said Peter.

"And a very rich one," said Lili.

"Have you known her long?" asked Paula, honest enough to know she was both intrigued and frightened by Haleli.

Peter shrugged. "Long enough to believe in what she's doing." He ordered a black coffee and kunafa.

"A sex workers' strike's a bit more significant looking for pieces of jewellery!" said Paula.

"Maybe. But if Haleli says what you're doing is important, then it is."

"Okay. Let's do it," said Lili. "I can't think about the strike for too long; it makes my head spin.

"I can't even get my head around it!" said Paula. "Changing the subject, then. Do you think our jewellery really could have come from the Queen of Sheba?"

"Or did someone fake them a few generations back and make up a good story to go with them?" Peter smiled and shook his head. "Not likely. Why bother just to have them hidden away under beds for hundreds of years? Some of the fakes are made the same way the originals were, with the same materials. It keeps traditional handicrafts alive and well! But there'd be no point with your pieces."

"I still think it's amazing that something could survive that long," said Paula.

"I've seen stranger things in my time," Peter said mysteriously.

"Like what?" asked Paula. "This is pretty strange, if you ask me."

Peter nodded. "That's true. I was thinking of the places where I've found some of my best treasures: five thousand year old jars in lean-to kitchens, cylinder seals from ancient Sumer propping up tables, enamelled scarabs in kids' toy boxes. Things that have been handled by pharaohs."

Lili spoke of some of the archaeological digs she had been on, and Paula started to think that necklaces from the Queen of Sheba might not be impossible.

They talked some more about the sex workers' strike, finished their coffees, and arranged to meet for dinner. Peter was spending the day visiting his usual contacts.

Lili walked Paula to the Old City and gave her a history lesson.

"This was once a small town in the hills, well away from the main trade routes between Egypt and the North. There had been tribes in these hills for centuries, but no one claimed the town as their own until King David wanted it for the capital of Is-rael."

"Were the tribes all Jewish?" asked Paula. "Or is that a stupid question?"

"Not at all stupid, but it depends who you ask. Remember that the answer can be used to establish who rightfully owns this piece of land that everyone seems to want a stake in."

"So who rightfully owns it?" asked Paula.

"They're all right and they're all wrong; it's like any story of conquest since the beginning of time. Who do you think owns Australia, for example? Who has the 'right' to the land? The original people who lived there for millennia, or the new settlers who had greater force of arms?"

"There's been some attempt to sort that out," said Paula. "Although it's too little, too late." The infant mortality rate among indigenous Australians was still one of the highest in the World. "What's happened back home is unofficial genocide. Terrible."

Lili nodded sadly. "The fight over who owns this land has been going on forever. But now we have Weapons of Mass Destruction, or the threat of them, and a global, media machine fuelling the fight. Do you have any idea how often Jerusalem has changed hands since David built his temple?"

Paula shook her head, certain that Lili was about to tell

her.

"Actually, I don't know exactly how many times it's been conquered and reconquered. David and his descendants had it for a few hundred years, and then the tribes split the Kingdom in two after Solomon's reign: Israel in the north and Judah in the south. Jerusalem was the capital of Judah. Then, in about 700BCE, the Assyrians took Israel and deported the tribes. Judah survived a bit longer but was finally destroyed by Nebuchadnezzar, the King of Babylon, in the fifth century BCE. They destroyed Solomon's Temple and carried off the treasures to Babylon, along with most of the people of Judah. Seventy years or so later, the Persian King, Cyrus, gave the descendants permission to return. Some stayed in Babylon, and those who went back to Judah became the ancestors of the Jews."

"So, that's where the Jews come in," said Paula.

Lili nodded. "But you have to remember that many non-Israelites also became Jews by religion. When it became politically expedient to claim direct descent from Abraham, the usual mixing of the tribes was conveniently forgotten. Anyway, when they returned from Babylon, they built a new temple in Jerusalem and settled down for five hundred years or so. Then Jerusalem changed hands a few times: Alexander the Great conquered the Persian Empire and Jerusalem came under Hellenistic Greek control, and then Ptolemy, and then the Seleucids. Then the Maccabean revolt established the Hasomean Kingdom with Jerusalem as its capital."

Paula looked around at the mix of old and new that seemed to exist in almost every part of Jerusalem. "And through all that, the Jews just went on living here."

"That's what it was like for most people at that time," said Lili. "Kings came and went, the tributes changed, and different soldiers imposed order, but life went on. Jerusalem became an important stop on the trade routes and a capital for whoever took control of the country."

"Who else took control?" asked Paula. "I guess the Romans must come in there somewhere."

"Romans, Byzantines, the Crusaders, Saladin, back to the Romans, then the Turks, the Marmelukes, more Turks, and then England and The League of Nations with the Mandate of Palestine to establish a Jewish state in the region."

"I think that was seventeen or eighteen," said Paula. "But I might have missed a few. No wonder there's so much angst about who it really belongs to."

Lili nodded. "I'm glad there's a homeland for the Jewish people, but I wish it was somewhere less prone to conflict."

"So, have I got this right? The Jewish people are the descendants of the tribes who returned from Babylon plus various others who became Jewish along the way."

"More or less," said Lili. "Scholars have traced the origins of the Semitic language. They say the Habiru, or wandering tribes, were originally scattered all over the Near East from Egypt to Mesopotamia, to the extremities of Assyria, along the coast of the Mediterranean through Canaan, and in the regions of Anatolia. Quite a range. They were the original, wandering Arameans, although their descent was Akkadian or Assyrian. It's this genetic line that produced Abraham. They had a deity whose name was unknown, an unusual thing in those days."

"And they first settled in Israel about three thousand years ago," said Paula quietly, wondering if the story Lili was telling had anything to do with their quest.

"What's interesting is how they established themselves as having a unique, genetic identity, whether it was strictly true or not. The original term, Habiru, disappeared from the ancient documents about the same time the name Ivri appeared, but only in relation to Israelites. The other Habiru must have become submerged by interbreeding with other tribes; it was only among the Ivri that the Habiru/Hebrew distinction survived. I don't know if it was far-sighted of the original, founding fathers, or if it's been used opportunistically in more recent times, but it supports the idea that Jews have a right to the lands promised to Abraham."

"And what do you think?" asked Paula.

Lili sighed deeply. "Like I said, I'm glad there's a homeland, but I wish it was somewhere where people could settle down to raise their children in peace."

"I guess that's the crux of it, isn't it?" said Paula. "The where of it has become more important than the how of it."

"Scripture says that the name, Israel, was bestowed on Abraham's grandson, Jacob, as a sign of his relationship with God. It was Jacob's twelve sons who fathered the tribes of Israel."

"Sounds like it's all tied up very neatly. Twelve sons? No mention of the mother, I suppose?"

"Oh, the mothers get a mention, but only in the background. Hebrew law centred around the male. Which is why they kept the women under lock and key; they needed to know it was their seed that produced the next generation of sons."

Paula pulled a face that said it all and wished there was something more useful to do than touring the Old City. At least Haleli was doing something, but could this crazy, sex workers' strike of hers really make a difference? Would it make people think more about how women were treated? Could it really change the way countries assumed the right to control and dominate Nature? Or was it just a grand gesture that would make no difference at all?

Paula and Lili spoke of little else for the rest of the day. Lili phoned Haleli every half hour, but there was no answer.

CHAPTER XLIII

Babillu (Babylon). c 30CE.

The desert environment is harsh and does not lend itself easily to the support of human life. Much of the Bedu territory receives only 4 inches (10 centimeters) of rain per year, and those 4 inches are scattered and unpredictable. Temperatures can go as high as 122° F (50° C) in the shade during the summer months, and as low as 32° F (0° C) during the winter. At night, the temperature drops dramatically, plunging as much as 86° F (30° C) from daytime temperatures. The beginning of summer is often heralded by violent sandstorms and scorching winds.[xxxvii]

The market day following her misadventure with the marjoram pot, Inna's father announced that the family would be leaving Babillu. Her body flushed hot and cold, and she choked on her bread. Did he know about her meeting with the brown-eyed man? Were they leaving because of her?

"It will be a better life," said her mother. "Joachim and his family sent word with the spice caravan that there are others like us in the West."

Inna knew her mother was referring to others whose ancestors had come from Ursalimmu hundreds of years ago, but it seemed a distant sort of connection. Would they be the same? Would they sing praises to the Queen of Heaven and honour the four directions? Would they know the ancient spells for Balance?

Her mother told her to stop asking questions and start packing their belongings into panniers for the asses.

Inna dutifully packed their belongings, but she still worried about her new life. What would they find in the West? Would she ever again see the man from the day of the wind?

Inna's family left Babillu without her catching sight of the brown-eyed man. Would there be men in the West like him, with a sparkle in their eyes at the thought of freedom? Or would they follow the Laws and obey their Fathers without question?

"Do not worry," said her Mother, guessing some but not all of her fears. "The men will treat you like a rare spice all the way from the Eastern paradise of Babylonia."

"I will miss Babillu," said Inna, crushing the wheat as if it was to blame for her exile. "I will miss my friends. And the colour of the sky. And the taste of the water." She said nothing of the dark-eyed neighbour.

"Babillu is in your blood," said her mother. "Our ancestors came from a great city in the South. For thousands of years they lived between the rivers."

"What do you mean? The tribes only left Ursalimmu two hundred years ago."

"That is true, but my mother's people came to Ursalimmu from the North, and from Urim before that. You know the songs . . ."

She sang a line from the morning and evening praises. "The holy Priestess of Heaven is radiant on the horizon."

Inna hummed the tune she had been singing all her life.

"There is no Queen of Heaven in Ursalimmu," said her mother. "The Ivri have honoured the one G-d for over a thousand years, but the Moon still changes with women's bleeding, and the morning and evening star still shines on the horizon."

"Why have you never told me about our ancestors?" asked Inna.

"I did when you were young, but you must have forgotten."

As they travelled Inna had her mother repeat all the old stories, until she knew them word for word. They sang the old songs, and Hazan said the camels liked them.

The Moon shone brightly in the desert, and the first daughter of the Moon, the radiant star that moved through morning and evening cycles, rose with the Moon while they travelled.

The man of the marjoram pot sometimes visited Inna in her dreams, and she often heard his words: "The desire for freedom is never foolish." Was it her desire for freedom that caused what happened?

Hazan had said the deadly sandstorms never struck so early in the season, but on their twelfth night in the desert, the sand began to whisper like wind in palm trees, and he pulled the camels into a tight circle and pitched a tent of goatskin in the centre. Inna huddled in the tent with her parents, Hazan, his three camel herders, and the other three families travelling West.

The children whimpered, and the parents crooned reassurances, but soon the small tent stank of fear.

Crouched between her mother and father, Inna took small breaths of the hot, sour air. The wind moaned like a creature in pain. One of the children cried pitifully. Then the sand hit the goatskins like a rainstorm.

Hazan and the herders hung onto the skins, pulling down with all their weight, their muscles like twisted ropes as they fought the wind that howled like jackals. The camels grunted and squealed as if they were being skinned alive by a thousand djinns.

A corner tore loose. Sand rushed in. Someone screamed.

Inna covered her face with her cloak. The sand stung her hands like tiny wasps.

Her father crawled over to help Hazan close the gap.

Inna huddled against her mother, trembling with fear.

With a wild cry, the wind tore away the goatskins.

Sand like knives rained on Inna's cloak. She curled into a ball and held her breath. Something heavy fell on her, and consciousness fled.

Inna opened her eyes.

She was blind.

A terrible weight crushed her chest.

She struggled to move, but her arms were trapped. Was she buried alive?

She turned her head and sucked in air. Sand filled her mouth, gritty and dry. Her throat closed against the dryness.

Desperate for air, she spat and coughed, but there was only sand. Tossing her head from side to side, she heaved against the weight on her chest. It smelled like camel. She screamed.

Someone yelled back.

The weight lifted off her chest.

Air rushed in, hot and gritty.

Strong hands lifted her and shook her so hard her bones rattled. She coughed up more sand. The shaking stopped. She opened her eyes.

She could see, but where was she?

Four strangers surrounded her, pillars of grey cloth with dark eyes in faces baked hard by the desert.

The desert. The sandstorm. Where was everybody?

A corner of goatskin stuck out from a mound of sand. With a cry, Inna fell to her knees and scrabbled at the sand.

"Mama?"

"Abba?"

Strong hands lifted her again. The man spoke, his voice surprisingly gentle. Inna could not understand a word he said, but she understood his meaning when he pointed to the mounds of sand and shook his head.

Dead? All dead? A scream rose up, wild like the wind that had attacked them. She howled at the sky, and the men carried her away.

One of them took her before him on horseback to a cluster of brown and white goats' hair tents sheltered between two dunes. Bedu tents. Hazan had told them tales of the wandering tribes that honoured Ishtar.

Dark-skinned women lifted her from the horse and carried her to a tent where all was shadowy and still. They dripped water into her mouth and washed the sand from her body, all the time chattering like birds in a language Inna had never heard. Then fever like fire claimed her, and the chattering birds turned into demons scouring the flesh from her bones, burning her life to ashes.

Six days later the fever left, but the women were still there. They fed Inna camel's milk and helped her stand on legs that had become skinny and weak. A glimpse of her face in a mirror of polished metal showed skin as rough as palm wood. Her tears ran like raindrops on parched soil.

Mama?

Abba?

Gone. Buried in the desert as if they had never been. How could they be gone and she still be breathing?

The women oiled her like a baby, and day by day the dead skin sloughed off to reveal new, unmarked cheeks. There was, however, no relief from the grief that made her bones ache.

Before she left the tent for the first time, they braided her hair and wrapped her in one of their heavy robes with the hood and face covering. The men, gravely courteous, treated her as one of their own.

When she had learned some of the language, Inna discovered that one of their people had been lost in the sandstorm, and the tribe accepted her as a gift from their Great Ones. No one asked her what she thought of the exchange, nor did anyone ever speak about her loss. It settled into a secret place in her heart, a dull ache that flared when the wind moaned and sand blew against the tents.

No one spoke of her loss, but they were kind enough. The women gave her tasks to do and taught her their language. Some of their songs were familiar, and their stories were of a great Mother who looked after Her children. How her own mother would have rejoiced in the songs and the new stories, laughing and chattering with the women. Inna felt her there, a silent presence who never left her side.

The seasons passed, from intense heat to bitter cold, from sandstorms to days of silence. Inna settled into the rhythms of the tribe, although her skin burned too easily to be a true desert woman. Nevertheless Avram invited her to share his tent, promising to feed her and treat her well. That may have been enough, but he also made her laugh, and coming together at night in the way of man and woman was . . . well, it was pleasurable and satisfying . . .and enough to make her stop thinking about the life she might have had on the other side of the desert.

Inna gave the tribe four children who looked like their father and ran after the goats on strong legs. Her two boys made their Grandfather smile with pride, and her two girls learned the old songs of Inna's family as well as the Bedu songs. She told them stories from Babillu, and the tale of her ancestors who had once lived in a great city.

Inna's children had children, and the daughters taught their daughters the old wisdom.

200CE--170 years later

Halala, Inna's seven times great granddaughter, shaded her eyes and scanned the horizon. Heat shimmered like flickering genies, but nothing moved on the ochre sand. The camels were restless, snorting and stamping like impatient old men waiting to be fed.

The jug grew heavy in Halala's hand, as if it were already full, although the camels had not yet produced a drop of urine. Even their daily treat of salt had not roused the usual interest. If there was no urine, there would be no medicine for her father's mother, whose belly rumbled and whose joints ached until she cried.

Halala's father strode past with his falcon perched on his arm. The bird fluffed his feathers and hissed like a snake, as if he, too, had a bellyache. Halala sniffed the air: burning camel dung. Food would be ready before her work was done.

"Come on. Who will be first?"

As if in answer, the old mother camel started. Halala ran forward and held the jug to catch the stream of urine before it soaked into the sand. It smelled like growing things, grass and trees, as if the camel remembered the oasis where they spent the hottest days of the dry season. Halala placed the jug carefully in a shallow hole in the sand and fed the camel a handful of dates.

Her father's falcon soared dark against the sky. For a moment Halala forgot the camels and flew with the falcon. Wind stung her eyes and ruffled her hair, and she could see forever.

Another camel moved to make water, and Halala came back to the warm sand and the smell of camel dung. Finally the jug was full, and she carried it back to the al-mahram. Her Mother was there, standing over the cookfire as she did every day.

"Wash your hands and dress for strangers," she said, not looking up from stirring the rice.

"Who is here?" asked Halala.

"Wear your best veil and clean your hands."

Halala's heart raced. It was time for them to find her a husband, but her cousins were all too young, and her Father had been fighting with the neigbouring tribes since before she was born. Who could it be?

She washed her hands and face and ran her fingers through her hair, releasing the sweet smell of ipomea. She settled a loose, black dress over her dishdasha and wrapped the veil around her head.

Her mother nodded, handed her a tray of rice and vegetables, and lifted the woven curtain for Halala to cross into the men's area. Her father and brothers sat in their usual places, with her uncles and their young sons opposite. There were no strangers. Halala poured habuk tea into gold-rimmed glasses and waited while the men filled their bowls with food.

The tent flap moved, and a young man entered. He bowed his head to Halala's father and sat between her brothers as if he belonged in the family. Halala's cheeks burned. Was he the one? She lowered her eyes behind her veil, slid her hands inside her sleeves, and breathed as quietly as a desert mouse.

She raised her eyes.

Her breath caught in her throat.

He stared at her with eyes like black stars.

Halala held his gaze through the veil. His eyes moved slowly to her feet and back again. He smiled.

Halala bit her lip. Heat flowed through her body like a fever. Was he the one?

Her Father waved her away. She felt the man's eyes on her back as she left.

Her mother was preparing the women's food and did not look up.

"Who is he?" Halala lifted her veil and splashed water on her cheeks.

"Suhail son of Salem son of Muhammad of the Bait Kathir. His Father has horses."

"Of course he has horses," said Halala. Her Father had always said her bride price would be an Al Kahmsa mare. "But where are their tents?"

"Close enough for me to nurse your children."

Halala smiled. So be it: she would choose the dark-eyed

man.

The next day, her Father informed her that Suhail would pay the bride price. She would be escorted to his tent on the next full moon.

Even if Suhail had not pleased her, Halala would have loved him for his horses. Three of the Al Kahmsa mares lived in the women's side of Suhail's tent like family. The mares warmed the tent at night when temperatures dropped, and they snorted to warn of the sandstorms that could strip skin from bone. Living there also was Suhail's mother, his unwed sister, Amahra, and a woman so old her skin was like leather.

Halala could never find out if the old woman was the grandmother or great grandmother of Suhail or one of his cousins. Perhaps no one knew for sure. They called her "old woman", and she sat all day on the mat where she slept at night, weaving goat hair into intricate patterns on a screen. Amahra washed her and helped her outside once a day to see the sky and relieve her bladder. She ate less than a lizard. They said she was blind, but she looked at Halala knowingly and nodded her head as if they shared a secret.

On the men's side slept Suhail and five unwed cousins.

Halala's first spring in Suhail's tents followed a good rain and lasted many weeks. The desert floor was covered in grasses and wildflowers so deep that Suhail's cousins teased him about the fertility of his new wife. When Halala heard their teasing, she clutched the khamsa her Mother had sent with her to ward off the evil eye; better not to attract the attention of the Great Ones through praise or pride.

Yet the mares all threw strong foals that season, and six of the mother goats had twins; their bleating kept everyone awake for five nights. Even the camels multiplied like desert rats.

"It is you," said Suhail, laughing his great, booming

laugh. "You bring luck."

Halala blushed and shook her head. All she had brought were the rituals taught to her by her mother and her mother before her. Before the Sun rose red and demanding in the east, she would leave the tent with a jug of camel's milk and four bowls. These she placed outside the four corners of the tent and asked for the blessings of the elemental spirits. So had the women in her mother's line done since the beginning.

The unusual fecundity continued, and everyone attributed it to Suhail's wife. Hadn't she borne twin daughters herself? Weren't they both dark as night? Some whispered that Halala must be coupling with Djinn's to bring such luck, but it was never said in Suhail's hearing.

Halala continued to rise before dawn and make her offerings. One morning at the end of her second winter, when spring was a promise on the air, she bent to pour milk.

Someone whispered in her ear.

She whirled around, splashing milk on the sand.

Was it a Djinn?

"Many are called but few are chosen." Deeply resonant, a woman's voice intoned the ancient words of initiation.

Halala gasped. She knew the words from her mother's lessons, but there was no one there. Who was speaking?

"Do you bring your feet to walk in Her Ways?" asked the voice. A warmth rose up from the sand. Halala nodded.

"You must answer, child," said the voice. "Do you bring your feet to walk in Her Ways?"

"I do," whispered Halala, shaking all over.

"Do you bring your knees to kneel in Her praise?"

"I do." Halala sank to her knees and lowered her head.

"Do you bring your sex to rejoice in Her Life-giving?"

"I do."

"Do you bring your breasts for Her abundance flowing?"

"I do."

"Do you bring your hands to do Her work?"

"I do." Halala placed the jug on the sand and held her hands before her, palms together.

"Do you bring your lips to sing Her acclaim?"

"I do." She smiled, remembering the songs her mother had taught her.

"Do you bring your eyes to see Her presence in all?"

"I do."

"Rise, child. You are chosen."

Halala stood. The first glow of the Sun touched the straight line of the Eastern sands. She picked up the jug and completed her offerings. With a joyful heart she sang the morning invocation that had come from her mother's ancestors in the East:

"My Lady looks down in sweet wonder from Heaven

Al Uzzah is radiant on the horizon."

As if in answer, the Morning Star shone brighter.

Soon other women joined Halala in the morning ritual, singing praises to the Queen of Heaven. The abundant fertility continued.

Suhail often came to her at night while the others slept, but it was the early weeks that she remembered while they came together quietly in the tent. The early weeks, when he had lifted her up before him on Rajhata, his stallion, and ridden off into the spring grasses to lie together as man and woman under the stars: him entering her like the Sun piercing the morning mist; she receiving him like the pull of the Moon. Their daughters, Amara and Suhala, had been conceived then. Perhaps that explained their spirit.

When the twins were old enough, after their brother was

born, they, too, joined the women in singing the praises. The rest of the time they ran free, chasing the goats, riding the mares, growing strong. Their laughter filled the camp all through the dry seasons when they settled near the tribe's wells. There was more time at the wells for weaving and embroidery, repairing the tents, and learning new songs, yet the girls still found time to run and ride. When they moved the herds to find grazing, Amara and Suhala helped their cousins herd the camels, tend the horses, and set up the camp.

c220 to 1970CE.

Amara and Suhala carried the gift of abundance with them when they moved to the tents of their husbands. It travelled with their daughters, granddaughters, and many times great granddaughters through the centuries. The lives of the women continued unchanged until midway through the Age of Pisces.

It was then that the tribes adopted the teachings of the prophet, Muhammad ibn 'Abdullāh, a new faith based on Jewish and Christian teachings as well as his own visions. This new faith, called submission or al-'islām, had already been taught in the cities for centuries, but time moved slowly on the desert . . .

The tribes gradually adopted the new faith, although they held to older beliefs and practices that had ensured survival in the desert for thousands of years: amulets and charms, lucky numbers, honouring the spirits. Their lives depended on reading the stars and listening to the wind. The voices of the desert guided them, and not lightly did they renounce them for one God, even one as mighty as Allah.

1000CE

Laleli held the khamsa so tightly the edges of the amulet dug into her palm. Her father and his brothers had been gone for five nights, chasing wolves. The evil creatures had been prowling the tents, stealing goats, and making the camels stamp and snort all night. It had been quieter since the wolves and men had gone, but the spirits of the night were growing bolder, calling Laleli to join them under the stars.

She clutched the amulet and prayed to Allah for protection. She also called on her Mother's spirit, reciting quissa learned from the women when she was young. The tales told of unseen spirits hovering at the edge of the tents to bestow blessings or steal virtue. Which would it be? And how could she tell the difference?

Laleli sighed deeply. The night wind froze her breath. Were not the wolves the embodiment of evil? Were not their camels the direct descendants of the spirits of the desert? How could one girl's prayers prevail against such forces?

The men returned in time for Eid al-Adha, the feast of sacrifice. Laleli's father boasted of their victory over the wolves--Subhan'Allah--and made sure to choose an especially plump sheep to commemorate Abraham's willingness to sacrifice his son.

Laleli's brother played the rabab as her father recounted their successful wolf hunt. It was a victory to be sure, but Laleli sat alone, wondering how the men could all be so pleased when the feast was in honour of some greybeard's plan to kill his child to please Allah. Maybe men needed to feel the power that comes from wielding knives and spilling blood. Yet Aban did play rabab like an angel . . .

Laleli's thoughts about the ways of men remained with her through her marriage the next season, the move to her husband's tents, the birth of three sons and a precious daughter. She taught her daughter and her daughter's daughters to honour the tribe but to place their faith in the unseen spirits that had guided her mother and the mothers before her since the beginning.

Season followed season in the eternal sameness of sand, wind, emptiness, and silence. Daughters were born and grew to bear daughters of their own, until one was born strong and fierce like her brothers, strong enough to flee while her sister died for the honour of her family . . .

CHAPTER XLIV

Jerusalem to Hungary c 33-1943CE.

Advance the eagles, Caius Placidus,
Even to the walls of the rebellious city!
What! Shall our bird of conquest, that hath flown
Over the world, and built her nest of glory
Even in the palace tops of proudest kings,
What! Shall she check and pause here in her circle,
Her centre of dominion? By the gods,
It is a treason to all-conquering Rome,
That thus our baffled legions stand at bay
Before this hemm'd and famishing Jerusalem.[xxxviii]

Miri-amne thought often of the softly-spoken dissident who had sheltered in her yard and made her welcome at the secret meeting. The group had moved away, but the man's voice had stayed with her, and the sadness in his eyes.

She was sweeping the courtyard before the evening meal, when Yesh-ua from next door came to her. Tears streaked his cheeks, and his eyes looked haunted.

"What is it?"

"They took him. He is dead."

"Who?" Although she knew.

"Yesh-ua. They took him last night and crucified him this morning. It wasn't even a fair trial." He cried so much it might have been his Father they had killed on their stinking, wooden cross.

Miri-amne hugged her friend close and stroked his back. Tears stung her eyes as well; it had been easy to cry since Mama and Bubba died.

"They said he called himself King, but it wasn't true. He just wanted freedom. They kill everyone who wants freedom."

"I have heard people speak of a King. Who will it be?"

"It's the old prophecy. They used it as an excuse to kill Yesh-ua. He was the best of us."

Miri-amne and Yesh-ua stayed in the courtyard until the sun set and it was time to light the lanterns. The flames seemed small against the darkness.

The dissident's voice floated through Miri-amne's mind. That night under the stars, he had spoken of freedom and of love. Did they always end in death?

Miri-amne was a grandmother when the struggle between the Zealots and Rome escalated into war. The peace of the last forty years had been uneasy; the Temple fire was not forgotten by those who had lost loved ones. But as long as the Ivri prayed for Rome, they were not unduly persecuted for their beliefs, not like the followers of the sad-eyed man the Romans had crucified when Miri-amne was a girl.

There had been unrest when one of the Emperors wanted his statue raised in the Temple, and Ivri had been prepared to die rather than have the Law broken in that way. But Rome had relented, and life went on . . .

Until Eleazar, son of Ananias, persuaded his fellow priests to stop offering sacrifices to G-d on behalf of the Roman Emperor. Perhaps it was because of what happened in Caesarea, where Roman troops had killed thousands in the upper market, women and children as well as men of rank. Or perhaps Eleazar did not care for the people at all, and was driven by his own desire for power. Whatever the reason, Miri-amne knew it was time to leave Jerusalem. Ivri were fighting Ivri now. Just last week, Ananias had been killed by the dissidents, and Eleazar had killed Agrippa's emissaries. The city was doomed.

Miri-amne's father had warned her it might come to this, but there had been years of tolerance, years for marrying, having children, and dreaming of independence from Rome.

Now the dreams were over, and it was time to leave. But how?

The dissidents had control of the heights and had ordered everyone to stay indoors. Roman soldiers were camped in the valleys, besieging the city. Food was becoming scarce, and the Romans were massing for one final battle. Miri-amne shuddered. Would it be another Caesarea?

She had dreamt of it: men cut down as they battled with sticks; babies smashed against walls; children screaming as their mothers and sisters were raped. The images haunted her through the day and besieged her at night; death, blood, and horror lay in wait for the people of Jerusalem, and there was no way out.

Miri-amne gathered her children--Amir, Eitan, and Mirele--and spoke of what they must do. Amir and Eitan were grown men with wives and children, and Mirele was already older than Miri-amne's mother had been the day of the Temple fire. Had it really been forty years?

"We must pack only what we can carry, food and clothes, and bribe our way out through the tunnels."

"What do we have to offer?" asked Eitan, a carpenter who eked out a living for his family.

"We have our land," said Miri-amne. "It will be of no value to us if we stay here and die."

"You would have us barter our houses?" asked Amir.

"Of course," said Miri-amne. "What use are houses with no one to live in them?"

"Are you so sure how this will end?" asked Ofra, Eitan's wife. She bit her lip and looked sideways at her husband, as if she may have spoken out of turn.

Miri-amne reached for Ofra's hand. She, too, was a mother who wanted to see her children have children of their own . . .

"I am sure that Rome is stronger than Jerusalem," said Miri-amne. "And we all know what happened in Caesarea. Why will it be different here?"

"I want to go," said Miriam, Mirele's daughter, standing close to Miri-amne. She was sixteen, the same age Miri-amne had been when she followed Yesh-ua to the gathering on the hill. So young.

"Me, too," said Reuven, Miriam's brother, a year older and desperate to do something, anything, to relieve the unbearable waiting.

"It is not your decision," said their Father, Aviram, frowning at Miri-amne. "We will discuss this and meet here this evening." He gestured for his wife and children to follow him home.

They all left, and Miri-amne went to pack a market bag with clothes and the bread and cheese she had saved. She left much behind, but none of it more precious than her children and grandchildren.

She climbed to the rooftop, thinking of swallows and hawks. Someone ran into the courtyard below.

"Bubba! Bubba! We are coming. It is decided. We are all coming!" Miriam ran up the stairs, eyes shining.

"I'm scared, Bubba. But we have to go. What should I take with me?"

Miri-amne sighed deeply. "With you young ones safe, it will not be so bad to lose the city. You already carry that which is most precious, but I have something else for you to take to this new place."

Miri-amne went off into the house, and Miriam waited in the courtyard. So many of her memories seemed to live there in Bubbe's house: the smell of barley toasting over fire, the taste of bread freshly baked on hot stones, the flavour of mint and fresh sheep's milk.

Why was she thinking so much about food? What about Bubbe's stories and the songs she sang to the evening star? And the sound of the fountain splashing into the pond . . .

"Many are called but few are chosen."

Expecting to see Bubbe, Miriam turned. The courtyard was empty.

The voice spoke again, out of the air. "Many are called but few are chosen."

Miriam sat on the rim of the pool and gripped the edge of the solid stone. Was she losing her mind?

The light changed, as if a cloud had covered the Sun.

"Do you bring your feet to walk in Her Ways?" asked the voice.

Miriam sighed deeply and nodded. Hadn't she just been thinking of Bubbe's songs to the Queen of Heaven?

"You must answer, child. Do you bring your feet to walk

in Her Ways?"

"I do," whispered Miriam.

"Do you bring your knees to kneel in Her praise?"

"I do." Miriam slid from the wall to kneel in the courtyard.

"Do you bring your sex to rejoice in Her Life-giving."

"I do," said Miriam.

"Do you bring your breasts for Her abundance flowing?"

"I do."

"Do you bring your hands to do Her work?"

"I do."

"Do you bring your lips to sing Her acclaim?"

"I do."

"Do you bring your eyes to see Her presence in all?"

"I do."

"Rise, child. You are chosen."

Miriam stood on shaky legs. There was still no one there, but she knew she would never be alone again.

Bubbe bustled out holding something close to her chest.

"Ah. I see you have heard Her voice. That is good."

"Whose voice?" asked Miriam, shivering despite the warm air.

"I call her the Queen of Heaven," said Bubbe, eyes shining. "This is Her gift."

Miriam took the bracelet from Bubbe. It was beautiful and very old, and it seemed strangely familiar.

"Carry it away from here to our new home and give it to your daughter or granddaughter when the time comes."

Even one hour earlier, Miriam would have asked how she would know when the time was right, but now she just nodded, slipped the bracelet back into it's goatskin bag, and tucked it inside her tunic. She hugged Bubbe and ran off to pack her bag.

Then a neighbour came to say the fighting had stopped. The Romans were withdrawing.

The city held its breath.

Would the Zealots accept this peace?

No. Eleazar attacked the Roman troops, and the cries of the wounded echoed through the valleys. Roman legions surrounded the city.

"We must leave tonight," said Etian. "Rome will avenge the soldiers, and the fighting will go on until the city burns or people starve."

Everyone was quiet. How could they leave the city now the Romans were patrolling every road?

"Yesh-ua's group will lead us out through the tunnel," said Etian. "We are on our own after that."

"Perhaps not," said Aviram. "If I can find Marcius, we can join his trade caravan. The Romans still want the pipes, tiles, and pillars from our kilns, and Marcius owes me a favour."

"Where will we go?" asked Miriam, hoping the favour was a large one.

"Antioch," said Aviram. "There are Children of Yisrael there."

"And Romans, too," said Reuven, clenching his fists.

Aviram nodded. "And Romans, too. But Marcius says there is a whole area given over to our people. They live peacefully and prosper there."

Miri-amne walked slowly through the house where she had been born, the house where she had birthed her own children. She climbed for the last time to stand on the roof where she had watched a swallow dip and soar and had yearned for freedom. Here she had seen Yesh-ua leave his house in darkness to meet with the dissidents on the hill . . .

Now Yesh-ua and his sons fought with the Zealots. Did

they really think they could win against Rome?

She walked slowly down the stairs, wondering what had happened to her own desire for freedom. She trailed her fingers through the water of the pond. The fountain was still now, but fish still nibbled at her fingers. Perhaps it was being a mother that made peace seem more important than freedom. Perhaps that was why the Zealots were all men . . .

She stepped outside. The air smelled of smoke. Smoke! Here she had stood watching her father return from the Temple without Mama or Bubba. Was it really so long ago?

Miri-amne left her home in the dark, walking quietly down the hill with her family. It was so still that the fighting might have been a terrible dream, but the smell of burning lingered, and the muffled sobbing of widows seeped through closed gates.

Miri-amne, too, was a widow, her husband long since dead from a sickness that leached the strength from his body and the reason from his mind. But she had done with sobbing. Her granddaughter, Miriam, had heard the Queen of heaven speak, and she carried the gift to pass on to her own granddaughters. If the Zealots were foolish enough to fight until the city was destroyed, that was their business, but it was Miri-amne's business to see that Miriam and the others lived to have children of their own . . .

They escaped the city through a drainage tunnel running alongside the Temple, a deep channel for the rains that turned the hills green and sent floodwater racing down the gullies.

Miriam dropped her bag down to Reuven and slid over the edge, hanging by her hands until he lifted her to the floor. By lamplight, it seemed the tunnel stretched on forever. Lined with stone blocks, it was high enough for a man to stand easily and wide enough to walk through carrying laden bags. Had the builders foreseen the need for a way out of the city for people as well as water?

Miriam shivered. There had been no rain for weeks, but still her heart beat like a trapped bird until they reached the end of the underground way.

She emerged near the river, beside the pool of Siloam, blinking her eyes to clear the afterglow of the lamps. The area was deserted; with so many Romans in the city, no one used the pool for ritual cleansing.

Yesh-ua's nephew, Yaniv, led them across the river and onto a path running towards the trade road. The night birds were silent, and even the frogs seemed to be hiding.

With a whispered warning to move with care, Yaniv left them on a goat track running South of the city. It was rocky and narrow, with pebbles rolling underfoot, but it took them around the soldiers to where Marcius waited with his laden asses.

The Roman said nothing as he handed each of them a dark, coarse robe and pointed to the centre of the milling asses.

Miriam and Reuven walked either side of Miri-amne, their faces swathed against the dust like the other ass herders.

"Where are the others?" asked Miri-amne.

Reuven pointed to another cluster of dark-robed figures ahead. "Father said we must travel separately so the soldiers will think we belong with the ass herders."

"It seems we do," said Miri-amne. "Forget not that we were all once slaves in Kemet."

There were others from Jerusalem on the road, families fleeing the city despite the Roman soldiers patrolling the area.

"What will happen to them?" asked Miriam.

"They will be taken by the soldiers. To Antioch or Rome, where they will be put to work as slaves." Miri-amne's voice was heavy with sadness. "But at least they will be fed, and they will live to tell their children and grandchildren about the fall of Jerusalem. I doubt we will see Yaniv or Yesh-ua again."

"How can you be sure Eleazar will not win?" asked Reuven. He had friends whose families had refused to leave, and he had whispered rebellious plans of his own to Miriam as they sat on the rooftop watching the stars.

"I think Eleazar seeks a grand story to feed the rebellion," said Miri-amne. "I have known men like him before. They care more for their own glory than for the lives that are lost."

"But Rome oppresses us," said Reuven, looking to Miriam for support.

"Rome seeks the prayers of our people," said Miri-amne. "If the priests will give Rome that, it may still be possible to live in peace." She spoke then of her childhood when the hand of Rome had, for a time, rested more lightly on Jerusalem.

"But we would not be free," said Reuven.

"Perhaps not," said Miri-amne. "But there are many who would still be alive if we had learned to live with Rome." She sighed again, a mournful sound.

Reuven looked sullen, but Miriam took her grandmother's hand. She knew the stories, and knew that Miri-amne still grieved for her mother who had been lost in the first Temple fire so long ago.

They walked until dawn, when Marcius called a stop to water the asses and share a meal of flat bread and goat cheese. That night, Miriam slept so deeply she did not feel the hardness of the ground nor hear the grumbling of the asses hobbled and tied at the edges of the camp.

On the second day, the air was so thick with birds it seemed like a warning. Were the birds fleeing the city, too?

On the fifth day, a legion of Roman soldiers thundered past, riding for Jerusalem as if chased by demons. Reuven lifted his head to watch them, squaring his shoulders and taking on the defiant stance of a fighter.

Miriam dug her elbow into his ribs. "Stop it! You need to look more like an ass herder and less like a Zealot."

Reuven slumped and looked down, scuffing the ground with his feet.

Late on the sixteenth day, they reached Antioch. The Syrian city glowed golden in the setting sun. Miriam's legs ached, and she was more tired than she had ever been, but hope stirred in her chest. Perhaps the stories of peace were true . . .

Marcius left the family by the South gate with directions into the Kerateion, the quarter where the Children of Yisrael lived. As they entered the city, Miriam held her grandmother's hand. Antioch was so much larger than Jerusalem, and bore the mark of Rome: paved roads, colonnades, and aqueducts in every direction. Yet some of the buildings were in ruins.

"Have here been riots here, too?" asked Miriam.

"Earthquake," said Miri-amne. "Marcius said the Romans are rebuilding the city. I have heard that Antioch is the equal of Alexandria and Byzantium."

"But it is not Jerusalem," whispered Miriam.

The gate to the Kerateion stood in a boundary wall of stone. The guards, Northerners, hook-nosed and dark-skinned, heard the family's story, nodding as if it were already an old tale. They sent for someone to find them a roof for the night.

A short man with a round belly came bustling up and led them to a large, covered courtyard where other travellers sat on reed mats, talking and sharing a meal cooked by women over an open fire.

"He looks well fed," said Reuven, inclining his head towards the round-bellied man.

Miriam nodded; perhaps the hand of Rome did rest more

lightly in Antioch. But still Antioch was not Jerusalem, and she grieved the loss of her home and her childhood friends.

Miriam's father used the coin he carried to secure a sprawling house that had been deserted after the last earthquake. The house was all on one level, with open pavilions and a garden. Miriam shared a room with her grandmother; they already shared so many secrets . . .

Life in Antioch followed a rhythm similar to life in Jerusalem. Soon Miriam knew her way around the market, and Reuven befriended the sons of their neighbours in the Kerateion.

Five months after they arrived, Marcius brought them the story of the fall of Jerusalem. Miriam cried for Yesh-ua and his family and for the city she had known.

Jerusalem began to fade from the notice of traders and Emperors but stayed alive in the hearts of those who had known the grace and charm of the old city and the sanctity of the Temple.

"Perhaps one day we shall return," they whispered.

But even the most ardent admirers of Jerusalem had to admit that the great city of Antioch was impressive with the marble-paved, colonnaded central road stretching as far as the eye could see, with the miracle of running water in all but the poorest homes, with Rome bestowing positions of authority on the children of Yisrael . . .

Miriam's family paid a tithe to Rome, as did all the children of Yisrael, yet Rome's hand rested lightly on Antioch. Miriam's neighbours prospered as bakers, bathhouse attendants, metal workers, and weavers. Some held positions as magistrates and councillors, and all observed the rituals and practices established in Jerusalem.

Reuven spent more and more time beyond the walls of the Kerateion, joining the Hellenes who worshipped in the groves outside the city and talking with the ever-growing group of people following the teachings of the prophet they called Christ.

"The Romans call them *Christiani,*" he told Miri-amne, who was avidly curious about everything in the city.

Miri-amne sighed deeply and nodded to herself.

"What is it, Bubbe?" asked Miriam.

"I think I met him, the one they call Christ. His name was Yesh-ua, and I went once to a meeting on the hill . . ."

Reuven looked shocked. "You went to a meeting of dissidents?"

"I was not always old," said Miri-amne, eyes sparkling.

Reuven snorted and went to help his father tally the sales of silk and spices. Antioch was perfectly placed for trade, and Reuven soon forgot his grandmother's stories, although he continued to venture beyond the walls of the Kerateion when his day's work was done.

As she had when she was a child, Miriam absorbed her Bubbe's stories; they lent her the courage to accompany Reuven to the sacred groves where the Queen of Heaven was honoured along with the Gods.

It was there she met Nereus and caused a minor scandal in the family by declaring her intention to marry outside the Kerateion. Nereus, however, was willing to adopt the ways of Miriam's family, and he moved into the Kerateion with his scribing tools.

Miri-amne died in her sleep three days after Miriam gave

birth to her first daughter. Miriam's grief was eased by the child in her arms and by the gentle smile on her Bubbe's still face.

Antioch continued as a city favoured by the Gods and Goddesses of the Hellenes, the one G-d of the children of Yisrael, and the new God of the Christiani. Neighbours joined in each other's ceremonies, and their children intermarried.

Miriam's daughters both found husbands outside the Kerateion: Mara married a Roman soldier, and Liliat married a weaver whose family had lived in Antioch for five generations.

Time passed, and those who had walked the lanes of Jerusalem died, leaving their children's children to walk the paved roads of Antioch . . .

Three hundred years after Miriam and her family began their new life in Antioch, a young reader from the academy, a student of Lucian, began preaching violent theories from his pulpit. Ioannis spoke bitterly against Christiani participating in Ioudaiōn festivals and other observances. His scathing rhetoric interrupted the centuries old communion of Christiani, Hellenes, and the children of Yisrael.

"Is it our fault the Christiani like the solemnity of our prayers?" asked Lili, Miriam's twelve-times great granddaughter. "Now people are blaming us for stealing the Christiani away from their churches."

"And for murdering children and worshipping avenging angels!" said her brother, Todros.

Twins, Lili and Todros often finished each other's sentences and completed each other's thoughts. From their mother, they had learned to respect the beliefs of others and to join their neighbours in the seasonal rituals and ceremonies held in the sacred groves. Would that stop now that Iaonnis was turning people against the children of Yisrael?

It seemed not. Even though some of the Christiani stopped visiting the groves, the Hellenes continued to welcome their neighbours to their ceremonies of song and abundance. Despite Todros's fears, the peace and harmony of Antioch continued for another twenty years.

Then Emperor Theodosius closed the shrines and temples of the Hellenes, and a child died in a village near Antioch. Children died all the time from illness and accidents, from hunger and snakebite, but they said this child was murdered, bound to a cross and scourged to death by Yisraeli men celebrating Purim.

Lili listened in horror as Todros told her the story. They were sitting together on the portico overlooking the garden, as they did every afternoon. Lili had grown too frail to manage the walk from the portico to the garden wall, and she welcomed Todros' daily visits.

"We were born together," he would say every so often. "So it is fitting that we wait for Death together."

Today his face was pale, and he twisted his big hands in his lap.

"Do you remember what Iaonnis said before he left Antioch?" asked Lili.

Todros nodded. "I remember. He spoke of our people murdering children. I thought he was a madman, but now he is a Bishop in Constantinople, and I have lived too long."

"We have both lived too long," said Lili, holding his hand. "But what of our children, and their children's children? What will this mean for them?"

Her question was answered the next month when strict regulations were placed on the celebration of Purim. Christiani were instructed not to have intimate or personal intercourse with Yisraeli and to avoid intermarriage.

Then a Yisraeli mob in Alexandria attacked and killed Christiani worshippers. Bishop Cyril expelled them all, rich and poor, scholars and carpenters, from the city. Some came to Antioch, but there was no longer an easeful communion between the different quarters of the city. Even the struggle against the Emperor's oppression failed to unite the people of Antioch.

"The young ones should leave," said Todros.

Lili nodded. What he said was true; the city had become increasingly hostile to the Judeii, as the Romans now called their people. "Where will they go?"

"I have heard of towns in the West, in Pannonia--Brigetio, Aquincum, Savaria--where our people have lived for generations.[xxxix] Sagiv's grandfather's brother was a soldier there, and his descendants still live side by side with Christiani and those who worship the old Gods, like Antioch before the troubles."

"Is it far?" Lili closed her eyes.   "I will miss them."

Lili and Todros died the same night, after an afternoon speaking spent talking of the future and the past. No one could explain how the two had died on the same day, but then no one was surprised either.

"Who knows with twins," said Lidor, husband to Lili's daughter, Mira.

Mira's daughter, Li'el, who was pregnant with her first child, had been close to Lili, and she told Mira about Lili's idea that they should leave Antioch.

"Did she see trouble here in Antioch?" asked Mira.

Li'el shrugged. "We can all see the trouble here, but I do not know if it will be better somewhere else." She stroked the tight roundness of her belly. "Perhaps we should ask Sagiv; he has family in Pannonia."

The men talked with Sagiv, who was only too happy to tell the tale of his seven-times-great grandfather, who had had fought for Marcus Aurelius and been exiled to Pannonia for his trouble. Sagiv's cousins lived in the town of Aquincum, on the West bank of the Danuvius, the great river that was said to flow all the way from the Silva Nigra, the endless forests in the North, to the Axeinos Pontos, the sea in the South.

Despite Sagiv's enthusiasm for the Western lands, Mira, Lidor and the others were still reluctant to leave the bountiful and well-appointed city of Antioch and risk a journey to an unknown place.

Then the Christiani burned the great temple of Apollo, and Lidor announced to Mira and Li'el that it was time to leave.

"Where will we go?" asked Li'el, thinking of her unborn child. "Pannonia is a long journey."

Lidor nodded his head in agreement. "We will go to Alma Roma. Roma's star fades, but there is a new star in Constantine's city."

"And it is on the road to Pannonia," said Lidor's brother, Joachim, who still yearned for the Western lands Sagiv had praised.

Once again precious belongings were sorted and packed. Once again, a daughter in the line of Mir-ri heard the Priestess speak and learned that the most precious treasure of all was the baby she carried. Li'el's daughter was born in Alma Roma, in a small house in the Chalkoprateia, where other Ivri lived in peace in the new Rome.

Li'el had never seen the old Rome, but it was hard to

imagine a city more beautiful than Alma Roma, the city that had once been named for the great Constantine, who had died the previous year. Shining water surrounded the city on three sides, and the harbours bristled with the masts of ships from Aegyptus, old Rome, and the ports of the Pontos Axeinos. The public spaces were filled with statues of the gods, and Christiani, Ivri, and Pagani lived side by side as they had once done in Antioch.

Li'el's daughter, Mara, was ten when riots caused a breach in the relationship between Christiani and Ivri, but the family continued to prosper in Constantinopolis for five generations. It was not until the year 720 that the Ivri were asked to accept baptism as Christiani or leave the city . . .

Eighty-five years after the family left Antioch, Li'el's four times great granddaughters--Miriam, Lilliane, and Rivka--travelled with their families to Pannonia, where they settled in Aquincum, on the west bank of the Danuvius River that flowed from the great northern forests to the sea.

It was another time of great change, and the family survived successive waves of migration by moving from town to town, adapting to changing customs while still holding to their Judaism. The Huns were followed by Gepids, Longobards, Avars and other long forgotten peoples of Germanic and Central Asian origin. The Avars were followed by the Franks, and the Danube again became the eastern borderline of a West European empire. In the ninth century Pannonia became part of the Morvian empire, and the Hungarians established the seat of their prince near the crossing of the Danube; Obuda, the territory of the city of Aquincum, became the first centre of Hungary.

The descendants of Li'el and Mara lived in the city that

became known as Budapest, where toleration and oppression followed each other like the changing seasons. The line of daughters continued, and the names of Miriam, Lili, and Mishka were passed down through the centuries.

In 1934, a baby girl called Miriam was born just before the Second World War and the terrible grief that would be visited upon the Jewish people of Hungary. In her ninth year, her great grandmother gave her a family treasure to take with her when she left Hungary. . .

CHAPTER XLV

Alexandria to Italy c 33-1959CE

When suddenly, at midnight, you hear
an invisible procession going by
with exquisite music, voices,
don't mourn your luck that's failing now,
work gone wrong, your plans
all proving deceptive--don't mourn them uselessly.
As one long prepared, and graced with courage,
say goodbye to her, the Alexandria that is leaving.
Above all, don't fool yourself, don't say
it was a dream, your ears deceived you:
don't degrade yourself with empty hopes like these.
As one long prepared, and graced with courage,
as is right for you who were given this kind of city,
go firmly to the window
And listen with deep emotion, but not
with whining, the pleas of a coward;
listen--your final delectation--to the voices,
to the exquisite music of that strange procession,
and say goodbye to her, to the Alexandria you are losing.[xl]

Meh-tan and her father dined alone in the courtyard.

"It seems they have found their Messiah," said Josephus.

"Where?" asked Meh-tan. It was the question that had been debated most intensely in the years since the Ivri had begun their talk of a King.

"Jerusalem," said Josephus. "The Romans crucified a dissident who had a following, someone they are calling 'King'."

"But how can he be King if he's dead?" asked Meh-tan. "What will it mean for the Ivri here in Alexandria?"

Josephus smiled. "Questions. Always questions, my daughter. How will we ever find you a husband when you talk so much?"

"If I talk too much, it is your fault," answered Meh-tan.

"It is my fault, I know it." Josephus laughed, and then suddenly looked serious. "They say the crucified one rose from the dead."

"Like Osiris," said Meh-tan. "But how do they know?"

"A good question, but irrelevant if the time is right for the fulfilment of the prophecy. The Ivri needed a King to fight the Romans, and now they have one. Although they may not want him if all I hear is true."

"What have you heard?" she asked, eager for the stories.

"Apparently he was one of the young dissidents who had been challenging the Elders. We will know soon enough what the Ivri make of it all"

"I wonder how long the stories will last."

"That depends on the times. Remember, it is turning of an Age. The Age of the Ram is giving way to the Age of the Fish. They say the followers of this Messiah have taken the fish as their symbol. We will not live to see it, but this may be the story of our time."

"What about Isis? Does she have a place in this story?"

Josephus looked thoughtful. "There have been stories of death and rebirth since the beginning. Osiris died and was restored by the love of Isis. She conceived Horus to rule Kemet while Osiris ruled the Underworld. It is an old story and will probably find its way into this tale as well."

"Will Isis be revered as the Mother?" asked Meh-tan.

"They will find a place for the Mother," said Josephus. "But I fear we might not recognise her."

Years passed, and Meh-tan had many more discussions with her father about the Ivri Messiah. Stories continued to come to Alexandria with those who fled Ursalimmu: there was a King; there was no King; the followers of the Messiah did not keep the Laws; the followers of the Messiah preached a new way to honour G-d.

Meh-tan turned sixteen and began to dress more carefully for the dinners and debates. One of the young men spoke particularly well, and his shiny black hair and glistening white teeth made her heart race. His name was Diamos, a mild name for a man whose hooked nose and piercing eyes made Me-tan think of a hawk. Diamos had come from Thebes to study Astronomy in Alexandria, and he brought the old wisdom of Kemet with him. He was the first one to mention the star that had appeared in the East at the turning of the Age.

"Many things will change," he said, with the far away look that Meh-tan loved. "People will follow the way of the Fish and forget the Neters. The change that began in the last Age will be complete. The old ways will be lost."

"But we can remember," said Meh-tan, recalling her

grandmother's lessons.

"Remember the way of the Mother," her grandmother had said every day of Meh-tan's life. She had taught her songs to praise the star that rose with the Moon and shown her how to honour the elements of air, fire, water, and earth. Most of all, her grandmother had taught her about Balance.

Meh-tan stroked the necklace her grandmother had given her before she died; lapis lazuli and gold, it had been passed down from mother to daughter for a thousand years.

"We can remember," said Diamos. "But much will be lost."

Meh-tan told him of the voice that had come to her as she walked alone by the Sea, the voice of Isis, Queen of Heaven and Earth, claiming her as her own.

Diamos kissed her hands and said she was blessed and beautiful, and he asked if she would consider him for her husband.

They called their first child Mah-ria. Josephus taught Mah-ria to read and use numbers, and Diamos taught her to see the patterns in the stars. Meh-tan taught her the old songs and showed her how to honour the elements. Mah-ria absorbed the lessons like a sea sponge, asking more questions even than her mother.

When Mah-ria was sixteen years old, Grandfather Josephus died. She wept for three days and nights, even though she knew he was a pure man and would pass through the Underworld to become one with Osiris.

On the fourth day, Meh-tan led Mah-ria out of her room and across the courtyard to the reading room. It looked the same: shelves lined the walls, laden with the books and parchments Josephus had collected over sixty years bargaining with traders from the East and travelling to Rome and Athens; patterned carpets covered the floor; couches with silk-covered pillows surrounded a low table in the centre of the room. It even smelled the same: leather and lamp oil, coffee and cinnamon. At any moment, Grandfather Josephus would appear, eager to talk about the latest treatise from Rome.

"It is yours now," said Meh-tan. "He left all this to you."

"But what about the boys?" Mah-ria wanted the books more than anything, but her Grandfather had instilled in her a deep sense of fairness and justice.

Meh-tan smiled. "Doman and Roburo will have the ship and can collect libraries of their own. Besides, it was you who spent most time in here with him."

Mah-ria walked slowly around the room. "I would rather have him here still."

"I know. So would I. But he said he was looking forward to the great adventure of death, so we must not hold him back with our grief."

"He said that often: the great adventure of death. I wonder if he engaged Thoth in a debate about Al Khemia."

Meh-tan smiled. "Of course he did. It is probably not over yet."

Mah-ria sat on a stool to sort through a pile of manuscripts on the table. "These came just before he died. We had just begun to look through them."

Meh-tan sat down to help. "Where are they from?"

"Thebes. I think they . . ." Mah-ria held up a yellowed parchment, the lettering feint. The first line made the breath catch in her throat.

"What?" asked Meh-tan.

"This one is written in Phoenician," said Mah-ria. She spoke slowly, translating as she read. "What is below is like that which is above, and what is above is like that which is below, to accomplish the miracles of one thing."

Meh-tan frowned. "It is like the songs about the Queen of Heaven and Earth and the Queen of the Underworld, the Balance between that which is above and that which is below."

"Yes," said Mah-ria. "I have read this before. There is a translation here somewhere, but Grandfather always said it was incomplete."

She lifted a pile of manuscripts down from a shelf and sat with them on her lap, leafing through them for the translation.

"Ah! Here it is. Listen to this: *In Truth, without falsehood and most real: that which is above is like that which is below, to generate the miracles of the one thing.* Do you see? They have only translated half, and it changes the meaning." Mah-ria took a deep breath. Her scalp tingled with excitement. "The Phoenician one says both: *what is below is like that which is above, and what is above is like that which is below.* It works both ways. Do you see how important this is?"

Meh-tan smiled. "You sound just like Josephus," she said, eyes shining with tears.

"Perhaps he is listening," said Mah-ria. "He thought most of the Philosophers were fools, dangerous fools. They speak only of Heaven and Earth and forget the Underworld."

"The Underworld will not forget them," said Meh-tan, laughing out loud.

Mah-ria loved the sound of her mother's laughter, like water running over rocks in the sunshine. She turned back to the parchment, her heart lighter than it had been since Josephus died. Perhaps not yet as light as Maat's feather, but light enough to spend the afternoon in the reading room, translating the rest of the text. Grandfather Josephus had taught her to read Phoenician when she was seven, and she could see that the text was some sort of recipe, but not for any ordinary food . . .

In Truth, without falsehood and most real: What is below is like that which is above, and what is above is like that which is below, to accomplish the miracles of one thing. And as all things have been derived from that one, by the thought of that one, so all things are born from that one thing by adoption. The sun is its father, the moon its mother. Wind has carried it in its belly and the earth is its nurse. Here is the origin point of every perfection in the world. Its strength and power are absolute when changed into earth; separate the earth from the fire, the subtle from the gross, gently and with great care. It ascends from the earth to the heavens, and descends again to the earth to receive the power of the above and the below. By this means, you will attain the glory of the world. And because of this, all obscurity will flee from you. Within this is the power, the force of all forces. For it will overcome all subtle things and penetrate every solid thing. Thus was the universe created. From this will be, and will emerge, admirable adaptations. For this reason I am called Hermes Trismegistos, having three parts of the wisdom of the world. What I have said of the sun's operation is accomplished.

Mah-ria stroked the parchment. In the way her mother had taught her, she settled her mind and followed her breath into her body. Her heart--beat, beat-beat, beat--marked off her moments in time like a water clock. Blood coursed though her veins. Suddenly she saw though the subtle thing that had fooled the Philosophers: the ancient treatise was not a recipe for transcending the body; it was about transformation in the body. There was no idealised place separate from human existence; above and below are the same. This was the true Balance.

Mah-ria imagined Grandfather Josephus smiling at her, his eyes bright, his face lined with wisdom. She wished him well on his adventure, but she would miss him all the days of her life.

Mah-ria followed the tradition of Al Khemi, the ancient wisdom that her many times great grandmother, Meh-tan, had learned from Pu-abi, the old woman who tended her husband's family in Thebes. Mah-ria followed the tradition and redefined it according to the deep understanding she had through the songs of her mother line, songs that went all the way back to Urim.

In time, Philosophers and Magi gathered in the courtyard to debate Mah-ria's translations. Some of them called her a prophetess, Mah-ria the Prophetess. It made her laugh, and she just went on studying and applying her theories to every aspect of her life.

In the kitchen, she devised a water bath for cooking the evening meal slowly while she studied. The Magi assumed she was distilling a powerful elixir and imitated her water bath in their laboratories. That inspired her to make a distilling apparatus from copper, with flour paste sealing the joints. She used it to make alcohol from grain for her healing tinctures, but the Magi once again copied her invention in the hope of making the elusive elixir of eternal life.

Mah-ria had one daughter when she was thirty-three, but she never revealed the name of the father. Her daughter, Josepha, also became renown for her scholarship and wisdom, and she studied alongside Mah-ria as she wrote her texts on Balance and the way of the elements. They still drew on the wisdom of the Phoenician treatise, finding the elements in the words that had baffled so many scholars: The sun is its father=fire; the moon its mother=water (did not the moon control the tides?); Wind has carried it in its belly=air; and the earth is its nurse. Fire, water, air, earth--the elements of life. They worked with the elements to accomplish the miracles of one thing: Balance.

Mah-ria saw in the second century of the millennium, sitting with her daughter and her daughter's children in the courtyard of the home where she had been born. Her reputation as a prophetess had grown over the years, although the clarity of her ideas had at times been obscured by the philosophy of the day. As her mother, Meh-tan, had predicted, the old ways of Kemet were being replaced by the cult of the Ivri Messiah who was said to have risen from the dead in Ursalimmu sixty years before. The new way of worship was sweeping through Rome and Alexandria, passing from mouth to mouth like a plague. And with it came the belief in one supreme G-d, the Yahweh of the Ivri, to replace the Neters, the principles of life and death that had guided Kemet for thousands of years.

Mah-ria's granddaughter, Marina, and great-granddaughters, Selene and Metana, lived through civil wars that destroyed parts of Alexandria; Ivri and Greek citizens fought over land and power and the face of God. Although Marina's mother line was Egyptian, her father's family was from Greece, and they honoured Isis as mother alongside Serapis, whose daughter had descended to the Underworld and returned.

Life in Alexandria continued. The cult of the Ivri Messiah, called "Christian" by the Romans, grew stronger, and the rebuilding of the city included Christian temples. Rome still hovered over the city like the shadow of an eagle hunting for prey.

A hundred years and four generations after the rebuilding, the Emperor Caracella caused more grief than the city had known since the beginning: he instigated the killing of all youths capable of bearing arms. It became known ever after as the "day of horror".

Mah-ria's seven times great-granddaughter, Mariama, wept bitter tears as her brother fled inland to avoid the slaughter.

"The Gods of war are too strong," she said, mourning for her city.

Like her mother, and all the mothers back through time, Mariama walked in the way of the Mother and of Balance. She called on the elements of air, fire, water, and earth, and she had heard the voice of the High Priestess.

But the old ways were fading. The religion of the Messiah was spreading, and everyone seemed to forget that the story of death and rebirth had been told before. What would happen to the Balance when people finally forsook the Neters and the elements for a supreme G-d? The Christian story had become the story of the Age, but where would it end?

For Mah-ria's descendants in Alexandria, it ended in the death of Hypatia, Mah-ria's ten times great granddaughter. It was nearly four centuries since the young dissident Yesh-ua had been crucified in Jerusalem, and the Christians were seeking more power in Alexandria.

Hypatia's mother, a daughter in the line of Mir-ri, taught her the songs of the mother line as well as the philosophy of her many times great grandmother, Mah-ria. Her father, Theon, a Mathematician at the Museion, introduced her to Hermetic and Orphic texts similar to the treatises of her ancestor, Mah-ria, called by some a prophetess.

As Hypatia matured, her reputation as a philosopher grew,

and scholars came from Egypt, Syria, Cyrene, and Byzantium to study with her. She ran private classes at home in the reading room lined with books and parchments, and gave public talks in the lecture halls. The Roman Prefect, Orestes, consulted with her on matters of ethics and planning, calling on her skills at discourse, her tolerance for the disparate religious groups in the city, and her willingness to support Rome's secular authority.

"We have a problem," said Orestes one day, as they sat in his courtyard. He was impeccably dressed, as always, in a full length white tunic, covered with a toga bordered with a thin purple stripe; purple for power. But his many rings and medals, symbols of his roles and responsibilities, seemed to weigh heavily on him.

"Theophilus destroyed the Temples," he said, "but the new Patriarch wants to rule Alexandria in the name of the Christian Church."

"Will the Emperor allow it?" asked Hypatia, twisting a strand of her dark hair until it was coiled tight. The future of her beloved city depended on the Emperor; if Cyril succeeded, only Christians would prosper there, and she and her kind would be exiled or worse.

Orestes shrugged and shook his handsome head. "Theodosius thinks Cyril too ambitious, but he has his own troubles in Rome. He may do nothing at all."

"There will be troubles here, too," said Hypatia. "Cyril needs to prove himself, so he must outdo his Uncle, and there are no more Temples to destroy."

Orestes scowled. He had made it clear he deplored the loss of the Temples, but Rome had been unable, or unwilling, to help. "Unfortunately, Cyril's ambition is greater than his common sense. I hope the fool does not cause another civil war."

"What will Rome do?" asked Hypatia again. It mattered very much.

"We will see soon enough," said Orestes.

Hypatia sent a prayer to Isis. "Without Rome to keep the peace, there will be more blood spilled in the name of the Christian G-d. Their Yahweh is like Seth, the quarrelsome One who killed Osiris."

"You must be especially careful," said Orestes. "Cyril fears your influence, and you are not one of them."

Hypatia was careful, but it became increasingly difficult to avoid the Christians who marched the streets carrying staves, bullying the Ivri and the followers of the old religion of Kemet. Even Orestes was attacked by a band of monks on his way to the Forum.

"The situation has become serious," said Hypatia one evening as she sat with her sisters and their husbands and children for the evening meal. "A messenger came today. Theodosius has decreed Christianity the official religion of Rome."

"Are the children safe?" asked Elexandra, her long fingers arranging and rearranging the food on her platter. Worry lines creased her beautiful face, and Hypatia wished they were young again, when she had been able to protect her sisters from neighbourhood bullies. If only it were that simple now.

"Cyril incites his followers to more violence," said Hypatia. "If they can attack Orestes, no one is safe."

"What should we do?" asked Theodora.

"Go to Athens. Take the children to their grandparents."

Hypatia was pleased to see Darius and Anteus nod in agreement. Her sisters' husbands were good men, merchants from Greece who had come to Alexandria in search of trade goods and found wives as well.

"You must come, too," said Theodora. "The people will turn against your teachings."

"It is not important," said Hypatia. "I do not need to be popular."

"But what if they attack you like they did Orestes?"

"I do not fear injury or death," said Hypatia. "I am growing old, and death is certain. What I fear is the destruction of the old wisdom. The Patriarch would have us all follow Rome and adopt the philosophy of the Christians."

"You must come away with us," said Elexandra, reaching out to grasp Hypatia's arm. "It is too dangerous here. The common people have long thought you practice black magic and divination. They have a superstitious horror of your astronomical studies and your religious interests. It would not take much to turn them against you."

Hypatia stroked her sister's hand. "If the Christians are truly rabid enough to attack a woman, then Alexandria is doomed. I will stay, but you must plan to leave for Athens. Marina and Sophira carry the wisdom. The way of Balance will not be lost."

A month later, Hypatia and Elexandra sat on the bench beneath the trellis, holding hands. Clusters of grapes hung above their heads, and dappled light sketched fleeting pictures on the paving.

"It is as I feared," said Elexandra. "The Patriarch's followers are saying you cast a spell on Orestes with your dark powers. They are spreading stories of forbidden practices and sorcerous activities. You must leave with us."

"As soon as my lectures are finished," said Hypatia, holding Elexandra close. "Though I am loath to leave Alexandria."

"I will have everything ready," said Elexandra. "The girls

will help me pack the library."

Marina lifted down another scroll from the top shelf and placed it gently in the crate Sophira had lined with linen and oiled ass skins. If they were fortunate, the lining would protect the parchment from moisture and salt damage on the sea journey. If they were not fortunate, they would have to rely on what they had stored in their memories.

"I am glad Hypatia is coming," said Marina. "She will know how to sort these when we set up our home in Athens."

"And she's the only one who knows what they all mean," said Sophira, wrapping another ornament in soft cloth. "I wish she would stop going alone to the Agora. What would we do if anything happened to her?"

Someone ran into the courtyard, screaming for help.

Sophira's face turned the colour of goats' milk.

Marina scrambled off the bench, heart pounding like a drum.

Josephus ran into the room, eyes wild. "The Christians have taken Hypatia! Help!"

Sophira screamed.

"Stay here," said Marina. "Look after Josephus."

"Where are you going?" cried Sophira. "They will take you, too. They hate all of us."

Marina ran to find her mother; Elexandra would know what to do.

But Elexandra was with Theodora at market.

Marina ran as fast as the drumbeat of her heart, down the lanes, through the gates, across to the agora. The sun shone down from a blue and endless sky. Surely nothing terrible could happen under a sky like that? The Christians heckled and threw fruit, but hadn't their prophet, the one who had died and been reborn like Osiris, hadn't he preached peace? Surely nothing really terrible could happen . . .

It was the silence that warned her. Alexandria was a crowded city, colourful and vibrant, and it was never quiet.

Now the silence was terrifying.

A woman ran past, knocking Marina against a wall. The woman stopped and turned. Tears made tracks in the dust on her round face. Her black hair hung loose and wild, but the most terrible thing was the blood. The woman's shift was splattered with it, and her hands were stained red.

Marina cried out in horror. "Hypatia! No!"

She ran into the square, clutching her shift with numb hands. Her ribs ached from lack of breath, and her eyes stung. Black birds circled in the blue sky.

A few Christians stood at the edge of the square. Marina hurried towards them, and they slunk away like jackals.

On the paving stones where they had been standing lay a pile of bloodied cloth. Patches of cloth still showed sky blue, the colour Hypatia always wore. A strange, thick smell filled the air.

Head spinning, stomach heaving, Marina studied the cloth. Amongst it lay the flesh and blood that had been Hypatia. Rage and grief surged through her body like fire, erupting in sound that echoed around the square and into the sky. The circling birds answered with the voices of the dead whose hearts had been weighed and found wanting.

Marina reached down to touch Hypatia's hand. It hung from her arm by a strip of flesh that had resisted the sharp edges of the pottery shards that littered the ground, bloody and terrible. Tenderly, as if her aunt were sleeping, Marina picked up the gold and lapis lazuli necklace that had come from Hypatia's mother. It was sticky with her blood.

Words came haltingly. "She is a pure woman, washed and fasted. May she soar high as sky. May she walk long roads past lotus pools. May she bask in the warmth of the Sun. May her heart go on. Neverending."

Then grief, scalding and bitter, stole her breath and her words. Clutching the necklace, she ran back through the lanes, sobbing for the brightest one of them all.

They left Alexandria two days later, bound for Athens, the birthplace of Marina's grandfather, Theon.

Marina and Sophira had helped their mother and aunt Theodora finish packing the books and parchments, and all else was bundled into cane baskets and loaded onto the two ships owned by their father and uncle.

As the ship carried her away from Alexandria, Marina revisited the Christian square in her dreams, standing again on the blood-soaked stones, hearing the voices of the dead, shaking like a leaf torn down by a storm. It came to her in dreams, and it was futile to sleep afterwards, so she spent those nights reading Hypatia's treatises and writing some of her own. The followers of the One G-d could kill those who did not walk in their ways, but they could not stop their thoughts or silence their voices.

Athens 395CE-500CE

Marina shaded her eyes against the setting sun and surveyed the harbour of Piraeus. Darius and her father, Anteus, stood at the prow of the ship, arms across each other's shoulders. They at least were coming home.

The harbour bristled with masts. On shore, a steady

stream of carts moved away from the docks towards the distant hills.

"How long now?" asked Josephus, hopping from foot to foot as if he could make the ship sail faster.

Marina crossed her arms and frowned at the harbour. Would Athens really be any safer than Alexandria?

"Are there Christians here?" asked Josephus, as if he sensed her thoughts.

"Rome is here," said Marina, shivering despite the warmth of the sun.

"And Rome has decreed Christianity the official religion," said Darius.

"Never fear," said Anteus. "Athens will be slow to abandon the old Gods and Goddesses. This is the home of philosophy and reason. The Patriarchs will not find people so ready to believe their lies."

"And Rome is looking elsewhere for conquest," said Darius. "They will not be looking so closely at what we do here."

Marina wrapped her arms around her chest and prayed to Isis that he was right.

They were rowed to the docks in a small boat manned by two red-faced men with long hair and wide smiles. Josephus was first ashore, stumbling around on unsteady legs as the others climbed slowly onto the docks.

"Is this Athens?" called Josephus, pointing at a cluster of low buildings.

Anteus laughed. "This is just the harbour, my son. Those are the storerooms for our trade goods. The city is over there." He pointed to hills in the distance.

"Do we have to walk?" Josephus looked so crestfallen even Marina had to smile.

Anteus laughed again; he seemed happy to be back in the country of his birth. Elexandra, was quiet, as if trying to sense the worth of this new land.

Darius called out to a group of men at the end of the dock. One of the men disappeared into a lane and reappeared with a cart pulled by a sturdy ass with mournful eyes.

Theodora, Elexandra, and the children rode in the cart. Anteus and Darius walked with the men, talking so fast Marina could only catch every third word.

"What are they saying?" asked Josephus.

"Talking about the city. Something about an old wall."

"Yes," said her Father. "We are reclaiming some of what was lost. In my great Grandfather's time, Athens was a city to rival Alexandria, but then the Barbarians came." He pointed to the wall they had been following from the Harbour: blocks of stone, broken pillars, and even carved friezes had been used to build it. Men worked there, fitting stones, mixing mortar, hammering, and chiselling.

"Once the city extended all the way to here," said Darius. "There were temples and schools, fountains and public baths. Perhaps we will see it all restored."

Darius and Anteus continued to talk about the places of their youth as they led the way into the inner city through an arched gate. It was more crowded than Alexandria and less ordered, but the smells and sounds were the same: spices and dung, women haggling over the cost of goods, goats bleating, asses braying.

They crossed a market square and trundled down countless lanes, finally stopping at a house with terracotta walls and white pillars. Anteus banged on the panelled door.

The woman who opened the door looked so much like their father--the same hooked nose and crooked front teeth--that

Marina knew it must be their aunt Grania, her father's older sister.

Grania screamed, hugged her brothers, pinched Marina's cheeks, patted Josephus's head, and kissed Sophira all over her face, constantly chattering about everything that had happened since Anteus and Darius left eighteen years ago.

"Enough, Grania!" said Anteus, holding her still. "There will be time for all the stories, but now we need food and a place to sit."

Grania slapped her own cheeks and ran inside, yelling to the rest of the household that her brother was home.

There was food, and somewhere to sit, and more cheek pinching, head patting, and kissing as they were welcomed by the rest of the family.

Marina stayed close to her Mother and aunt Theodora, who both smiled and nodded and answered endless questions about Alexandria and the journey. No one mentioned Hypatia.

Theodora and Darius pleaded tiredness and retired. Marina sat with Sophira and Josephus on a low couch while the rest of their father's family told stories. Josephus was yawning. Sophira rested her head on Marina's shoulder and closed her eyes.

Grania bustled them off down a hallway and up a flight of narrow stairs to a bedroom. An oil lamp glowed softly from a table under the window, and the air smelled like flowers. There were three sleeping pallets.

"This is your room," said Grania, patting Marina's cheek.

"It's lovely," said Marina. "Thank you."

"You are a good girl," said Grania. "You will look after the others." She hurried back to the stories.

Josephus claimed the pallet nearest the window and lay down. "I don't like it here," he said. "My cheeks are hurting, and everyone yells."

"Maybe they only yell when they're excited," said Sophira, sitting on the pallet near the door.

"Maybe we should go to sleep and see what Athens is like in the morning," said Marina, blowing out the lamp.

The next morning their boxes and baskets arrived in two carts. Josephus took one look at the pile of boxes and ran off to count the rooms in the house. Marina and Sophira helped their Mother unpack the clothes and books

"What do they say about the Romans?" asked Marina, folding the linen cloths in which they had wrapped the oldest books.

Elexandra sighed deeply. "The Christian influence is strong. Already some temples have been closed, but there is a new Gymnasium, and two schools have been rebuilt. The Academy still operates outside the city. We will watch what is happening and decide."

"Why do they destroy what they don't understand?" asked Marina, remembering the silent square and the circling birds.

"They fear what they cannot control," said Elexandra. "It is a big thing to claim power for one God above all."

"But they want people to believe what they say without thinking about it." Marina snorted to show what she thought of that. "Hypatia said it was better to think wrongly than not to think at all."

"And she was right," said Elexandra. "But that is not the only reason the Christians feared her. She taught that dogma must always be questioned by self-respecting people. The Christian patriarchs could never accept that."

Marina hugged the folded linen cloth to her chest. "I fear them."

Elexandra sighed. "It is sensible to fear them, but we

cannot allow fear to fetter our thoughts or blind us to the truth. We will live in Athens and honour the old ways. If it becomes dangerous we will leave."

The family settled into their new life.

Anteus spent his days at the docks, taking inventories of the trade goods shipped in by Elexandra's brothers: glass from Egypt, fine textiles from Kos, fish from the Black Sea, grain from Sicily. He used his scholarly skills to bargain with tax agents and merchants, and to prepare the lists for the next shipment of oil from Athens.

Marina liked to visit her Father at the docks, to touch the pots of oil and dried fish and grain that had travelled so far. She traced over the destinations scrawled in pitch on the pots: Alexandria, Rome, Antioch.

"At least merchants are still welcome in the Christian cities," said her Father, crossing his arms over his chest and sighing deeply.

"What is it, Abba?"

"Everyone welcomes a merchant with his goods. They forget to ask which God he worships or which philosophy he follows. I have spoken with Josephus; he will leave with your uncles on the next run."

For a moment Marina wished it was she who would be sailing away . . .but her place was there, continuing Hypatia's work.

Her Father spoke as if he had read her mind. "The old ways are still strong here. With Roman power split between the old city and Byzantium, Athens is safe enough." He smiled the crooked smile that made him look like a boy. "Perhaps there will be another Emperor like Julian, and we can stop looking over our shoulders for trouble."

Marina shook her head. "It is the time of wolves. But we

must use what time we have to teach and write so the old ways are not forgotten."

Anteus uncrossed his arms and held her hands between his. "You are a true daughter of your Mother line. I am proud of you."

Marina sighed. "I wonder how long we have?"

More than the docks, Marina loved to visit the Academy outside the city. Rebuilt on the ruins of the original Akademia, it was still a place of study and debate.

She first went with Elexandra, Theodora, and Darius. They were welcomed by a teacher called Plutarch who was eager to read more of Hypatia's treatises. Plutarch's daughter, Asclepigenia, a philosopher and teacher at the Academy, embraced Elexandra, Theodora, and Marina like family.

"Their philosophy seems sound, but the Academy itself is inferior to the school in Alexandria," said Theodora, after their first visit.

"We must stop finding everything less than it was in Alexandria," said Sophira. "They killed Hypatia."

"And Plutarch and Asclepigenia teach the Theurgia of Iamblichus," said Marina.

Elexandra nodded, but Sophira shook her head and sighed. "The what of who?"

"Rituals," said Marina. "Iamblichus wrote about the Southern mysteries, about knowing the Gods and Goddesses directly through rituals. He argued that matter is as divine as the rest of the cosmos."

"Of course it is," said Sophira. "As above so below; as below so above, just as Hypatia taught."

Marina smiled. Sophira did not embrace the work with the same rigour, but she knew the truth of it. She was not as interested in the finer points of philosophy, but she was content to be among scholars and to copy the works of Porphyry and Plotinus in her fine hand.

Marina, however, affixed herself to Asclepigenia, who willingly took on Hypatia's niece as a student. Marina read and debated philosophy, practised ritual, and won herself a place in the Academy as a teacher.

She married a quiet man, born and raised in Athens, who studied at the Academy. They had three daughters.

Sophira also married a scholar, and her three sons chased each other and squabbled with Marina's girls, disrupting the meditations of their grandparents.

Throughout Marina's house were altars to the four elements: Air, Fire, Water, Earth. Marina taught her daughters the old songs and rituals:

"Hail! Lady of the Morning. We invoke you and call you. Radiant One of the dawn, Winged One of the morning Sun, Come! Bestow on us your laughter, love and inspiration. Lift us on your wings so golden."

"Hail! Lady of the Daylight. We invoke and call you. Fiery One of the midday heat. Mighty warrior, fierce protector, be our shield and our defender."

"Hail! Lady of the Evening. We invoke you and call you. Flowing One of the Watery Depths, Twilight One. Sibyl, soothsayer, seer, speak your truth that we may hear."

"Hail! Lady of Night. We invoke and call you. Black One of the Midnight Hour, Stone, Mountain, Life Giving Soil, Cow-eyed one whose arms are open, be with us through the night."

When Marina's oldest daughter, Armina, was sixteen, they were sitting together in the small library room at home, translating a bundle of treatises Josephus had found in a market place in Alexandria.

"It's amazing this wasn't burned by the Christians," said Armina.

"Most of them cannot read," said Marina, frowning over an indecipherable line. "Their priests want all the power for themselves, so they do not encourage study or debate amongst their followers."

Armina made a disgusted sound that reminded Marina of herself at sixteen. "Listen to this: 'What should be said of us, who are forced to live piously, not by devotion but by terror?'"

"Who said that?" asked Marina.

"It was in a sermon by Maximus in Turin. What happened to him?"

The question hovered in the air.

The front gate creaked and opened slowly. An old man shuffled in.

No, it was Anteus. His usual sprightly step was slow, his eyes downcast.

Marina hurried out to meet him.

"Are you all right, Abba? Has something happened?"

He rested his weight on her arm. "Augustine has decreed against us. He has proclaimed us wicked and justifies the persecution the Church of Christ inflicts on the wicked."

"How can he call us wicked?" Marina clenched her fists and bit her lip. Hot anger burned through her body. Even Augustine had turned against them; Augustine, who had preached tolerance and moderation. What was it about the religion of the one God that made men believe they had a right to dominate the whole of the known World?

"What will we do?" asked Armina, who had come to stand behind Marina.

"We will wait to see how his words are interpreted in Athens," said Marina. "If necessary, we will find somewhere else to live."

"How will we know when it is necessary?" asked Armina.

Marina closed her eyes. In the darkness behind her eyelids she glimpsed blood and shredded blue cloth.

"We will know."

But with Rome's attention split between East and West, Athens faded in prominence, and the city had time to regain some of its former grace. Buildings grew out of the rubble: a new Gymnasium, a restored Library, grand homes. Scholars returned to study and debate philosophy, and Marina's family found a place at the Academy. For a time it seemed that the Gods and Goddesses could stand against the tide of Christianity.

By the time Armina was recognised as a teacher at the Academy, Marina was close to the age Hypatia had been when she was killed. She often sensed her Aunt with her as she gave a dissertation on the exact wording of a line in a new treatise.

Syrianus replaced Plutarch as head of the Academy, and a scholar arrived from Alexandria with renewed enthusiasm for the work of Plato. Proclus was a mathematician who emphasised structure over imagination, but Marina enjoyed his intensity and the debates it provoked.

"His teachings weaken the cause of polytheism against Christianity," argued Armina as they walked between the city and the Academy. "Augustine already says the Christians should convert our work to their use. How he will rejoice to see the reason and structure of Proclus' texts!"

"Fear not," said Marina, "Proclus is aware of Augustine's greed for our knowledge. He knows the Bishop names us 'unjust possessors' of our philosophy. Do you think he wants our work to be plundered like the gold and silver of the Egyptians?"

Armina sighed. "He may not want it, but his love of mathematics blinds him to human nature. Christians like Augustine will stop at nothing to see their One God exalted above all."

"It is true," said Marina. "I am glad there are young ones like you to fight for the truth."

Proclus listened to Armina's arguments as he did to all the scholars, and he wove them into his systematic philosophy. Armina remained wary of how Proclus' words would be used by the Bishops and Priests, and she gathered around her a dedicated group of scholars who advocated for the imagination of the individual as the one true path to experience the Divine in Nature.

Marina stopped attending the Academy when her swollen legs made the trip from the city too painful, even by donkey and cart. She missed the debates; Proclus was attracting students from Phoenicia, Gaza, and Syria, and Armina's work was recognised in Alexandria and beyond.

Time passed, and Armina's place at the Academy was taken by her daughter, Mara. Mara's daughter, Maria, was more interested in gardening than philosophy, and her sons followed their uncles as merchants. It was Maria's daughter, Myia, named for the daughter of Pythagorus, who took up the mantle of her motherline as a student of philosophy. Myia began attending the Academy in the time of the Scholar Damascius. It was the year

518, and Christianity was finally displacing the old ways throughout the Empire.

Myia held to the old teachings of her family, writing tracts opposing the use of Athenian philosophical works for Christian purposes. Her brother, Atolos, his dark eyes serious, warned of increased Christian zeal in Rome and Alexandria.

Myia shrugged off his warnings. She knew about Augustine's decree, and she had heard the story of Hypatia's murder, but Athens was the home of philosophy and free thinking . . .

Then in the year 529 the Emperor Justinian banned the teaching of philosophy by non-Christians:

We wish to widen the law once made by us and by our father of blessed memory against all remaining heresies (we call heresies those faiths which hold and believe things otherwise than the catholic and apostolic orthodox church), so that it ought to apply not only to them but also to Samaritans [Jews] and pagans. Thus, since they have had such an ill effect, they should have no influence nor enjoy any dignity, nor acting as teachers of any subjects, should they drag the minds of the simple to their errors and, in this way, turn the more ignorant of them against the pure and true orthodox faith; so we permit only those who are of the orthodox faith to teach and accept a public stipend.

Atolos became more strident with his warnings. There were stories from Rome of property being confiscated and temples destroyed; tales from Bithnya of massacres; rumours from Byzantium of further Christian decrees.

The Academy closed. Philosophers and scholars packed up their belongings for extended visits to relatives in the countryside. Damascius fled to the East with a small group of followers.

Atolos returned from a trading trip and insisted that the whole family leave Athens.

"Where will we go?" asked Myia. "The philosophers of Byzantium use our words to strengthen their Christian texts, and Alexandria is too uncertain."

"Your destination does not need to be a city," said Atolos. "One of my men comes from a village in the mountains of Lakonia. His family honour the old ways, and there are no Christians."

"But what of my work?" Myia looked to her father, who had supported her to attend the Academy.

"You can still write in the country," said Atolos. "I will come to you on my way from Athens, collect your words of wisdom, and sell them for a fortune in Alexandria."

Myia bit her lip and wished she had left with Damascius. What would become of her in a village so remote that her brother could reach it easier by Sea than by land?

Atolos hugged her as he had when they were younger. "It will be different from Athens, but it is far from Justinian and his decrees. And remember, Rome is fading. The power is in the East, and they will not be looking to the South. Many are settling in Magna Graecia from Syria, Palestine, Egypt. The philosophers will come to you." Atolos looked pleased with himself.

"I bow to your wisdom, brother, but I will kill you if I end up milking goats."

"Considering how much you talk, they will be the best educated goats in Lakonia," said Atolos.

Myia threw a pillow at his head and went to start packing her parchments and codices. She saved the oldest of them, the original ones from Alexandria, to lay on top.

Her grandmother found her there and helped clear the

shelves.

"The Christian tide is strong. What is it Justinian said? '...one finds persons possessed by the error of the unclean and abominable Hellenes, and performing their practices, and this arouses in God, in his love for mankind, a righteous anger.'"

"A righteous anger in the Emperor more like," said Myia.

"And it is the Emperor who has soldiers to punish the 'abominable Hellenes'," said Avia Mara. "We will survive this, Myia. Remember, you are the daughter of an unbroken line of mothers and daughters that goes back to the beginning."

"That didn't save Hypatia," said Myia, pacing the room, picking up scrolls and placing them back down. "They are too strong."

"Their star is rising, but the Moon always returns after the nights of darkness."

"Oh, Avia. I wish I could be as strong as you."

"Listen for Her voice," said Avia Mara, leaving as quietly as she had come.

Myia had no time for the voice of the Goddess. Atolos spoke endlessly of his plans to resettle them in Lakonia, his voice like the harsh cawing of the crows that perched on the city walls on market days.

"How will Lakonia serve us better than Athens?" asked Myia, who had never met anyone from the Southern state.

"They live according to their own Laws. Philosophy would not be unwelcome there. Perhaps you could start your own Academy."

"Name one philosopher of note from Lakonia," said Myia, daring Atolos to respond.

"Myson of Chenae," he said, shaking his head. "And I thought you were the scholar."

Myia snorted in disgust. "Myson may have come from

Chenae, but there are only soldiers there now. We would be better off in Arkadia, living like shepherds."

"That could be arranged," said Atolos. "But fighters may be needed before this is finished."

"So more people can die in the name of their God," said Myia, scowling in disgust. "And what would we do if it came to fighting?"

"That is why I am taking you to Lakonia. There are no temples to destroy, no Christians to attack women in the streets. Anyway, if it comes to fighting, then you can move to Arkadia, or the mountains of Magna Graecia."

Grandmother Mara patted Atolos on the shoulder and agreed that Lakonia would be a good place to live. Myia stopped arguing and went to pack up her life.

The family--Myia, her mother, father, grandmother Mara, and a cousin, Lorta, who had studied at the Academy--left Athens in two carts pulled by stocky mountain ponies.

The city was in uproar. Carts loaded with tables, urns, and children jostled for right of way on the narrow streets leading to the city gates. Everyone knew the stories of what had happened in Bithnya.

They were fortunate to have Atolos' trading ship waiting at the Harbour. He had his men load their belongings and ponies alongside his amphorae of oil bound for Alexandria.

As the sun settled in the West, Myia stood on the deck and watched the Harbour fade. She was seventeen years old, but felt more like seventy, thinking of endings. Someone interrupted her reverie, a woman speaking in a strange accent.

Myia turned to see who was there.

No one. Was she hearing voices now?

"Many are called but few are chosen." The voice spoke again, out of the air.

Myia held the railing, the wood solid under her hands. The light changed, as if a cloud had covered the Sun.

"Many are called but few are chosen."

"Do you bring your feet to walk in Her Ways?" asked the voice.

Myia gasped. The voice was real. Had she lost her reason along with her home?

"You must answer, child. Do you bring your feet to walk in Her Ways?"

"I do," whispered Myia.

"Do you bring your knees to kneel in Her praise?"

"I do." Myia knelt.

"Do you bring your sex to rejoice in Her Life-giving."

"I do," said Myia.

"Do you bring your breasts for Her abundance flowing?"

"I do."

"Do you bring your hands to do Her work?"

"I do."

"Do you bring your lips to sing Her acclaim?"

"I do."

"Do you bring your eyes to see Her presence in all?"

"I do."

"Rise, child. You are chosen."

Myia stood, her body strangely light. From across the deck, Avia Mara nodded knowingly at her, eyes shining.

"Listen for Her voice," whispered Myia to herself. Maybe this strange journey was about more than survival after all.

On the third day out of Piraeus, Atolos put them ashore at the ruined port of Gytheio, the town shattered by an earthquake

414

years before.

"It looks welcoming", said Myia, scowling at her brother.

"Be thankful the dock still stands," said Antolos. "Besides, priests and inquisitors will not be looking here for apostates."

"I know, brother. I know you have done your best for us," said Myia, hugging him one last time. "Come back soon and save us from the Spartans." She kissed him on both cheeks and stepped away to load the ponies.

"Don't talk the ears off the goats." Antolos, having the final word as usual.

Myia smiled though her tears.

They loaded the ponies with baskets and crates until all that showed were their heads and legs and their short tails. The rest of their tail hair had been chewed off by the goats on board ship.

Myia trudged after the ponies through the ruined town, hoping it was not a bad omen to begin their new life amidst ruins. Antolos had said they would be safer to begin from Gytheio than one of the fishing villages but, right at that moment, Myia just wanted to be home in Athens. At the top of the hill, she turned to wave to the departing ship.

Diodotus, Atolos's crewman from Lakonia, had drawn them a rough map that led them through the town and up an overgrown track into the hills. The land was dry and harsh, but the vista back over the sea was breathtaking. Atolos's ship floated like a leaf in a pond, and Myia wondered how it would be to have stayed on board and sailed to Alexandria.

"Many are called but few are chosen," the voice had said. And that was exactly what she was doing, following her calling in this rocky, mountainous, isolated place.

"No wonder the people have not been converted," said her

Father, leading a pony up another steep path. "Atolos says the way in is even harder from the North. We won't find monks climbing these trails."

"I hope not," mumbled Myia, wondering what they would find. Would the local people even speak the same language? Would they be unwashed and smell like wet dogs? Would they . . .

The villagers of Liakada were not at all concerned with how others saw them. They and their forebears had lived in the mountains of Lakonia for centuries, mostly undisturbed by wars, plague, and Emperor's decrees. They honoured the seasons and the elements and lived well from the produce of their terraced gardens and the meat and milk of their pigs and goats.

The men, women, and children of Liakada gathered to watch the newcomers toil up the track. Dogs barked and geese honked a rustic paeon of welcome. A grey-haired, round-bellied man stepped out from the shade of an olive tree to greet them.

"Welcome to Liakada. I am Eirenaios, father of Diodotus. He sent word of your coming."

The others all clustered around to greet the travellers.

Myia's parents responded as if they were visiting old friends, but she and Lorta held back. Why was everyone so old? Where were the young people? Had they all left as Diodotus had?

Eirenaios took charge of the ponies and led the way up a path to the house Atolos had bought for them. Myia and Lorta followed the procession of villagers, dogs, and goats, rolling their eyes at each other and mumbling about leaving with Atolos when he came for his first visit.

Their new house stood alone near the top of a terraced hillside. At the bottom of the slope was a rocky river bed, and across the valley was another house the same: mudbrick and stone walls with small vellum-covered windows and a thatched roof.

"The roof is grass," said Lorta, frowning at the house.

"There were roofs like that in Athens when I was a boy," said Myia's father. "These are made from wheat stalks, if I am not mistaken." He looked to Eirenaios for confirmation. "You will be glad of the shelter they give."

Lorta shrugged. "I am sure I will."

"We must learn how it is done," said Myia's Father. "The walls here are made from mudbrick. They are not strong enough for tiles, even if Antolos could bring us some. I think we will be needing to repair the thatch every season."

Eirenaios nodded. "We will help. Always we help each other."

They reached the house, and everyone crowded into the courtyard of packed earth. One old woman came close and peered into Myia's face as if reading her soul through her eyes. She nodded once, smiled toothlessly, and patted Myia's hand.

"That must mean she likes you," said Lorta.

Myia sighed miserably and went to inspect the house.

Clustered around the courtyard were six small rooms under one roof with a narrow verandah running the whole length. At the end was an open-sided area for cooking, complete with a stone fireplace and a grinding stone. A roofed sitting platform stood separately beneath a huge bay tree.

Myia's mother stood by the platform, studying the courtyard, no doubt planning a garden. That meant someone would have to cart water . . .

"That must be the dining room," said Lorta, pointing to the platform.

Myia rolled her eyes and went to claim a room for her

work. The one nearest the cooking area had shelves, but it would fill with smoke when the fire was burning.

"We'll need that storeroom," said her father. "There is no market like there was in Athens."

Myia sighed deeply. It might come to carting water and milking goats after all.

Lorta beckoned from the room at the far end. "Look. It has a window in both walls."

More light for reading and writing. But no shelves.

They unpacked the long-suffering ponies with willing help from the villagers. Myia carried her bedding and basket of belongings into the small room next to the library, as Lorta had named the end room. Then she and Lorta stacked the boxes of parchments and codices, vellum, inks, and pens in the new library.

Myia was opening the first box when more people came running into the courtyard. Lorta nudged her and they went to stand on the verandah. Milling around the courtyard, laughing and talking loudly, were about twenty more villagers, all of them young.

"Come meet my daughters," called Eirenaios, waving Myia and Lorta over. He proudly presented two smiling young women about Myia's age.

Lorta flushed and stuttered a greeting. Myia didn't blame him; the girls were beautiful.

"They have been picking olives on the mountain. It is young people's work. This is Korinna." Eirenaios pushed the taller one forward. "And this is Ligeia." He propelled the shorter woman towards Myia. "You will be good friends."

The girls grabbed Myia, one hand each, and pulled her over to meet the others. They all called out their names, more names than Myia could remember. Liakada suddenly seemed more friendly.

Over the next days, as they settled in, two or three of the younger ones came to watch Lorta line Myia's room with shelves made from the packing crates. When Myia finally sat on a stool at the low, wide shelf Lorta had built for writing, an audience crowded the verandah.

"Atolos was right," said Lorta. "You could start a school."

It was not the Academy, but Myia gladly gave the villagers lessons in writing and reading, and she was surprised to find some who wanted more. The debates about religion and freedom introduced Myia to Lakonian philosophy, an ancient understanding based on profound respect for Nature. The Lakonian seasonal rituals honoured the World Soul in a way that taught her more about the true nature of her relationship with the Divine than she had learned from any of the codices.

Part of the revelation lay in the everyday tasks that had not been part of her life in Athens: sweeping the courtyard, collecting wood for the cooking fire, and helping her mother prepare the meals. Despite her promises to Atolos, she also learned to milk the goats her father purchased from Eirenaios.

They hired a stocky, bearded man called Platon to tend the olive trees, and her father spent his days out on the terraces, digging in manure, pulling weeds, and admiring the silvery beauty of his trees.

Her mother planted seeds carried from Athens and diligently watered the seedlings until the courtyard came alive with vines and potted flowers. Myia's arms grew strong carrying water from the stream.

Atolos came twice a year with tales of the rest of the World. At first he brought them oil, salted fish, and other items of food much sought after in Alexandria and Antioch. After his first visit, he conceded that the oil from the olives grown on the terraces of Liakada surpassed any he carried, and the local honey was like the Gods' own nectar. He finally convinced the villagers to let him trade their local dish--pork smoked with thyme, oregano, and mint, and stored in lard along with orange peel--but only on the condition that he never reveal the source to anyone.

Five years after arriving in Liakada, Myia married Solon, a quiet man with serious eyes. They had three sons and a daughter. Lorta married and had three children, and the family compound grew. Life went on much as it had for centuries in Lakonia.

Fifteen years after he had left his family on the shores of Lakonia, Atolos sold his ship and came to live in the village.

"Will you miss the cities?" asked Myia.

Atolos shook his head sadly. "Much has been lost in the name of the Christian God. I am weary of the strife, and I long for the old ways." He gave her a hug and went to help Solon and Lorta build another room.

Time passed, and Myia's daughter gave birth to three girls who learned the seasonal rituals of the village along with their grandmother's philosophy. They did not leave the village, and there was less news from outside as Rome's might shrank . . .

The Empire that had once stretched from Britain to Armenia and Egypt fragmented into successor states, and even the Byzantine Empire dwindled. The cities of the Greco-Roman world shrunk and decayed.

Throughout Europe, the religion of Christianity adopted increasingly severe legislation to drive the old religions underground. Christian Inquisitors attacked a secret temple of Zeus in Antioch. The Gentiles were arrested, tortured, and sent to Byzantium, where they were thrown to the lions. When the wise creatures would not tear them to pieces, the Inquisitors crucified the apostates.

In rural areas like Lakonia, the old Gods and Goddesses persisted as guides to the changing of the seasons, the planting and harvesting of food crops, and the cycles of birth and death. It took centuries more before Christianity began to penetrate the population of rural Europe, and even then the old ways were still practised. As always, it was the women who held the memories . . .

Lakonia. c 930CE.

Sixteen generations after Myia sailed from Athens to Lakonia, her many times great granddaughter, Mariana, walked softly through the fallen autumn leaves, making no more noise than a summer breeze. Dark shapes moved through the trees to either side of her, women gathering in the moonlight to honour the Mother. Mariana's skin prickled. Would the wolves come tonight?

Nona Armania said the women had been gathering there since the beginning of Time, but the wolves had only appeared three gatherings ago, eyes shining in the moonlight, smelling musky and wild. They had come every time since, as if they, too, called down blessings from the Moon.

And why not? Did She not look down in wonder on all living things, bestowing her life-giving power on women, wolves, trees, and on the men and children who stayed at home on full Moon nights?

Mariana sighed deeply and slowed her steps. She was troubled by the wolves. She could read signs in birdsong and weather patterns, in the first setting of the olive crop, in the shape of the clouds that hovered over the mountains like a shroud, but the wolves were a mystery.

She walked on slowly, guided by the moonlight. What message did the wolves bring? She had read the old stories in which wolves were friends to humans. Had they come to warn them of trouble?

All Mariana's life, trouble had meant Christians. The Christian God was a jealous God, and rumours abounded of the violence done to those who did not convert. But the priests and inquisitors never had come to Liakada, hidden as it was in the Southern mountains where the wolves were as big as horses, and witches still met under the full Moon. Mariana had never left the village where she had been born, but she had heard the tales: in the World outside Lakonia, men fought battles for power and land, women and children suffered, and the priests and inquisitors converted everyone to Christianity.

She shuddered and gave thanks that they were safe in Liakada: babies were born; people died; the rains came or did not come; the Sun rose each morning, and Spring followed Winter just as day followed night.

She slipped into the circle between Carmena and Anna; the twins were new to the circle and might need her there to steady them through the ritual. At least they knew better than to speak while the dark shapes of the other women glided into place under the trees.

Nona Armiana stood in the centre and held up her arms. Mariana and the other ten women became as still as statues.

Nona Armiana turned to face East.

"Hail, Keepers of the Light. Golden eagle of the dawn. Rising Sun. Come! By the Air that is Her breath, be here now."

Did the breeze answer?

Nona Armiana faced South.

"Hail, Keepers of the Flame. Flaming one. Summer's warmth. Come! By the Fire that is her spirit, be here now."

Nona Armiana turned to the West.

"Hail, Keepers of Water. Rainbringer. Grey-robed twilight. Come! By the Waters of Her living womb, be here now."

Nona Armiana faced North.

"Hail, Keepers of Earth. Feared and fearless Lady of the Night. Come! By the earth that is Her body, be here now."

Nona Armiana knelt, head bowed.

"We are between the worlds, beyond the bounds of Time, where She waits."

Mariana sank to her knees. The twins settled beside her, hands clasped before them in prayer.

Mariana bowed her head and waited. Sometimes the Mother spoke in whispers that made her shiver; sometimes She came as a sudden wind or a stirring of the forest creatures; sometimes She was silent as Death.

The wolves came quietly, shadows among the trees. Mariana sensed them but kept her eyes closed. Alongside her Carmena shivered.

Then the wolves started to howl.

Mariana opened her eyes.

Nona Armiana stood and raised her arms.

A rock hit her head with a dull thud. She fell slowly, like a tree chopped by an axe.

Carmena screamed. Mariana grabbed for her, but the

younger girl rushed blindly away.

The wolves stopped howling, but they were close, their eyes glowing in the shadows. Mariana pulled Anna to the ground and signalled for her to follow.

Men ran into the clearing, shouting prayers and curses. Women screamed.

Mariana crawled into the shelter of the trees and kept crawling, grabbing at the ground with her hands, lifting her knees, moving away from Death. Don't think. Keep moving. Grab the ground, lift her knees, keep moving. . .

The cries faded behind her. Her hands were bleeding and her knees burned. Her heart raced like a captive bird's. The wolves had disappeared.

Where was Anna?

Mariana was a child again, filled with aching loss as she had been when her Mother died giving birth to a baby brother who had only lived a day.

She stumbled to her feet and ran. And ran. And ran.

When the Moon dropped into the West, Mariana turned back towards the village, following the stars home as her brothers did after taking the goats to the far pastures. Dawn could not be far off, but it was still full dark.

Why were cookfires burning in the village?

Mariana's heart beat like a drum. She crept to the edge of the trees.

Not cookfires. The village was burning.

And no one was trying to save the houses, protect the olive trees, rescue the children. No one at all. Papa? Arturo? Donato?

Were they dead? Taken by the priests for judgement?

Mariana shivered.

"Go," her Nona had told her. "Swear it. If the priests ever

come, you will go. Leave me, I am too old to run. But you must go. You carry the gift."

Mariana gripped the necklace her Nona had given her when her Mother died.

"Take Her gift and go. Pass it to your daughters."

Mariana hid in the shelter of the trees until the houses burned down to ashes. Then she walked slowly through the ruins of her life, gathering what she could use: a basket, a charred cloak, the blade of a knife, a handful of coins. She scooped soiled grain onto a sheet and tied the corners to make a bag she could carry over her shoulder.

Nona's room of words was ruined; the thatch had fallen in and crushed the remains of the crumbling parchments she said came from their ancestor who had been a philosopher in Athens. Mariana picked up a scorched fragment of vellum. Nona had promised to teach her to read and write, but somehow they were always too busy. Mariana had long since guessed that the real reason they never had the lessons was because Nona barely remembered what her own grandmother had taught her so long ago.

And now there was nothing left at all . . .

There were no bodies, so the others had not been killed, but what would happen to them in Sparta or Athens? Mariana shuddered. They all knew the fate of heretics.

She waited one full day and night in the trees outside the village in case anyone else had escaped. It was unnaturally quiet, as if the Earth were in mourning. Even the dogs had run off.

On the second morning, she found Anna at the stream, pouring water over her legs and moaning like a woman giving birth. The water ran pink with blood, and Anna's face was black with bruises.

"Come, little one. We must leave."

Anna rubbed at her legs as if to scrape the skin away.

"Stop this, Anna. We must go."

Anna looked up.

Mariana recoiled. A madwoman looked out through Anna's eyes. With a cry like a stuck pig, Anna pulled away and ran down the track away from the village.

Mariana followed, but her cousin was fast in her madness, and soon she was gone. Perhaps she would be waiting at the foot of the mountain, or perhaps not. It was beyond Mariana. Everything was beyond her but the next step, the step she took because she had sworn to Nona that she would go. Nona, who never tired of the stories . . .

"They are strong, the priests. They will force the Governors to convert everyone. It has happened before. We are here because it was not safe for our family in the city. Have I told you what happened to your many times great Grandmother in Alexandria?"

And, of course, Nona had told the story countless times before, but Mariana had always listened as if for the first time. Now she alone carried the stories . . .

On the fifth night away from the village, Mariana came upon a family setting up a shelter. Two hollow-cheeked, round-eyed children watched their parents gather wood, start a fire, and stretch a goatskin between saplings for their roof.

Mariana coughed and clapped her hands to warn the parents of her approach. She held before her as an offering the two kouneli she had snared that morning. Meat was always welcome on the road.

The man stepped between her and his family. Mariana

held out the kouneli.

The man looked at them and licked his lips.

"Affliggere?" he asked. Are you on the road because of Plague?

Mariana shook her head; even the Plague had not dared to climb all the way into the mountains. "Christians," she said, bracing to run.

"Ah." The man nodded, his eyes sad, and took the rabbits.

Mariana stayed with them that night, telling her story and hearing theirs. They, too, were fleeing persecution and were glad of company on the road.

They headed North, following forest paths and goat tracks to the coast, where a cousin of the family rowed them across the Straights and gave them the name of someone who could arrange passage to Magna Graecia.

Mariana used her coins to secure five places in the hold of a trading ship that took countless, stomach churning days to cross the Ionian Sea. They stumbled ashore on a rocky coast and walked South until they found work picking olives for a Don who fed them, gave them a shed to sleep in, and paid them as little as possible. He made all his workers pray to the Christian God in a house he built on a hill. No one lived in the house; it was God's house, a capella. Mariana knelt and prayed with the other workers, but she never understood why a God needed a house when there were trees and streams and the endless sky.

"You do not like the capella?" asked one of the workers, in a Southern dialect Mariana barely understood.

"Why do you say that?" she asked.

"You frown at the walls as if they offend you," said Antonio.

"I prefer the trees and sky overhead."

His smile made his eyes sparkle.

Mariana married Antonio and went home with him when the olive picking season finished. He wanted her to sell her necklace so they could build a house on his grandfather's land, but she said it was all she had left of her family, and he let her keep it.

The necklace was passed from mother to daughter for a thousand years, through forty generations, through famine and plenty, through war and peace, through good times and bad.

Mariana's daughter and granddaughters did not learn to read or write. Some of them heard the voice of the High Priestess and answered her call, and the old ways persisted down through the generations despite the priests. The worst of the Inquisition bypassed the village where Mariana and Antonio had settled, and the family survived wars, plague, and the passage of Time.

In 1926, in a village in Calabria, in the south of Italy, Maria and Antonio dePasquale had a daughter, also called Maria, for her mother and grandmother. Maria's family had lived in the village and surrounding area for longer than anyone could remember. Like all the girls of her village, she grew up a Catholic, yet on Christmas Eve she gathered with the other women to perform a ritual in the Church that no man was allowed to see. The words she spoke would have been familiar to her many, many times great grandmother, Meh-tan, who once met a Queen in Ursalimmu.

It did not occur to Maria that the ritual was not in keeping with the teachings of the Church; it was what her mother and all the mothers before her had done on Christmas Eve to honour the Great Mother.

Maria and her husband, Rocco, emigrated to Australia just in time for their first child to be born in Melbourne in 1959. They had two boys and, ten years later, a girl they named Paula.

CHAPTER XLVI

Jerusalem. May 20th 2015.

On their fourth day in Jerusalem, Lili and Paula set up their computers early at the café, ordered coffees-- Paula's a long black, Lili's a double shot latte--and set to work searching for references to the elusive *me*. Peter joined them, bright-eyed and obviously excited about something. He ordered a black coffee and spoke quickly, drumming his fingers on the table in time with his words.

"Things are really moving with this sex workers' strike. The market's all over the place, and I couldn't get any sense out of my usual contacts. I checked the inventory from the Baghdad museum, and it seems there was a piece the same style as your jewellery."

"Was?" said Paula. "It's gone?"

Peter nodded. "You have no idea how much was lost when the museum was looted. Even before that, pieces were stolen to sell on the black market. What use are antique ornaments in a museum when your children need food?"

"Are you justifying the looting?" asked Lili, eyes blazing with indignation.

Peter threw up his hands. "Even I, opportunist that I am, would rather it hadn't happened, but the scale of things here is different from America or Australia."

Lili nodded. "I'm sorry, Peter. Sometimes I forget. I just have to look at Jerusalem. People have been fighting over this small patch of land for more than three thousand years."

Paula remembered the voice asking her if she thought it was a game. She had decided she might never understand what drove someone like Haleli, or what truly fuelled the conflicts in Israel, Palestine, and Iraq. It all seemed to go back so far . . .

In an upstairs room of a modern hotel in the heart of Jerusalem, Ahmed smiled his predator's smile. At last his leader had spoken the words that meant he could act.

"With that jackal helping them, there must be some connection with Haleli. Frighten them away, Ahmed. Kill the scavenger but not the women. It would bring unwanted attention."

Ahmed prepared himself for the following day's work.

Pereira, Colombia. Updated May 21st 2015
A wave of violence in Colombia has stretched Police capacity to breaking point. Killings have doubled in the wake of the crossed legs strike, with most of the victims women refusing to return to the sex trade.

Claudia was one of the first women in Colombia to die.

Her family in Santa Rosa de Cabal said three men came to their door and took her while she was sleeping. When they contacted the police, they were told Claudia's body had been found by the river. No one was in any doubt that Jorge had been involved.

Women and children had fled the city, returning to villages, hiding away with relatives, queuing to leave the country with the money provided by the organisation directing the strike. Not all left, but enough to throw the sex industry into chaos. The central Directorate of Criminal Police formed a special sub-Directorate to manage the increase in violence.

Maria and Angie left late one night with their children and the belongings they could carry. Miguel was snoring in the next room, sleeping off too much aguardiente. He had threatened to kill one of the children if Maria took the money and stopped work; it was that more than anything that made her decide to leave. They crept down the lanes to meet aid workers from the Organizacion Femmina Popular. The OFP workers had stepped in to support women and children to leave cities throughout Colombia, relocating them in villages and communities far from the madness unleashed by the sex strike. The cities had never been safe, but they had become even more dangerous as pimps, accustomed to control and manipulation through brainwashing, terror, beatings, and the occasional murder, embarked on a campaign of desperate force.

The OFP trucks were carrying building materials to the Cauca River Valley, and Maria, Angie, and their three children sat uneasily amongst the bricks and cement. Eventually, after three more truck rides, two close encounters with guerilla fighters, and a night spent hiding under a bridge, Maria and Angie arrived at a remote settlement in the Llanos Orientales, the eastern plains of Colombia. Named after one of the river birds, the settlement was an oasis, offering work and safety, and a place for their children to grow with no weapons, no police, and no jail.

Not all of the women from Pereira found such a refuge, but many used the money they received to stop work to leave the city. Women died, but the "big crossed-legs strike", as it came to be known, was not broken.

London: City Police Headquarters, Old Jewry. May 21st 2015.

"How could millions of women all over the world have just stopped working? In the same week?" asked Inspector Willi Durham. It was a question that had been asked a thousand times.

Willi was speaking at a meeting of Police Chiefs from around the country. Called to address the unprecedented wave of murders, rapes, and various other violent assaults perpetrated on sex workers, the meeting had bogged down in the impossibility of what was happening.

The sex workers had shut up shop, women were leaving the cities like rats from a drowning ship, and the pimps had gone crazy.

"What the hell is going on?" demanded Willi.

CHAPTER XLVII
Jerusalem. May 21st 2015.

When examining the LIL root of deity in ancient Sumer, the meaning is thought to be that of AIR. In Sumer, EnLIL was the name of a male deity and NinLIL the name of a female deity. Enlil and Ninlil ruled the earth and heavens. Ninlil, a deity of destiny, was sometimes identified with Inanna. [xli]

"What the hell is going on?" asked Thom, glaring at Paula on the Skype screen. "The whole World has gone mad with this sex workers' strike, and we haven't heard from you in days."

"Sorry," said Paula. "We've been busy. It's not so bad here. Is everyone okay?"

They talked about the children, and Paula promised to call more often. When she ended the call, Lili asked a question with her eyebrows.

"Thom was worried," said Paula. "I haven't called home for two days, and the news is full of violence and riots. I didn't even mention the idea of staying longer."

"Did you tell him it's quiet here?"

"Uh huh. But it's unusual for me not to call. I'm just so caught up in all this." She pointed to her computer screen.

Lili hugged her. "I'll remind you to call every day."

They returned to their laptops, sitting either side of a wide table at the internet café that had become their second home. They drank coffee and freshly-squeezed lemonade, checked emails, and talked about the sex strike.

The morning news reported ongoing violence and unrest and restated the demands of those behind the strike: cooperate not dominate. The demands were for World leaders to implement policies to act in unison to close down sex trafficking, to ensure protection for women and children from exploitation, and to address the environmental crisis.

"How long can they keep it up?" asked Paula.

Lili shrugged. "It's a miracle it even happened. I still wonder where she got the money."

"Oil money?" said Paula.

"Not likely among the Bedu," said Lili. "She may have support from Saudi, or the money may have come from dealing drugs or guns. Who knows."

Haleli had still not answered their calls.

Paula was talking and typing at the same time, something she had learned to do while completing a doctorate with four children calling for her attention. She was unusually anxious, jumping at shadows, seeing movements out of the corner of her eye, sensing figures looming from behind her. When she turned to face the shadows, they resolved into waiters going about their business or a curtain blown by the overhead fan.

She was about to say something to Lili about the courage of the striking sex workers, when another movement caught her eye. Walking purposefully towards the café, staring straight at them, was the man who had been following them.

"Lili! It's him." Paula stood and pushed her chair back from the table.

Lili looked up, startled.

"Let's get out of here," said Paula, backing away from the table.

"Let's see what he wants," said Lili. "He can't do anything in broad daylight."

"No! We have to go now!"

Lili stood, looking determinedly at the man.

"Come on," said Paula, pulling at Lili's arm. "He's got something in his hand."

Paula pulled Lili away from the table, through the café to the small, kitchen area, and out into a back lane cluttered with boxes and bins of rubbish.

Lili grabbed Paula's hands and made her stop. "Okay, that's enough. You look like you've seen a ghost, but no one's following us. You're imagining things."

Paula pulled away. "It was the same man, and he had a knife or a gun or something."

"The biggest risk right now is that someone will steal our computers," said Lili, turning back to the kitchen door.

Paula grabbed her arm again and pointed through to the café entrance.

Silhouetted against the light was a man holding a knife.

"Shit!" Lili's eyes went wide with shock.

They turned and ran along the cluttered lane. Paula reached the end first and dashed around the corner -- straight into a man whose arm closed around her chest.

She screamed, but a strong hand smothered the sound.

She tried to bite, but the man pulled her head back against his chest.

Then she looked up.

Peter looked down at her, shaking his head. Paula sagged against him. He loosened his hold and held his finger to his lips for silence. Lili slumped against the wall, chest heaving, eyes wide with fright.

Peter motioned for them to follow, and they hurried after him down more lanes, taking hidden turns squeezed between buildings. How did he know where to go?

They finally stopped at the edge of a small plaza.

"Have we lost him?" asked Paula.

Peter shrugged. "If he's a local, he'll know the lanes better than I do."

"What about our computers?" said Lili.

"I'll call the café and have them sent to my hotel," said Peter. "You've been there often enough for them to look after your things. You'd better have your luggage sent to my room as well."

"But what if he's after you?" said Paula.

"How would he know me?" Peter looked surprised.

"How does he know us?" said Paula. "And who the hell is he?"

Ahmed watched the three of them from a doorway on the other side of the plaza. They were cowering like frightened children, but the women would be even more frightened soon.

The scavenger led the women across the plaza.

Ahmed did not follow them; he knew exactly where they were going. He turned and walked in the opposite direction.

Paula and Lili followed Peter across the plaza and through more lanes where people sat on back steps smoking, and everything seemed like business as normal. Paula began to think she had imagined the knife, but she still looked back over her shoulder, checking for the man. Several times she had to run to keep up with Peter as he led them through lanes that twisted and turned as if the city had been built as a labyrinth.

Where were they going?

Paula stumbled over a pile of empty cartons and kicked them out of her way. Two lanes later they finally they reached a plaza near Peter's hotel. There was no sign of the man.

"I'm glad most of that was downhill," said Lili, breathing fast.

"Do you think he followed us?" Paula asked Peter.

He shrugged, a casual movement that made her want to hit him. Then she noticed a muscle clenching along his jaw; he might not be as calm as he seemed.

"Wait here," he said quietly. "I'll check my hotel and call when I'm in my room." He held up his mobile.

Paula leaned against the wall, the brick rough against her back. Lili crouched on the cobblestones, still breathing heavily.

"I haven't been that frightened since I was a kid," she said, holding her phone ready for Peter's call.

Paula nodded. "That man's dangerous. I can feel it."

Lili nodded. "You were right. Sorry for not believing you."

The phone rang. She held it to her ear, listening intently.

Paula moved restlessly, looking back down the lane.

Lili cried out and scrambled to her feet, eyes staring in horror at something Paula couldn't see.

"What?" she asked. "What's wrong?"

Lili just stared at the wall and shook her head.

"Lili! What?"

Lili took the phone from her ear. "He said it was clear. Then he grunted. Then nothing. Something's happened to him."

"Ring the Police," said Paula.

"What's the number?" Lili looked terrible, face deathly pale, black rings under her eyes.

Before Paula could answer, Lili's phone rang again. They both stared at it like it was a bomb.

"Hello?" Lili's face went impossibly white. She nodded once and ended the call.

With a frantic glance towards the hotel, she grabbed Paula's hand and pulled her back down the lane.

"Lili! What's happening? Who was it?" Paula skidded to a stop, pulling on Lili's arm.

"He said Peter's dead. He said for us to go home. Leave it alone. Go home. Peter's dead." Lili spoke fast, her eyes so wide the whites showed all round.

"Dead?" said Paula. "Who said he's dead?"

She let Lili pull her away. They ran up a lane Paula didn't remember, dodging more steps and boxes.

Lili looked back over her shoulder.

A woman stepped out from a doorway with a broom.

Lili ran straight into her, tumbling to the cobblestones in a tangle of limbs, twisted up in the dark fabric of the woman's burka.

Paula caught herself on the wall, scraping her palms raw.

The bodies on the ground heaved and struggled. Lili crawled out from under the burka, and the woman sat up, her eyes flashing through the mesh face cover.

"Are you hurt?" asked Paula, bending to help the woman, who waved her away.

She laughed, a sound like water running over pebbles. "Never could I be hurt by one of Mir-ri's daughters. Never." Her accent sounded like a mix of Arabic and French, with a hint of music.

Lili, on all fours on the cobbles, stared open-mouthed at her.

"You mean us?"

"Who else?" said the woman, standing unaided, apparently unhurt by the fall.

"Who are you?" asked Lili, scrambling up with Paula's help.

"They call me Old Lil."

"That's my name," said Lili, as if she met someone like this every day. "Almost. I'm Lili. This is Paula."

Paula shook Lili's arm. Wasn't Peter dead? Weren't they running for their lives?

Suddenly everything went quiet, as if someone had turned down the volume. It must be shock. Paula' legs started to shake.

"Come," said Old Lil, beckoning them through the doorway. "Whoever is chasing you will not find you in here."

Paula followed Lili through double-doors into a walled courtyard. Flowering vines covered the walls with a rainbow of colour, a small fountain bubbled in one corner, and a fire burned beneath a hotplate in an alcove.

Old Lil closed the doors and dropped a bar to secure them. She ushered Paula and Lili to a bench under the overhanging branch of an acacia tree, and then lifted off her burka to reveal a nondescript dress, grey hair coiled and fastened high on her head, and a lined face with high cheekbones and wide, almond-shaped eyes, dark as night.

"Let me see where you are hurt," she said.

Paula opened her hands to reveal the scrapes. Lili lowered her slacks, wincing as the fabric pulled away from a bloody gash on her thigh.

Old Lil filled a kettle with water, placed it to heat above the fire, and disappeared inside through an arched doorway.

Lili grabbed Paula's arm. "Did you hear what she said?"

"She sounds crazy," said Paula. "We should go."

Lili seemed dazed. "She said something about daughters. I wonder how she knows."

"Knows what?" asked Paula, walking towards the gate.

"About the daughters marked at birth."

"Oh, stop it! Enough about the prophecy. What if Peter's really dead? What are we going to do?"

"Did you say someone was dead?" asked Old Lil, reappearing with a basket of bottles, and jars. She placed the basket on the table, poured boiling water into a bowl, and added powders from the jars and bottles.

"Our friend. Peter Moneghi. A man said he'd killed him." Paula felt dizzy and sat down again.

"The treasure hunter?" asked Old Lil.

"Do you know him?"

"I know of him," said Old Lil. "There have been some like him in all the ages of the world."

"Huh?"

Old Lil picked up Paula's hands and washed away the blood with her potion. It stung horribly.

"We think he's dead," said Paula again.

"People die," said Old Lil. "It is not so bad."

"Not so bad? Are you crazy? He was a friend. We have to call the Police." Suddenly her head felt clearer.

"Even friends die," said Old Lil, turning to tend Lili.

Paula found her phone and dialled 100, the emergency number she had memorised before leaving home.

"I think there's been a murder," she said to the woman who answered. Classic B-grade movie.

"In a hotel. No. I'll ask."

"Do you know the name of Peter's hotel?" she asked Lili.

Lili shook her head. "On Jaffa Road. Near the Convention Centre. Not the really big one."

"Did you hear that?" asked Paula. "Peter Moneghi. He's a friend." She waited.

"A man phoned to say he was dead. No, I don't know his name."

She had to give her name, her passport number, and the address of her hotel before the woman would let her go.

"She sounded like it happens every day." Paula moved restlessly around the yard.

"You have done what you must," said Old Lil. "Now come and sit."

Paula sat down again like an errant child. Who was this old woman?

"I have wandered the city streets and the desert," said Old Lil, as if she had heard the question.

Paula frowned. Lili had her eyes closed, gritting her teeth at Old Lil's ministrations.

"There. Now you will heal," said Old Lil, straightening from her task. "I will make tea."

"Thank you, but we should be going." Paula stood again and moved towards the gate.

"Not yet," said Old Lil, in a voice that sent shivers up Paula's back.

"But we have to go. What if the Police need us? What if the man's still looking for us? We have to go." Paula reached for the cross bar to open the gate.

"Wait, Paula," said Lili.

Paula hesitated and frowned at Lili, who still sat with her trousers around her ankles. At least her leg was bandaged.

Lili turned to Old Lil. "Who are you really?" she asked.

Old Lil smiled, deepening the lines etched on her face. "I am Old Lil."

Lili waved her hand in a signal for old Lil to say more.

"I am Old Lil, the one who wanders and waits. I have walked the banks of the Buranun to welcome the dawn; I have crossed the desert, sailed the Sea to Zara, where all the colours of the world could once be found: saffron and indigo, white lead and lapis lazuli, and the purple taken from sea creatures for the robes of Kings and Queens, Priests and Priestesses."

Paula moved closer to Lili. Shivers rippled up her back. What was going on?

"I have seen cities rise and fall, and I have waited through the time of Kings for two Ages of the world. I am Old Lil."

Paula sat down. Every cell in her body hummed. She was still deathly afraid for Peter, but she no longer wanted to be anywhere else. She just wanted to listen to Old Lil forever.

Lili sighed deeply and closed her eyes.

"Let me tell you a story," said Old Lil, sitting on the wide rim of the fountain pool. "At the beginning of time, at the very beginning of time, before the world had filled with people, there lived a man and a woman. Do you know who they were?"

Lili shrugged. "Adam and Eve?"

"Half right," said Old Lil. "And half wrong."

The silence deepened. Birds twittered in the vines, and the distant traffic hummed. A siren wailed its distress call, making Paula's breath catch. Was Peter really dead?

Old Lil opened her eyes and looked intently at them. "Before Adam lived with Eve in the garden between the rivers, there was another woman. Long has she has been forgotten. This is her story."

Lili's face was flushed, her eyes shining. "Most people think Eve was the first woman," she said. "But you must be speaking of Lilith. She is named in the old stories."

Old Lil smiled. "What comes first, the bird or the egg? The time of sun or the time of rain?"

Paula shivered; someone walking on her grave.

Old Lil went on with her story. "There is no beginning and no end. So it is, and so it has always been. The green shoot is nourished by all that has gone before. It grows and, when the season is done, it returns to the earth."

The words were familiar. Were they from the Bible? Paula couldn't place them.

"The very first woman--Lilith as you call her--was strong and free," said Old Lil. "She knew the true names of every living thing. When the first man saw her, he wanted to be with her like the lion was with the lioness, like the horned gazelle was with the doe. "But the fierce one knew that men and women could come together in a different way. She tried to show him, but the man turned his back and refused her wisdom. One night, as frogs called from the rivers and crickets sang from the earth, the man tried to force the woman to do what he wanted. She rose up and uttered words of power, and the World changed."

Bees hovered around the flowers on the vines, making a sound like a summer breeze in dry grass.

Old Lil nodded her head. "Where the woman had stood

was a Serpent, scales shimmering in the moonlight. When Eve came, the Serpent was waiting."

"What happened?" asked Lili.

"First the Serpent spoke of earth: *I am the womb of life. From me you come and to me you shall return. Nothing is wasted. Do not fear.*" Old Lil's voice sounded like the hissing of snakes.

"Then the Serpent spoke of air: *I am the breath of life. From me come the winds of change. Nothing remains the same. Do not fear. To live you must leave the safety of the womb. To eat you must crush the wheat. Nothing remains the same.*"

Paula closed her eyes and leaned forward to rest her arms on her knees, her fears for Peter dissolving in the dreaminess of Old Lil's story.

"Then water," said Old Lil. "*I am the beginning of life. From me all things come forth. Nothing is forgotten. Do not fear. The primal vortex of destruction is also the central wellspring of creation. Nothing is forgotten.*"

"Finally, the Serpent spoke of the golden light of the Sun and the glowing flames of fire. *I am the heart of life. From me comes the searing heat of desire. Nothing is unknown. Do not fear. The barley and the corn agree to live in the Sun and die in the flames, to give you food. Nothing is unknown.*"

Old Lil smiled. "The first woman carried the life-giving power of the Earth."

"I know of her," said Lili.

"Of course you do," said Old Lil. "Her name was almost lost, but some remember. Although you may have not heard this story before. History says she became a demon, living in the netherworld, tormenting men's dreams. But that is not what happened."

"What really happened?" asked Paula.

Old Lil smiled at her as if she had just done something clever. "She took many different forms--serpent, wise woman, harpy, priestess, prostitute--coming to women when they were ready to hear her story. Through the Ages, she kept alive the original dream of the Earth. She has even been a 'bag lady'."

Paula laughed, a sort of hysteria that brought tears to her eyes.

"Why didn't the Serpent speak to Adam?" asked Lili.

"Because men can't hear Serpents speak," said Old Lil, laughing like a mad woman.

Old Lil was still chuckling when Paula's phone rang. She jumped in fright, shivers rushing up her spine.

"Yes, this is Paula Matthews. Yes."

Lili leaned forward.

"Where? Yes, yes. We'll be there." Paula turned to Lili. "He's alive."

Lili hugged her. "Where is he?"

"Hadassah Hospital. They want us to go."

Old Lil was watching them intently. "Go," she said. "But may I offer advice? Visit your friend, then go to your hotel and pack your bags. Let it be known you are leaving Jerusalem. Go to the airport and disappear."

"Disappear?" said Lili, frowning.

Old Lil smiled and produced a bundle from behind the bench.

"Burkas. No one will notice you if you emerge from the airport as two Muslim women. But you must walk like Muslim women and speak as they speak. Or not speak at all."

Lili pulled up her trousers and picked up a burka. Old Lil showed her how to wear it. Paula picked the other one up. It was surprisingly light.

Old Lil gave them a plastic shopping bag each to carry

them.

"No one ever looks at a plastic bag," said Lili. "I had a friend in New York who carried her money around in one instead of using a handbag."

They were both quiet in the taxi that carried them through the early evening traffic. Paula was thinking of her family and what Thom would say if he knew about the man with the knife. Lili called Haleli, but there was still no answer.

They found their way to the Intensive Care ward at Hadassah and sat close together in the waiting-room. Before they could see Peter, two policewomen arrived to take statements. They spoke to Paula while Lili waited in the corridor, and then swapped to take Lili's statement. The policewomen seemed bored.

"Does this happen often?" asked Lili, when the women called Paula back into the room.

"Often enough," answered the younger of the two. She had introduced herself, but Paula couldn't remember her name.

"Will you catch him?" asked Paula. "He's been following us since Amman."

The older woman looked at her notes and raised an eyebrow. "Tall, close-cropped dark hair, sunglasses, leather jacket. There can't be too many like him in Jerusalem."

Paula flinched at the sarcasm, and the younger woman apologised for her partner, explaining that they had been working since the night before. Paula shrugged and went to wait by the door.

Lili tried calling Haleli again. No answer.

When the doctor came two hours later, Paula was still leaning against the door frame. Lili was curled up on the couch, eyes closed. The doctor, a woman about their age, came in and sat down. She beckoned Paula over to the other chair. Lili stretched and sat up.

"The admission form says Mister Moneghi has no relatives here, but he named you as close friends."

Paula nodded. Close enough to have the same enemy.

"I can tell you that his condition is now stable. The knife missed his kidney by a prayer, but there is some tissue damage, and there was significant blood loss."

"Can we see him?" asked Lili.

The doctor stood. "For a short time. He's drifting in and out on the painkillers."

Peter was wired to several machines and looked terribly pale. He opened his eyes when he heard them walk in, but only managed to squint at them briefly before closing them again.

"Hello," he whispered, trying to smile. "Thanks for getting help."

Paula squeezed his hand.

"I'm not sure you should be thanking us at all," said Lili. "That man was following us, remember."

Peter shook his head slightly. "No mistake. Men like that. No mistake."

"You mean he was after you?" asked Lili.

He nodded. "Be careful," he whispered. "Call Haleli."

They stood helplessly by the bed for a few minutes and then went back to sit in the waiting room. Lili tried Haleli again, and this time someone answered, but Paula was too tired to make sense of a one-sided conversation.

"She didn't seem surprised," said Lili. "I think the attack might be more about her than us."

"The sex workers' strike?"

Lili shrugged. "She suggested we leave Jerusalem as soon as we can. Go to Amman or Italy or Greece."

"You didn't say anything about Old Lil," said Paula.

"Maybe we should just go home," said Lili quietly, looking at the floor.

"I'm not sure I can," said Paula, her throat tightening painfully.

Lili looked puzzled. "Why not? It's not safe here. What about your family?"

"It's not a game," said Paula quietly.

"But what do we really have?" said Lili. "Two pieces of very old jewellery and a prophecy. I don't think it's enough to change the World. And I'm damned sure it's not enough to get killed for." Her foot tapped a tattoo on the linoleum.

"But you really believed in this," said Paula, searching her friend's face.

Lili shrugged. "I don't know what I believed. I needed a change, and your enthusiasm was infectious, but I don't think we're going to find the *me,* and I don't think the *me* can save the World. I believe in global change, but I think Haleli's sex strike is more likely to make a difference than what we're doing."

"She said this was important," said Paula. "Maybe we've been thinking about it the wrong way. What if the prophecy's not about something physical. What does it say? *Hidden in stone soaked in sweetness, Riding the wind burnished bright."*

"What's it about then?" asked Lili. "I'm the one who can read cuneiform, and I have no idea what it means."

Paula sighed. Had Lili always had those doubts? "We have to keep going," she said, holding Lili's hands. "I know we're going round in circles, and there's someone chasing us, but I don't want to leave yet. It's crazy, but I feel safe with Old Lil, even if she acts like she's four thousand years old."

Lili managed a smile. "She certainly tells great stories."

They visited with Peter again briefly and were reassured to find a policeman guarding the door to his room.

"Be safe," he whispered as they left.

They arrived back at Old Lil's four hours later, having collected their computers and their bags, gone to the airport, changed into the burkas, and caught another taxi back.

"I feel like I'm in James Bond movie," said Paula, sitting with Lili in the back seat of a taxi, her voice muffled by the fabric covering her face.

"It still feels like Raiders of the Lost Arc to me," said Lili. "I never saw James Bond."

"You never saw James Bond?" said Paula, loudly enough to make the taxi driver look up. Dark eyes watched them from the rear vision mirror.

Lili was quiet, but Paula could see her eyes smiling.

Old Lil opened the gate as soon as they knocked. "How is your friend?"

Paula heard Lili answer. Then something happened to the light.

"Many are called but few are chosen." The voice came out of the air.

Paula staggered to the bench and sat with her head in her hands. The air hummed with distant music.

"Paula? What's wrong?" asked Lili, sounding scared.

Paula couldn't answer. The words repeated in her head. "Many are called but few are chosen."

She stood. Her legs shook as if she had a fever.

"Do you bring your feet to walk in Her Ways?" asked the voice.

Paula nodded.

"You must answer, child. Do you bring your feet to walk in Her Ways?"

"I do," whispered Paula.

"Do you bring your knees to kneel in Her praise?"

"I do." Paula knelt.

"Do you bring your sex to rejoice in Her Life-giving?"

"I do," said Paula, suddenly hot all over.

"Do you bring your breasts for Her abundance flowing?"

"I do."

"Do you bring your hands to do Her work?"

"I do."

"Do you bring your lips to sing Her acclaim?"

"I do."

"Do you bring your eyes to see Her presence in all?"

"I do."

"Rise, child. You are chosen."

Paula stood, her body strangely light. Old Lil nodded knowingly at her, eyes shining.

"What happened?" asked Lili.

Paula told her.

"It is very ancient," said Old Lil. "The words were spoken by the High Priestess of the Temple of Nanna in Urim when a girl entered to become a priestess."

"I've heard some of it before, at home," said Paula. "I used to think it made me special. Then I thought I was going crazy. Then I just accepted it. It's been there for a long time."

"But it is only now that you have chosen," said Old Lil.

"That *I* have chosen?" said Paula. "I thought it said few *are chosen*, as in chosen by someone else."

Old Lil chuckled. "The choosing can only ever be one's own. Many are called, but few take up the calling."

Shivers rippled up Paula's back, along her arms. "No

wonder the voice persisted! It took me long enough to choose."

"And now you have chosen," said Old Lil. "It will bring you closer to what you are seeking."

"I wonder whose voice it is," said Lili, frowning at Old Lil.

Old Lil smiled. "The words are always spoken by the High Priestess. But now I will make coffee."

Paula sat on the bench. What did it might mean to have finally chosen? Did it change things?

Her mobile phone rang. An sms from Thom.

At Children's hospital with Mary. Talking in sleep. Can't wake her. Vital signs okay. Doing tests. Where are you?

Spider's legs of fear crawled up Paula's arms and along her neck. Not Mary. Please, not Mary. She called Thom's number. A recorded voice said something in a foreign language. She called again. Same voice.

"What's happening?" asked Lili.

"Can I use your phone?"

Lili handed it to her, and Paula dialled Thom's number. The foreign voice again. "Not in local network" appeared on the screen.

"What's going on? I can't call home." She brought up the sms and pressed "reply". "Emergency calls only" flashed on the screen.

"This is a fucking emergency!" She threw the phone onto the table.

Lili picked it up. "What? What's happened?"

"Mary's in hospital. I have to call." The spiders' legs were running all over her body.

Loud voices sounded in the lane.

Three knocks shook the gate.

A man yelled something in Arabic.

Lili's eyes went wide. Old Lil hurried out, holding her finger to her lips, shaking her head.

"We must go," she whispered. "They must not find us." She pointed to narrow stairs leading down under the courtyard.

"They? Who are they?" asked Paula. "I have to call home."

Old Lil picked up her burka and hurried to the stairs.

"Let's go," said Lili, grabbing the shopping bags and following Old Lil.

The angry shouting from the lane grew more urgent.

Paula gave up on the phone, picked up her shoulder bag with her computer, and followed Lili to the top of a steep flight of stairs.

The gate shook with the force of the knocking.

Paula stepped down onto the first stair. The rise of each stair was so tall that she had to squat and step sideways onto the one below. Old Lil scrambled ahead like a mountain goat. Lili came behind, grunting and swearing quietly. About six steps down, she slipped and fell heavily against Paula.

"Aahhh! Sorry. These stairs were made for giants."

They went more slowly, bracing each other at every step. Above them, the banging on the gate became more urgent.

Finally the steps gave way to hard-packed earth in a cellar lit by a single light dangling on a cord with exposed wires. There was nowhere to hide.

Paula thought instantly of the assassination of the Romanovs; the fate of Anastasia had haunted her as a child.

"This can't be good," murmured Lili.

Wood shattered in the courtyard above. More yelling.

Old Lil disappeared behind one of the supporting pillars. Paula followed. Another set of steps. How far down could they go?

These steps were also made for giants, and with each one the light faded until it grew dark as a moonless night. Paula clung to the wall, sliding her feet along each step. Lili came down close behind, her breath coming in gasps and groans that broke the velvety silence.

The stairs ended, and Paula sank to her knees. "Will they follow?"

"They will not find us," said Old Lil. She lifted Paula to her feet and led them further into the dark silence.

"Who are they?" asked Lili.

"Men who destroy what they cannot control. They are angry now because Laylareeh has tricked them."

"Who?"

"The teacher. She has opened a window so fresh wind can enter."

"Haleli?"

"Yes. The teacher."

Paula no longer cared if the old woman was crazy; she just didn't want the men to find them. She walked faster. The ground seemed to be rising, but it was hard to be sure.

Old Lil stopped abruptly. Paula walked into her back, Lili into hers, all three of them sandwiched against a solid wall.

Old Lil waved her arms, and the wall moved. Chinks of light appeared, blinding after the dark.

They slipped through into a courtyard just like the one they had left. Had it been ten minutes ago? Twenty?

Harsh cries echoed from the darkness behind them. Old Lil touched the mechanism, and the heavy door closed, silencing the men's voices.

"Where are we?" asked Paula, crossing to the gate. Cooking smells made her mouth water, but she just wanted to find a phone.

"Salaam, Mareka," said Old Lil to an even older woman flipping vegetables with a spatula and dousing the grill with oil.

Mareka grunted, but kept her eyes on the food.

"Is there a phone here?" asked Paula. Her mouth was so dry it hurt to talk.

Old Lil scooped water from a large clay jar and handed her the ladle. Paula drank and passed it to Lili.

"Please. I need to phone home. My daughter's in hospital. They can't wake her up."

Old Lil frowned. "Does your daughter have the mark?"

Paula's chest tightened. She nodded.

"The time of reckoning draws near," said Old Lil. "Your daughter feels the call, but she cannot answer. The circle has stretched too far. You must close the circle, or she may never return."

Paula made growling sound deep in her throat. "Close what circle? This is Mary! Not some cryptic crossword in a foreign, bloody language!"

"I will take you to where it all began," said Old Lil. "To close the circle, restore the Balance."

"No!"

"You'll take us to Iraq?" asked Lili, as if Old Lil had just suggested they go to the moon.

"I'm going home," said Paula.

"You heard Her voice," said Old Lil. "You have chosen."

"My daughter needs me." Paula pulled at the handle on gate.

Someone knocked loudly on the other side.

Paula stumbled back into Lili. Old Lil called out and was answered. She opened the gate.

In walked a man with oiled dark hair, pockmarked skin, and a smile like a toothpaste advertisement. He smelled of cardamom and cloves.

Mareka looked up from her cooking and grinned toothlessly at him.

"Ami," said Old Lil.

"Do you have a phone I could use?" Paula mimed holding a phone to her ear in case he did not understand English.

"No phone. Wait." He brushed her aside with an abrupt hand movement.

Old Lil put a hand on her arm. "You can use your phone now."

Paula tried again.

"Paula? Thank God! Where are you?" Thom sounded as young as Jon.

"I'm still in Jerusalem. How's Mary? What's happening?"

"Fucked if I know. She went to bed as usual, slept for a few hours and then started talking in her sleep. It disturbed Rinna, so I tried to get her to stop talking. She wouldn't wake up! It was horrible, like she was possessed, talking and talking but sound asleep. I didn't know what the hell was going on, so I called an ambulance. They've admitted her, but they say she's fine, no fever, no sign of infection, her blood pressure's okay. They did a CAT scan in case there's a tumour or a bleed in her brain. Nothing. She's just asleep. And talking."

"What's she saying?" asked Paula.

"What?"

"What is Mary saying?"

"Hell, I don't know. Something about calling or choosing or something. What does it matter?"

"Many are called but few are chosen," said Paula, holding the phone so tightly her hand cramped.

"That sounds right," said Thom. "Has she done this before?

"No, but I've heard the words before."

"Don't get mystical about this! It's Mary we're talking about."

"I know, but it's all connected. The prophecy. The birthmark."

"What are you talking about?" He yelled the words so loudly Paula jumped and held the phone away from her ear. "Are you mad? Our daughter is in some sort of coma, and you're talking about a prophecy. Unfuckingbelievable!"

"I know it's weird, but it really is all connected: what I'm doing, Mary's coma, all of it."

"Is Lili there?" asked Thom, speaking slowly as if to a child, or to someone having a psychotic episode.

Paula handed the phone to Lili and shrugged helplessly.

"Hi, Thom," said Lili. "She's okay. She's beside herself about Mary, but the coma does seem to be linked to what we're doing here."

Lili's knuckles were white on the phone as she listened.

"No, we're not crazy. We've heard the same words here."

"Exactly the same."

"Uh huh. Is she stable? Have they got her on a drip?" She listened intently, frowning and nodding. The she handed Paula the phone and raised her hands helplessly.

"It's me," said Paula, bracing for Thom's anger. Who could blame him? If someone told her a mother of a nine-year-old girl was babbling about a prophecy while her child lay in a coma . . .

"Okay, Paula, listen to me. I want you on the next plane home. Forget the prophecy. Forget Lili. Come home." He sounded exhausted.

Paula closed her eyes. "I'm on my way. I'll call from the airport."

The line started to crackle, and the phone went dead. Old Lil handed her a coffee, black and sweet.

Lili sat on a low wall with a cup in her hands, staring into space. Mareka lit lanterns. Was it night already?

"I can lead you to what you seek," said Old Lil.

"I have to go home," said Paula. Why did that sound so wrong?

Old Lil turned away.

Lili shook her head. "We're so close. I can feel it."

"I know," said Paula. "But I have to go."

Lili nodded. "Of course you do. I'll keep going, and maybe you can come back."

Paula felt sick. "I'm sorry." She turned to the gate.

Ami stepped up, as if to open the gate for her.

Instead he spun around and threw a burka over head. Quick as a viper he grabbed her, pinning her arms to her side.

"Hey! What are you doing?" cried Lili. Then she grunted and went quiet.

Paula kicked and struggled, but the man was strong. Someone--Old Lil?--helped him tie her arms to her side. She screamed, but the heavy fabric muffled the sound. Bile rose into her mouth.

"Take them to the car," said Old Lil.

Ami lifted her like a sack, carried her for ten steps, and shoved her into a car. She kicked and squirmed, but the more she struggled, the tighter the bonds became, cutting into her skin through the burka. Hot tears burned her eyes; helpless rage churned her stomach.

The door opened and something heavy landed on the seat beside her.

"Lili?"

No answer.

"Lili!" Black terror flooded Paula's body, and she screamed Lili's name until she was hoarse.

She stopped for breath. It was very quiet. Tears overflowed and ran down her face. Thom would be waiting for her. And Mary . . .

The car doors opened again. Two people settled into the front seats, speaking in clipped tones. Paula couldn't understand a word, but Old Lil's voice sounded the same, wise and kindly. Paula wanted to strangle her.

"What have you done to Lili?" she asked through clenched teeth.

"She will sleep for a while," said Old Lil.

"She wanted to go with you. You didn't have to hurt her."

"She did not want us to take you."

"So why take me? Where are we going?"

"First we are going to Amman," said Old Lil. "It is not far as the crow flies, but crows do not have to pass through traffic and border crossings. We will take the northern road, across the Sheikh Hussein bridge."

Now she sounded like a tour guide. Crazy.

"We will be like all the others on the road," said Old Lil. "Women who fled the war and are now returning to visit their husbands and brothers. Most will start from the Mahat'ta in the early hours of the morning. With Ami we can make our own time."

The car sped along, wheels hissing on the road. Old Lil reached across and twisted Paula's burka around so she could breathe through the face veil. She sucked in air and leaned towards the window. They sped along a narrow, two-lane highway, passing SUVs, laden sedans, and station wagons as if their car had wings, or as if they were being chased by demons. The desert rolled by, and Lili lay still as death

The headlights turned the desert into a scene from a post-apocalyptic movie, relentlessly brown and dreary, strewn with rocks, plastic bottles, and soft-drink cans. They flashed past signs warning of camels crossing, but the camels must have thought better of it because not one dared the crossing.

Paula lapsed into a dream-like state in which she had been crossing the desert forever . . .

When the car finally stopped, she thought she was still dreaming.

"Is this Amman?"

"We have passed Amman. Now we will untie you so you can walk and use the toilet. Do not try to run."

Passed Amman? Where were they?

The binding came free, and blood rushed into Paula's hands like ants biting. She rubbed her arms and staggered from the car.

The roadside stop was a large open-fronted shed surrounded by trucks like dinosaurs at a watering hole. In the shed, two young men with greasy hair kneaded dough into flat bread as large as a car seat. To the side was the toilet, a smaller shed over a foul-smelling pit.

Paula emerged from the toilet and thought about running. She had no idea where she was, and running into the desert did not seem like a good idea. She hurried past the trucks and climbed back into the air-conditioned Mercedes. Smiling like a benevolent father, Ami handed her a bottle of water. She scowled at him, but she lifted the burka and drank.

She rested her other hand on Lili's back. She was breathing rhythmically, as if asleep.

They drove on.

Hours later, the Mercedes slowed to crawl. Huge, arched gates appeared like the entrance to Heaven. Or Hell.

"The border," said Ami, sounding pleased with himself.

Old Lil turned to Paula. "Be quiet. It is dangerous for foreigners."

Paula bit her lip until it bled. Should she scream for help? Would the border guards save her or shoot her?

They coasted up to the gates. The blood on her tongue tasted bitter.

A soldier strolled over to the car to tell them they would have to wait until morning. Paula dozed until the red light of dawn brought out a group of Jordanian and Iraqi officials who looked at the papers Ami gave them at least six times each, talking excitedly. Ami was so deft at handing the papers back and forth, it was hard to see if he passed any money across.

"It is normal," said Ami, as the car crawled forwards, sandwiched between a new SUV filled with young men and an old station wagon filled with boxes of laundry powder.

Paula closed her eyes and did the breath meditation she had learned when she was pregnant with Mary: breathe in, breathe out, count one . . .breathe in, breathe out, count two . . .

An argument broke out between the paper stampers and someone in the SUV. Not enough money? Not enough papers? Or maybe it wasn't an argument; maybe they were long lost relatives, yelling with excitement at finding each other alive. Without the language, Paula had no idea.

Breathe in, breathe out, count . . .what number was she up to? Maybe she would grow old there, stuck like one of Dante's sinners in her own circle of Hell.

Ami was saying something in an excited voice to the officials. Paula opened her eyes. Everyone was smiling and nodding. She sighed with relief; it seemed she wasn't going to be shot after all.

The car crawled across the border into Iraq.

Lili groaned and sat up.

Paula handed her the water.

"What happened?" Lili sounded drunk.

"Old Lil kidnapped us," said Paula, bitterness stinging her throat.

"What?" Lili pulled up her burka. "Where are we?"

"We just crossed into Iraq."

Surprisingly, the road on the Iraq side widened into a six-lane highway.

"German aid money," mumbled Lili, as Ami pressed his foot to the floor.

"Better to go fast," said Ami. "Snipers."

"Great," said Paula.

The desert flashed past, littered with abandoned cars, charred buses, and so many bomb craters it looked like the Moon. Paula opened the window a chink for a better look. It was like opening an oven door.

"No!" cried Ami. "Sand storm. See the wind?"

The ground did seem to be moving, the sand sliding.

"Does anyone live out there?" asked Paula.

"Camels," said Ami.

"Bedu," said Lili.

Was this where Haleli came from? Images of proud-looking robed figures riding camels and Arabian horses drifted through Paula's mind. Proud-looking figures who killed women for honour.

She finally stopped thinking about the desert and closed her eyes. The movement of the car became the drone of an airplane taking her home to Mary.

Paula woke to Ami talking excitedly.

"See the green! We have reached Baghdad. Twelve hours and fifteen minutes. It is good time."

The desert gave way to palm trees and scrubby bushes; the leaves were dusty, but definitely green.

"The Euphrates brings water," said Old Lil. "The river of life. The Buranun it was called."

Lili whispered something Paula couldn't hear.

The dusty palms led into a city of contrasts: new buildings alongside burnt-out shells where people must have suffered horribly; shiny SUVs parked next to vacant lots piled with abandoned tanks and overturned trucks. And people everywhere, shopping, walking, filling the city with sound.

"It is the way of the World now," said Old Lil. "Men have their wars, people die, and the rest go on trying to rebuild." She sounded weary.

The sun was high overhead by the time they stopped at a two-storey building on the far side of the city. Ami said they would rest for the afternoon and drive on in the cool of the evening. He shepherded Paula and Lili up steep, external stairs. Lili kept tripping over her burka.

"If the snipers don't get us, these bloody steps will," she said, grunting all the way to the top.

The room was shadowy and cool, with couches and a low table.

"Don't tell me the toilet's downstairs," said Lili, throwing off the burka and looking around the room. There were no internal doors.

An anonymous woman in a burka brought them their bags and a tray of food: flat bread, rice, lamb, and beans. She also left a jug of iced lemon drink.

"This has to be the best drink I've ever had," said Lili,

refilling her glass.

"You sound like a tourist," said Paula. "That old woman has kidnapped us, and you go on about a lemon drink!"

"I'm sorry she took you like that, but I think this is what we're meant to be doing." Lili finished her drink.

Paula nodded reluctantly. "But where is she taking us? And what about Mary?" She wanted to shout, but her throat was raw from the screaming she had done in the car. "I feel like I'm going crazy. One minute I'm a True Believer, the next I'm going home to my daughter, and now I'm sitting in a room in Baghdad. And you're almost as bad."

Lili shrugged. "You're right. It's hard to trust something as weird as all this. Not logical, at all! But I honestly think we can help Mary best from here."

Paula scowled.

"I still don't think Old Lil should have kidnapped you."

"Hmmph." Paula tried the door handle. It was locked. "What if we need the toilet?"

The anonymous woman opened the door and pointed down the hallway.

Paula shook her head.

"Is this where Ami lives?" asked Lili.

The woman shook her head.

"He is from Basra," said Old Lil, pushing past the woman. "We will go there tonight."

"And then?" asked Lili.

"From Basra you shall find what you seek," said Old Lil.

"How do you know what we seek?" asked Paula. "We have never mentioned the *me*." She was too tired and too angry to be careful.

Old Lil laughed. "Many daughters through the Ages have thought the treasure was made of gold and precious stones, but what you seek is not solid."

"It's not?" Lili choked on her second drink. "What is it, then?"

"It is the treasure Mir-ri carried out of Urim before the fall."

Lili frowned. "Mir-ri. You said that name when I ran into you in the lane. 'Mir-ri's daughters', you said. Who is Mir-ri?"

Old Lil told them the story of the girl who entered the Temple of Nanna to become a priestess. She told it as if she could see it unfolding: the daily rituals, the gardens, the House of Tablets. She spoke softly as she described how the girl had grown into a woman who met Eresh-ki-gal and returned, who studied at the E-dub-ba, loved one of the scholars there, and left Urim bearing a child.

"So the child was the treasure," said Lili.

Old Lil nodded. "Daughters marked at birth."

"But how could a child born four thousand year ago make any difference now?" asked Paula. "And what has all this got to do with Mary?"

"Even a small thread changes a tapestry," said Old Lil. "And this was a very large thread. The child's mother was Mir-ri, a daughter of Ki-en-gir. The child's father was Abram, who left Urim to find the One God and establish a dynasty through the line of sons."

"Abraham." Lili turned to Paula. "You were right. Remember what you said in Amman: it started with a love affair. You even talked about it being Abraham."

"But what about Mary?" asked Paula.

"Complete the circle," said Old Lil. "Restore the Balance."

Paula sighed with frustration. It was an amazing story, but how the hell did a four thousand year old love affair send a child into a coma? She shivered despite the heat.

Lili's mobile phone rang.

Old Lil pointed at their bags by the door and nodded.

Lili rummaged in her bag and surfaced with her phone. She mumbled something and covered the mouthpiece. "It's Peter. He's out of hospital and wants to know what we're doing in Iraq. I told him we're following our noses. He swore at me in Yiddish."

"Tell him we've been kidnapped." Paula glared at Old Lil.

Peter was yelling so loudly, Paula could hear him.

"Do you have a guide?"

"Yes. We met her in Jerusalem."

"Who is she? Who does she work for?"

"She's just herself. I don't think she works for anybody."

"You sound strange. Have you been drugged?" asked Peter.

"Kidnapped," yelled Paula.

"What? Who's that yelling?"

"No one."

"Where's Paula? Let me speak to her."

Lili frowned at Paula and shook her head. "She's busy."

Paula lunged for the phone. "Help! We've been kidnapped."

Lili ended the call.

"What are you doing?" cried Paula. "He could help us!"

She rummaged through her own bag, but her phone was missing.

CHAPTER XLVIII

Basra. May 22nd 2015.

. . .the "Descent of Inanna" poem. . .has many elements that show that it is one that has undergone change. Perhaps originally it was a poem in praise of a goddess who combined the characteristics and realms of Inanna and Eresh-ki-gal , she who was the source of all becoming, the reason why the cycles rolled back on themselves and the world continued.[xlii]

Basra was like a beautiful woman who had suffered a terrible calamity. The beauty lingered in the wide streets, graceful buildings, perfumed air, but the scars of war were deep. Yet the canals still flowed, and a kingfisher flashed through the slanting sun to catch a fish.

"Why do we do so much harm to each other when there is so much beauty?" said Lili.

Old Lil squeezed her hand, an answer of sorts.

Ami drove through the back lanes to a narrow road leading out of the city, away from the coast. They passed through villages where women sat at roadside stalls next to mounds of dates, dogs ran carelessly in front of the car, and children walked hand in hand, their feet dusty, their faces sometimes bright, sometimes sullen.

About two hours later, Ami stopped the car by a hill rising like a ziggurat from the plains. The terraced rows were overgrown with grey-green shrubs, and three trees reached twisted branches to the sky.

"What is this place?" asked Lili.

"You will see," said Old Lil, turning to lead her up a goat track.

Paula followed, heart racing, legs itching to move faster, desperate fear for Mary burning in her chest

Old Lil stopped in front of a large, flat rockface. She pointed to a low cleft in the rock and indicated that they should enter. Lili squatted to peer into the entrance. With a shrug, she dropped to her hands and knees and crawled into the darkness.

Paula hesitated. Were there bats? Spiders? A strange smell tickled her throat, like aniseed and lavender together. She dropped to her hands and knees and crawled after Lili.

The cleft opened into a larger space. Lili stood, hands outstretched to feel the walls.

"I come here to hear Her voice," said Old Lil from behind. "This room is very old."

"Is there a way out?" asked Paula.

Old Lil lit a candle. They stood in the centre of a circular room with a low ceiling of stone. Old Lil used the candle to light more candles set on platforms at four points around the room.

"The way out is through," said Old Lil, holding the flame to a bowl of charcoal and blowing until the charcoal glowed red. Smoke rose in spirals, filling the room with musky incense.

She pointed to a trickle of water running down the rock face.

Lili scooped water into the palm of her hand and drank. When she was done she wiped her wet hands on her face, leaving streaks like war paint.

Paula paced the small room. The cleft through which they had entered had disappeared into the shadows.

"Your daughter needs you to walk the path of Inanna," said Old Lil. "Descend and return, and she will return with you."

Lili put a hand on Paula's arm and pointed to one of the platforms. Suspended above it, a white carving of a bird hovered in the candlelight as if alive.

"Celestial dove," said Old Lil, her voice loud in the subterranean silence. "She bestows radiant love. We call on Her for laughter, lust, and inspiration."

Lili crossed to the dove and knelt on the hard-packed earth.

"Come, Paula. It is the old story, descent and return. It is the way through."

Paula looked around the walls once more and knelt beside Lili. Despite her fears, peace filled her body, and warmth settled in her bones.

"She lifts us on Her golden wings." Old Lil's voice rose as she lifted her arms above her head, backs of her hands meeting like wings.

Lili lifted her arms and took on the pose of the dove. She seemed to be glowing. Paula mirrored the movements, the life of the dove filling her arms.

Then Old Lil pointed to the next altar. A statue of a lioness watched them with topaz eyes.

"Lioness of battle," said Old Lil, her voice deep.

Paula trembled.

Lili whispered. "There are tales from Sumer of the great mother lions roaring to stop the hearts of goats, to take the breath from gazelle and antelope."

Old Lil nodded. "She brings strength invincible. Mighty warrior, fierce defender, She is the protector of women and children." She raised her hands to her shoulders, elbows held close to her sides. Her fingers curled outwards, forming the shape of lion's claws, tensed, ready to fight.

Lili stood to one side, hands raised in the pose of the lioness. Paula took on the posture and moved closer to the altar.

The great beast blinked.

Paula gasped. Had she imagined it? Had the incense clouded her mind?

Lili tapped her gently on the shoulder and led her to the next altar while the lioness watched.

Something moved in the shadows. Snakes!

They writhed like a living painting with soft-patterned scales, glittering mosaic eyes, tongues darting in and out.

"The West is home to the sacred serpent who holds the ancient wisdom. Sibyl, soothsayer and seer, She speaks Her truth that we may hear." The words slid into Paula's ears, into her senses.

Old Lil raised her hands before her forehead and moved them down and up in front of her body, palms crossing in the undulating movements of the snakes. Lili's hands moved in time with hers. Paula let the movements take her.

When stillness returned, Old Lil lifted two of the smaller snakes. Raising her hands slowly, Paula reached for the snake . .
.

. . . and murmured with surprise at the velvet-smooth warmth of the creature. The snake's tongue darted in and out as it swayed closer and closer.

"She's beautiful," Paula whispered, holding it to her face. The snake's skin slid softly against her cheek, and its tongue

KAALII CARGILL

probed gently on her eyelids. Old Lil placed the snake back on the altar, and Paula walked with Lili to the last altar.

In beaten copper, mounted on a base of lapis lazuli, rested the curved horns of the crescent Moon. The moon had sailed over the horizon just like that in Amman; no wonder the ancients thought of it as a boat sailing the heavens.

"The Horned One," said Old Lil. "She brings blessed fruitfulness, the life-giving power of the womb, of women, of the Earth. Her arms are always open, from Her breasts abundance flowing."

Paula knelt by Lili's side at the altar to receive the blessings of the Queen of Earth, the Mother of all. She followed Old Lil's movements, extending her arms out to the side, bending her elbows and opening her hands so that her palms faced up to the heavens. The sign of the Cow-eyed One felt natural, as if her arms knew what to do.

They walked again to the centre. The symbol woven into the mat was an eight-rayed star. Lili smiled knowingly and whispered, "The sign of Inanna, Great Lady of Heaven."

"We return always to the centre," said Old Lil. "To the formless Chaos. To the Primal Waters. To the beginning. It is from this we come and to this we must return. The centre holds the Balance."

Paula studied the symbol. Balance. Restore the Balance. Was this it? The key to the prophecy?

"Sit," said Old Lil. "I will tell you a story."

Paula sat cross-legged on the woven mat, Lili beside her.

"You have heard of Inanna," said Old Lil.

Paula and Lili nodded.

"She was the favourite of An, and came to womanhood in his Palace." Her voice seemed to come from all directions at once. "She won the sacred measures from Enki, Great Ones of Wisdom. They drank beer together, toasted and challenged each other, and Enki said, 'In the name of my power! In the name of my holy shrine! To my daughter Inanna I shall give The high priesthood! Godship! The noble, enduring crown! The throne of kingship!'

"And how Inanna said, 'I take them!'

Alongside Paula, Lili shivered. Of course she knew all the old stories of Sumer. But even she must feel something to be hearing it like this.

"You know that Enki gave to Inanna Truth! Descent into the Underworld! Ascent from the Underworld! The art of lovemaking! The kissing of the phallus!

"And that Inanna said, 'I take them!'

"You know the story of the courtship of Inanna and Dumuzzi. How the holy Priestess chose the Shepherd who was conceived on the sacred marriage throne."

Lili's eyes shone in the candlelight. She smiled at Paula and squeezed her hand.

"You know the story of Inanna's descent to the Underworld," said Old Lil.

Lili nodded.

"Tell me," said Old Lil.

Lili took a deep breath and spoke the story as she remembered it from the translations. "Inanna, holy Priestess of Heaven, turned her thoughts to the Great Below.

"From her seven Holy Temples she gathered the seven Holy Measures and prepared herself.

"She placed the Crown on her head.

"She tied the single strand of Beads around her neck.

"She let the Double Strand of Beads fall to her breast.

"She wrapped the Royal Robe round her body.

471

"She bound the Breastplate around her chest.

"She slipped the Gold Ring over her wrist.

"She took the Measuring Rod and Line in her hand.

"Inanna told Ninshubur to watch for her, and if she did not return, to go to the Great Ones, so that the holy Priestess of Heaven not be lost in the Underworld."

The hairs on Paula's neck tickled, as if ants were crawling on her skin.

Lili went on. "When Inanna arrived at the outer gates of the Underworld, She knocked loudly.

"She called for the door to be opened.

"Neti, the Gatekeeper, left Inanna on the doorstep to speak with the Queen of the Underworld.

"Eresh-ki-gal told the Gatekeeper to bolt the seven gates of the Underworld. They would be opened one by one, just wide enough for Inanna to enter.

"And so it came to pass that at each gate Inanna had to surrender one of the Sacred Measures. Only then, naked and bowed low, could She face the Holy, Dark and Eternal Eresh-ki-gal."

Paula's stomach tightened, her head throbbed. She bit her lip and waited for Lili to tell the rest of the story.

"Inanna faced the Annunaki and was judged.

"Eresh-ki-gal turned the eyes of Death on Inanna and hung her body on a hook."

The breath left Paula's body as if it were she who hung in the Underworld, condemned by Eresh-ki-gal. Spots danced before her eyes like mosquitoes.

"After three days and three nights, Inanna had not returned.

"Ninshubur sought help from the Great Ones, so that the holy Priestess of Heaven not be lost in the Underworld.

"Father Enki sent help, and Inanna was restored as Queen of Heaven and Earth."

Old Lil nodded. "That is good. But it does not end there. Inanna was restored. Balance was restored. That which is above is the same as that which is below; That which is below is the same as that which is above."

Paula let her breath out in a long sigh. She guessed what Old Lil was going to say next, but could a flesh and blood person really walk in the steps of Inanna? Could she really go to the Underworld and return?

Old Lil spoke slowly, as if reciting another verse. "The initiate makes the seven sacred Measures, using only what is offered by the Great Ones in the gardens. She speaks no words. She sits in her chamber for two days and nights. Her thoughts are of the Underworld realm of Eresh-ki-gal. Strange images haunt her, dreadful sounds assault her, and terrible feelings assail her: she knows that Eresh-ki-gal waits with Her eyes of Death."

Paula's heart sat heavy as a lump of clay in her chest. The prickling on her skin grew stronger, like ants biting her arms, her legs, her belly. Surely no one ever died in rituals. Did they?

"Come," said Old Lil. "She waits."

Paula stood, holding tightly to Lili's hand. A shadow moved behind the altar of the dove.

Paula screamed and stumbled backwards into Lili. Lili sat down heavily on the floor. Paula fell onto her lap like a child.

The shadow extended a hand. "I am sorry. I startled you."

"Haleli?" Lili pushed from behind, and Haleli helped Paula up.

Paula and Haleli took a hand each and lifted Lili to her feet.

"Of course," said Old Lil. "The three streams, daughters

of Mir-ri."

"Of course," whispered Lili.

Of course.

Old Lil took up a candle and led the way to another cleft hidden in the cave wall. They emerged into a larger chamber.

Old Lil lit more candles and pointed to a shallow pool of water caught in a natural hollow in the rock. Haleli slipped out of her clothes and washed, as if she had done this before.

Haleli stepped back, and Lili shed her clothes and completed the cleansing ritual.

Paula did the same, the cold water sluicing away some of the jumbled thoughts. Fear still pricked her skin and tightened her throat.

Old Lil handed them robes, dark-colored fabric, soft as swanskin. Paula slipped hers on over her head. It smelled of herbs. Lavender? Pine oil?

Old Lil pointed to a pile of objects on the floor. Paula picked up the top one, an arrangement of twigs and dried leaves. She hung it around her neck as Old Lil indicated. Lili and Haleli also donned strange necklaces that covered the front of their bodies. They looked like ancient warriors, or priestesses. Hadn't Lili said a breastplate was one of the sacred *me*?

As if she had heard Paula's thoughts, Lili smiled and nodded, a look of wonder on her face. They all knelt before the other objects on the ground.

Instructed by Old Lil, Paula settled a Double Strand over the Breastplate, placed a Single Strand over that, fitted the Gold Band over her wrist alongside the bracelet from her mother, and lifted the Crown onto her head. She took up a long staff, draped with leaves. If these were the *me*, they were not made of gold and precious stones, but crafted from grass and wood and things of Nature. It seemed so obvious now.

But were they really going to walk the way of Inanna? Meet Eresh-ki-gal? Who would play the part of the Queen of the Underworld? Would an enactment really help Mary?

Once again Lili smiled and nodded as if she was reading her mind and trying to reassure her.

Old Lil led them to a corner of the chamber. Paula peered down a rough stairway descending into the earth.

Haleli spoke the ritual words. "If I am not returned when three days and nights have passed, seek help to secure my return."

Lili repeated the words slowly, as if reciting from memory.

Paula stumbled over the words, and Lili said them again so she could repeat them. Spider legs of fear scuttled along Paula's arms and across the back of her neck. Were they really going to do this? Sweat dampened her underarms and inner thighs. She wrinkled her nose at the sharp smell of it.

The air thickened, making it hard to breathe. With a final look at Old Lil, Paula followed Lil and Haleli down the stairs. Bare feet touched steps wide and worn in the middle. Others had passed this way before.

Breathe . . .

Hands brushed the sides of the tunnel, smoothed by others who had passed this way.

Breathe . . .

The steps ended in a room of earth with a low ceiling, walls glowing in the light of coals smouldering in a bowl on the floor. Smoke clouded the air, pungent with incense. A wooden door lay three steps ahead. A heavy stillness in Paula's body cautioned against movement.

Breathe . . .

The coals died.

The room darkened.

Three steps to the threshold.

Lili moved first, and Haleli moved to stand beside her.

Paula moved one foot, her mind thick and slow from the incense and the fear. Moved the other foot. Stepped to the door.

Lili's knuckles sounded loud on the wood, and Paula remembered that knocking was part of the story.

Nothing moved.

The last glow of the coals faded, and Lili hammered at the door with her fists, like a child begging to come in from the dark.

"Who seeks entry to the Otherworld?" asked a voice like night.

Paula's lips stuck together, mouth too dry to speak. She licked her lips and swallowed.

Lili answered first. "I, Lili, seek entry," she whispered.

"I, Haleli, seek entry."

"I, Paula, seek entry."

"Wait," said the voice.

Cold seeped from the walls.

"You may enter," said the voice.

The door moved to make an opening lit by the glow of a single candle held by a dark-robed figure. Paula strained to see beneath the hood, but there were only shadows. Was it Old Lil?

Paula followed the others through. The door slammed shut behind her. Hands reached for the Crown, pulled it free from her hair.

"What is this?" she said. Lili and Haleli cried out the same words.

"Quiet. The Ways of the Underworld are perfect and may not be questioned."

Paula's legs trembled. She bit her lip. The weight of the

rock above pushed down. Whatever waited below pushed up. Between the two, Paula's senses cracked like grain between grinding stones. She fell into blackness.

Her thoughts returned to an absence of pressure. She shivered in the cold darkness. Had she slept? Had she fainted?

She pressed her hands against the floor, the soil hard-packed, smooth and dry. The Crown was gone, but the earth remained solid beneath her hands. She picked up the staff and stood. Lili and Haleli breathed and rustled alongside her. Paula reached up to touch the ceiling. Like the floor, it was solid, smooth and dry. *That which is above is the same as that which is below; That which is below is the same as that which is above.*

How long had they been there? There was no way to tell. Paula remembered the story and reached out to find the next door.

She beat loudly on the wood with her fists. The door opened. She walked through. The others followed. Hands took the Single Strand from her neck.

"What is this?" she asked, her teeth chattering. Once again, the others spoke the same words. Could they say anything else?

"Quiet. The Ways of the Underworld are perfect and may not be questioned."

Paula's head spun as if she had been turning in circles. Dots of light flashed like stars, becoming brighter, bigger. One rushed at her and exploded against her forehead.

She was on the ground again, head pulsing with pain like stabbing knives. Was it meant to hurt like this?

She stood on shaking legs to reach for the next door. Her hands met Lili's back. She felt around for her staff, picked it up, and followed the others into the chill.

Her feet told her that the path sloped downwards, but her other senses were baffled, no way to tell how long they walked before meeting the next door. Her body trembled and fearful thoughts flooded her mind, but she joined with the others to hit her hands against the wood. The slapping sound and the stinging of her palms reminded her that she was alive.

The door opened. She walked through. Hands took the Double Strand. The ritual words burst forth from them all: "What is this?"

"Quiet. The Ways of the Underworld are perfect and may not be questioned."

A fight welled up inside Paula; like fire and wind all at once, it raged in her chest, her arms. A cry like birth burst from her mouth, leaving a wound in her throat.

Surely she was meant to be there, surrendering the necklace. Then why was it so hard? She sat down abruptly, heat coursing through her body. Had Old Lil tricked them? Were they going to die there?

When the fiery wind of doubt stopped raging, Paula rose and walked on. It was so dark she could not even see her fingers when she held them before her face. The air shifted as Lili and Haleli moved alongside her, but she saw only blackness. If not for the glimpse of light at each door, she might think they had taken her eyes as well. She felt for them then, scrabbling with her fingers, breath coming in gasps.

They were there, safe.

Lili and Haleli had stopped, waiting at the next door.

They knocked. It opened. They walked through.

Hands grasped the Breastplate, lifted it over Paula's head.

"What is this?" they all asked.

"Quiet. The Ways of the Underworld are perfect and may not be questioned."

This time Paula stood quietly as the dim light disappeared, no sound except the slow beating of her own heart. Crossing her arms over her chest, she imagined the Breastplate, sensing it as part of her body, something that could not be taken.

She moved more certainly to the next door and knocked with the others on the smooth wood. The Golden Band of wheat was taken from her arm. It stripped the skin from her arm, leaving her raw and bleeding.

"What is this?" she asked with Lili and Haleli.

"Quiet. The ways of the Underworld are perfect and may not be questioned."

Blood dripped onto the ground, falling onto Paula's feet as if eager to leave her body. The candlelight began to flicker, dissolving into blackness as her eyes lost focus. She fell.

When awareness returned, it brought pain. Her head hurt. Spots danced behind her eyelids. Her arm throbbed as if it had been scraped raw, but the flesh was unbroken. Had it been fear alone that had weakened her?

Water dripped from the low stone ceiling, falling onto Paula's face with a small, wet sound. It reminded her of thirst, of her body struggling to live despite being buried in timelessness. A rush of warmth filled her chest, a rush of love for the life that pulsed in her body. She moved to catch the drips of water on her tongue. It tasted of metal and earth.

Truly, she reasoned, no one had done her any harm. Fear alone had overwhelmed her. Perhaps that was what she must learn: to overcome the power of fear to rob her of will and life. She rolled to the side and stumbled to her feet, still tempted to cradle her left arm in front of her. She refused the image of flayed skin and dripping blood, and the illusion left like a sigh.

Paula picked up the staff and moved with Lili and Haleli

through the darkness until they came to the next door.

The all knocked against the wood. The door opened. They walked through. Hands took the staffs.

"What is this?" they asked.

The voice of night answered. "Quiet. The Ways of the Underworld are perfect and may not be questioned."

They walked to the final door and waited. Was it moments or days that they stood there? What strange crossings had brought them to this place? Had this final crossing been waiting since the beginning? Waiting for daughters of the lineage that began in ancient Sumer and spread across the Middle East and from there to Europe, America, Australia?

As Paula confronted the unanswerable questions, the silence deepened around her. She stood between Lili and Haleli. They held hands. Were they strong enough to take the next step?

They released each other's hands, and Lili knocked. The door opened. They passed through.

The Gatekeeper took the Robes, leaving them naked.

"What is this?" they whispered.

"Quiet. The Ways of the Underworld are perfect and may not be questioned."

They walked together, naked and bowed low, to meet Eresh-ki-gal. Queen of the Underworld. Holy, Dark and Eternal Eresh-ki-gal.

Paula's cheeks flushed, like a child caught at something shameful. Would The Queen of the Underworld see through to all her secrets? Would she turn the eyes of death on her?

A terrible wailing filled the air with unspeakable grief. Images writhed in the grief: corpses piled high as hills; hills weeping blood from wounds too deep to heal; rivers running dry like scars; oceans rising to flood the land; trees felled faster than seeds could grow; fish harvested too plentifully to breed; arable land sold to the highest bidder to cover with concrete.

Paula sank to her knees, covering her ears. Never had she heard such a sound; it was as if the Earth wailed in torment. She cried out in sympathy. Alongside her, Lili was moaning as if in great pain, but Haleli looked ecstatic, hands raised, eyes glowing, smiling.

"Ancient Mother, I hear you calling," she cried. "Your pain is my pain. Your flesh bleeds. Your body trembles. Your salty tears overflow. I bleed with you. I tremble with you. My tears overflow." She sobbed, tears dripping off her chin onto her chest.

The wailing stopped. A voice older than Time echoed in the chamber.

"Have you the wisdom to hear beyond my wail? I am the catastrophe, the devourer, the necessity. Impaled on my teeth, you shall be blessed for you will glimpse truth. I am the living power of water, the cry that catches in the throat, the sob that shatters stone.[xliii] Have you the courage to lift up my veil? Have you the courage to welcome my voice? Have you the wisdom to embrace the choice?"

As if she had been walking towards this moment all her life, Paula surrendered to the necessity, offering up her body, her blood, her life.

Lili cried out in wonder.

Haleli spread her arms wide and sang an ululation that echoed into a hundred voices. A thousand voices.

When the last echo faded, there was silence, deep, eternal silence.

Haleli's voice rose to meet the silence. "Holy Eresh-ki-gal, great is your renown. Holy Eresh-ki-gal, your praises I sing. Holy Eresh-ki-gal, great is your renown. Holy Eresh-ki-gal, your praises I sing."

Lili joined her, repeating the words over and over. Paula found the rhythm and sang until her throat ached and her heart filled with joy.

CHAPTER XLIX

Basra to Amman. May 22nd 2015.

"Lil" means "air", "breath", and "spirit" in Sumerian.[xliv]

Paula, Lili, and Haleli returned to the light of a new day, wearing their own clothes, which they had found exactly where they had left them. Hot air greeted them as they crawled out into the open from the cleft where Old Lil had led them. Was it only yesterday?

Paula turned a full circle, looking for Old Lil. They were alone on the hillside.

A phone rang, the familiar sound of Paula's birdsong ring tone. She ran to where their bags had been stacked against a low wall.

"Hello?"

"Thom?

"She's awake?"

"Good. Good."

"As soon as I can."

"Everything's fine."

"Love you, too."

Paula looked up to see Lili and Haleli smiling and crying as if it was their daughter who had woken from a coma and asked for something to eat.

"Old Lil?" Lili tuned back to the cleft through which they had entered and returned.

"Gone," said Haleli, eyes shining with tears.

"Who was she?" asked Paula.

Haleli shrugged. "Old Lil."

The voice that had called to her in Old Lil's courtyard whispered in Paula's mind, and the breeze caressed her skin like a promise.

"Not gone," said Paula. "She is in the air."

"And in the water. In fire and in the earth," said Lili.

Haleli stood between them. "Seven times the Guardian spoke, taking each time the sacred me. Hidden in stone soaked in sweetness, riding the wind burnished bright. Seven times the Guardian spoke, taking each time the sacred me. When men forsake the task of life, and bitterness floods the land, Daughters will come marked at birth to find the *me,* remember the Queen, Restore the Balance for eternity."

"The prophecy," said Paula. "It was about the elements: air, fire, water, earth. About Nature."

"And about the Queen," said Lili. "The life-giving power of the Queen."

"The same thing," said Paula. "The Queen, the Mother, Nature. The same thing."

"That which is above is the same as that which is below," said Lili. "That which is below is the same as that which is above."

"But what about the *me*?" asked Paula, grasping the lapis necklace that had been waiting with her clothes.

Lili smiled. "The treasure never was a piece of jewellery, a robe or a staff. The treasure is the life-giving power of Nature, of the Mother. When we truly know this, we have Balance."

Haleli smiled knowingly and whispered the words of the prophecy again.

They picked up their bags and walked together down the hill. Paula wasn't surprised to see a car heading towards them, stirring up a cloud of dust.

Lili stopped walking when she saw the car. A shiver moved across her skin, like someone walking on her grave. In the first story, Inanna had to send someone to Eresh-ki-gal in her place. Inanna had refused to send her faithful companions, but she had found her consort, Dumuzzi, indulging himself with no regard for his kingship. She had turned the eyes of death on Dumuzzi, and he was taken to Eresh-ki-gal.

What would they all be required to send to Eresh-ki-gal in the days and weeks and months to come?

Paula and Haleli waited for her and, holding hands, the three of them went to meet the car at the bottom of the hill.

Peter emerged slowly from the passenger side of the dusty black SUV, hugged them all, and handed out bottles of water, just like a tour guide collecting his charges after a day's outing. He looked older, pale from his brush with death, but his smile was the same as ever.

Before anyone could say more than "How are you?", he ushered the three of them into the back seat and settled back into the passenger seat, motioning for the driver to take them back the way they had come.

"If we drive straight through, we can cross the border in the morning," said Peter.

Haleli leaned forward and put her hand on his shoulder. "What has happened?" she asked.

Peter turned and smiled again, teeth dazzling despite the dust on his skin and the lines of exhaustion around his eyes.

"What hasn't? People marching in the streets everywhere. Internet activist sites going crazy. Governments promising to stop trafficking, clean up the sex trade. A world summit on everything from HAARP to coastal development. You name it, it's happening. And they want you there. The University President announced it yesterday."

Haleli settled back against the car seat and closed her eyes. A smile hovered at the edge of her lips.

The drive back to the border was surprisingly uneventful, but what could compare with passing through the seven gates and meeting the Queen of the Underworld?

Paula slept with her head on Haleli's shoulder, lulled by the whoosh of the tyres and the warm certainty of Mary's safety. She woke several times to hear Peter and Haleli speaking in Arabic like old friends--or long-time conspirators.

They stretched their legs at the crude roadside stops, but somehow the toilets seemed less foul smelling, and the flat bread tasted delicious. Lili was quiet, but every so often she held Paula's hand and smiled tiredly.

Peter dozed while they waited at the border crossing into Jordan, waking just in time to get them through without any trouble. Paula watched closely, but she still couldn't tell if money changed hands.

The last stretch to Amman seemed to take forever, with smaller roads and more traffic. It wasn't until they stopped outside the Hillside Hotel that Paula thought to ask Peter how he had found them, like the logical question that comes after waking from a dream of something wonderful and impossible.

He shrugged and looked at Haleli.

"Desert magic."

CHAPTER L

May 25th 2015.

As for what happens —
Of the past you can only see what is past,
Not what is always present. That is what matters.
                    TS Eliot, The Family Reunion, 1939.

Two days later, Lili left for home. Paula flew out the same night, her computer and other luggage safely restored by more of Peter's magic. She slept most of the way, not sure if she was flying or being driven across an endless desert. Twice she woke to find someone standing over her.

"What is this?" she asked, remembering the timeless weight of stone.

The flight attendants apologised for disturbing her and offered her a drink. Very polite. Very civilised.

They were all there to meet her: Thom, Hayley, Jon,

Rinna, Mary. Paula laughed and cried and let the warm embrace of family envelop her. There would be work to do when Haleli and Lili called for her, but today was for the simple joy of being alive in a World where there was hope for the future . . .

NOTES

i
http://earthquake.usgs.gov/earthquakes/eqarchives/year/eqstats.php

ii

http://www.acehtsunami.com/index.php?option=com_content&task=blogsection&id=5&Itemid=27

iii http://en.wikipedia.org/wiki/Astrological_age

iv D Hill (1998). http://www.naturepark.com/cricket.htm
The actual calculation is Temperature=50+(Number of chirps per minute-40)/4.

v Adapted from Ralph Ellis's understanding of the Gilgamesh epic as a story of the constellation Orion; "an epic tale of a battle between Taurus and Aries - between the biblical patriarchs, (who were known as shepherds - Arians) and the Apis Bull worshippers (Taureans)" © 1998, 1999 by R. Ellis. Gilgamesh the Hunter.
http://freespace.virgin.net/kena.edfu/gilgamesh.html

vi http://www.webofdebt.com/excerpts/chapter-5.php URL accessed 18/6/2010

vii Ibid.

viii http://www.suppressedhistories.net/articles/priestesses.html

ix A Watkins (1991). Reclaiming the Temple. Words and music on cassette Catalogue No 202. Used with kind permission.

x ibid.

xi B Gilbert (2003). Words used in seasonal rituals, Australia. Used with permission.

xii http://preview.farmsresearch.com/publications/books/?bookid=21&chapid=112

[xiii] J Stuckey (2005) Inanna and the Sacred Marriage, MatriFocus Cross-Quarterly for the Goddess Woman, Samahin 2005, Vol 5-1. http://www.matrifocus.com/

[xiv][xv] The number systems of 10 and 6 were used in ancient Sumer. The calculations for 360 degrees in a circle, 60 seconds in a minute, 60 minutes in an hour, 24 hours in day all came from ancient Sumer. The measure for weight was a "mina", with 60 shekels in a mina (approximately one pound in weight).

[xv] The Electronic Text Corpus of Sumerian Literature http://www-etcsl.orient.ox.ac.uk/section1/tr141.htm

[xvi] N Ellis (1988). Awakening Osiris: The Egyptian Book of the Dead. Grand rapids, MI: Phanes Press, p. 169. Copyright permission granted by Red Wheel Weiser.

[xvii] T Frymer-Kensky(1992) In the Wake of the Goddesses: women, culture and biblical transformations of pagan myth. Fawcet Columbine, New York.

[xviii] J Stuckey (2005). Inanna and the "Sacred Marriage". In MatriFocus, CrossQuarterly for the Goddess Woman, Imbolc, 2005, Vol 4-2. http://www.matrifocus.com/IMB05/spotlight.htm

[xix] Ibid.

[xx] T Jacobsen (1978). The Treasures of Darkness: A History of Mesopotamian Religion. Yale University Press, pp. 87-90.

[xxi] N Ellis (1988). Awakening Osiris: The Egyptian Book of the Dead. Grand rapids, MI: Phanes Press, p. 169. Copyright permission granted by Normandi Ellis and Red Wheel Weiser.

[xxii] Ibid.

[xxiii] http://en.wikipedia.org/wiki/Arrapha

[xxiv] S Roffé. The Jews of Aleppo. http://www.jewishgen.org/sephardic/aleppojews.htm

[xxv] V Shiva (1988). Staying Alive: Women Ecology and Development, p 24. Cited in http://en.wikipedia.org/wiki/Ecofeminism

[xxvi] K Turner (cited in J Stuckey, Inanna and the "Sacred Marriage", op. cit.) Beautiful Necessity: The Art and Meaning of Women's Altars. Thames & Hudson. p. 29.

[xxvii] E Neumann (1963). The Great Mother., Bollingen Series, Princeton University Press, p 43.

[xxviii] Read more at Suite101: The Ancient City of Aleppo Syria: The Umayyad Great Mosque of Allepo – a City Treasure http://ancient-middle-eastern-history.suite101.com/article.cfm/the-ancient-city-of-aleppo-syria#ixzz0rHValjw6

[xxix] http://en.wikipedia.org/wiki/Solomon%27s_Temple
According to secular historians, the Temple would have been completed in around 960 BCE and destroyed by the Babylonians in 587/6 BCE. Traditional rabbinic sources state that the First Temple stood for 410 years and based on the 2nd-century work Seder Olam Rabbah, place construction in 832 BCE and destruction in 422 BCE (3338 AM), 165 years later than secular estimates. The Second Temple was subsequently built and destroyed on the same site and Jewish eschatology includes the belief that a Third Temple will also be built there. Due to the extreme political sensitivity of the site, few archaeological excavations have been conducted on the Temple Mount itself. To date, no archaeological evidence for Solomon's Temple has been found and the only information regarding the First Temple in Jerusalem is contained in the Hebrew Bible.

[xxx] Before her visit to Solomon, Makeda is said to have told her people:

"I desire wisdom and my heart seeketh to find understanding. I am smitten with the love of wisdom.... for wisdom is far better than treasure of gold and silver... It is sweeter than honey, and it maketh one to rejoice more than wine, and it illumineth more than the sun.... It is a source of joy for the heart, and a bright and shining light for the eyes, and a giver of speed to the feet, and a shield for the breast, and a helmet for the head... It makes the ears to hear and hearts to understand."

"...I will follow the footprints of wisdom and she shall protect me forever. I will seek asylum with her, and she shall be unto me power and strength."

"Let us seek her, and we shall find her; let us love her, and she will not withdraw herself from us, let us pursue her, and we shall overtake her; let us ask, and we shall receive; and let us turn our hearts to her so that we may never forget her." From Budge, Sir Ernest A. Wallis, translator, THE QUEEN OF SHEBA AND HER ONLY SUN MENYELEK, (THE KEBRA NEGAST), Oxford University Press, London, 1932, chapter 24.

xxxi

http://www.jewishvirtuallibrary.org/jsource/judaica/ejud_0002_0016_0_16220.html

[xxxii] http://www.jcialeppo.com/about-aleppo.htm

[xxxiii] In the centuries leading up to the new millennium--the Age of Pisces--the land of Kemet became a great centre of trade and learning. A small town at the mouth of the Nile became the city of Alexandria, named for the young, Greek war-leader whose armies had conquered most of the known World. Built between the lakes of the Nile delta and the shores of the Marimara, the mother Sea, Alexandria was the jewel in the crown of the Greek and Roman empires.

[xxxiv] http://www.ancientsites.com/aw/Places/Place/419305

[xxxv] Article Source: http://EzineArticles.com/1075970

[xxxvi] The Habiru in Babylonia at the start of the new millennium were descendants of the tribes that had been exiled from Ursalimmu hundreds of years before. The exile had long since ended, but many remained in Babylonia where they had been born. In this context, the term "Habiru" is used to represent the people who later become known as "Hebrew"--although the names appear to have the same derivation, there is still debate about whether the terms should be used interchangeably.

xxxvii http://www.everyculture.com/wc/Rwanda-to-Syria/Bedu.html#ixzz1cQojXNu8

xxxviii HH Milman (Rev), 1820. The Fall of Jerusalem. John Murray: London. Not in copyright.

xxxix R Patai (1996) The Jews of Hungary: history, culture, psychology. Detroit, Michigan: Wayne State University Press.

xl C.P. Cavafy, 1992. Collected Poems. Translated by Edmund Keeley and Philip Sherrard. Edited by George Savidis. Revised Edition. Princeton University Press.

xli Some of this information is from: "Ninlil" in Encyclopædia Britannica. Encyclopædia Britannica Online. Encyclopædia Britannica, 2011. Web. 23 Jun. 2011. http://www.britannica.com/EBchecked/topic/59492/Ninlil

xlii J Stuckey (2005). Inanna's descent to the Underworld. In Matrifocus, Cross-Quraterly for the Goddess Woman, Beltane, Vol 4-3.

xliii N Ellis (1988). Awakening Osiris: The Egyptian Book of the Dead. Grand rapids, MI: Phanes Press, p. 169. Copyright permission granted by Red Wheel Weiser.

xliv http://web.archive.org/web/20011120212809/http://www.lemurian-imports.com/lilitha/drkgodes.htm

ABOUT THE AUTHOR

I write fiction that asks "What if . . .?"

When I was young, my imagination populated the world with wolves, dwarves, a king in the moon, a troll beneath the hallway floor, and a friend called Miss Shell. These figures were as real to me as my family, and they befriended, terrorised, and entertained me for years. It may have started with my father's stories about the souls of the dead . . .

At thirteen I left my "make believe" world and exchanged the wolves and dwarves for the lure of romantic love. My childhood companions waited patiently through the highs and lows of relationships, marriages, and parenting.

Early one morning an old man came to me while I was sitting on a veranda in Bali, overlooking the northern ocean. He told me a story:

I am an old man dozing. I have seen my share of mornings. When the Sun comes gliding over the mountains wearing His robe of silver grey cloud. When the cocks crow their welcome and cook fires flavour the breeze. I am an old man dozing in the shade. The cat stretches nearby, whiskers sensing movement. I have been like that, alert to life, ready to act. I am an old man dozing in the shade of a Nabab tree. Holy tree, sacred tree, trailing tendrils in the breeze. Reaching deep to the heart of things. Touching the sky. Dreaming of colour and ceremony, music and laughter . . .

Thus I met the ancient Warden, Garamen, and the fantasy trilogy, THE ELEMENT SERIES, unfolded as a living story. Since then I have written and published short stories, won some writing prizes, and completed DAUGHTERS OF TIME.

I live in a rambling home in south-eastern Australia, with ample walls for my murals and a leafy garden for the elements. I have altars in my home for Air, Fire, Water, and Earth, and I use many of the invocations spoken by the Wardens in *The Element Series* and by the priestesses in *Daughters of Time*. The "real" world and the world of the imagination interweave more gracefully these days.

Questions and comments welcome:
kaalii@kairoscentre.com
www.kaalii.wix.com/soulstory

What people are saying about DAUGHTERS OF TIME:

Across a 4,000 year line of descent, an epic struggle arises to restore balance to a world gone awry...Weaving ancient Sumerian myth and legend into a modern story of intrigue and mystery, Kaalii Cargill brings to life an epic struggle across four millennia. Myth becomes strength, tales held and transferred through the years as a counterweight to written history, to arise in a time of need. In the end, Cargill creates a strong message of empowerment through a fascinating set of characters compelled always to move, but never to forget, handing down their message from mothers to daughters -- the Daughters of Time. **W.B. Hafford, University of Pennsylvania Museum of Archaeology and Anthropology, author of Archaeology in the digital age: creating an online research tool for the ancient city of Ur.**

I absolutely LOVED this book! It soothed me on SO many levels - and confirmed many of my thoughts and memories. The history and daily life of the Priestesses, the strong link of the mother-daughter lineage down through time, the sacredness of our daily lives and the celebration of our own sacredness as women and the temple of our female body. A rip-roaring mystery yarn as well - while the author called it fiction, I believe the truth was jumping off the page in many places as chills ran up and down my spine. **Maree Lipschitz, Director/Facilitator/Coach at The Midlife Midwife; Senior Leader/Cofounder of 'Pathways into Womanhood' Teenage Girls program at Pathways Foundation Ltd.**

Reading 'Daughters of Time' by Kaalii Cargill was an experience like no other. I felt like I was able to put names and faces to times and places. Reading this book was an interesting and exciting way to engage with our Herstory. **Jane Hardwicke Collings, author of Becoming a Woman: A Guide for Girls Approaching Menstruation and Thirteen Moons: A Cycle Charting Handbook and Journal**

Kaalii Cargill is one very smart writer. The depth of Daughters of Time is astounding as an ancient mystery unfolds and unfolds while moving back and forth through time. It is a story of an ancient prophecy, a forgotten bloodline that continues to exist into the present and a secret that is passed down through time. **Christos Morris, author of Digging at the Crossroads of Time**

Made in the USA
Charleston, SC
16 June 2014